Shadow of Fear

Jane Peart is a prolific author of romantic fiction who lives in Fortuna, California. She is the author of the Orphan Train West series and the International Romance series.

Shadow of Fear

Jane Pearl

Fleming H. Revell
A Division of Baker Book House Co
Grand Rapids, Michigan 49516

Published by Fleming H. Revell
a division of Baker Book House Company
P.O. Box 6287, Grand Rapids, MI 49516-6287

Printed in the United States of America

2 in 1 ISBN 1-56865-332-8

I had to change coaches in London. I stepped down into the bustling stagecoach courtyard. All was noise and confusion. At least three coaches were being readied for travel—their harnesses checked, luggage strapped on top and behind by coach hands. The clatter of horses' hooves on the cobblestones mingled with the voices of dispatchers yelling at the stable boys, drivers shouting out their destinations, passengers calling for porters, porters rattling by with baggage carts and clamoring for people to make way.

The October morning was dark, the chill air dense with fog. Prospective passengers clustered in little groups, their shoulders hunched against the damp. In spite of my merino cape and fur muff, I shivered, though perhaps more from nerves than from actual cold. This was the first time I'd traveled so far and alone. I stood looking about me in utter bewilderment, wondering whom to ask for the information I needed.

I spotted a burly man wearing a battered beaver top hat, a long fringed muffler wrapped about his neck. He was standing near the open door of one of the coaches as he supervised his helper, who was loading luggage on the top. I hurried toward him.

"Please, sir, is this the coach for Meadowmead?"

"It is," he said gruffly.

"And does it stop at Tynley Junction?"

"It does."

"Oh, good." I sighed, digging into my small purse for the ticket I had purchased beforehand.

"You may as well get in," he said, taking my ticket. "We're about to leave."

Although outwardly I managed to keep my demeanor composed, inwardly I was filled with anxiety. I was setting out on a journey fraught with uncertainties, hazardous even, its outcome unknown. My heart beat wildly. The purpose of my journey was cloaked in lies and deception. For a person who held personal integrity in high regard, this weighed uneasily on my conscience.

Once inside the coach, I settled into a corner of the carriage. Thrusting my kid-gloved hands deeply into my squirrel muff, I felt the edges of the envelope containing Nanny Grace's letter, the reason I'd embarked on this uncertain mission.

A flurry of activity outside and the sounds of raised voices attracted my attention. Suddenly the coach door was yanked open, admitting a draft of cold air. The shovel-bonneted head of a sharp-eyed woman poked inside. Her head turned as she made a quick survey of the interior, then it disappeared. Soon the soberly dressed owner of the bonnet reappeared, climbed in, then turned to assist an elegant elderly lady, obviously her mistress, aboard. Swathed in a fur-lavished, claret-colored cape, the elderly lady wore a bonnet that quivered with egret plumes and framed a thin, finely lined, aristocratic face with a high-bridged nose. She called crossly over her shoulder to someone outside, "Now, not another word, Nicholas!"

While, with a great deal of rustling of taffeta, she took her seat opposite me, she continued speaking to the unseen person outside. "I'm not risking an attack of ague by staying another hour in this wretched weather."

Her words were immediately followed by those of a male voice, tinged with irritation. "This is really unnecessary, Aunt Isabel. Another day and the broken axle on *my* carriage will be fixed. You will be able to travel home in comfort, not in a crowded public conveyance."

"I would hardly call this crowded, Nicholas," the lady replied archly, casting a sharp glance over at me. "There is only one other passenger."

A moment later two hatboxes, a wicker hamper, and a leather tea case were handed inside. Then the head of a man, who would have been extraordinarily handsome were it not for the scowl that brought his heavy dark brows together over piercing gray eyes, leaned in. His mouth was grim as he looked around then let his eyes rest on me.

His gaze made a sweeping inventory from the brim of my bonnet to the tips of my boots, making a swift evaluation of his aunt's traveling companion. I felt my cheeks grow hot, blushing under his calculating appraisal. My instinctive reaction was to tuck my feet under my braid-trimmed skirt. Otherwise, no doubt, he would have counted the buttons on my boots.

Indignant at his steady regard, I wanted to show my annoyance. Certainly this was not a gentlemanly thing to do, even though he *was* dressed like a gentleman in an impeccably tailored caped coat of fine tweed with a velvet collar, and leather gloves. As I stared back at him with as cool a look as I could manage, a strange thing happened. I experienced a sudden sense of recognition. Was it possible we had met somewhere before? That seemed unlikely. I certainly would have remembered. His face—with its classic Greek nose, gray-blue eyes the color of a winter sea, firm yet sensitive mouth—was a face that, once seen, could not easily be forgotten. It was a ridiculous idea, I told myself, yet the feeling of recognition lingered.

Confused, I turned my head away from his riveting eyes to peer out the misty window. I pretended a great interest in the loading of the luggage on top of the stage, being conducted with much loud discussion.

My attention was then demanded by the woman he had called Aunt Isabel. "Well, young lady, as it seems we are to be fellow travelers on this miserable morning, let me introduce myself. I am Lady Bethune. My maid, Thompson. That fierce-looking gentleman is my nephew, Nicholas Seymour."

Forced to acknowledge the introduction, I murmured, "I am Challys Winthrop."

"Challys! What an odd name!"

I thought her comment rather rude. However, perhaps a person past sixty, especially one of her class, felt she had leave to say anything that popped into her head. I did not feel compelled to explain that Challys was a proudly inherited Winthrop family name, nor that most of my family and friends called me Lyssa.

I had much else on my mind other than to pay heed to the somewhat arrogant Lady Bethune, born-to-the-purple though she might have been. I had a long journey ahead of me and much to think about. I turned away from the curious gaze of my companion, pretending to study the dreary scene outside the carriage window.

Try as I might, it was almost impossible not to overhear the continued bickering between Lady Bethune and her nephew.

Finally she said, "Enough, Nicholas. I'm settled, and that's the end of it." She added grudgingly, "I'll send a message as soon as I'm safely home."

With a somewhat ungracious good-bye to his elderly relative, he slammed the door, causing the carriage to rock a little. I got the feeling Nicholas Seymour was not used to defeat and did not take it well.

With a great jangling of harnesses, shouts from the driver and the stagecoach station manager, and a few jolting half-starts, we at last got under way. The heavily loaded topside of the carriage caused the body of the stage to sway and groan ominously on its wheels, which brought muted squeals of alarm from Lady Bethune's maid for which she was abruptly reprimanded by her employer.

"Don't be such a ninny, Thompson."

The coach rumbled through the sleeping city streets, cobbles shiny with heavy moisture. Gas lamplights shed a dim, eerie glow on the tall buildings we passed, which loomed over us like dingy, brick canyon walls.

Past the outskirts of London the landscape changed, but still heavily veiled by fog, it was indistinct. I soon became used to the motion of the stage as we were now on country roads beyond the city. The jolting sensation had a certain rhythm. After a while, I noticed a steady purring sound. A quick glance toward the other occupants of the coach revealed they had both slipped into shallow slumber. Lady Bethune's bonnet was knocked askew, giving her a rakish air. Thompson's neck was tilted at what appeared to be an uncomfortable angle, and through her prim mouth, slightly open, soft snorting noises emanated.

With both my traveling companions asleep, I was afforded a bit of privacy. I drew out Nanny Grace's letter and began rereading it.

Nanny Grace had been both my mother's nurse and then my nurse. Actually, having been educated above her station, she had been more than that. When my mother and I had each reached the proper age, Nanny had served as a governess, teaching us our letters and to read and write. I unfolded the page and read again the few terse lines hurriedly written because of the urgency of the message. As I replaced the letter in its envelope, I felt my stomach tighten from anxiety.

But the die had been cast. There was no turning back now. I had no alternative but to proceed with our desperate plan.

I leaned my head back against the seat. Closing my eyes, I let my thoughts wander.

I had never known a father's protection. I was but an infant when my young soldier father was killed. My mother, hardly more than a child herself at seventeen, went to live with her guardian and godmother, Lord and Lady Hazelton, at their country estate, Briarwood Manor, where I grew up.

As the only child in a household of adults, I was pampered, my every need anticipated, any wish happily granted.

My earliest memories were of my pretty mother, with her golden-brown curls, her sparkling sapphire eyes, her low sweet voice and musical laughter, the feeling with which she would read Bible stories, teaching me even at an early age to trust God. I remember Nanny's warm comforting presence, nursery teas and glowing hearth fires and bedtime stories, the Hazeltons hovering over us with affectionate indulgence, that beautiful house with its polished floors, shining windows, filled, it always seemed, with light, luxury, and love.

My childhood was, as I recall it, a completely happy one until I was twelve, when my mother remarried.

I did not like Henry Muir the first time I met him. I believe I could sense his aversion to children. Of course, at that first encounter, I had no idea my young, unsophisticated mother was planning to marry him.

I had been playing in the garden, Nanny seated on one of the iron lace benches nearby, knitting, when Mama came outside with a tall, dark-haired man.

"Darling, I want you to meet a very special friend of mine, Mr. Muir," Mama announced, a happy lilt in her voice.

My Irish wolfhound's deep-throated growl at Mr. Muir's approach should have warned me further, since animals often seem to have an instinctive awareness of evil. Ran had been my father's dog and so was especially beloved by my mother. At my birth, he became my loving protector and guardian. Now, he pushed his great bulk between me and my mother's companion. My mother did not seem to notice; she was gazing up adoringly at Henry Muir.

"So this is little Challys," a deep voice said.

I looked up from where I had been making a miniature garden, into a pair of the coldest eyes I had ever seen.

I felt an immediate revulsion. Everything about him was in sharp contrast to my pretty, delicate mother. His coarse-featured face was swarthy, his eyes the color of dull pewter, his mouth harsh, even as he tried to smile.

I stumbled to my feet, feeling threatened by his great height, his intimidating gaze. He was holding out his hand to me, and I was forced to put my own into it. I withdrew it hastily, wiping his clamminess on my pinafore. I thought at first my gesture undetected, but then I saw his mouth curl into a kind of sneer that frightened me.

Only Mr. Muir and I were conscious of this strange exchange that set once and for all our adversarial relationship, our mutual dislike. After that first meeting, I could not think of him without shuddering.

2

*C*hildren are much more sensitive to what goes on than the adults in their world realize. I soon sensed Nanny Grace did not like Henry Muir either. After Mama had flitted in and out of the nursery schoolroom for a quick visit before going off for an afternoon ride with Mr. Muir in his shiny black phaeton or out to an evening musicale or party, Nanny would shake her head grumbling, "Innocent as a lamb being led to the slaughter." I didn't know exactly what she meant, but I did feel uneasy about Mama's seeing so much of Mr. Muir.

When Mama, happy as a lark, declared they were going to marry, the Hazeltons put as good a face on it as they could. However, I don't think Uncle George and Aunt Evelyn were happy about the match either. Childless themselves, they treated my mother and I as if we had been their own, but they had to accept the marriage and that we would all be moving away to Muir's residence, Crossfield Grange, in a remote part of northern England.

The Hazeltons were unworldly, trusting people, and Henry Muir was a master of deceit. He had gone to great lengths to ingratiate himself with my mother's guardians until the betrothal was official.

I shall never forget the day of my mother's wedding. Sitting between Aunt Evelyn and Uncle George in the small, candlelit village church, watching my mother come down the aisle on the arm of a man I'd already begun to fear and distrust, I felt small and helpless. I wondered bleakly how she could look so radiant when my heart was near breaking.

But for all our private miseries, the four of us who loved Mama best saw her off on her wedding trip with Mr. Muir, not knowing how much all our lives would change.

While they were still abroad, Nanny and I traveled to Crossfield Grange. Ran and my Shetland pony, Betsy, were to be sent later.

With Nanny I always felt safe and secure, even during this tremendous upheaval. But at my first glimpse of the timbered Tudor house, with its overhanging roof and dormered windows, located on a rocky hillside and brooding over acres of rough, tuffetted moors, I felt a tremor of apprehension. The day itself was overcast; smoky gray clouds cast a depressing pall. Instinctively, I reached for Nanny's hand. I heard her quick intake of breath, as if she too found the sight daunting. Then she patted my hand. "It'll come right, dearie, by and by." However, her voice sounded quavery and unsure.

Inside, the house was also gloomy. Dark wood paneled and furnished with heavy, carved pieces, it was as depressing as the exterior. We found Crossfield Grange had a meager staff, only a cook, a downstairs maid, a scullery maid, and Mr. Muir's valet. Evidently, having been arranged beforehand, three of the servants from Briarwood Manor had been sent to work here—James, our footman; Marsden, the groom and coachman; and Lily, Mama's maid.

A week after our arrival, my mother and Mr. Muir returned, and I learned what direction my life would take. The day they came back I was called into the drawing room, where they were having tea. I had been outside romping with

Ran, and as he always followed me wherever I went, he came along into the room, his great paws and toenails making a scratching sound on the polished floors. It was then—at least to *me*—Mr. Muir showed his true colors.

At our entrance, he turned to Mama. "Surely, you don't allow that great brute of a dog in the house, Maria?"

Mama immediately looked anxious. She gave Muir a quick glance, then said to me in a gentle but worried voice, "Darling, why don't you take Ran out to the hall. Ask James to put him outside for now."

"But Ran is always allowed in at teatime," I said, puzzled by this unusual suggestion.

"Yes, darling, I know but—"

"Maria." Muir placed his hand over hers and said firmly, "Let me handle this, dear."

He turned his lusterless gaze on me. "Children should not argue with their elders, Challys." His voice was edged with ice. "Do as your mother told you."

I looked at Mama, expecting her to say something in Ran's behalf, but she only bit her lower lip and fiddled with the tea tray, nervously rearranging the sugar bowl and creamer.

Resentful that I should have to obey Muir, I tugged at Ran's collar and started pulling him toward the drawing room door. He resisted, and I had to drag him, sliding and whimpering, out to the hall. James, who had been standing in the hall, gave us both a sympathetic look and took the still-protesting dog.

As I turned to go back into the drawing room, I heard Muir remark to Mama, "Remember, my dear, children need a firm hand. A child must be trained to instant obedience. An unruly child is as unwelcome as an unruly animal."

I felt a hot rush of anger. Stepping back into the room, I glared at Muir and met a look that chilled me. There were triumph and satisfaction in his eyes, and also a threat.

That incident was an indication of what was to come. I soon found out Muir had no intention of including me in his new domestic arrangements. Within three weeks after their return, I was informed I would be going away, that Muir had enrolled me in a boarding school.

"A very fine institution for young ladies," he told my mother and me. "Its emphasis on discipline, orderliness, and deportment is just what Challys needs."

He turned a patronizing look on Mama. "Maybe you did not realize it, my dear, but it is certainly obvious to anyone else that your elderly relatives spoiled the child outrageously. She is self-willed and careless. All this is most deplorable, as I'm sure you'll agree. Challys will benefit greatly from this change."

"Of course, Henry," Mama murmured, but her eyes shining with unshed tears and her trembling mouth were not convincing. I knew sending me away was Muir's idea, not hers. I knew at that moment from then on *he*, not my tenderhearted mother, was to be in charge of all that concerned me.

A red-nosed, sniffling, tight-lipped Nanny Grace helped me pack my trunk. Loyal to my mother as she was, I knew Nanny did not want me to go. For both their sakes, I tried not to express the sense of abandonment I felt at being sent away. I attempted to tell myself staying at Crossfield Grange did not guarantee much happiness either. Still, as I drove away in the carriage on my way to Miss Elderberry's Academy, I pressed my face against the window, keeping in sight as long as possible the figures of Mama and Nanny Grace on the steps waving good-bye to me. We passed the bend in the road, and they were out of sight. I had just passed my thirteenth birthday; it was the end of my childhood.

It was hard to adjust to the strict regimen at boarding school after the easy, flexible way of life I had known at Briarwood Manor with the doting Lord and Lady Hazelton.

Still, I had to reconcile myself that, with my mother's remarriage, my life had changed irrevocably, and I had to make the best of the new circumstances. At school I soon made friends and settled in, reminding myself I could look forward to spending the school holiday with my dear mother in a few months.

To my dismayed disappointment that was not to be. At the end of the term, when I should have been leaving for the summer, the headmistress received a message from Mr. Muir that my mother was unwell and it would be best for me not to come to Crossfield Grange. I was desolate at the prospect of spending the holiday with a few other students whose parents were army or diplomatic personnel stationed in one of Great Britain's colonies too far away to visit. At the last minute, however, I was rescued. Evidently Nanny Grace had written the Hazeltons, and they came to get me.

I spent a happy enough holiday with them, for they did everything to make it so. After that one time, however, Muir sent word that I should remain at school during holidays if, for some reason, I couldn't come to Crossfields, explaining to the headmistress that "surely Challys would benefit from some added time given to her studies." In the thoughtless way of children, and with no one to prompt me, I failed to write to my elderly relatives, and gradually we lost touch.

As the school year continued, I began to worry about my mother more and more. I'd had only a few letters from her. In them she had said little about her new life at Crossfield Grange. Instead, her notes were filled with questions about my life at boarding school, and always ended with her hopes that I was happy and repeated reassurances of her love, even though it was necessary for us to be separated.

I didn't really understand why this had to be so. I decided I could manage to tolerate my stepfather if it were possible for me to stay with my mother and enjoy at least a semblance of our happy, old life together.

I was also puzzled why, if she was not seriously ill, I could not have gone to Crossfield Grange instead. In the past, when we had lived at Briarwood Manor, I had often sat on her bed, reading aloud to her when she had a headache or was slightly indisposed. Mama had always loved having me near her, no matter what.

When I was allowed to come to Crossfield Grange for the Christmas holidays, I got some idea of what I had not been able to read between the lines of her letters. I was certainly unprepared for the atmosphere I found upon my arrival there.

I had anticipated Mama would be at the stagecoach station to meet me. Instead, a newly hired, unsmiling coachman met me. When I asked about Marsden, he replied shortly, "Gone, Miss," then transferred my luggage to the rack on the end of the one-horse barouche. His brusque reply made me wonder what other changes I would find when I reached Crossfield Grange. Would James and Lily be gone as well?

When we arrived at the house and came to a stop in front, I drew a sigh of relief when I saw Nanny hurrying down the steps to greet me. I was out of the carriage in a flash, being hugged. While Nanny fussed, declaring I looked thin and needed fattening up, over her shoulder I saw a tall woman standing in the front door. Had Muir hired a housekeeper?

Nanny took my hand and we started up the steps together. At the top we halted, and I recognized something familiar about the woman's features, her severe expression. Her graying, dark hair was drawn plainly back from a center part. She wore a high-necked black dress with no adornment except for a large onyx brooch, glittering so like a big black beetle, I had to suppress a shudder.

"Good afternoon, Challys. I am your stepfather's sister. You may call me Aunt Sybil." Her voice was as cold as the hand she extended. As I touched it, I felt the same strange chill I had felt when I first met her brother.

I murmured something I hoped concealed my surprise and sounded polite.

Sybil Muir then turned to Nanny, and speaking as though used to giving her orders said, "You may take her up to see her mother for a few minutes, then Mr. Muir wants her down for tea at four."

As we went up the stairs, Nanny tried valiantly to prepare me. Mama had been ill, she whispered, so I was to speak quietly and was not to excite her or tire her out with too much chattering. That was indeed a difficult charge for one who was returning after a first separation from an adored mother.

. In spite of Nanny's gentle warning, I was devastated by the startling changes in my beautiful, young mother.

I did not know my little brother's birth was imminent. Children were not told such things. I just thought how tiny and frail Mama looked in the big, canopied bed. For all her pallor she was still lovely, her glorious, golden-brown hair spread out like silk floss against the pillows.

She gave a little cry of welcome when she saw me and held out her arms to me. The ruffles of her shell-pink nightgown fell away from her arms as she did, and I was shocked to see how thin they were.

"Darling girl!" she called, but her voice seemed weak and lacked its usual lilt. I rushed over to her, snuggled in beside her on the downy quilt.

She kissed me and hugged me, told me how glad she was to see me, but even with my limited experience, I identified what I saw in her eyes as unhappiness.

A moment later, without knocking, Mr. Muir strode into the room. His harsh voice broke the spell of our happy reunion. "So you're here, Challys."

I felt my mother's thin fingers tighten convulsively on my arm.

He walked over, stood at the foot of the bed, and spoke to Mama without any softening of tone. "Well, Maria, you must not tire yourself with prolonged rejoicing over the prodigal's return." He used the term sarcastically.

To me he said, "Your mother needs rest. My sister says tea will be served in fifteen minutes, and you will join us in the drawing room." It was not anything like a cordial invitation. It was an order.

I would much rather have stayed and shared a quiet tea alone with my mother—I had so much I wanted to ask her and tell her—but Muir remained standing there as if waiting for me to obey. I glanced appealingly at Mama, hoping she would plead the same thing. Instead, an expression of anxiety came into her eyes, and she pressed my hand, gently urging, "Go along, darling. We shall have plenty of time to visit while you're here."

I could not help but notice she said *here,* not *home.* I think I knew then that Crossfield Grange did not feel like home to her either. I left reluctantly, tense and troubled. Something had entered my mother's room with Mr. Muir. It was fear.

A half hour later, I sat rigidly in the drawing room facing the Muirs, each ensconced in a straight-backed armchair flanking the black marble fireplace. I was very hungry after my long trip but couldn't eat my sandwiches or scones for having to answer the Muirs' rapid questions. I felt like a prisoner at the Inquisition.

"So what exactly are you studying, Challys?" Sybil asked, stirring her tea so that the silver spoon clinked against the side of the porcelain cup.

"Well, we have classes in grammar, botany, sums, music, and French—"

The spoon stopped abruptly.

"What? No religious or moral education?" she exclaimed, turning to her brother as if shocked. "That certainly was not the curriculum where *I* attended school."

"Oh, we do have chapel and Scripture study," I hastened to tell her.

She speared me with a withering glance. "It doesn't seem to have had much effect if you so quickly omit mentioning it."

She turned to her brother. "Surely, this is a lack you should investigate, Henry." She put down her teacup on the piecrust table beside her chair. "I think you should seriously consider sending Challys to my old school—Glenhaven in Scotland. There students are taught the fundamentals, not foolishness like French and dancing!"

Scotland! My stomach lurched at the thought of being sent even farther away from Mama. Desperately I tried to think of some way of improving the worth of my education at my present boarding school before Muir took it in his head to follow his sister's suggestion.

3

*E*ven the slight possibility that Muir would send me to a boarding school in Scotland might have motivated me to try to please my stepfather by good behavior in order that he would not consider such a drastic move, if it had not been for two separate but devastating discoveries.

After tea, I excused myself and went in search of my dear, devoted Ran. To my horror, I found him chained out near the stables, and I learned he was never allowed in the house. Seeing my approach, he went into a frenzy of joy, barking wildly, struggling to be free. I ran to him, threw my arms around his neck. Tears streamed down my face. "Poor old fellow. Poor boy," I said over and over as I caressed him and felt his warm tongue on my cheek.

When I finally got the chain loosened from his collar, he had a hard time standing. I realized his legs were weakened from lack of exercise and constant inactivity. The callous, young village youth who had replaced our old groom, Marsden, seemed indifferent when I complained about Ran's treatment. I was determined to protest to my stepfather. But there was more to come.

The second blow came when I found out that Muir had sold my pony. The next morning at breakfast, when I mentioned I thought I'd go for a ride, he offhandedly told me. I dropped my fork. "*Sold* Betsy?" I gasped.

"You're much too old for a pony, Challys. I shall look for a proper mount for you at the next horse fair."

Fury welled up within me in a fiery spasm. I pushed back my chair, stood up, fists clenched at my side. "You had no right to do that!"

"I had every right, young lady," he replied coldly. "All your mother's and your property now legally belongs to me."

I stared at my stepfather, hatred hardening my heart. Then I ran out of the dining room and rushed upstairs to my room where I flung myself on my bed, sobbing bitterly.

"I will never forgive him," I told Nanny Grace when she tried to comfort me.

All during those miserable three weeks I kept my distance from my stepfather, speaking only when spoken to, avoiding him as much as I could.

I took long walks on the desolate moors surrounding the house, trying to restore Ran's leg muscles as much as I could while I was there. He seemed to have lost his old energy and often limped far behind. Sometimes he just stopped and looked at me in a way that broke my heart. I would sit beside him, holding his head on my lap, weeping. Instinctively, I knew that the next time I came to Crossfield Grange Ran would be dead.

So went my first Christmas holiday in my new home.

Holiday? Certainly my time at Crossfield Grange that dark December was not worthy of the name.

My heart aches even now . . . remembering those dismal weeks. We were supposedly celebrating the most festive time of the year, but Crossfield Grange was a complete contrast to the joyous Christmases we enjoyed at Briarwood Manor. There, the rooms were gaily decorated with fragrant cedar boughs and holly, bright with red berries. The delicious smells of baking pies, roasting goose, and all the other tantalizing, delightful aromas associated with the holiday filled the whole house. Sweet-scented candles glowed in every window, welcoming the constant flow of visitors arriving for parties and balls. Music, the sound of dancing feet, and the excited cheers when the Yule log was brought in or the Christmas pudding, aflame and smelling heavenly of spices and rum, was placed on the table echoed through the house.

On Christmas Eve, snow was usually falling. Just at dark, carolers from the village were heard outside singing "O Little Town of Bethlehem" or "God Rest Ye Merry, Gentlemen," and we stood on the terrace, shivering, listening. Then Aunt Evelyn had cups of steaming cider brought out for the carolers. A little later we went to church, where the glorious story of the Christ child's birth and the shepherds' arrival at the stable was read. After riding home through the frosty night, we opened presents around the tree with its sparkling candles.

At Crossfields there was no such gaiety, no sense of the holiday spirit or the meaning of the holiday.

I returned to school after the holiday feeling depressed. Perhaps in the spring things would be better.

They were not. In fact, I found things were much worse.

To my dismay, I learned that not only had Sybil Muir extended her visit, she was now established as a permanent member of the household. I no longer had easy access to Mama. We were never alone. We were always in the company of either Mr. Muir or his dour sister. My mother seemed smaller, more fragile, intimidated not only by her husband but also by his sister. She kept to her room, often to her bed, and rarely joined us for tea or dinner. The piano remained closed, and the mother I had known, who laughed, danced, and sang, seemed to have disappeared. A kind of invisible yet palpable check seemed to discourage all spontaneity.

Again I returned to school heavyhearted.

The one bright spot in all this was the news of the arrival

of a baby brother. This announcement was delivered to me by the headmistress. The excitement it brought was diluted with the further information that his birth had taken all my mother's strength and that I was not to come home until the end of the term. Unhappy as that made me, I was assured I could come for his christening that summer.

Disappointments such as this were becoming routine in my new life. It was not until much later that I realized Muir had contrived deliberately to set me apart from my mother and little brother. If he thought he could alienate me from my mother and brother, however, he was sadly mistaken. When I was at Crossfield Grange, I tried in every way to make up for the long periods I was not there.

The baby was duly christened Tyrone. I had the privilege of holding him during the ceremony at the village church because my mother was still not well. Assisted by a young maid, Nanny Grace had taken over his care, and while I was there, I was constantly in the nursery. Ty, as Nanny and I began to call him, was a beautiful baby, favoring my mother, thank goodness, with tufts of red-gold curls, big, dark eyes, rosy cheeks, and a sweet smile. I adored him from the minute I saw him, and I was very sad to leave him when my summer holiday ended and I had to go back to school.

How strong the bond between us grew would be proven later. During the next two years, even though I was away from him for months at a time, my little brother grew dear and precious to me.

Because of my own affection for Ty and how remarkable I thought him, I found it very odd Mr. Muir paid little attention to his son and heir. He seemed indifferent as Ty grew into a sturdy little boy with obvious intelligence and a lovable personality. All the things Nanny and I thought marvelous about Ty seemed of no interest to Mr. Muir. I questioned Nanny about this.

"Most men don't think much of babies," she said. "When

he's older and running about, talking and such, Mr. Muir'll likely pay him more mind."

However, from the lift of her eyebrow and the curl of her lip when she said this, I didn't think Nanny really believed that would happen. Although she never said it in so many words, I could tell by a sniff or a shrug that Nanny did not care much for either of the Muirs. She was absolutely loyal and devoted, however, to my mother and Ty. Sad as I was to part with Mama and Ty each time a holiday was up and I had to return to school, I felt better knowing Nanny was there looking after both of them.

Still, the situation at Crossfields remained nearly always on my mind. I worried about Ty growing up in that stern and loveless environment with such a father.

Also, now that I was getting older and had my own romantic fantasies, I often wondered how my mother, with her delightful sense of humor and love for music, dancing, and company, had ever seen anything to love about Mr. Muir. He seemed the most humorless, negative man I'd ever known. Of course, he and I had little to say to each other ever. I had never forgiven him for selling my pony or the cruel way Ran had been exiled. It still hurt me to think about it. The dear old dog had been put down because of his deteriorating condition. I still missed him.

When I was at Crossfield Grange, we lived in a suspended state of truce. I knew Mr. Muir had the power to make my life even more impossible, so I kept my tongue and avoided him as much as I could when I was there. This was not difficult. Muir was often away. Nanny told me he was sometimes gone for days at a time, with no explanation to my mother or the staff. He came and went at will, leaving his formidable sister in charge. When Muir was absent, Mama usually did not come down, and I had to endure long dinner hours with "Aunt Sybil." She asked me questions about my studies and was critical and disparaging about everything and everybody.

Crossfield Grange was not a happy place. Indeed, if it hadn't been for Mama, Ty, and Nanny Grace, school would have been preferable to my time spent there.

It was Nanny who kept me informed of every detail of Ty's progress—his first tooth, his first word, his first steps. I read every word, longing to be there myself, even though that would have meant enduring the Muirs.

Over the next few years, it was Nanny who alerted me to the dire events that began taking place at Crossfields. Gradually her hints became stronger. Eventually she reported Muir's indifference to my mother and brother had become worse: unkindness, neglect.

As a young widow, my mother had been left a sizable fortune by my father, who had been an only child as well as the favorite nephew of an earl. Mama had brought that wealth to her second marriage. But I learned from Nanny that Muir was going through it with such rapidity that soon nothing would be left. Certainly there would be no inheritance for Ty if things continued unchecked.

During my final year at school, I learned how bad our financial situation had become when the headmistress called me into her parlor. With considerable tact she informed me that my tuition had not been paid for months. Regretfully, she said, if my fees were not caught up at once, I would not be able to return to school for the next term. Humiliated and shocked, I stammered that there must be some mistake. I promised I would write my mother immediately about the matter.

I explained the situation in a hastily written letter to my mother and sent it off by the next post.

A week went by, ten days, and still there was no answer from Mama.

I was again called into the headmistress's office.

"I am very sorry, Miss Pomoroy. I can't imagine why I haven't heard anything from my mother," I began in a shaky voice.

"Our contact has been with your stepfather, Mr. Muir. Perhaps you best write directly to him, Challys. He gave me the impression your mother was an invalid. Maybe it would be better not to disturb her, whatever the problem is."

The idea that Muir had described my mother as a helpless invalid infuriated me. Although she was much changed, *intimidated* would be a better description of her situation. She was still fully capable of understanding my tuition had not been paid and of remedying it. If she knew, she would be distressed that I had suffered such embarrassment.

I murmured something, and Miss Pomoroy kindly excused me.

In that same day's mail I received a letter from Nanny. In it she said that things were entirely out of hand at Crossfield Grange. She asked if I could possibly come home.

Dearest child,

I hope you can find a way to come to Crossfields as soon as possible. I cannot describe vividly enough the extent of what has been happening here. Half the staff has left because their wages have not been paid. Cook, who is too old to go elsewhere, remains, as does Muir's surly valet, for reasons of his own. Of the few who came with us from Briarwood Manor, only Lily and I remain. I stay because of my devotion to your dear mama. Lily, though young enough to easily get another lady's maid position, has become engaged to a local farmer. She'll probably go when they marry. Of course, I shall never leave as long as I'm needed, but something must be done. I don't know what else to tell you, except please come as soon as you can. See for yourself.

Ever,
Your loving Nanny Grace

Frightened, because I knew Nanny would not exaggerate, I determined I must leave at once for Crossfield Grange and find out exactly what was going on there. Pleading an emergency at home, I went to the headmistress for permission. Since she already knew something was amiss in my family, she granted my request. I had the further embarrassment of having to ask her to lend me traveling money, assuring her it would be paid back along with overdue tuition fees.

When I arrived at Crossfield Grange, I found the situation far worse than I could have imagined or than Nanny had described.

4

*I*n the months since I had been home on summer holiday, Sybil Muir had departed, driven away by Muir's drinking bouts and rages. My mother, in a state of nerves, remained secluded in her room most of the time. Muir, it seemed, spent long periods of time away in London at gaming houses, drinking and gambling away what was left of my mother's fortune. He was not at Cross-field Grange when I arrived, and I had time to assess the dire state of affairs.

Everything was in disarray. The estate was beginning to deteriorate. The staff, demoralized and without direction, had become lazy. The whole house had an air of neglect.

To make matters worse, at age four Ty had begun having frequent and severe bouts of asthma, which Nanny felt were brought on by the stress created by my stepfather's behavior. In spite of all Nanny Grace's efforts to protect him from the bleak situation at Crossfield Grange, my little brother, like my mother, had become Muir's victim.

The evening I arrived Ty was suffering from an attack, aggravated by his excitement at seeing me. I sat with Nanny in his bedroom until he went to sleep. Nanny kept a kettle of steaming water on the spirit burner near his bedside to help him breathe easier.

I was appalled by all I had discovered. "Whatever shall we do?" I asked Nanny.

Nanny shook her head sorrowfully. There seemed no solution for all the problems. My mother, she said, had given up. Nanny, herself, now getting old and rheumatic, had all she could do caring for Ty.

Late that night, we heard my stepfather return. I went to the stair landing, ready to march down and face him, explain to him the reasons for my arrival, and demand from him some explanation for the way he was treating my mother and Ty. But when he roared for his manservant and called my mother downstairs, demanding a bottle and dinner at once, Nanny held me back. "No use, dearie," she whispered. "It will only make things worse." Now, I saw firsthand what my dear mother and my precious little brother had been enduring. Then and there I promised myself, whatever it took, I would free them from this unbearable situation.

Nanny and I sat up most of that night discussing possible ways out of this seemingly hopeless dilemma. Toward dawn, we decided on a plan. When she felt it was warranted, she would send me a message that the time was right to put it into action. It was a reckless and dangerous plan for a girl of eighteen and an old woman to devise and initiate. However we both realized that the desperate plight of my mother and brother, helpless to act on their own behalf, demanded extreme measures.

Nanny did not need to point out to me the obvious. My mother was failing, fading before our eyes. She was thin to emaciation, her once beautiful eyes sunken in her hollow-cheeked face. Neither of us could bear to admit aloud that she had lost the will to live, probably even hoped to die. She blamed herself for the misery she had brought on us all by her marriage to Muir.

If I had allowed myself to speak of or to dwell on these realities, I would have lost heart completely. I could not give way. Everything now depended on me.

The day before I was to return to school, Nanny motioned me into Mama's room. Mama sat up in bed and beckoned me closer. Weak as she was, I found her very agitated. She drew a small packet of money from under her pillow and pressed it into my hand. In a hoarse voice she told me she had secretly sent Nanny to sell some of the inherited pieces of jewelry she had kept hidden from Muir, afraid he would confiscate them and use them to pay off his gambling debts. Since English law decreed a married woman's property, money, and possessions belonged to her husband, Muir already had access to and control over the money Mama received in monthly cheques from my father's estate. Selling her jewelry was the only way Mama could get any money without going through Muir.

Mama also furtively slipped me a chamois bag containing her set of diamond and sapphire pendant and earrings, a gift from my father on their wedding day.

"These would rightfully come to you anyway, my darling. I'm afraid if left here they might disappear upon my death, so best you take them now." She whispered even though Muir was noisily sleeping off his latest drunken stupor downstairs.

"I don't know what will happen in the future, my darling, and this is all I can do at present," Mama said, her large eyes haunted and brimming with tears. "God willing, I will find a way so that you and Ty will not be destitute but—"

She paused, biting her lower lip to keep from breaking down. "Forgive me for bringing this disaster upon you. If only I'd known—"

She began to cry and I took her in my arms, rocking her gently, trying to soothe her. Her body felt as delicate and weightless as a little bird's.

It hurt me to see my mother so beset, her eyes ringed with purple shadows, her once beautiful face haggard, her expression tense and troubled. Rage and vengeance toward the man who had caused this terrible change in her rose within me.

"If anything happens to me, Lyssa, you must take care of Ty."

"Oh, Mama, don't say that. You're not going to die!" I cried out, but my words held no conviction.

Her hands clutched mine convulsively and I almost winced with pain. "Listen to me!" she pleaded earnestly, her eyes burning. "Nanny's too old. It's up to *you*. You must see he is safe. Promise me, no matter what, you will be responsible for Ty. Promise?"

Tears rushed and spilled down my cheeks and I nodded. "I promise."

She sighed, then seemed to lose what strength she had mustered to command that promise. Her hold on me loosened, and she fell back against her bed pillows obviously exhausted. Weakly, she instructed me to pay my school fees and repay the money Miss Pomoroy had lent me for traveling expenses, to keep the rest of the money, and not to hesitate to sell the jewels if ever I found myself in circumstances of need.

Nanny came in just then to say the carriage was waiting to take me to the stagecoach station. Heartsick with grief, Mama and I bade farewell to each other, not knowing if it might be the last time. I hugged and kissed Ty and said goodbye to Nanny, with a silent confirmation of commitment to our plan. Then, with deep foreboding, I left to return to school.

I was back at school hardly a fortnight when word came of my mother's death.

The sad day of my mother's funeral is etched forever in my mind. It was a desolate, overcast day, heavy with clouds. Rain-blown wind whipped at my cape, tugged at my bonnet strings, tore the remaining leaves from the trees that lined the cemetery road and sent them scattering across granite headstones.

Holding Ty's little hand, I clung to Nanny's with my other and looked across the gaping gravesite, into which they had just lowered Mama's coffin, at the harsh face of my stepfather. How I despised him, the source of Mama's misery. Surely he had also hastened her death. I vowed I would do anything and everything in my power to rescue my little brother from the control and power of this evil man.

Since we assumed Muir had notified Lord and Lady Hazelton of Mama's death, they being her closest relatives, we were puzzled that they had not come for the funeral. Not a letter, a telegram, or even a wreath of flowers for her grave had been sent. I tried to explain their absence away, telling myself the shock of the news, their grief, or the distance of the trip had prevented them from coming for the funeral. Perhaps their age or physical condition had also been a factor.

With the long day finally over and Ty tucked in bed, Nanny and I stayed up until midnight making our final plans. It was decided I would write to the Hazeltons and ask their permission to come with Ty to stay with them. Because of my memories of a happy childhood at Briarwood Manor, I felt sure they would welcome us. My confidence in their caring love for us went so far as to predict they might even adopt Ty and make him their heir.

Until I heard from them, I would return to school to finish my last year, preparing me for a teaching or governess position, which I would certainly need. Although my penniless plight was in some ways the same as Ty's, it was also different. Muir had gone through any inheritance I might have received from my own father through Mama. Without Mama's fortune, I was left without a dowry and so with no prospects for a prestigious marriage, an unenviable position for a young woman, though marriage was far from my mind.

Muir had already informed me that he would not be paying any more of my tuition, that it was—in his words—"high time you started earning your keep for all the years I've supported you."

I had to check my anger at this and not fling back at him the truth, that it was my mother's money that had paid for everything. There was too much at stake. Outwardly meek, I accepted his dictum, glad that Mama had given me money for tuition.

Back at school, as soon as Nanny sent word "when," I would leave school, meet her with Ty at Tynley Junction, and take Ty on to Briarwood Manor.

Nanny's urgent message came sooner than I expected and before I had received a response from Briarwood Manor. We would have to move very quickly, she wrote, before Muir came out of the most recent of the stupors into which he had been drinking himself since Mama's funeral. Nanny had requested and been given permission to take Ty with her to visit her widowed sister at her cottage in Kent for a few days to comfort the little boy on the loss of his mother. What Muir would do when he sobered up and found all three of us had disappeared I dared not imagine.

I would cross that bridge when I came to it. The important thing for me to concentrate on was meeting Nanny and taking Ty. Once Ty and I got to Briarwood Manor, I felt sure Uncle George would do whatever was legally necessary to safeguard us, even though he might be shocked by both our arrival and our circumstances.

And such now was the mission of my journey. I was on my way to carry out my part of the plan Nanny and I had agreed on before my mother's death.

Suddenly Lady Bethune's sharp voice jerked me back to the present. "So, young lady, I suppose you are on your way from London after a whirl of a social season."

Still preoccupied, I looked at her blankly, her comment seemed totally unconnected to my troubling thoughts.

As I hesitated, she frowned, her mouth pursed petulantly. "I find it strange that a young lady of quality like yourself is traveling without a chaperone, or at least a maid."

She paused, as if awaiting an explanation, and I realized

that while I had been preoccupied with thoughts of my uncertain future, Lady Bethune must have been surveying me carefully, drawing her own conclusions about my age, status, and probable reason for traveling out of London on this miserable morning. She would have been surprised, I was sure, to know she had drawn all the wrong conclusions, even though my general appearance, the fine material of my well-made traveling outfit, and my upper-class accent indicated much of what she conjectured about me was true. In her wildest imaginings, she surely would not have conceived that I was actually a *fugitive*, that I had lied to the headmistress of my school, that I was on my way to meet my accomplice and complete my part of a criminal conspiracy to kidnap a little boy.

Demurely as I could, I replied, "No, Lady Bethune, I have not been enjoying a social season in London. I am recently bereaved and am on my way to meet my brother and travel with him to our relatives' home where we shall live now."

She seemed somewhat taken aback by this reply, and as I turned again to stare out the window, she was, momentarily at least, abashed enough by her mistaken assumptions not to initiate further conversation.

The closer we got to the village where Nanny's sister lived, where I was to meet Nanny and Ty, the more nervous I became. Suppose something had happened to prevent their coming? Perhaps Ty had suffered one of his asthma attacks. What if, heaven forbid, Muir had uncovered our plan somehow and snatched Ty back for whatever devious reasons of his own? Involuntarily, I shivered and, too late, saw that Lady Bethune was still watching me curiously.

As the coach suddenly lurched to a shuddering stop, I realized we were at Tynley Junction. My heart was pounding as I gathered my skirts and pressed forward, impatient for the coach door to open. It was jerked wide, letting in a cold, damp wind, and the driver shouted, "All out that's stoppin' 'ere! We got twenty minutes' rest whilst we change horses."

Lady Bethune, peering out the window next to her, exclaimed, "What a hovel the station looks. What a dismal place for a rest stop. Good thing we brought our own tea, Thompson."

Then she glanced sharply at me. "And where do you think you're going, young lady?"

I thought it none of her business, but having been taught to be polite to my elders, I replied mildly, "This is where I'm to meet my brother."

"Ah! And how old is your brother?"

"Five, almost six."

She looked aghast. "An infant! You mean we're to have a babe on our hands for the rest of the journey? I hope he's well behaved. I can't abide noisy, spoiled children."

I was immediately on the defensive, and I replied coldly, "My brother is *very* well behaved, I assure you. And bright and sweet natured as well," which was more than I could have said for *her.*

Though her remark had made me dread the rest of the long journey ahead, I was determined not to let a fussy old woman, used to having her own way as well as her own private carriage, bother me. I had come this far, overcoming hurdles she could never dream of, and had only the second part of our plan to complete—the journey to the blessed safety of Briarwood Manor.

My heart melted at the sight of Nanny, huddled in a voluminous hooded cape, sitting on a wooden bench under the shelter of the dripping overhang of the dilapidated stagecoach station. Ty was cuddled close, Nanny's arm protectively around him. When he saw me, he jumped up and ran to me, grabbing my waist as I leaned down to hug him.

"Lyssa! Lyssa, you've come!" he said over and over, lifting his round, rosy-cheeked face to look up at me, smiling.

Nanny hobbled toward us, and my heart ached to see how bent she was. She seemed to have aged even in the few weeks since my mother's death.

"Dearest child, thank God you've come. I've been worried. Afraid something would happen—"

"I know, Nanny, I know. I have too, but everything has worked out as we planned. It will be all right now. As soon as we get to Briarwood Manor, we'll be fine."

I wished I felt as certain of the outcome of this risky venture as I claimed. There was still the matter of not having received a response from Briarwood Manor, and in the back of my mind I was troubled by the knowledge that the plan was built on lies, no matter how necessary they were, no matter how critical the cause.

"And you, Nanny, will you be all right? You're not going back to Crossfield Grange, are you?"

She shook her head vigorously. "Never! Not to that blackguard or to that place that was your dear mother's prison."

"All aboard that's goin' wi' us to Dorset!" The harsh call of the stagecoach driver rang out through the misty air.

"You best go now, my dearies," Nanny said, her voice cracking a little. "I won't worry about you two anymore. In a short while you'll reach the home of your dear mother's relatives, where I know you'll be safe."

We hugged.

"Be a good lad, won't you, Ty? Don't give your sister any trouble. Just do as you're told, won't you?"

"Yes, Nanny!" Ty nodded, looking from one to the other of us, his little brow puckered with concern, for we were both crying.

"Here, I've fixed a wee basket of goodies in case the stage is late and you get hungry." Nanny thrust a small wicker hamper into my hands. "I know when you reach the manor they'll have a feast for you."

I didn't want to tell Nanny I had not yet heard from Lady Hazelton. When I had received Nanny's urgent message that we had to put our plan into action immediately, I just came. There was no use worrying her.

After hugs all around, we took leave of Nanny, her "God

bless" following us. Holding Ty tightly by the hand, I walked back toward the waiting stagecoach. Lifting Ty up over the high step into the carriage, I saw we had gathered four new passengers for the rest of the trip. I noticed Lady Bethune's martyred look as she moved to the end of her side of the seat. She gave several exasperated sighs as the portly Thompson was squeezed between her and a stout man who, with much huffing and puffing, wedged himself into the leftover space.

A couple with pinched faces and disapproving glances made room for me and Ty as we boarded. Contrary to my belief that children were universally loved, I discovered that others felt as Muir did. The fourth new passenger had opted to ride on top next to the driver and his helper.

I felt Lady Bethune's curiosity double as we settled ourselves. I helped Ty off with his bulky jacket and removed the knitted cap I recognized as Nanny's handiwork. I looked down fondly at my handsome little brother, ruffled his russet-gold curls affectionately. He looked up at me with eyes so much like our mother's I felt my throat tighten. He smiled, showing his dimples, and I pulled him onto my lap with a hug, returning Lady Bethune's stare, as if to say, who could resist this dear little fellow?

Totally unaware he might be the target of unwelcoming thoughts, Ty grinned happily at the other occupants of the carriage as he munched contentedly on the apple I dug out for him from Nanny's basket. It was growing dark as we got underway, and the coach moved at a fast clip in spite of the fog and drizzle.

Having earlier been roused out of his warm bed into the chilly morning, Ty's head soon began to nod, and leaning against my shoulder, he went to sleep. Troubled with worried thoughts, I was not as lucky. At least we were on our way to safety. Eventually I began to relax, and lulled by the rocking motion of the carriage coupled with my own exhaustion and stress, I drifted off.

Suddenly, I was startled awake by a crashing jolt. The terrified screams of my fellow passengers rent the air as the carriage swayed, shuddered, then tilted precariously. Everyone slid to one side. I gripped Ty, who had awakened and now began to cry.

"We've had an accident!" someone shouted.

The man on the other side of the coach struggled free from a tangle of skirts, hatboxes, and reticules, and managed to scramble up. He pushed open the door and peered out into the murky morning.

"I'll see what's happened," he announced to no one in particular, then disappeared from sight. To our horror, there followed an ear-splitting cry and a splash. Sickeningly I realized the stagecoach must be overturned and pitched sideways, suspended over water.

We heard the frightened horses shrieking in terror. As they lurched to right themselves, they sent tremors through the dangerously tipped carriage. Inside there were only the sounds of muffled groans, rapid breathing. We were all too afraid to speak.

5

$\mathcal{F}$inally the other male passenger's steady voice broke through our collective fright.

"We must be very still or the whole carriage will turn over. Be calm, or none of us will make it. Someone is bound to come and help us."

I felt Ty's clinging arms tighten almost to a stranglehold around my neck. I patted his quivering little body and murmured soothingly, hoping to keep him quiet. My own common sense echoed the other passenger's cautionary warning that the slightest motion might send the whole coach and its occupants hurtling into the icy water I knew was below. I closed my eyes, prayed silently, and tried to comfort Ty.

I don't know how long we hung there, literally between life and death. Maybe it was only minutes; it felt like hours. The waiting seemed endless. However long it took, eventually the man who had spoken those reassuring words was right. The coach driver's husky voice called to us, "Hold on, now, we're comin' to get you out!" A few seconds later his head, illuminated by the lantern he was carrying, emerged into the carriage.

"Folks, we've got the horses unhitched and moved away. We've put rocks under the wheels so as not to tip this whole thing over. Now, we'll get you out of here one at a time. Move slowly, carefully. Easy does it."

I was in agony as I kept Ty still, holding my breath, afraid nearly to breathe. First, the whimpering Thompson was guided forward, Lady Bethune shoving her from behind. Then "milady" herself, with no hesitation at all, followed. Next, the prune-faced woman on my right, her eyes wide with fear, was helped by her stoic husband through the carriage door. Then it was my turn. With Ty in my arms, I inched on the slanted floor of the coach toward the open door.

"Hand me the lad," the driver ordered.

I did so, releasing Ty from my stiffened fingers.

"There you go, laddie!" the driver said as he took Ty from me. A minute later the driver was back. "Hurry, now, miss, don't know how long we can keep this vehicle from slidin'."

I felt strong hands grip my upper arms, pull me up roughly, and swing me around. Then at last I felt my boot soles on the soggy ground of the riverbank and knew I was safely out of the wrecked carriage. I looked around and saw Ty standing with the other rescued passengers a little farther up, near the road. Slipping a bit on the rain-soaked grass and mud, I made my way up to join them.

We were all a little dizzy from relief. On the edge of hysteria, I suppose. Some were making humorous remarks about our mishap, others laughing, if uneasily. We all knew we had barely escaped death.

But in a few minutes it began to drizzle, dampening the strained humor of the situation. The attempts at jokes turned to grumbles and complaints, in some cases to mumbled swearing with little care that ladies and children were within earshot.

My skirt hem was already wet, and I was shivering. Ty was

wide awake now and finding it all a great adventure. We women stood a little apart, and the male passengers joined the driver and his helper, huddling in a small circle discussing the problem.

An earlier storm had blown down tree limbs. The driver surmised a large fallen tree branch might have been the obstacle the stagecoach's wheels struck, overturning us. Either that or a dislodged boulder that, loosened by the soaked ground, had rolled into the road.

We were stranded, it seemed, in the middle of nowhere. I looked around at the unfamiliar countryside. Below the embankment where we were all gathered like bedraggled refugees, the river, swollen with rain, rushed in a mighty current, the huge hulk of the half-sunken stagecoach barely visible. It looked like a beached whale. In the distance I saw the outline of an arched bridge we had been about to cross when the accident happened.

After what seemed like a great deal of time, the driver came over and informed us that he was sending his helper to hike to an inn, which was a regular stagecoach stop. There he could get us help. The driver was sure they'd send a wagon to fetch us and give us shelter for the night. It would be morning before they could get the damaged coach righted.

"Then, we'll get word to the next stagecoach station, and they'll dispatch another coach and have you ladies and gents on your way 'fore long," he said heartily.

I'm not sure any of us believed him, but there was nothing we could do but agree that his was as good an idea as any. We watched the man set off with one of the only two lanterns. As his lonely figure merged into the darkness and disappeared, I believe a common mood of depression about our plight settled on the group. Standing there in the misty chill, none of us thought things could be worse, but we were all wrong. Soon the drizzle turned into rain, and within minutes it began to rain steadily. In time the rain became a downpour. There was absolutely nothing we could do but stand there and become soaked. I wrapped my pelisse as best I could around Ty, who had begun to shiver violently. What this exposure might do to him, given his susceptibility to taking cold, added to my other worries.

We were all miserable by the time we saw lanterns bobbing in the distance. As the lights moved closer, we could see our driver's helper arriving with a man driving a large farm wagon pulled by two workhorses.

Drenched by the rain and shuddering from the chill, we were herded into the wagon and seated on the rough boards that lined each side. My bonnet was hanging around my neck from its strings, and without its covering, my hair was dripping wet. As we bumped along the rutted road, I hunched over Ty, hoping my body heat would offer him some protection from the cold. By the time we reached the inn, however, Ty's breathing was labored, and with a sinking heart I knew that he had caught a bad chill.

We entered the main room of the inn where a fire had been started for our benefit. The innkeeper's wife, a stout, florid-faced woman, introduced herself as Mrs. Brindle. She made noisy, clucking sounds of sympathy as she ladled out bowls of warm broth. I tried to get Ty to take a few mouthfuls but from his eyes, glassy with fever, and his skin, hot to the touch, I knew I had a new problem. To ward off a serious illness, I knew I had to get him in bed at once. I asked the innkeeper's wife if there was a room available.

She took one look at Ty and said, "Come along."

I followed her up the stairway with Ty in my arms.

She showed me into a small but neat room and turned back the patchwork quilt on the bed. The linen was fresh, the coverlet clean.

As I lay Ty down, his small body was shaking. Mrs. Brindle gave him a sharp look and said to me, "The lad's caught a bad chill, for sure. You best keep him snug and warm. I'll have Peg heat a brick, wrap it in flannel, and slip it under the sheets. That'll warm him up quick."

She bustled out of the room and I heard her heavy, clumping footsteps going back downstairs. I was filled with apprehension. From Nanny's descriptions of Ty's other illnesses, I recognized he was very sick.

A few minutes later a sleepy-eyed young woman appeared, obviously resentful that she had been awakened to help with a crowd of unexpected travelers. She carried a flannel-wrapped square, which she held out to me. With poor grace and a sullen look she said, "Here 'tis."

I took it from her, murmuring my thanks, too worried about my brother to say more.

There was an extra quilt in the blanket box at the foot of the bed, so I took off my own wet, outer clothes and wrapped myself in it. I drew the one straight chair up to the side of the bed where Ty lay, flushed and breathing laboriously.

Keeping a lonely vigil through the night, I wondered what in the world I would do if Ty were too sick to continue our journey. Toward dawn I got up, stretched my stiff muscles, and walked over to the window.

The morning sky was lighting, but it still looked ominous. The old adage "Red sky at morning, sailors take warning" spun through my head. More storms ahead. I glanced anxiously over to the bed where Ty restlessly slept. Leaning over him, I placed my hand on his forehead. It was burning hot.

I knew, whether or not the stagecoach company sent another carriage for the stranded passengers, my little brother was too sick to continue our journey. We would have to stay here until he was well.

Of course, staying at the inn meant using more of the small sum of money I was hoarding so carefully. Extra days of lodging and meals would speedily reduce the amount that had remained after I had paid my overdue tuition, and if I had to summon a doctor for Ty, he would have to be paid as well. Still, it had to be done for Ty's sake. He certainly couldn't travel in his condition.

How would I get word to the Hazeltons? After receiving

my letter telling them what I intended to do, Aunt Evelyn would be beside herself with worry if we did not show up as planned. I must send a message explaining the delay. Perhaps, knowing Ty was ill, Uncle George would send his own carriage and coachman for us.

I would have to ask the stagecoach driver to take my letter, paying him of course, taking the chance he *would* post it, not just pocket the money.

Even knowing that Uncle George would generously reimburse me for expenses incurred, I still felt a gnawing anxiety about our predicament. That was nothing, however, compared to the horror I experienced a moment later—my purse was missing! A frantic search through my skirt, jacket, and pelisse was futile.

In all the confusion after the accident, my mind had been preoccupied with getting out of the carriage safely and making sure Ty was okay. I must have dropped my purse somehow. I couldn't think, couldn't remember, if it had been on my lap, beside me on the seat—where. It didn't matter. All the money I had left was gone! How could I have been so careless? What was I to do?

Then I remembered Mama's jewels. My stomach lurched. I felt sick, dizzy. I reached for the small chamois bag that I had tied around my waist under my petticoats. In it was all that was left of her jewelry, my insurance against disaster to be used only in an emergency.

It would be easy to say this was it, but I knew better. Priceless heirloom jewels could not be used for common tender. You didn't pay a country inn bill with valuable diamonds and sapphires. An innkeeper would not even know the value of such gems. No, the jewels would not solve my present problem, nor was I ready to part with them—at least not yet. Once the Hazeltons knew of our situation, I had no doubt they would take care of all our expenses. My main concern had to be Ty, getting him well.

I went back over to the bed and looked down at my little

brother. My heart swelled for him. The full weight of the tremendous responsibility that was mine pressed down on me, as did my feelings of inadequacy at the thought of having to protect and care for him. I sank to my knees beside the bed and prayed earnestly for guidance. My task to get us safely to Briarwood Manor seemed impossible, but "with God, all things are possible." I had to rely on that bedrock of faith, as well as keep my head and use my wits.

A tap on the door drew my attention. I opened it to a kerchiefed maid, a different maid than the one who had brought up the heated brick the night before. This one was a country lass, rosy cheeked and cheerful.

"Mornin', miss." She bobbed a curtsey. "The mistress says to tell you she's servin' breakfast now for the passengers. Another stagecoach's come over from the junction to carry the passengers who was dumped last night. They'll be on their way in an hour, she says."

"I must have a word with your mistress," I said as calmly as I could. "Would you mind staying here with my little brother for a few minutes while I speak to her?"

"For sure, miss." The girl nodded, walked over to the bed and peeked down at Ty. His cheeks were red from fever, his russet curls a tangled mass against the linen.

"He's a bonnie one, ain't he?" she whispered, meeting my gaze. "I'm gettin' married meself come next month, and I want to have a half dozen of me own."

Sensing her love for children, I felt I was leaving Ty in good hands and went quietly out of the room. As I went downstairs, I rehearsed what I would say to Mrs. Brindle. She had certainly seemed kind and helpful the night before. That, however, was when she'd believed I was a paying guest. It might be a different kettle of fish when she knew I had no money. I was sure she had assumed from my dress and speech that I had the means to pay for our room and Ty's care for the length of time necessary for his recovery. Innkeepers were in business for profit, not charity.

The innkeeper himself, Mr. Brindle, whom I had hardly noticed nor spoken to the night before, was much in evidence this morning. He had the look of a drinker. I'd learned the signs from seeing Muir drunk. Mr. Brindle's face was blotched, his nose bulbous, his eyes bloodshot and bleary. Obviously it was his wife who ran things. Mr. Brindle was talking in a loud voice with the stagecoach driver, waving in one hand a tankard that I guessed contained ale not coffee.

Lady Bethune and the other passengers were seated in the taproom at one long trestle table. I cast a wary eye at Thompson, who looked vaguely uncomfortable. This was probably the first time she had sat at the same table with her employer.

I found myself wondering if any of the others had found themselves in a predicament similar to my own. Surely not all of them had been thinking about gathering their belongings, though perhaps each had held on to whatever seemed most important at the time. To most it *would* have been their money, not having a small child to look after. I had been most concerned about Ty.

The smell of sausage frying rose tantalizingly to my nose, and I realized I was hungry. Great platters of potatoes, fluffy eggs, rolls, thick slices of homemade bread, and mounds of creamy butter were being passed around, and everyone was helping themselves and eating heartily.

I put the thought of food out of my mind. I had more urgent matters to deal with.

6

J glanced around the room for the innkeeper's wife. I saw her through the doorway into the kitchen. She was red faced, bustling about, bossing the cook, and overseeing the serving.

Then for some reason my gaze met Lady Bethune's. She was studying me speculatively. The thought crossed my mind to confide in her. Most certainly *she* would have held on to her purse. All I needed to do was mention Lord and Lady Hazeltons' names to assure her that she would be repaid. But as my gaze lingered on her elegantly held head, the faint disdain I saw in her expression and her air of detachment from the rest of the now convivial group of survivors caused me to recoil.

I couldn't. I was too proud.

Besides, Lady Bethune—well, she had not impressed me as the most compassionate person in the world. She was likely too self-centered to care for the problems of others, not one who would readily offer either sympathy or monetary help. I would not ask for either. I would face this myself in the most dignified, honorable way I could.

I made another decision, standing there with Lady Bethune gazing at me intently. Though I was not comfortable with it, in this case discretion seemed the better part of valor. I would not tell the innkeepers the truth about my purse, that I no longer had the ability to pay for the room and the service I would need. I would wait until Ty was well and say nothing about the state of my finances until then. Only time would tell if this was a wise decision, but right or wrong, I felt it was the *only* one, the expedient thing to do in terms of Ty's well-being.

When Mrs. Brindle came out of the kitchen, bringing another pot of coffee, I beckoned her over. "My brother's fever is still high, his breathing worse; I fear we cannot continue our journey. Could you send for a doctor? I would feel so much better if I had him looked at by a physician."

"The poor little tyke is worse then?" She seemed genuinely concerned. I thanked God that this unlucky twist of fate at least had brought us to an inn kept by someone as understanding as she appeared to be. How misleading appearances can be I was not to find out until later. I myself was trying to protect the appearance of a well-born lady acting in a proper manner given difficult circumstances. It seemed to work. Mrs. Brindle immediately offered to summon the local doctor.

"Dr. Hardin lives not a stone's throw from here. He always stops here for a morning coffee, either on his way out to make sick calls or on his way back from an all-night delivery, as the case may be. I'll send him right up."

I thanked her and started to turn away.

"Don't you want a bit to eat, miss? Nursing takes all your strength."

"I should get back upstairs. I asked your maid to stay with Ty while I spoke with you—" I hesitated.

"At least, have some good, hot tea. Here, let me pour you a mug to take up with you. I'll send Peg up with a tray of food so you can have it while you wait for the doctor."

"That's very kind of you. Thank you." I gratefully took the mug she handed me. The tea was strong and sweet. As I took a sip and felt its warming strength flow through me, Lady Bethune got up from her place and moved slowly toward me.

"The child is ill?" she demanded. "You won't be continuing on with us then?"

"Ty has a bad cold and isn't up to traveling. No, we won't be going."

"What about your relatives, the ones you said were expecting you? Won't they be waiting at the stagecoach station for you?" Her high-arched eyebrows drew together over curious eyes. "I could take a message, telling the reason for your delay."

"That's very kind of you, Lady Bethune," I began, touched by such unexpected thoughtfulness on her part. Then caution checked me.

I had no assurance that the Hazeltons knew we were coming. Maybe they had not received the note I'd posted before I left school. Worse still, by this time Muir might have found out that Ty was not going to Nanny's sister's, but that *I* had taken him. If that had happened, Muir might already have contacted the Hazeltons, threatened them, reminding them of his legal rights. By what little I knew of the courts, I was afraid Muir would win any custody dispute. Even worse, what if Muir gained knowledge of our whereabouts, came after us, and forcibly took Ty?

I decided I best not give out any more information.

"That won't be necessary, but thank you," I said, my voice cooler than I intended because of my own fear.

She shrugged. "As you please. I know I would be upset if I were expecting two young people I cared about to arrive and they didn't show up. Word of our accident has most probably already gone out. Bad news always travels fast, wrong accounts even faster. They might be saying by now there were no survivors, that all of us perished instead of crawling out of an overturned coach like scurrying monkeys." She sniffed and started back to the table.

I hoped I had not offended her by my refusal. She turned around and, frowning, asked again, "You're sure?"

"Yes, but thank you very much."

She shrugged and went back to the table and took her seat beside Thompson. I saw her say something to her maid, who glanced my way. I assumed they were discussing me. I was sure they thought me rather odd, but they knew only part of my circumstances.

I set down the mug and went back to the stairway. Halfway up I heard the driver's loud voice announce, "We're ready to load up, folks. All going to Dorset!"

Although their possessions had not been retrieved, the other passengers had decided to continue on their journey. The driver had assured us that as soon as the rain stopped men would dive to find and bring up the luggage that had plummeted into the water when the coach overturned. The stage company would contact the owners so they could identify and claim their salvaged belongings. My trunk and Ty's trunk had either been swept downstream or had settled in the mud at the bottom of the swollen river.

How I longed for us to be on our way again to the haven of the Hazeltons' home. Every day Ty was away from Crossfield Grange intensified the danger of discovery. I was deathly afraid of Muir's actions should he find out what Nanny and I had conspired to do and then actually done.

From the window of our room I saw the stagecoach depart. As I watched it drive off and disappear around the bend of the road beyond the inn, a strange desolation overwhelmed me. The feeling of being friendless, forsaken, and destitute left me momentarily weak. I wished then I had at least given Lady Bethune the names and address of Aunt Evelyn and Uncle George. But it was too late, and the sensation of being truly alone with the responsibility of my sick brother became frighteningly real.

Resolutely, I put such thoughts from me. I must be strong, for Ty's sake. He was still asleep, tossing and mumbling feverishly. I knelt beside the bed, took his hot, little hand in my own, and prayed as I had never prayed before, for his recovery and for our continued protection and safety.

Within twenty minutes a doctor with a craggy, weather-beaten face and a bushy beard arrived to examine Ty. He was so cheerful and optimistic, my own low spirits lifted. He ordered poultices be placed on Ty's chest and a steaming kettle be kept nearby for vapor to keep his lungs from becoming congested. "Good nursing and a few days' rest should have him right as rain," Dr. Hardin assured me heartily.

Although Mrs. Brindle had been particularly solicitous about Ty, I worried constantly about her reaction when she found out the state of our financial situation. During Ty's illness she had sent up fresh linens and towels every day. Trays, too, for both of us as Ty began to take nourishment. All these services were rendered by an unwilling Peg, who made her reluctance to do this extra work evident. It seems the other maid was actually a village girl who came in to help only when the inn needed her.

As far as I could tell from what I overheard when downstairs, little had been recovered from the wreck. All the luggage on the top of the stage had toppled into the river, and most of that was ruined by water. All Ty and I had were the clothes we were wearing when we were rescued.

True to Dr. Hardin's prediction, a few days later Ty was better. Then came my moment of truth. I knew I could not put off telling the innkeepers about our predicament any longer.

That evening, after I'd finally gotten Ty settled in bed, I took courage and went downstairs. With all the forthrightness laced with gratitude I could manage, I haltingly explained my situation to the Brindles.

They stared at me, aghast, as I told them of my penniless state. Quickly their expressions changed from disbelief to indignation and finally to anger. Mrs. Brindle was quicker to react than her husband, who was in a besotted state.

Her eyes protruded, her face reddened, and her expression turned ugly. "Well, I must say, this is a fine state of affairs. Not only did I give you the best room in the inn, which rightly should have gone to her ladyship and her maid, but *you* insisted on special services besides. You've got a fair nerve, my girl! We should call the sheriff that's wot! Can't pay, eh? Well, we'll just see about that!"

"You have every right to be upset, Mrs. Brindle. Believe me, I understand. But it wasn't my fault my belongings, including the purse containing all my money, were lost in the stagecoach accident. All I could think of was taking care of my little brother." I swallowed hard, and attempting to appeal to their sympathy, added, "I am all he has in the world."

"Yes, well, be that as it may, remember we had the doctor up to see the lad—come out in all the storm, he did—and that's an extra charge." Mrs. Brindle pushed out her lower lip aggressively.

Her statement was not quite true, but I was in no position to argue. I merely nodded and went on. "I know. I much appreciated that, and I'm very grateful. Maybe it was wrong of me not to tell you right away about the money, but what else could I have done? Ty could not travel farther and—"

I paused, searching both faces for some understanding, some hope of kindness. I met with stony, blank faces. "I fully intend to pay you back for everything."

"Just how do you expect to do that, miss?" Her mouth twisted. "Have your fairy godmother wave a wand and magically bring all the money you owe us?"

"I will work it off. I'll do whatever you say until I've paid back every penny."

"You!" she scoffed. "What can you do with them lily-white, soft hands, them delicate bones?" Her narrowed eyes moved over me scornfully.

I drew myself up. I had to convince her. Visions of debtors' prison, Ty in an orphanage, rose in my fevered imagination. "I'm much stronger than I look."

Mrs. Brindle still looked skeptical. What more could I say to soften her? Had I been entirely mistaken about this woman? She had seemed so kind, at least about Ty. Of course, she *had* thought I was gentry, that she would be well recompensed for all her trouble.

She eyed me with cold contempt.

Swallowing my pride, I took another tack. "Mrs. Brindle, the stagecoach accident was no one's fault. I cannot help it if my brother and I are alone in the world. I have offered you a fair deal, I believe. I am willing to work off my indebtedness."

Mr. Brindle's bloodshot eyes made a slow, rather insolent appraisal of me, which brought the blood rushing into my face. Then for the first time he spoke. "She's got a point, Molly. I could use her in the taproom. I'm always short-handed these nights, pertickerly Saturdays. She's surely strong enough to pull a pint, carry trays, serve customers, and wash up after closing."

Mrs. Brindle shot him a scathing look, but I could see she was considering his suggestion. She chewed her lower lip for a moment, gave me another long look. I felt like a horse at auction. It was humiliating to have them evaluate me as if I were livestock.

Then almost as if thinking out loud she said, "Well, she's pretty enough, I 'spect. We'll give it a try."

In another minute a bargain was struck. It was agreed that I would work as a general housemaid during the day and as a barmaid in the evenings when the taproom opened for business. Mrs. Brindle would figure out the total I owed for room, board, and services rendered.

From that moment I was treated as a servant. Mrs. Brindle had the last word and all the power in the situation, telling me that if my work wasn't satisfactory, there was still the possibility of turning us over to the authorities. Thus she cleverly hung over us, like the Sword of Damocles, the threat of debtors' prison, an orphanage, and, that of which she was not even aware, discovery by Muir and the very real possibility that he would take Ty away from me forever.

7

*S*o began a time in my life I would always look back on as something out of a nightmare. It took less than an hour for my new status to be known throughout the inn. Ty and I were removed from our comfortable room and sent to the attic, a cubbyhole under the eaves. The day after I confessed the truth to the Brindles I was handed a gray muslin dress, a rough, faded, blue cotton coverall to wear over it, and a calico scarf to tie over my head. My hair was to be braided and pinned up, Mrs. Brindle ordered, instead of falling in its natural waves to my shoulders. My high-heeled boots were replaced by sturdy clogs to be worn with heavy woolen stockings.

I, who had been brought up in luxury, waited upon and served, now found myself the lowest in the pecking order of the inn's staff of servants. I was immediately placed in the kitchen as the cook's helper and set to tasks for which I was completely unprepared—washing dishes and greasy platters, cleaning cooking pots and pans, scrubbing potatoes until my hands were raw, stirring stews in a steaming pot over a hearth fire.

It was a far cry from anything I had ever known. With vir-

tually no experience, I had to be shown how to do everything, and I was awkward and clumsy. This made me the
target of irritated tongue-lashings from the cook and the
scullery maid.

After my morning chores in the kitchen, Mrs. Brindle sent
me to help Peg clean the guest rooms, change the linens, and
make the beds. Peg had been a rather sullen girl even when
she thought I was a guest. Now she treated me with utter
contempt. She seemed to take pleasure in assigning me the
most odious jobs: emptying the slop jars, collecting the ashes
in the fireplaces, dragging heavy baskets of used sheets down
to the laundry shed and returning with heavier loads of
ironed linens. I had to trundle the large brass vats downstairs
and out to the well, fill them with water, and lug them back
up to fill a washstand jug in each room.

Although I thought I'd mentally prepared myself for the
physical work I would have to do to pay our debt, I was not
prepared for the daily disgrace of being a servant. The staff
members treated each other harshly. There was no gentleness, no tactful suggestions, no compliments on jobs well
done, only name calling and ridicule. I never heard so much
as a please or thank you. My sudden downfall to this lowly
position made me the butt of rude jokes, the topic of coarse
humor.

In the afternoon I put on a clean apron and head scarf and
reported to Mr. Brindle behind the bar. I had to sweep and
spread fresh straw on the floor before the place opened for
business. By five o'clock, yeomen, farmers, millers, black-
smiths, and shopkeepers began to come in for their nightly
convivial ale or spirits.

I may have been able to withstand the hard labor of the
daytime work if it had not been for my assignment to the
taproom at night. I found it the worst possible form of pun-
ishment, humiliating in the extreme. Worse still, after my exposure to Muir's abuse of spirits, and its ruinous effects on
the lives of my mother and little brother, the thought of work-

ing in a place that dispensed it, as well as nightly being around people who consumed it, was repugnant to me. However, I had no choice but to comply with the terms of my agreement with the Brindles.

Weary as I was from my daily chores, the evening seemed endless. In the beginning I only washed tankards and mugs behind the bar, keeping Mr. Brindle supplied with clean ones as the press of crowd grew. Mr. Brindle often drank along with the customers, becoming less coherent, more blurred of eye and slurred of speech as the evening progressed. Within a week or so, he had me serving the tables. This I disliked as much as anything else I had to do.

Each night when the tavern finally closed at midnight, I climbed the steps to our attic room, almost in tears from weariness and exhaustion. The knowledge that this situation was only temporary kept me from giving in to despair.

As an early and useless bid for sympathy, and more importantly because I did not want the Brindles to contact Muir, I had told them that Ty and I were orphans, which in my case was true, and that we were on our way to our only relatives when the accident occurred. Most of the time I held back the fear that somehow Muir would find out where we were. Sometimes, however, I awoke in the middle of the night shaking from a bad dream in which he had found us.

I tried to put a brave face on our situation for Ty's sake. Using all my storytelling ability, I made our plight sound like one of the adventures I used to make up for him. I wove a tale that we, the prince and princess of a faraway kingdom, had been put under a spell and were being held captive, that we would have to plan and plot secretly our escape.

"You mean some witch has put a spell on us, Lyssa?"

"Something like that."

Completely caught up in this pretend game, Ty's eyes shone with excitement. "But we *will* find our way out some day, won't we?"

"Of course," I said, wishing I were as sure as I sounded.

His little brow puckered, then he asked, "Is Mrs. Brindle the witch?"

"Oh, Ty, don't ever let her hear you say that!" I was unable, in spite of our serious situation, to keep from laughing. "Actually, she's been kinder than we had any right to expect, likely kinder than most innkeepers would be. After all, I do owe her a lot of money. I'm working very hard to free us from the spell."

"I know. I will too, Lyssa." He looked serious. "I can feed the chickens and bring in the eggs for Cook."

I hugged him hard. "You're a champion, Ty!"

"Just maybe a prince from another country will come and rescue us like in *Briar Rose*. Do you think?"

I shook my head doubtfully. "I don't think so, Ty. I think we're going to have to work this out ourselves."

Though I had enjoyed reading fairy tales as a child, I'd never quite believed in the fairy-tale solution of a handsome knight on a white charger coming to save a fair damsel and take her away to live happily ever after. That had been too contrary to my experience of the *real* world.

All our hardships notwithstanding, at least Ty was well. In fact he was thriving. He had become the pet of the place. The cook had taken a fancy to him and saw that he got the best food. During the day he played with the cat and her kittens and helped in the vegetable garden. He was such an appealing child, merry and sweet natured, it would have been hard for anyone not to grow fond of him. I do believe *he* was the reason the other servants' attitudes toward me gradually improved.

This was true of all the servants—all except Peg, the overworked general housemaid. She was the one holdout not won over by Ty, but who could blame her after finding out that the *lady* who had demanded so much extra service— frequent hot water, clean linens, trays and extra pots of tea— was not only poor as a church mouse but, by deceiving the

Brindles, was also, in her opinion, no better than a common thief.

Her hostility was unrelenting. All my attempts at friendliness failed. She ridiculed me, pointed out my mistakes, made ugly, cutting remarks to me, and complained to Mrs. Brindle about me. I understood why she resented me. From birth our destinies were ordained to be different. My situation, no matter how low, was temporary, while Peg had been born into poverty, and with no education, her position would remain the same. I could not disguise my accent nor hide the fact that I had been used to another kind of life. No wonder Peg hated me.

Gradually our lives took on a sort of pattern. The account I was keeping of our indebtedness was steadily growing even. Soon I would be able to pay off the Brindles, and Ty and I would be free to leave and continue on our journey to Briarwood Manor.

I did not mind the hard work in the daytime but I greatly disliked working in the taproom in the evenings. There I had to ignore the ogles and remarks made to me or about me as I served. I kept telling myself it would soon be over. Soon this wretched experience would be a thing of the past.

Then one morning something happened that jolted me. As I was coming downstairs with a bundle of sheets piled in a willow basket, the front door of the inn burst open and a tall man, his dark cape billowing behind him, strode into the center of the room. The blustery wind caught the door, slamming it against the wall and making his entrance even more dramatic. Startled, I almost dropped the laundry, and Mrs. Brindle, standing behind the counter, turned around with a jerk.

He stood, looking around him, and from where I stood on the staircase I could see his face clearly. It was Lady Bethune's nephew, Nicholas Seymour! His heavy, dark brows drew together as his penetrating gaze met mine. Instinctively I drew back. While I recognized him immediately, I was sure he would never recognize the grubby maid I had become. He would never make the connection between the well-dressed young lady, his aunt's traveling companion, Miss Challys Winthrop, and a scruffy maid working at a country inn.

There was, however, an instant of hesitation as though he were about to take a step toward me or speak, but Mrs. Brindle, sensing a paying customer, bustled forward, all warmth and welcome. "Good day, sir. What can we do for you? A room for the night? Your horse stabled?"

Her tone of voice was noticeably different from the one she used toward the servants, far different from the one in which she usually addressed *me*.

Seymour turned toward the woman. "No, madam. Thank you very much." His voice was deep, authoritative. "I have come to inquire whether any of the belongings of the passengers on the stagecoach that met with the accident several weeks ago have been retrieved from the river? My aunt, Lady Bethune, was among the unfortunate travelers marooned here afterward. She is missing some very valuable belongings. I thought they might have been brought here for identification."

Mrs. Brindle seemed flustered, and afterward, when I thought about it, rather furtive and defensive in her manner. I passed it off at the time, thinking she was offended by Seymour's remark about "unfortunate travelers marooned here." "No, sir, none as I know of. What was brung up was done by a salvage company hired, I think, by the stagecoach line. I dunna heard of anything of value being found. It was a very stormy night indeed, the night of the accident. The current in the river is treacherous. Like as not most things was swept downstream."

"Well, then, that's that." Seymour brushed his hands together in a dismissive gesture. "Luckily, her maid held on to her jewel case containing most of the irreplaceable items, but since I was on my way to my aunt's for a visit, she requested I at least stop and inquire. Thank you, madam, and good day to you."

As he swung around to retrace his steps to the front door, he again glanced toward where I stood, trying to make myself invisible. He halted, and again our gazes met—I flattened myself against the wall, feeling heat rise into my face. He seemed to hesitate as he pulled on his leather gloves. For a few seconds he remained motionless, as if he were grasping at something that eluded him. He frowned, then giving his head an almost imperceptible shake, marched toward the door, yanked it open, and went out.

With the door's slam, I felt my tension ease, but in the next minute I felt a scalding resentment. Until I was in the position of a servant, I did not realize how people treated them. To Seymour I was no more than a part of the woodwork. Of course, I had not wanted him to recognize me. Still, I was determined that when I got out of my own bondage, I would be aware of those serving me and treat them kindly.

After Seymour's departure, to my surprise, Mrs. Brindle hurried to the window, peered out as if to make sure he had gone, then went to the cellar door and opened it. "Brindle!" she called. "Come up here at once! I got sumpin' to tell you."

I heard a muffled reply from below where Mr. Brindle was gathering stock for tonight's tavern trade from the wine cellar.

Mrs. Brindle stood there, hands on her hips, tapping her foot impatiently. "*Now,* I said, Brindle!"

Within minutes I heard the clump of boots and the rattle of glass as a red-faced, puffing Mr. Brindle emerged through the door behind the counter, carrying a wooden box of bottles. "Whatja want?"

I tried to slip down the rest of the steps and disappear out through the back hall to the laundry shed, but Mrs. Brindle turned and spotted me. "What are you gawkin' at? Gwan wi' your work."

I hurried past but not before I heard her say to her husband, "We got a bit of trouble, unless—"

Unless what? What kind of trouble did she mean? What, if anything, did it have to do with Nicholas Seymour's unexpected visit?

or the rest of the day I felt depressed. Seeing Nicholas Seymour—handsome, well groomed, expensively dressed, assured of his position—made my present situation doubly hard to bear. It was all I could do to get on with my chores. My evening stint in the taproom loomed, even larger than usual, and with it my other worries.

I should write Nanny Grace at her sister's address, where she was supposed to be visiting with Ty, at least to let her know where we were. Yet, how could I let Nanny Grace know what had happened to us, especially with the Brindles watching my every move, keeping me busy from sunrise to sunset. And what if, having discovered Ty was gone, Muir went after Nanny and threatened her? Having witnessed his frightening rages, to be the target of one would be terrifying. Letting Nanny know where we were might put her in greater jeopardy. No, I couldn't take that chance. And I couldn't risk the possibility of Muir finding us. What I'd done was criminal—kidnapping! Children were the property of their father. I had taken Ty without Muir's permission, even his knowledge. He could drag me into court, have me thrown into prison. A young woman like me would stand no chance against a powerful man. I shuddered at the possibilities should Muir find us.

All these complicated thoughts churned in my mind as I entered the taproom to take up my duties that evening. To my disgust I found Brindle had been tippling earlier, even before the evening had begun. He was far into his cups.

He was flushed of face and slurred of speech, refilling his own glass whenever he filled one for a customer. At this rate he wouldn't last the evening. This was not a new occurrence. More than once I had been forced to summon Mrs. Brindle to help him to bed. Then I'd been left to clean and lock up on my own.

It was, as usual, crowded and noisy, and I was kept constantly on the go, clearing tables, serving round after round of drinks, picking up empties, and taking back refilled mugs. I'd learned, for the most part, to ignore the bold ogling, the coarse remarks, sometimes purposely made loudly enough for me to hear, as I moved about. Mentally, I gritted my teeth, repeating to myself, *This too shall pass.*

That night a frequent customer was there, one who was remarkably different from the regulars. I'm not sure when I first became aware of Francis Vaughn, but by the time he had come in several evenings in a row, I had noticed him.

He was young, boyish looking almost, with rounded features, a soft beard, and thick, curly, dark hair. He was slight of build, and he spoke in a low voice with an accent I couldn't place. The thing about him that stood out most to me was that he was always polite, thanking me when I served him, leaving an extra coin as a tip. The other unusual thing about him was that he brought a small sketchbook with him and spent the evening sketching the other patrons. One night I could not help but see a rendering he'd made of the village baker, a man with strong features and interesting facial expressions.

"That's very good," I said. I knew nothing of art, but it did seem to be somewhat of a good likeness from what I could tell.

"Only a quick impression." He shrugged, then he looked

up at me and said intently, "I'm an *artist*. My name is Francis Vaughn." He smiled. "Remember it. Some day I'm going to be very famous."

He sounded very sure of himself. Boastful, even. I started to move away, but he stopped me with a question. "What is someone with the face of an angel doing in a place like this?"

I must have looked startled, for immediately he apologized, saying, "Please don't be offended. It's just that I noticed you right away. The first time I came in here. As an artist, I'm always looking at people as possible models and naturally—maybe, you don't realize how—well, what an interesting face—I'd love to paint you."

He went on to tell me he was living near the village in a small cottage turned into a studio. He seemed eager to talk more, but just then an impatient customer banged his empty mug on the bar top, and I looked over my shoulder nervously. "I have to go."

"If you'd consent to pose—"

"Oh, I couldn't. I have no time."

"Not even one day a week?"

Mr. Brindle's loud voice reached me then, and I had to hurry off.

When I came by his table again, Vaughn ordered another drink and whispered, "If you would pose for me, I can pay you in a few days what it would take you a month to earn here as a serving girl." He went on to say he had received a commission for a special kind of portrait for a prestigious gentlemen's private club in London, but he had not found the right model yet.

By this time in the evening, the noise level had risen along with the amount of alcohol consumed. The crowded room was hot, filled with the smells of men who had come straight from field, forge, and barn, and loud with argumentative voices and the clatter of tankards against wooden tables. The heavy tobacco smoke from a dozen tar-encrusted pipes hung in the air. My head pounded, my feet hurt, my back ached. Anything that promised escape from this nightly scene would have sounded tempting, but I hesitated. "Think about it, will you?" Vaughn persisted as he pressed a piece of paper into my hand.

The rest of the night I did not have much time to think. Mr. Brindle was hardly any help, huddled in one corner of the bar with two unsavory-looking fellows whom I did not recognize as regulars. I had to fill the pint-sized beer mugs myself, as well as collect the empties and wipe off the counter.

I reminded him when it was time to close. To my surprise he waved me off, telling me I could leave, that he'd shut down the place. He was still with the two men I'd noticed earlier. Well, it was nothing to me. Mr. Brindle would have to answer to his wife.

Wearily, I plodded up the steps, ready to fling myself on the lumpy mattress for a few short hours of sleep. As I undressed, I found the slip of paper in my apron pocket that Vaughn had given me. I took it out and read it. In a distinctive, curling hand he'd written the directions to his studio-cottage and the hourly rate for modeling. He was right. It was more than I made here in a day.

I got into bed and pulled the thin blanket over my shoulders. Every muscle twitched from fatigue. Anything would be better than what I was doing. I had discovered that barmaids were notoriously underpaid. Although allowed to keep whatever tips customers left, I could see it would be slow going indeed to pay back the amount Mrs. Brindle figured we owed her. All the "extras" we had enjoyed when Ty was ill had added up to a tidy sum. If I could hasten our leaving even by a few days, wouldn't it be worth it?

But could I trust Francis Vaughn? Artists were not really respectable. Except, of course, for those whose work was hung in the Royal Gallery. What did I really know of Vaughn?

I closed my eyes and was soon asleep. Vaughn's offer, then,

might have just as easily been forgotten except for two un-foreseen events.

As I said, the cook had become fond of my little brother, though I did not know how fond until the fair came to the village and she gave me time off to take him. I was surprised that morning when instead of giving me my orders for the day she provided me with the excuse to give Mrs. Brindle. Besides the carnival attractions—clowns, magicians, and puppet shows—local farmers set up booths to sell their produce of vegetables, fruit, and specialties of all sorts. The cook handed me a list of items to bring back, adding gruffly, "No need to hurry. Give the lad a chance for a treat and a ride or two."

I realized she was doing this from a heart recently thawed by a little boy's smiles. Nonetheless, I appreciated the chance for a day off, and so with a feeling of freedom I had not ex-perienced for weeks, Ty and I took off for the village.

Even before we saw the bright tents and flapping flags, we heard calliope music and the sounds of a large crowd. The nearer we got to the village the more chaotic the scene around us became. Everyone seemed to be going to the fair. People on foot, in carts, carriages, and coaches, as well as riders on horseback, added to the confusion. The noise of shouts and laughter grew louder. Holding Ty's hand, I quickened our pace, a sense of anticipation mounting with every step.

We passed through the entrance, jostled on every side by people. The holiday air was contagious. Ty gave a little skip and, swinging my hand back and forth, asked excitedly, "What shall we do first, Lyssa?"

"Let's take a look all around, then decide." Besides the money the cook had given me, I'd brought along a few coins of my own from tips earned in the taproom. I'd squirreled them away without guilt, given, as they were, directly to me. Now was the perfect time to use some of them. I'd have to account for the cook's purchases when we got back, and the little extra money she'd given us did not amount to much. But I wanted Ty to have a good time. The poor little fellow had been so good and patient all this time with no playmates and only the small kitchen yard in which to roam, not to mention the long evenings he had to spend alone upstairs while I worked in the taproom. I wanted him to have at least this one day of fun. Still I'd have to be careful and pick and choose how to spend our tiny amount.

We wandered through the tented fairgrounds thronged with people. Everywhere there was color, movement. The midway was lined with booths of all kinds on every side, the owners hawking their wares. Booths decorated with streamers boasted baskets of rosy apples, golden pears, pumpkins, dark, leafy, green vegetables, bright orange carrots, and striped turban squash. Most of the sellers were pleasant, cheerfully greeting potential customers. Vendors sang out from wheeled wagons as they sold hot chestnuts, candied apples, fruit tarts, and sausages on buns.

The whole scene was such a direct and pleasant contrast with our grim existence that I was soon caught up in the merriment all around me. My one nagging wish was that we could somehow get lost in this crowd, slip away, and escape from our dreary serfdom to the Brindles.

It was then I saw Francis Vaughn.

He was sitting on a canvas stool outside a small tent in front of an easel. Before him in another chair sat a weathered-faced fisherman with a woolen cap pulled around large ears, red with cold. His blue eyes twinkled as he drew on a long-stemmed pipe. A plump woman with wispy gray hair stood nearby nodding approvingly. Vaughn was busy with his paintbrush, working steadily on the old man's portrait.

A sign nearby read, PORTRAITS, 1 shilling.

Almost at the same moment I saw him, he looked up and saw me. He smiled and beckoned me, his hand still holding the brush. I moved around behind him to see the small canvas propped on the easel. To me it looked like a good drawing, at least the cap and pipe were well rendered.

"That's very good!" I declared, nodding to the couple who beamed happily.

Vaughn worked swiftly and, with a few more strokes, signed his initials with a flourish at the bottom left side and handed the picture to the woman. She, in turn, counted out the fee into his outstretched palm.

"Next?" Vaughn said hopefully, turning to me.

"Oh, no." I shook my head. "We're here to have fun."

"Don't turn me down. I'll do one of your brother here free if *you* will sit for me. I've been wanting to sketch you since I first saw you." He snapped his fingers. "I've got an idea. Your brother can ride the carousel while you pose. It's right over there." He pointed to the gaily painted merry-go-round a few yards away. "You can keep your eye on him while you pose for me."

"Oh, please, do say yes, Lyssa," Ty begged. "Can I?"

"*May* I." To Vaughn I said, "I don't know—"

"I'll be fine, *really,* Lyssa!" Ty tugged at my arm. "You can see me from here." He hopped from one foot to the other in his eagerness.

"Smart lad! Of course you'll be fine. Here's the price of two rides." Vaughn handed him a fistful of change.

Before I could protest, Ty was off and running toward the carousel.

"Take a seat, turn your head just so. I'd like a profile first." Vaughn began sharpening his charcoal stick.

It was a joy to see Ty having such a good time, and almost without thinking, I turned my head this way and that as Vaughn made several sketches. He made little murmuring sounds as he worked. The sound of the calliope lulled me, and Ty's smiling face and excited wave each time he came around on the merry-go-round made me glad. Strangely enough, I didn't even examine Vaughn's sketches. I was just happy to be free, at least for a while.

When his two rides were over, Ty came running back. We wanted to explore still other parts of the fair before we had to return to the inn, and Vaughn decided to close up shop and accompany us. As we wandered about, stopping at this booth and that, he told me more about himself. Although he was rather mysterious about it, he hinted that he had a famous London artist as a mentor. In fact, it was one of this artist's wealthy patrons who had lent Vaughn his weekend cottage outside the village. The man had seen some of Vaughn's work and had given him a commission as well as a place to paint. It was a great opportunity for a struggling artist.

"My dream, of course, is to have my work hung in the Royal Academy exhibit. You have to be really good; however, it doesn't hurt to have connections, people in high places within artistic circles to promote you."

We stopped, and Vaughn bought us all meat pies and cups of sweet cider. We sat on one of the benches in the little park set aside for picnickers.

"What I have in mind—that is, if you would consent to pose for me—is something like I've seen in the works of Millais and Rossetti. My patron is a great admirer of the Pre-Raphaelite painters."

"Pre-Raphaelite?"

"They were a group of idealistic artists that specialized in painting religious and allegorical themes. When I said you had the face of an angel, I meant that literally. You would be perfect for a painting I have in mind."

"But wouldn't such a painting take ages and ages?"

"It would take only three or four sittings. As you can see, I work quickly. And you would only have to pose for the face and figure. The background and details can be painted in afterward. As I told you, I can pay you very well. I already have a commission for the painting, and my commissioner is willing to pay the expense of a model."

"To tell you the truth, I don't think I'll be here much longer," I said, then, in a burst of confidence, I told him about the accident, Ty's illness, and our delayed journey to the home of our relatives.

"So you see, I have no time of my own. I must pay off our debt so we can be on our way."

"You'd get the money much faster, be on your way sooner, if you'd pose for this painting. Surely you can get off for a few hours on a Sunday?"

I thought that over. Mrs. Brindle reluctantly let her help off to attend services on Sundays. Since the taproom was closed on that day as well, there was very little to be done at the inn. Ty usually became restless during the church service. Only my promise of some special treat afterward made it bearable for him to sit still that long. If the weather permitted, that meant a picnic. If the cook was in a good mood, she let us pack a few apples, some cheese and bread, for our lunch. Maybe I *could* combine one of our outings with a few hours' posing for Vaughn.

Since I still had Cook's list of purchases to buy, I told Vaughn we needed to get going. We got up to leave.

"Think about it, won't you?" Vaughn urged.

"Yes, I will," I replied, not at all sure I would. I promised to let him know, and we parted.

When I think back on that afternoon, it all seemed friendly and harmless enough. Yet, as life so often teaches us, the things that cause the most trouble, those that bring the most regret, often start innocently.

9

*F*rancis Vaughn's offer the day of the village fair soon faded from my memory. Although Mrs. Brindle was supposedly keeping an account of what I was earning against what I owed, I kept my own tabulation. My tips each night were accumulating. I'd discovered the key to getting generous ones—being pleasant when I didn't feel like it, smiling when I'd rather frown. The sad truth was that the later it got and the more ale that was consumed the better the tips became.

We had been at the inn nearly two months by the time I figured we had enough to pay back the Brindles in full. We would need some additional money for our travel expenses. A couple weeks longer and we would be free. Knowing my days in bondage were nearing an end, I worked with more energy than ever.

I told Ty we would soon be leaving. Of course, since he did not have any of the same happy memories of Briarwood Manor that I did, he expressed mixed feelings at my announcement.

"I'll be sorry to leave Cook," he said doubtfully. "Tabby too." Tabby was the barnyard cat he had made his special pet. "She's just had kittens, just begun to let me handle them."

"But, Ty, I'm sure Auntie and Uncle George will let you have your own cat and a dog, if you like, probably even a pony. I did when I was a little girl and lived with them at Briarwood."

That seemed to encourage him, and he entered into my plans more enthusiastically.

The night before I planned to leave, I laid out our clothes for travel. Ty had shot up like the proverbial weed over the last two months and had outgrown the things he'd worn on our journey. I was grateful Cook had passed along some clothes that had belonged to her numerous nephews. My one outfit, water stained and spotted from that night, was all I had. I cleaned and brushed it, made it as presentable as possible. I had not dared buy anything for either of us in the village, not even new ribbons for my poor battered bonnet. Knowing how the smallest scrap of gossip in a small town flies, I didn't want to risk having Mrs. Brindle confront me as to how I could spend any money when I hadn't paid her back. Better that we go as we were, even if we looked rather shabby.

The following morning I rose before dawn and dressed before waking Ty. My heart thumped anxiously. I didn't relish the encounter with Mrs. Brindle, even though it would be my last. I helped Ty with buttons and lacers, and we started down the attic steps.

To my dismay we met Peg coming up from the kitchen. Her mouth dropped open in surprise when she saw us.

"Wheredja think yer goin' dressed up like that?" she demanded. "You should have taken out the slop jars and fetched hot water afore this. We have two new lodgers, ya know."

I let go of Ty's hand and very deliberately drew on my gloves, carefully smoothing each finger. "Not *this* morning, Peg. Not *any* morning after this."

Her pale green gooseberry eyes popped wide, and the look on her face would have made me laugh if I hadn't been so nervous. Before she could regain either wit or tongue, I brushed by her with Ty in tow.

However, once we'd passed she leaned over the banister and shrilled, "Jest you wait till the missus hears about this!"

I didn't have to wait long. Mrs. Brindle evidently had heard our voices and was waiting at the foot of the staircase. Her startled expression turned to outrage when she saw us dressed for traveling.

"And what's all this about? Leaving you say? Without no notice. After all we done for you?"

"You must have realized we would be on our way as soon as I paid back the money I owed you, Mrs. Brindle."

"What makes you think you done that?"

"I've kept track of all I owed and the amount of work I've done. It tallies." I took out my ledger page and showed her.

"Wait jest one minute, miss high and mighty," she said after studying it. "I don't see any for the room you've been occupying and for the meals you've been eating since you started working off your first bill." She looked at me with narrowed eyes, her arms folded belligerently.

I was stunned. Surely she didn't expect payment for our miserable room and the skimpy meals we'd eaten?

"Did you expect charity after trying to cheat us out of what was our due when your brother was sick and we did all we could for you?" Her chin jutted out. "No, miss, not so fast. You still owe me." With a great show she turned the ledger around and started checking my figures. "The way I figure it, you still owe us two months of labor."

I bit back the words I felt like flinging at her. I felt Ty's hand tightening in mine. I knew I could not fight this. Mrs. Brindle had the upper hand. She could still make a case for the authorities if she had in mind to do so. If the sheriff were called, he might investigate, discover Ty and I had run away from Muir, and send Ty back. Furious but defeated, there was nothing I could do but agree either to pay the added amount, which I didn't have, or work it off.

75

For one rash moment I was tempted to pull out the chamois bag containing Mama's sapphire set that I had kept hidden beneath my mattress all this time and cast it into Mrs. Brindle's sneering face. It would more than pay our "ransom." But good sense prevailed. I would not waste my precious inheritance on such an unworthy cause. It would be like the biblical equivalent of selling my birthright for a mess of porridge. No, my mother's wish had been that I keep the jewels to protect my future, to sell them only as a last resort. This was not the emergency she had feared. I was young, strong, and healthy. As long as I could work, I would do what was necessary to settle this debt on my own.

With dragging feet, Ty and I remounted the stairs. Peg stood sneering on the landing as we reached it. I knew she had listened to every word of my confrontation with Mrs. Brindle. As we went past her, she hissed something vicious, but I ignored her.

"Never mind, Ty," I said as soon as we were in our room. "It will be all right. You'll see. They can't keep us here forever. I'll pay what she says we owe, but after that, we'll go. Don't worry."

His trusting eyes wide, he nodded solemnly. I'd never felt the responsibility of my little brother more heavily.

That day all my chores seemed more onerous than ever. I couldn't believe I was still the Brindles' indentured servant. We'd been so close to freedom that this added sentence seemed unbearable. That night when I climbed the stairs to the attic, I felt completely worn out. As I wearily undressed, I caught a glimpse of myself in the cracked mirror above the washstand. Suddenly Francis Vaughn's request came back to me.

Holding my stub of a candle closer to get a better look, I studied my face. My high cheekbones were more prominent now that I had grown thinner. My eyes were large, long-lashed like Ty's, and like those of our mother. My mouth was rather full, my nose a little long. However, maybe to an artist, it seemed an interesting face to paint. I remembered the amount he said he would pay me for modeling.

Desperate times call for desperate measures, I had heard said. Now I realized just how desperate I was. After all these weeks I'd been slaving at the inn, I still owed the Brindles money, and I would need enough for the traveling expenses too.

The candle sputtered, then went out. I was left in the dark to grope my way over to the cot. How wonderful it would be when I no longer had to scrub another floor, clean another grease-caked pot, or serve another foaming pint of ale to a leering customer in the taproom.

Perhaps encountering Francis Vaughn was a stroke of luck, even the answer to prayer. Then and there I decided to tell Francis Vaughn I would pose for him.

The very next evening Vaughn came to the taproom. When I brought him his lager, I told him of my decision. Delighted, he started to tell me how to get to his studio-cottage. "I still have the directions you gave me," I whispered just as Mr. Brindle hollered from the bar, "Get a move on there, girl. There's customers waiting."

"I have to go," I said and hurried away to pick up another order. I was too busy the rest of the night to speak to Vaughn again, but before he left, he managed to slip me a piece of paper on which he had written "Sunday afternoon. FV."

Of course, Ty had to be in on our secret. He was excited. He remembered Francis from the fair and thought he was a "jolly fellow." Always game, my little brother made it sound like a great adventure.

The next Sunday, using the directions Vaughn had given me, we turned down a crooked road just before getting to the village, then followed a winding path to a fenced cottage nestled under leafy oaks. The cottage had a sloping thatch roof, diamond-paned windows, and a flagstone walkway leading to its red-painted door. It was actually quite charming, I thought as I knocked.

Vaughn opened the door almost immediately and greeted us enthusiastically. He ushered us into the large front room, a parlor, one end of which he had made into a studio. The canvas was concealed on a large, cloth-draped easel. Vaughn said he would incorporate some of the sketches he'd made of me at the fair with some full-length poses he'd make today. That was his method of working, starting with sketches and shifting to an oil painting later.

He said he was planning this composition in an Oriental style, much the fashion among artists just then, with a Chinese screen, perhaps, as background.

"May I see what you've done so far?" I asked, filled with curiosity.

He shook his head. "I never show a work in progress." His eyes twinkled mischievously. "You'll see it when it's hung in the Royal Academy exhibit."

He refused to answer my questions about the mysterious person who had commissioned the painting.

"I can say this, however. I've discussed my idea for this particular painting with my mentor, and he thinks it's fine. Now, it's time I gave you the tea I promised." He smiled.

Francis turned out to be a lively if rather clumsy host, dropping napkins, sloshing into our saucers the tea he poured from a brown, earthen pot. The tea was hot and fragrant, and we toasted crumpets on long forks over an open fire he'd built in the small fireplace. I remember the coziness of that Sunday afternoon, in sharp contrast to the gloomy weather outside.

After we'd had our tea, Vaughn found a box of old tin soldiers somewhere and a wooden Noah's ark with a menagerie of little animals. Ty was kept happily occupied while I posed.

"Will you paint me in this?" I asked, looking down at the dress I wore under my coverall as a maid.

"When I go up to London next I'll go to a costumer's and select something. It won't matter for now. Here—" he flung a length of Prussian blue material around my shoulders and arranged it. "This will do, the color is all I want to get. Loosen your hair. Let it fall—thus. Wonderful!" Vaughn seemed elated, high spirited that day.

He seated me on a high stool a few feet from his easel. It was my first such experience, other than that brief time at the fair, and I soon grew tired and stiff. My muscles ached from holding the pose. Francis, however, worked feverishly. I could hear the scrape of his brush on the rough fabric of the canvas. He seemed almost to forget me until I cleared my throat a couple of times and reminded him it was getting dark and I must get back to the inn.

Afterward, when I protested the amount of money he pressed into my hand, Francis assured me, "Money means nothing to the man who commissioned this painting. You've earned it."

He walked through the woods back to the road with us. "Will you come next week?"

"Yes." I said. "Same time?"

"Wonderful." He smiled.

As it turned out, I posed only a few more times for him—four Sunday afternoons out of a lifetime. Yet those hours were to have profound effects on both our lives.

10

It was a strange interlude, a drastic change from my workaday week. The cottage tucked into the dense woodland seemed a world set apart. Francis Vaughn was like no one I'd ever met before. He matched the image I'd held of artists, meteoric and moody by turns, sometimes talkative, other times morose. I came to accept his erratic personality, though I never knew how he would be when I arrived. Sometimes silent, other times he talked constantly as he painted. Those times he seemed angry, speaking bitterly about less talented fellow students at art school who had connections. He criticized artists whose names even I recognized, saying they were unfairly elevated in the art world. Often he declared confidently, almost arrogantly, his assured future success.

"One day I *will* be well known, have clients clamoring for me to paint their portraits," he told me.

I simply listened, not always too attentively, my mind preoccupied as it was with my dilemma.

I do remember one particular day, though, when I found him quite depressed. He said he had wakened with a screaming headache brought on by a recurrent nightmare, and had been sleepless the rest of the night. He had a glass of wine in his hand as he let me into the cottage and offered me one from the half-full bottle on a table near his easel. I refused and said I should leave, that he probably did not feel like painting.

But he would have none of it. "I want to paint, I *need* to because—you see *that* is the nightmare. I dream I'm paralyzed somehow and can never paint again. I have lost the inspiration, the talent."

"Has this happened before?" I asked, feeling rather uneasy.

"It used to happen a lot. Before I met the man I told you about who sees my potential." Vaughn took a long sip of his wine.

"It all goes back to my childhood," he explained. His father, a once prominent merchant who had not encouraged his son in his art, had later been thrown into debtors' prison. Vaughn was plagued with the horror of suffering a like fate and with terrible guilt because he had not gone into business with his father and perhaps could have helped him avoid failure.

"I have to succeed," he told me fiercely. "I don't want you to go. You pose, I'll paint. If I'm alone, I'll drink too much."

I had seen him at the tavern a few times when I thought he'd had too much to drink, so I reluctantly consented to stay that afternoon. Things went all right, although Vaughn continued to talk erratically, the large onyx signet ring on his little finger flashing as he waved his hand about to emphasize some point he was making. I was shocked to hear that in the past, in times of deep depression, he had taken chloral, a powerful drug, to induce sleep so he could shut out his demons.

"I don't anymore," he said. "I *know* if I keep at it I *will* succeed. Now, someone believes in me."

Francis told me he would be going up to London the next day to show the preliminary sketches for the painting to his

81

patron. I suppose I should have been more curious about this wealthy man to whom the cottage belonged and who was sponsoring Francis. However, my mind was usually pre-occupied with other concerns.

While I sat modeling, I daydreamed of how wonderful it would be when Ty and I were at last at Briarwood Manor, safe and secure. It was then that I thought of a solution to my constant worry that no one knew where we were or of our sorry plight. When finally Francis said we were finished for the day, I got down from the stool on which I was perched and asked, "Francis, may I have some paper and the use of a pen? I'd like to write a note to my relatives who are expecting Ty and me and tell them of our delay."

"Of course," said Francis. He tore off a sheet of paper from one of his sketchbooks and handed it to me. I scribbled off a hasty note with only the merest of explanations. It was time to get back to the inn. Hurriedly, I folded it, addressed it, and handed it to Francis.

He glanced at it then raised his eyebrows and exclaimed, *"Lord and Lady Hazelton of Briarwood Manor* are your relatives?" He seemed impressed. "No wonder. I had an *uncanny* feeling about you. I knew you didn't belong in the Brindles' tavern." He paused, regarding me curiously. "These people are your relatives and you're working as a barmaid in a place like that?"

"It's a long story," I said quickly, wondering if I'd already revealed too much. "Too complicated to go into right now." I looked over at Ty, then said, "We must really get back. Come along, Ty."

Francis pocketed the letter in his smock, saying, "Not to worry. I'll take care this reaches its right destination."

The next Sunday Vaughn greeted me with unusual joviality. "I have some exciting news," he declared. My commissioner has seen the sketches, and he is very pleased. He especially likes the model!" He laughed. "His very words were, 'What a stunner,' so you can see, it all looks very promising."

"May I see the painting?" I asked.

"Not yet. I still have some final touches. But you have been very patient, and I'm grateful."

At the end of the session, Vaughn seemed particularly pleased with his afternoon's work. He still wouldn't let me see the painting, but he did press an extra coin into my hand as Ty and I were ready to leave, waving away my protest. "Actually, your part is finished, though I hope you will pose for me again. I have another idea in mind for which you'd be the perfect model."

"I doubt it, Francis. You have helped me enormously with this payment. But I will be leaving—very soon." I stopped, wondering how much I should confide in him. No one from the inn knew where we spent Sunday afternoons, nor of my association with the artist, and he had been warm and helpful, providing me with an unexpected windfall of cash. "This has helped me pay off our debt, and I'm very grateful. I hope we can soon leave for my relatives'."

He frowned. "I don't understand why you didn't contact them right away. Surely they would have sent you money, being who they are. Members of the aristocracy and all."

Quickly I explained that Lord and Lady Hazelton were elderly and I did not want to distress them. I held up the money he had just given me. "With this, we should be on our way much sooner. Thank you."

"We shall *all* soon be very well off. Both of us freed of our shackles of poverty," he said grandly, giving me a conspiratorial wink. "This painting will make me famous. I feel it."

Mondays were always busy in the taproom. Men deprived of their pints with their fellows on Sunday swarmed into the tavern early, drank heartily and long. Brindle not the least. I gathered he spent most Sundays in solitary drinking. He certainly opened the taproom on Mondays somewhat the worse for his Sunday indulgence.

The same rough-looking men I'd seen him huddled with before showed up, and again the three of them went to a table at the far end of the room, leaving me to tend bar. It was a job I detested. As we were doing a brisk business I soon noticed the supply was getting low, the shelves of bottled spirits emptying rapidly.

Finally, I went over to Mr. Brindle and whispered, "Excuse me, sir."

He turned around, obviously annoyed at being interrupted. When I told him the problem, he snarled, "Here, go down to the cellar and bring up a dozen or so bottles—the red."

He thrust his ring of keys at me. I stood there for a few seconds, holding them. He'd never before entrusted me on such an errand.

As I hesitated, he snapped, "Whatja waitin' for? Get a move on. Customers waitin'." He turned back to his companions and lowered his head, clearly continuing the conversation I'd interrupted.

I had to pass by the register counter, where Mrs. Brindle was nodding at her post. She gave a kind of snort as I went by but did not waken.

There were several keys on the ring, and I had no idea which one to use. I went down the narrow stone steps to the lower part of the house. When I reached the bottom of the stairway, I held the candle high and looked around. The space was circular, with three wooden doors. Which one led to the storage room for the tavern? They looked similar. I'd just have to try to find the right one.

Starting at my left, I tried one key, then another, but I couldn't get any to slide in or turn easily. I tried the second door and found a key that twisted slightly. I gave the key a push, and the door squeaked open. Raising the candle, I peered in.

It was a storage room, but not the one containing the wine. There were no shelves or barrels. It was hardly bigger than a pantry. Something caught my eye, however, and I stepped forward cautiously and slowly turned around. I saw a number of trunks and assorted luggage. There was even a wicker hamper, very much the worse for wear, dented, bent out of shape, its willow strips broken. I took another step in, tipping the candle to shine in front of me so I could get a better look.

Seeing something familiar, I crept closer. A small humpbacked trunk. When I bent nearer I saw it bore the initials CW on the metal plate below the lock. *My* trunk! The one I thought had been swept away when our stagecoach toppled into the river! My breath came shallowly as I glanced around. I recognized more articles. A now water-stained, expensive alligator tea kit. Wasn't it the one Lady Bethune's maid had carried? Had all these things been pulled from the wreckage? The very things Mrs. Brindle had assured Nicholas Seymour had *not* been recovered?

What were they doing stashed away under the inn? What were the Brindles up to? Were they selling these expensive items? Were they collaborating with thieves? I had thought the Brindles mean-spirited, conniving, and penny-pinching, but I had not thought them to be criminals. The two men I'd seen Brindle with in the tavern recently—*they* had the sly, dangerous look I would have suspected of crooks. Were they selling these stolen goods for the Brindles and then splitting the profits?

I began to shake. The candle in my shaking hand dripped hot wax on my skin, and I gasped. Were Ty and I literally trapped in a den of thieves?

Just then I heard heavy footsteps on the ceiling above. With a creak of hinges, the door to the basement opened, and Mrs. Brindle's voice bellowed down, "What's keeping you?"

Hastily, I backed out of the room, closing the door but not relocking it. "Coming!" I called back. "It's a heavy load."

I hurried to fit the next key on the ring into the lock on the third door. It opened easily. This was the wine cellar. I grabbed the nearest wooden box of wine bottles, lifted it, set it on the lowest step of the stairway, then shut and locked the wine cellar door behind me.

For the rest of the night, all I could think of was that room filled with my belongings and those of my fellow travelers. What should I do? Should I go to the authorities? Tell the Brindles I knew, confront them, threaten them? The thought made my knees weak, almost buckle. They wouldn't hesitate to accuse me of defrauding *them* and turn Ty and me over to the authorities who would possibly find out about Muir and notify him as to our whereabouts.

As I mechanically served drinks, washed mugs, and wiped counters and tables, my one compelling thought was that I must get Ty away from here before anything worse happened. Then I remembered Nanny Grace telling me she had sewn extra cash into the lining of Ty's trunk in case we should be delayed or need it on our journey. I hadn't seen Ty's trunk. I could only pray it was there. I had left the door to the storage room unlocked. Somehow I must go back down there before that was discovered, find the money, and take it. It was ours. Then Ty and I must escape.

It was difficult to work in the tavern the rest of that evening. I could think of nothing but the money sewn into the lining of Ty's little trunk, and how to get it without being caught. Should I even try on my own? What about all the other goods I had seen? Did the storage room contain items in addition to those belonging to the stagecoach passengers? Were the Brindles involved with thieves? Did the disreputable-looking fellows I'd seen whispering with Mr. Brindle bring their stolen goods here to be stored until they could be sold?

Every time I glanced at Mr. Brindle, a feeling of revulsion came over me. Maybe I *should* go to the town sheriff, tell him what I'd found. Let the law take care of it. But would they believe me? Might not my word be discounted as that of a disgruntled employee getting back at her employers? Wouldn't

I be accused of swindling the Brindles out of two months' room and board? I wished I had someone whose advice I could trust. But who?

Francis Vaughn? He was the only friend I had now. All evening I anxiously looked for him, hoping he'd come into the tavern, but he didn't show up. I decided to go over to his studio and tell him what I'd discovered. Maybe he could help me decide what I should do.

Usually I had about an hour late in the afternoon when I was supposed to wash up and change my apron and head scarf to prepare for my work in the taproom that evening. The following afternoon I hurriedly washed and changed, then slipped out the back door and ran practically all the way to Francis's cottage.

When he opened the door, he had a half-full wineglass in his hand. "Lyssa!" he exclaimed. "What a surprise."

"Francis, I need to talk to you."

"Come in."

Noticing he was dressed in a coat, wearing a shirt and cravat, I asked in dismay, "Are you going somewhere?"

"I'm going to London for a couple days." He seemed especially cheerful. "But there's time. What's the matter?"

As I stepped inside I saw a large, square package wrapped in brown paper and tied with string propped against the wall.

He saw my glance. "I've finished your painting, and I'm taking it to London to show my mentor and commissioner, then to have it framed."

"I haven't even seen it!" I exclaimed. Disappointment momentarily distracted me.

"I had a real inspiration about the background and worked round the clock to complete it." He smiled. "I've called it 'Lovers' Farewell.' You'll see it when it's on display in the Royal Academy."

All that seemed unimportant compared to my frightening discovery, the dreadful knowledge I now carried like a heavy stone. I poured out my story while Francis listened. By the time I finished, I was trembling.

He went to the cupboard for another glass, poured wine into it, and handed it to me. "Poor girl. You've had a dreadful shock. Here. Drink this."

I waved it away, shaking my head. "No. But, Francis, what should I do?"

"Nothing," he said flatly. "Unless you want to be tarred with the same stick. Accepting stolen goods is a crime. Knowledge is a crime. Concealing it could make you an accessory. The Brindles would probably twist the whole thing around so *you* would get into trouble. The police might even suspect you of being an accomplice." He took a long sip of wine. "If I were you, I'd say nothing. Get you and your brother out of there as fast as you can."

"But *my* things are among them. I could identify them."

Vaughn shrugged. "Then do as you like. I'm only giving you my opinion. They're a bad lot up there at the inn." He put down his glass. "I'm truly sorry I can't be of more help, Lyssa. I have to go or I'll miss the stage. My commissioner's expecting me for a celebration dinner at his club. I really must go."

"Of course." Obviously Vaughn was more concerned with his own affairs than he was with mine.

I went to the door; he followed.

"Take care. Don't do anything foolish."

Dejectedly I hurried back along the woodland path, the shortcut Francis had showed me, to the inn. I dreaded the night ahead more than ever. The discovery I'd made was dangerous. It had put Ty and me in even greater jeopardy. I had hoped for help from Francis Vaughn and had been disappointed. If the Brindles ever found out I knew—my heart jumped wildly.

11

After my discovery, working alongside Mr. Brindle in the taproom the next few nights was the hardest thing I'd ever done. Knowing what I now knew and seeing no possible solution, every time I glanced at his beady eyes, his rum-flushed face, I had to fight to keep from shuddering.

The Brindles were not only hard and unforgiving, eking out the pound of flesh for what I owed them, they were involved in criminal dealings. Vaughn's advice was right. We had to get away. We *had* to.

As I went about serving, wiping tables, picking up mugs, taking orders, I asked myself *how* I would manage it. I'd have to wait until the middle of the night when the household was asleep, slip down to the storage room, open Ty's trunk, if it was even there, and find the money Nanny had hidden. Then I would look for my own things, take whatever I could carry, and quietly sneak back upstairs. With the money from Ty's trunk, I would have more than enough money to pay back the Brindles in full and pay our travel expenses.

Toward the end of the evening Brindle was well on his way to being drunk, stumbling behind the bar, eyes at half-mast, tongue thick. When his attention was elsewhere, I took the knife with a sharp blade, the one Brindle used to slit the cork hood off wine bottles, a candle, and some matches. I slipped them into my apron pocket.

Just thinking about the possible repercussions of being caught set my heart thudding like a wooden clapper. A terrible inner debate ensued. Mr. Brindle was getting loud and argumentative with one of the customers, and Mrs. Brindle came in once or twice to check on him. This made me uneasy. Nothing escaped her eagle eye. A missing knife, a candle, would be spotted. Luck was with me, however. At closing time Mr. Brindle was head down on folded arms at the end of the bar. Mrs. Brindle marched in and, while berating him, half dragged, half pushed him out of the taproom and down the hallway to their room back of the lobby. Over her shoulder she ordered me to clean and lock up.

This was my chance. Alone, unwatched, I could slip down to the storage room. But I would have to be careful. The cellar door was behind the register counter at the front, which was *her* usual post, the spot where she remained until the tavern was closed. If she was busy putting Mr. Brindle to bed to sleep it off, she would be in their living quarters on the other side of the lobby. Still, the slightest noise might alert her and bring about my discovery. I remembered the squeaky hinges on the door to the cellar. I would have to take care of them. Some tallow or a bit of oil would do it—that is, if I waited another day. Perhaps I *should* wait another day. No. I couldn't afford to wait. I couldn't count on Mr. Brindle being this drunk again so soon. This might be the only night—my only chance.

I made as much noise as I could while cleaning up the taproom, shoving chairs on the tile floor, banging metal mugs, closing the shutters. I rattled the ring of keys loudly as I hung them on the hook behind the register. I let my heels clop on the steps as if I were on my way to the attic. At the bend of the stairway I crouched down, scarcely breathing, to wait until the house settled down for the night.

I don't know how long I sat there, hunched up, waiting. It seemed endless. I slipped off my clogs, crept down in my stocking feet, eased back along the wall until I was behind the register counter. My hand shook as I turned the knob of the door to the cellar.

I held my breath as I opened the door just enough so I could slip through. I bunched up my head scarf and thrust it between the door and its jam so the door couldn't bang shut and trap me. I felt along the wall for the worn, irregularly spaced steps leading down. I was afraid to light my candle until I got to the bottom.

Once there I took a long, shaky breath. My fingers searched my pocket and brought out the candle. I struck a match on the stone wall. My hand was shaking so much I didn't get the wick lit on the first attempt. The match burned my fingers, and I had to drop it.

"Oh, God, an ever present help in time of trouble. *Please!*" I prayed desperately.

I'd been taught not to presume on God's mercy if I did something reckless or took unnecessary risks. I knew I was doing something foolhardy and dangerous, but this was a matter of life and death, every bit as much for me as it had been for David when he was pursued by King Saul. Wasn't it? I fervently hoped so. I prayed as if it were.

My candle finally lit, the circle of light wavered as I started forward. Suddenly my mind went blank. I couldn't remember which door was which. Sweat formed in my palms, on my forehead, trickled down my back. Panic swept over me, and my whole body trembled.

Why hadn't I brought the keys with me, just in case? The thought of crawling back up the dark, twisting stairway, groping for the ring of keys, and making the descent again left me sick with fear. I desperately hoped the door was still unlocked.

Still praying, I took a few steps and pushed the flat of my hand on one of the doors. To my relief, it gave. I gulped as though I'd been drowning and just surfaced for air. I leaned my shoulder against the door and slowly it opened.

I would have to work fast. I did not know for sure how much time had passed since the taproom closed. If Ty and I were to get out of here, we would have to do it under cover of darkness. The Brindles would never let us leave otherwise. But now I couldn't think beyond finding the trunk and our money, then making it safely out of the cellar and back to the attic.

As long as I live I shall never forget those moments I searched frantically in the near dark for Ty's small, leather trunk. I hoped I could recognize it—if it was there at all. It might have floated away in the choppy river that stormy night. It had been one of the lightest, smallest objects. Still, I had to try to find it.

I felt like a beetle, scurrying around in the dark among the luggage, the odds and ends of bundles and boxes. I held the candle high. Its flickering flame shed only weak light. All I can now believe is that the Lord or my guardian angel guided me, for I was beginning to feel hopeless when, all at once, I saw Ty's little trunk. It was piled lopsidedly on top of a sagging willow basket in the corner behind a large gun case. I felt the stinging edge of tears as I scuttled over to the trunk. I tipped the candle, dripping some wax on the floor beside me, then stuck the end of the candle into the soft puddle so I would have both hands free. The trunk was wedged in so tightly, I had to work to shift heavier objects away so I could loosen it and pull it out. Luckily the lock had been broken by someone else in an attempt to open the trunk. When I lifted the lid, I saw that the once neatly packed clothes had been rumpled through, as if someone had been looking for valuables. Of course, such a cursory search would never have revealed a hidden cache of bank notes carefully sewn into the lining.

I reached for the knife. In my haste, I caught the sharp side of the blade. I drew in my breath as it cut into my flesh. Instinctively I stuck my finger into my mouth, sucking the blood the knife had drawn. Quickly I ran my other hand along the inside of the trunk. Under the lid I felt a ridge. The cloth gave easily. Soon I felt the reassuring thickness of a packet of notes. Thank goodness! The package was bound with ribbon. I thrust it into my apron pocket.

I made a quick job of investigating the whole interior lid, sides, and bottom, but found no more. After all, this had been taken from Nanny's own small savings. It was enough, I was sure, to get us on the stage and on our way to the Hazeltons—at last.

I had no sense of time. All I knew was that I was in a fearful race. I dared not think what would happen if I should be caught down here. My breath was coming fast and sharp. Once I was sure I had all the hidden money, I did not dare take the time to collect any belongings from my own trunk. Escape was more important. Ty and I must get away.

I retraced my steps quickly. Closing the door to the storage room, I thought again I should have brought the keys and relocked it. What would happen when the Brindles or one of their accomplices found it unlocked?

Well, I couldn't worry about that now. I had to get up the stairs and rouse Ty so we could get away before dawn broke.

12

*T*y, Ty! Wake up. There's a good boy." I shook him gently. He sat up, sleepily rubbing his eyes. His small mouth opened in what probably was a yawn, but afraid it might be a loudly voiced question, I quickly placed my hand over it. While he pushed at me indignantly, I whispered, "Listen, Ty, this is important. I'll explain later, but we have to leave *now*, without waking the Brindles or getting caught."

I leaned closer. "You must do exactly as I tell you and try not to make a sound. Promise?"

I felt his indrawn breath against my palm, and he nodded. I removed my hand. "Get dressed. Hurry."

There was not a minute to lose. Time wasted getting ready increased our danger of discovery. I got out of the despised maid's outfit and into the only other clothes I had, my traveling suit. I discarded my work clogs, but I kept on the heavy wool stockings. I tied my boots by their lacers to my waistband.

With Ty's help I wound the end of the sheet around the post of the bed and knotted it as hard as I could. We pushed the bed closer to the high dormer window on the slanted ceiling wall and pushed the window open. It had been drizzling earlier, and the shingles would be slick. It would be difficult getting down to where the rain gutter ran along the edge of the roof, where we could drop to the ground. Dangerous, too, but we had to do it. I couldn't risk both of us stealing downstairs and out through the front door.

As agile as Ty was and as strong as I now was from the months of hard physical work, I felt we could make it. We *had* to. I knotted the thin blanket to the sheet and threaded it out through the window, letting it slide across the roof and dangle over the edge. There was still a good five-foot drop to the ground.

Should I go first, test the strength of the sheet and blanket, leave Ty to follow? Would it be safe to leave Ty in the room in case something went wrong, the sheet ripped, or I fell, or—I had to take the chance. He was a brave little fellow, but even so, it would be better to test my weight on the makeshift rope. If it held me, it would surely hold his much lighter body. Resentment at the thought of our stolen belongings stored downstairs along with those of other passengers drove my energy. But anger was a luxury I could not afford at the moment. I had to focus on our escape.

The packet of pound notes was my security, and I felt a curious satisfaction in having outwitted the thieves, who had not searched more thoroughly. I knew my self-satisfaction was probably wrong. I battled my conscience on this issue, but I felt no guilt for taking what was ours.

Even in my feverish haste to get away, I knew I had to take certain precautions. In their outrage at our departure, the Brindles might report us to the authorities, who would then be on the lookout for two fugitives on the road. I had to do my best to eliminate the possibility of pursuit. Therefore, I carefully counted out the money Mrs. Brindle said I still owed them and left it in plain sight on my empty cot. Although I doubted the amount to be true, I wanted to give them no reason to call us thieves.

Thrusting Mama's bag of jewels and our few other belongings into my shawl, I tied the ends together, knotting them securely.

"All right. We're set, Ty," I whispered. "Ready? I'll help you out, then you wait until I slide down and jump, then you come. When you jump, I'll be there to catch you. Can you manage?"

"Yes!" he said, his voice hoarse with suppressed excitement. For a lad his age, this was high adventure.

I lifted, shoved, and supported Ty as he climbed out the window, then I pushed our bundle of belongings through. Ty crouched outside the window on the slanted roof holding our bundle while I followed. It was much harder for me, with my skirt and larger body. I heaved myself up, squeezed through the narrow opening, and slid out, breathless and panting.

"You all right?" I asked Ty.

Quivering with excitement, he nodded.

"Stay here until I'm on the ground, then toss me the bundle. Carefully inch down to the gutter, then jump. I'll be right below."

The night air was chill and damp. It was dark, the moon hidden behind the clouds of the promised storm. Poised precariously at the top of the roof, I felt as though I were looking down into a bottomless pit. Panic knotted my stomach, tightened my throat. Breathing was painful. I'd come this far. I had to go on. There was no going back.

I clung to the thin material of the sheet, my lifeline to the edge of the roof, then to the ground and safety and freedom.

"You all right, Ty?" I asked again.

"Yes."

"I'll go ahead then," I said, still clinging to the makeshift rope, struggling to gain courage. Gradually I slid inch by inch down the splintery shingles, catching the material of my skirt as I did. My heels hit the tin gutter. I winced and gasped. Slowly I exhaled then took several deep breaths.

I turned my body so I lay stretched out, stomach down, suspended. With one hand I grabbed hold of the metal gutter, my other hand still clutching the end of the blanket. I would have to twist my body and grip the gutter with both hands, swing over the edge of the roof, and drop to the ground beneath.

I took another long, shaky breath and closed my eyes. Between clenched teeth I implored God for help. Then I twisted, grabbed, and went over the side. I felt my fingers slip on the slimy gutter, held my breath, and let go.

The fall was harder than I anticipated. I fell on my knees and elbows and toppled sideways onto dew-wet grass.

As soon as I caught my breath, I scrambled to my feet. Cupping my mouth with both hands, I called quietly up to Ty. "I'm down, Ty. It's all right. Come on."

Down tumbled the bundle, nearly hitting me on the head. I put it to one side and squinted up through the darkness, watching the small figure inching his way to the end of the steep roof. The next thing I knew a solid weight of little boy landed in my arms. For a minute I held him close, tears crowding my eyes. "What a wonderful, brave fellow you are!" I whispered over and over as I hugged him.

"Where do we go now, Lyssa?" he asked as I set him on his feet.

His question caught me off guard. It was damp and cold, and the clouds moving across the moon looked dark and frightening.

I'd only managed to think as far as getting out of the inn. We weren't safe yet. Discovery would come with first light, when I was supposed to be up and fetching water from the well, lugging it up to the few occupied guest rooms. Peg would surely sound the alarm if I wasn't on the job.

Then I thought of Francis. He had said he was going to London for a couple days. Surely he was back by now. Of course, *Francis*. No one at the inn knew anything about my friendship with him. It seemed logical we should go first to his cottage. He would be sympathetic, glad we had followed his advice. We could stay there until it was light, then walk to the crossroads.

"I think we should go to Francis Vaughn's cottage. We can wait there until it's light enough to meet the stagecoach."

I picked up our bundle and grabbed Ty's hand. "Come on, Ty. Once we're at Francis's we'll be safe."

It seemed farther to the cottage than I remembered, burdened as we were by our bundle and the darkness. Hurrying along, I hoped I would be able to find the path that turned off the road leading to the village. I realized I was walking too fast for Ty's little legs and forced myself to slow down.

It was slowly getting light when we finally came in sight of the cottage. The relief I felt was, however, short-lived. There was no answer to my repeated knocking. When we both went around and looked in the windows, there seemed to be no one inside. There was no smoke coming from the chimney, nor any sound of movement inside. Ty sat down wearily on the little porch while I wondered what to do next.

Only a little while later we saw a shawled woman approaching. When she saw us, she eyed us suspiciously. To my cheerfully managed "good morning," she just gave me another hard look and a humph. She came right up to the front door without speaking. Her eyes were skeptical.

"We are friends of Mr. Vaughn's."

"Well, he ain't here," she said. "I've come on directions from the owner to clean the place up."

"But Mr. Vaughn—"

She gave me a short grunt and another glance.

"You one of his—" She paused significantly before finishing. "One of them models?" She used the word as if it were something distasteful, wrinkling her nose as she said it.

I drew myself up, feeling offended by her attitude. I knew we looked bedraggled and not at our best; however, I didn't think she had any cause to be so rude.

She got out a key, turned it in the lock, and opened the

door. "There's no use you staying around. He's gone. But left me a job to do, I'll tell you! Paint spots on the rug, rusty, smelly cans he'd used to mix paint and oil! Never saw such a mess. Don't know what he used the kitchen for. Not to cook in, I warrant."

I was ready to ask her if we might come in, perhaps even have a cup of tea, but she was already inside and about to close the door.

"Did Mr. Vaughn leave a message of any kind?"

She shook her head vigorously. "Nor did he leave anything for me, not even a shilling! Just took off, he did. I suspect that's the last we'll see or hear of *him*. Can't see why the gentleman who owns this cottage rented to the likes of him. Humph. An artist." With that she shut the door squarely in our faces.

"Come on, Ty," I said, gathering up our bundle.

He got up a little reluctantly, tired from interrupted sleep, our hazardous escape, and the long walk.

"Where will we go now, Lyssa?" he asked plaintively. "I'm hungry."

"I know, Ty. So am I. But we still have to get away from this village. Once we're on the stage—well, then at the first rest stop, we'll have an enormous breakfast." I tried to sound sure of myself.

"When will that be? Where is the stagecoach?"

For some reason—and all I can credit it to is pure inspiration—the word *sanctuary* came into my mind. I remembered reading that pilgrims, fugitives, and refugees could find a safe place to stay in a church by claiming *sanctuary*. Their captors or pursuers could not violate that.

Not far down the road from Vaughn's cottage I saw the steeple of the gray stone village church rising through the morning mist.

"We'll go to Christ Church, Ty. We can wait safely there until it's time to catch the stagecoach."

We walked the short distance to the church without further conversation.

Cautiously, I pushed the heavy, nail-studded church doors open. At once the combined smell of old wood, cold stone, beeswax, and the faint, decaying scent of wilting flowers prickled my nostrils. This being an Anglican church, I felt sure there would be matins. Soon a sexton would be lighting tapers on the altar, and a handful of faithful parishioners would start coming in for the early service. Surely someone could give us the information we needed.

I tugged Ty's hand and we went inside, almost on tiptoe, as though not to disturb the unearthly quiet. We slipped into one of the back pews. Gray light palely filtered through the high, stained glass windows on either side. I had no idea what time it was. The lack of sleep sent waves of fatigue through my body, which was numbed by the chill and dampness of the early morning.

Ty gave a big yawn and leaned his head against me.

I had to find out from someone when the next stagecoach was due. If I approached the vicar when he appeared, I hoped he would be kind and not ask too many questions. I rehearsed my story nonetheless. He more than likely knew all his regular church members and would recognize that we were strangers. I would just say we were on our way to relatives and had missed our connection. That was literally the truth, though a slightly incomplete version of it.

With a heavy sigh, Ty nestled his head on my lap and curled up on the bench beside me. He was soon sound asleep.

I prayed. This was, after all, a house of prayer. I reached for the prayer book in the narrow wooden niche on the back of the pew in front of me and turned the pages. I came to one called Prayer for Travelers. In the dim light I read the short verse then repeated it silently.

O Lord, our Guide on all our life's journey, protect us from all danger as we travel, that accompanied by Thy holy angels we may arrive safely whither we are going. Amen.

For the first time in weeks, a sense of tranquility descended like a warm blanket around me. I'm not sure how much time had passed, for I must have drowsed a little myself, when I heard a stirring, the shuffle of footsteps. An acolyte came out to light the candles on the altar. Behind me I heard the church door squeak as it opened and an elderly woman entered. She looked at us and smiled as she passed to take a seat in a front pew.

I eased Ty's head off my lap and slipped the shawl-wrapped bundle under his head for a pillow, then made my way up the aisle to where she sat.

As it turned out she was the vicar's mother, visiting him from the next village, and she had come in on the stagecoach a few days before. She told me that a stage was due in less than an hour. If we waited at the crossroads, it would stop for us.

I thanked her and went back to where Ty slept peacefully. I hated to wake him, but I didn't dare miss the stage. We had come this far without trouble, but I wouldn't feel entirely safe until we were on board the stage and on our way to Briarwood Manor and our relatives.

13

Since it was still early, the stagecoach was occupied by only two other passengers, both nodding sleepily. A few minutes after we boarded, we were settled comfortably, Ty fast asleep.

I was still too tense to relax. I could hardly believe we had made our escape and were finally on our way to our original destination. We had met with so many unexpected delays, endured so many unforeseen hazards, encountered such mean, unsavory characters. The fact that we had survived it all was surely due to God's grace and dear Nanny's prayers.

As soon as we arrived safely at Briarwood Manor, I would write to her and tell her about all our adventures. I had to smile in retrospect, recalling how Nanny appropriated Scripture to fit her purposes—or rather *mine*. "You must be wise as a serpent. The world is a wicked place, and you two are going out there, two lambs where wolves prowl," she had said.

However, considering what had actually happened to us, I realized we had been in more dangerous territory than Nanny could ever have imagined. I had certainly had my eyes opened and was no longer the innocent I had been when I started on this journey.

The unknown threat of Muir still hung over us. I had no idea what he had done or might be doing given Ty's disappearance.

I must have drifted off because the next thing I knew the coach had stopped and I heard the driver bellowing, "Meadowmead! All out for Meadowmead."

"Come, Ty, wake up. We're here!" It is hard to describe the relief I felt. Soon I could turn over the responsibility of my little brother to those older and wiser than I.

We got off the stage in the town square. I was stiff, my muscles cramped and aching from the long trip.

"Just think, Ty, we're almost to Briarwood Manor. You're going to love it there." I picked up our meager belongings wrapped in my shawl.

"How far is it, Lyssa?"

I knew the Hazeltons' estate was quite a distance from the village. I remembered riding to and from the village in my pony cart. However, Ty had already traveled quite a distance, and I didn't want to discourage him at the outset. "Not too far."

Ever willing to accept my word, Ty smiled up at me and we started off. Happy hearts carry a light load, and knowing a warm welcome awaited us at the end of our journey, we were cheerful travelers. We sang some of the songs Nanny had taught us and managed to cover quite a distance before Ty's steps began to lag. His little legs, so much shorter than mine, tired sooner. We stopped by the roadside and rested, then pushed on.

I encouraged Ty by telling him of the delicious lemon sponge cake the Hazeltons' cook made and of the sweet grape juice from their own arbor. Even those promises did not manage to sustain his sore feet, and we sat down under a leafy oak tree.

All I had with me was a crumbling currant bun I'd bought from a vendor the last time the stage had stopped to change horses. I handed it to Ty. Since he was more thirsty than hungry, it did not prove very satisfying.

About this time, we saw a carrier cart coming along. When the driver saw us, he reined his horse and asked us where we were headed. When I told him Briarwood Manor, he offered us a ride.

"Goin' right past it." He nodded. "Come on, get in."

Gratefully I lifted Ty up on the seat beside him, then climbed aboard myself. The driver flicked the reins, and the horse plodded along the rutted country road. The man turned and looked at us. "Is the old lady hiring new help, then?"

At first, I was puzzled by his question. Then I realized how shabby we must have looked. Obviously he thought I was applying for a servant's position at the Manor. When I informed him Lady Hazelton was my mother's aunt, he looked startled.

"And how long is it since you visited your aunt, miss?"

Not willing to tell him my whole sorrowful history, I just said, "Five years."

At this, his bushy eyebrows went up alarmingly. He gave his head a slight shake. "Well, miss, I'm afeared you'll find many changes up at that house."

I felt a sense of uneasiness at these gloomy words, but I hesitated to ask more. In another mile, around another bend or two, we would be there. If there was bad news, I'd learn it soon enough.

The driver didn't offer further comments or questions, and we rode the rest of the way in silence. At length we came in sight of the tall, scrolled iron gates with the arched bridge across the top, the Gothic letters spelling BRIARWOOD MANOR.

The driver brought the wagon to a stop.

"Thank you very much," I said, gathering my things together and preparing to get out.

"You're sure now, miss, this is where you want me to leave you off? It's a long way back to town."

I tried to ignore the uncertainty in the man's voice, but it caused my heart to beat nervously. "Of course," I said briskly as I got down. I helped Ty down. "Thanks again."

He did not reply. Unsmiling, he tipped the beak of his cap, slapped the reins, and drove off.

Resolutely I pushed back the doubt he had triggered in my mind. "Come on, Ty."

I leaned against the gate and pushed it open. It gave a protesting creak, for it was badly rusted.

We went through and started up the driveway. I'd forgotten the house was set so far back from the road. Distances are often distorted in the memories of children.

"How far?" Ty's voice sounded plaintive.

"Not far. Not far at all, now," I answered, knowing it was about a quarter of a mile to the house. "Just think how happy they'll be to see us."

Although determined to be optimistic, the farther we went along the winding drive, the more wary I became. On either side, where I remembered acres of velvety lawn, there was only tangled underbrush and thistles. Weeds seemed to have sprung up everywhere. When we came in sight of the rambling Tudor house, I was shocked to see it standing in the midst of untrimmed hedges that had grown to gigantic height. Shaggy rhododendron bushes drooped with wilted, browning blossoms.

The closer we got to the house the lower my spirits fell. I looked up at windows that had once shone like sparkling jewels from their diamond-shaped panes and saw that they were shuttered. My steps slowed, and a premonition of dread overtook me. Ty began to drag his feet. He was catching my growing sense of dismay.

There was no sign of life anywhere. A kind of stillness hung over the house.

"Isn't anybody home, Lyssa?" Ty's voice was low, a little frightened. "It looks—empty."

It looked worse than that to me. *Haunted* was the word

I'd have chosen. I swallowed hard. "Oh, I'm sure somebody's there, Ty. We'll just go knock on the door. Surely somebody will come. Anyway, we'll see, shall we?" I tried to sound optimistic, something I certainly did not feel.

Ty's little hand tightened in mine as we went up the terrace steps to the front door. I raised my trembling hand to lift the badly tarnished brass knocker. All sorts of dreadful possibilities marched through my mind as we waited for the door to be opened, ones I did not dare pursue. I held my breath, then knocked a second time, somewhat harder.

Had Ty's observation been right? Was the house empty? Had some terrible tragedy taken place without my knowledge? Were my relatives ill or even—I couldn't quite finish that thought.

No communication had taken place between Briarwood Manor and Crossfield Grange for the past five years. My stepfather had curtly cut off my mother's oft-expressed wishes to invite Lord and Lady Hazelton to visit. Even her pleas to have them come for Ty's christening had fallen on deaf ears. My poor mother loved her aunt and uncle dearly and had wept bitterly when they had been banished so cruelly from our lives. I wasn't even sure Muir had notified them of her death.

The Hazeltons were both close to sixty when my mother and I had lived with them before she married Muir. It was possible they had succumbed to the ravages of age in the years since I had seen them. Like their once beautiful house, perhaps they too had deteriorated under the sickle of time.

The longer we stood in front of that closed door, the more frantic I became. If something *had* happened to the Hazeltons, what would I do? Where would I go? How would I care for my little brother?

My heart was literally in my throat. Ty sagged against me. We had come too far, traveled too long under hazardous conditions, to be faced with this. Please, *please,* someone come! I prayed desperately.

As I prayed, my ears pricked up at the sound of slow steps advancing on the other side of the door. The latch slipped back, and the door was inched open.

"Yes, what is it? What do you want?" a quivery voice asked.

I could not see through the narrow crack created by the open door. I bent closer but still could see nothing.

"It is Challys Winthrop, Maria's daughter, and my brother, Tyrone. Are Lord and Lady Hazelton here?"

There was a soft exclamation, like a sigh. Immediately the door swung back, and a small, gray-haired lady stood holding out her arms to me. "Dear little girl!"

It was Aunt Evelyn. I stepped forward into her embrace, my tears of relief mingled with her tears of joy.

"Oh, Auntie Evelyn, I'm so glad to see you. So happy to be here. We've come such a long way—" I almost sobbed. Then drawing away, I reached out for Ty and pulled him forward. "This is Ty, Auntie. We've come to stay. If you'll have us."

"Of course, my darling. Of course!" She hugged me tightly. Then as we drew apart, she looked down at Ty. "And this is Maria's dear little lad. How I've longed to see you."

Aunt Evelyn put her hands on his shoulders, looked down at him. Ty smiled angelically.

"Come in, both of you. There's so much I have to ask."

"There's so much I have to tell you." I was too exhausted and too relieved to be careful. "Mr. Muir hasn't contacted you, has he?"

"Oh, no, my dear. We haven't heard from him in—well, since your sweet mother passed away. We wrote at once to Muir, explaining that we would be unable to come because of George's health, and enclosing a bank note, requesting it be used for a headstone for our dear Maria's grave. But we never heard back from him, and we never learned how the money was spent." She shook her head sadly. "Probably gambled away . . . But we mustn't dwell on those unhappy times. We have to celebrate your coming. Just wait until George hears. Wait until he sees this young man."

Auntie Evelyn beamed, her wrinkled face appearing magically younger, her faded blue eyes sparkling as she regarded us fondly. "Come along, he's in the library."

She beckoned us to follow her down the hallway. "He will be overjoyed to see you. It will do him a world of good to know you have got away from that monstrous man—oh, Challys, George has had much to bear, if you but knew. Now, don't be alarmed. Through all his trials, all his tribulations, George has remained . . ."

She paused, pressed her fingers to her mouth for a few seconds. "Although, you'll find him aged, his spirit is still valiant and . . . Well, come along, dear. See for yourself."

In spite of Aunt Evelyn's euphemistic description, I was shocked to see Lord Hazelton. The tall, erect man I remembered was bent of shoulder, his eyes vague, his face deeply lined. At first, he didn't even seem to know who I was. Aunt Evelyn had to repeat my name several times, saying, "It's Maria's little girl, George, all grown up now. She's come and brought her little brother."

Gradually understanding broke through, his face lit up, and I saw a glimpse of the jovial, energetic gentleman I had known as a child.

I was badly shaken by this visible deterioration in the person on whom I'd planned to unload my burdens, the person of whom I planned to ask advice and direction.

Auntie declared we must celebrate our homecoming, and Uncle George insisted we open one of the few remaining bottles of fine wine still in his once well-stocked cellar.

I tried to enter into Auntie's enthusiasm and hide my shock at the changes that had taken place at Briarwood. The whole house was in a run-down condition due to lack of proper care by a greatly reduced staff. At dinner, I noticed the silverware was tarnished, the elaborate lace tablecloth torn and unmended, the jacket worn by their old butler, Manning, shiny and missing buttons. It was all I could do to put on a good show and help Auntie as she tried to act as though everything was just as it used to be.

Toward the middle of dinner Uncle George became silent, then his head sank to his chest. At a nod from Aunt Evelyn, Manning assisted him out of his chair and led him out of the room. Aunt Evelyn's glance followed his progress anxiously, and she suppressed a deep sigh.

Soon after that I took Ty, who was heavy-lidded and yawning, upstairs to put him to bed. A trundle bed had been placed in the hastily aired room I was to occupy. I tucked him in, and he was soon asleep.

Bone tired and weary as I was, sleep did not come easily for me. The haven I had dreamed of reaching had been an illusion. Here at Briarwood all was ruin and chaos, with as unpredictable a future as my own.

14

*T*he next afternoon, while Uncle George napped, my aunt and I had the opportunity to really talk. We went into her sitting room decorated with flowered wallpaper and lace curtains, a room I remembered as being as feminine and dainty as Aunt Evelyn herself. Now, both seemed a little worn and faded. She told me she had been devastated by the news of Mama's death but had received no word from Muir since. She never received the letter I sent her from school saying I was on my way to Crossfield Grange to get Ty, so she was appalled to get a letter weeks later from Nanny Grace, inquiring if we had arrived at Briarwood.

"After that, I prayed every day for your safety. I worried endlessly about what might have happened. I was terrified that dreadful man had done something with you two. I never trusted him, not from the first moment he came courting Maria. I was proven right."

Auntie shook her head, bit her lower lip. "Nanny warned me not to try to find out anything through him if you had not yet come. She said you had a good head on your shoulders and would take every precaution to cover your tracks so Muir couldn't find you. And that, she suggested, might mean your arrival here would be delayed. That's what I counted on."

I should not have been surprised that my aunt had never received the note Francis Vaughn had promised to post. Given his erratic personality and his self-absorption, I should not have counted on his carrying out my request.

I told Auntie about the stagecoach accident, Ty's illness, and how I was forced to work off our indebtedness to the Brindles. I didn't, however, tell her about posing for Francis Vaughn, nor of my discovery of the stolen goods in the inn's basement. Auntie had about all she could handle at the moment.

"To think you both might have been killed in that accident! And you, poor dear, who had never done a day's work in your life—a scullery maid and tavern worker! At least your dear mother was spared knowing."

From this reaction, I realized it was well I hadn't revealed all I'd endured, witnessed, and been involved in, especially posing for Francis Vaughn. An artist's model was considered on a par with an actress, or worse. Auntie would need more than a whiff of smelling salts if she knew I'd done that.

Although I kept some distressing revelations from my aunt, there was much at Briarwood that could not be concealed from me. After being there less than twenty-four hours, it was clear the Hazeltons had fallen on hard times. The evidence was everywhere—the worn rugs, the upholstery that needed replacing, the shredded lining of faded velvet draperies, the furniture that needed dusting, floors polishing. Of course, what could be expected when the house servants, who used to number twenty, were now reduced to the elderly cook, a laundress that came twice a week from the village, and Manning, almost as doddering as Uncle George.

Gently, I questioned Aunt Evelyn as to how all this had happened. Reluctantly, she confided what had become of the Hazeltons' once vast fortune.

111

During her disastrous marriage to Henry Muir, my mother had turned to them on several occasions to borrow large sums of money, first from the trust fund they had set up for her as her guardians. When that was depleted, they lent out of their own bank account.

"Maria promised to repay us, and I know she meant to. We had no idea what her life was really like with that man. It was only through rumors that we learned of his profligate behavior. Then our bank manager, an old friend of your uncle's, came down from London to talk to us personally. He told us Muir was well known as a gambler, that he frequented notorious gambling houses in the city and was rarely lucky. Thus we assumed some of the large sums we loaned to Maria were to cover Muir's losses."

Although I had been away at boarding school while all this was going on, I wasn't surprised to learn the man I so despised was worse than I had even suspected.

"George was still going up to London to his club in those days," continued Aunt Evelyn. "There he heard Muir was also a heavy drinker. Gradually, we realized the money would never be paid back. Not that we begrudged it, not a cent of it, if it would have helped Maria, whom you know we thought of as a daughter. It was just that, in the end, it made things worse."

The story got even more depressing as Auntie went on. About the same time they had extended Muir credit, Uncle George suffered some severe financial losses of his own. Sugar being highly valuable and its sale here in England quite profitable, Uncle George had invested in several trading ships sent to obtain the prized commodity from the plantations of the Caribbean islands. Several of the vessels were shipwrecked in tropical storms, their entire cargo lost at sea.

"So you see, we became unable to help Maria anymore, and Muir cut us off from her. I suspect he intercepted our letters to her and her letters to us. He wanted to isolate her so he could conduct his derelict lifestyle without any interference."

Tearfully, Aunt Evelyn glanced at me. "I can't tell you how glad I am you are here, Lyssa. I haven't known what to do, and George, dear fellow, well, you see how it is, don't you?"

Auntie looked suddenly old, hopeless. Impulsively, I reached out and covered both her thin, blue-veined hands with my own. Hard as it was for Auntie to tell me all this, I think in a way, it was a comfort to have someone with whom she could share her terrible burden.

It took me only another day at Briarwood to realize Uncle George had only a tenuous hold on reality.

The first night I was at Briarwood, I told them both how important it was to safeguard Ty's future. Uncle George had seemed attentive and lucid. He promised he would discuss it with his lawyers, arrange for me to become Ty's legal guardian, claiming Muir was neglectful and abusive, that he had recklessly squandered what little remained of the estate that was rightfully Ty's through our mother. It was *her* inheritance that had maintained Crossfield Grange. The house and land otherwise would have gone to pay off Muir's gambling debts.

Two days later, when I asked Uncle George if the lawyers were going ahead with the necessary legal procedure, he looked at me blankly. With a sinking heart, I realized he had no memory of our conversation. That's when I realized how dire the situation at Briarwood really was.

That afternoon I went outside into the gardens, or what was left of them, overgrown and choked with weeds as they were, and walked along the gravel paths between the neglected flower beds. I was unable to put my thoughts in any kind of order.

One by one, I counted off the main problems confronting me.

My stepfather's dissolute habits had bankrupted the Hazeltons and destroyed Ty's inheritance. I had hoped to shift *my* problems to responsible relatives. Instead, *their* problems had become *mine*. There was no one else. I would have to take on all I had hoped to relinquish, and more. Uncle George was fast slipping into senility. Auntie was helpless, Ty a mere child.

Everything depended on me.

Because I had no experience in household management, at first I thought the sparse meals served were due to the fact the cook was old, no longer eager to show off her culinary skills. Auntie's explanations seemed feeble. The kitchen garden yielded only a few vegetables because it had been left untended. In the orchards, unharvested fruit fell rotting to the ground. When I offered to do the grocery shopping, having gained some knowledge from my experience at the inn, I found the horses were gone, the three carriages sold. There was no vehicle in which anyone could go to market.

Since I'd volunteered, I took a large wicker basket and walked into town. There I received a further cold dash of reality when the butcher refused to put the roast I selected on Lady Hazelton's account.

"Sorry, no more credit," he retorted, then rudely turned away to wait on another customer, leaving me standing at the counter, red faced and humiliated.

With my empty basket I headed back up the road to Briarwood. Something would have to be done. At once. Or we adults would end up in the poorhouse and Ty in an orphanage or, worse, back with Muir. I had to find a way to earn some money.

What could I do? Ironically, the only kind of work for which I had any qualifications was that of a maid. What good was my fine education at Miss Elderberry's Academy to me now? I could read and speak a little French, play the piano adequately, do five embroidery stitches. I had fine penmanship. Hardly skills that paid well.

I might get a job as a governess. However, that meant living in a home with the children to be tutored. I couldn't leave Ty with Auntie and Uncle, who needed to be taken care of themselves.

Another restless night followed. I woke at heart-pounding intervals, tossing and turning, all the problems and possible solutions tumbling in my troubled mind.

Still distracted the next morning, I tried tidying up the downstairs. The dust and general messiness of rooms once spotless and neat was getting on my nerves. The parlor maid had long ago departed. It was amazing how much clutter collected daily in a house where people, used to servants, never picked up anything or put anything away.

The library was the worst. Uncle never emptied the ashtray where he dumped his tobacco whenever he sat smoking his pipe in the big leather chair. He was, further, in the habit of dropping sections of the newspaper to the floor as he finished reading them. I started gathering them up, then something caught my eye—the classified advertisement section of the *Country Journal*. Picking it up, I sat down and perused the listings under Help Wanted. One seemed to leap right off the page.

SOCIAL SECRETARY TO A LADY. Non-residential position for refined, well-educated gentlewoman, skilled in social protocol, excellent penmanship. Special consideration given to someone who can do calligraphy suitable for dinner party menus, invitations, place cards. Three days a week. Location local. Personal interview after receipt of letter of application. Reply Box 47, this paper.

I read it over twice. Refinement, social grace, good penmanship. It sounded like the requisites taught at Miss Elderberry's. In these, I certainly qualified, and the position was local. The opportunity sounded almost too good to be true, and I had nothing to lose by answering.

A quick search for stationery turned up only a few sheets with the Hazelton crest engraved at the top. It would never do for a letter of application for a secretarial job. I felt it would be inappropriate to associate myself with the Hazeltons. I knew Auntie would recoil at the thought of her niece having to earn money. However, since my last name was different from theirs, I could keep my relationship with them a secret. Pride might be a sin, but it was one of which the gentry of the day were all guilty. I wanted to protect my relatives from malicious gossip.

I decided to walk to the village and purchase some plain, good quality paper. I would say nothing unless, of course, I got the job. Then I would explain to Aunt Evelyn. Crossing bridges as I came to them seemed to have become a way of life for me.

I set off on foot for the village, my thoughts wandering back to my recent escape from the inn. What had been the Brindles' reaction when they had found us gone? Had they discovered the storage room door unlocked? If so, what had they made of *that?*

I shuddered. I wished I could forget that terrible episode in my life. The present was what was important. I turned my mind to the possibilities of being hired as a social secretary, being able to bring some much needed income to Briar-wood.

In the stationery store, I looked through the samples of stock, searching for paper that would give a good impression yet was not too expensive. I happened to glance up. Through the front display window of the shop, I saw a tall man crossing the street. Dressed in a caped, tweed coat and fine leather boots, carrying a riding crop in one hand, he was striding directly toward the stationery store. Nicholas Seymour. What in the world was he doing in this remote village such a distance from London?

Immediately, two incidents flashed into my mind—the fog-shrouded morning when he had put Lady Bethune on the stagecoach, and the time he had burst into the inn demanding from Mrs. Brindle an account of his aunt's missing luggage. What would *he* think if he knew what had happened to it? Surely he would have gone straight to the authorities.

All at once I felt guilty. I *knew* about a crime and had not told anyone. Did that make me an accessory? Liable to arrest and imprisonment? A shiver ran up my spine. Instinctively, I stepped back and nearly tipped over a bin of lithograph prints behind me. It tottered precariously and the store owner at the counter glared at me as if I'd done it on purpose. I righted it, then glanced around for a place to hide should Nicholas come into the store. However, I was spared the necessity.

Just as he reached the door, someone hailed him. He turned to greet another gentleman hurrying toward him. Nicholas removed his hat, providing me with a good view of his handsome profile. A brisk wind lifted his thick, dark hair, blowing it back from his well-shaped brow. After a minute or so, the two men broke into hearty laughter and, still talking, strolled back across the street toward the pub and restaurant, The Golden Peacock. As they disappeared inside, I realized I had been holding my breath.

I hurriedly made my choice of stationery, purchased it, and left the store. My avoidance of a man who would hardly recognize me seemed ridiculous. Walking home, I told myself I was being foolish. I'd been able to avoid encountering Nicholas Seymour face-to-face, but it was not as easy for me to stop thinking about him.

That dismal October morning of our first meeting, which now seemed long ago, almost in another lifetime, I'd been too troubled, too preoccupied, to be fully aware of him. However, I had been conscious of a strange current that passed between us. The second time I saw him I'd been too miserable and ashamed to do anything but hide. Yet when Francis Vaughn urged me to imagine saying farewell to a *real* beloved in an attempt to catch the right expression on my face for his painting, it was Nicholas Seymour's face my imagination summoned.

Oh, it was all too absurd. I commanded myself not to be

so silly. To concentrate on the task at hand. To write the letter of application and hope to be hired as a social secretary.

I spent the rest of the afternoon and most of the evening composing my letter, practicing my handwriting, and finally copying the text onto the new stationery in my best penmanship.

The next morning I walked to the village post office and opened a letter box so I could receive mail without giving Briarwood Manor as my return address.

Two days later when I checked the box, I found a letter inside. I examined the address to be sure the letter was for me. The handwriting was a spidery Spencerian, the smooth paper sealed with red wax stamped with a crest. I was astonished to get so prompt a reply, then wondered why we are so often surprised when our prayers are answered.

However, it was the letter's signature that startled me more than its timeliness. It was signed, Isabel, Lady Bethune, Elmhurst Hall, Meadowmead. Nicholas Seymour's aunt! My fellow traveler on the ill-fated stagecoach.

15

$\mathcal{I}$ walked home, conflicting emotions churning within me. A chance for a job had come, just the opportunity I had prayed for. But the identity of my prospective employer was a shock. I had certainly never expected to see Lady Bethune again or to learn that she lived so near Briarwood Manor. The letter said I was to come for a personal interview the following afternoon. Should I go? Would Lady Bethune recognize me? Would she question me about my relatives? Would my need to work reveal their dire circumstances, opening them up to embarrassing village gossip? Instead of helping my aunt and uncle, would I be betraying them? First, I had to tell Aunt Evelyn.

When I went in the house, Aunt Evelyn looked at me curiously. "What is it, Challys? You look very pale, dear. You're not ill, I hope."

I handed her the letter to read. Then, as gently as I could, I explained. She wept a little, saddened that things had come to this. "Not that I blame your dear mother," she quickly assured me. "She was young and foolish and trusting. It's that villain Muir. I blame George and myself as well. We should have seen past his slick facade and kept Maria from making such a terrible mistake. Now, you and dear little Ty are also the victims of our failure."

I comforted her as best I could, and in the end she understood. In fact, she helped me put together a proper outfit to wear for my interview with Lady Bethune.

"You must make a good impression," she said firmly and went to search her armoire for something we could alter to fit me. As so many ladies of her social station, Aunt Evelyn had acquired complete new wardrobes for each season. She still had many hardly worn outfits, although most were two or three seasons out of fashion.

We decided on a blue foulard promenade dress with a fitted jacket and flounced skirt that could easily be lengthened to accommodate the three inches I had on Aunt Evelyn. The material was still beautiful, and when we finished the few nips and tucks necessary for a perfect fit, it looked quite stylish.

We put new ribbons on my bonnet, and Auntie found a pair of kid gloves she had never taken out of the box. A lucky thing, too, because my hands had not recovered from the ravages of my work at the inn. The total effect we created was that of a young lady who may have fallen on hard times, but still had a certain chic and panache.

The following afternoon I walked to the end of the road, waited for the postman's cart, then asked for a ride to the gates of Elmhurst Hall.

Elmhurst Hall was very grand. Built of gray stone, it had turrets and towers and statuary. In the marble-floored foyer, to which I was admitted by a formidable butler, massive portraits of important-looking ancestors lined paneled walls.

The butler showed me into the morning room and told me her ladyship would be with me shortly. The room, filled with sunlight from floor-length French windows that looked out onto terraced gardens, was furnished with gold-leafed antiques, baroque-framed mirrors, and priceless vases containing hothouse flowers—pale pink peonies and amethyst irises.

As I sat there waiting, I tried to guess whether or not Lady Bethune would recognize me from our shared adventure. Probably not. Perhaps the incident itself had become an amusingly told story to relate to friends at dinner parties. It would be far-fetched to think that with her busy social life, the dozens of people she likely met at the rounds of parties she attended, she would remember someone she had met *literally* by accident.

I heard the rustle of taffeta skirts and the staccato tap of heels on the polished floor. The door opened, and Lady Bethune, tall and elegant, swept into the room. Regardless that she was leaning on a gold-topped cane, she carried herself like a queen.

I rose to my feet.

"Good day, Miss Winthrop." She inclined her beautifully coifed silver head. "You are very punctual. I admire that in a person. It shows respect for others' time, a courtesy I find sadly lacking in today's society. Too careless to be prompt, people seem to care nothing for keeping others cooling their heels."

She sat down in a needlepointed chair with gracefully curved arms and pointed to its twin with a ring-encrusted hand. "Do sit down."

When I did so, she said, "Now tell me about yourself."

Briefly I recounted my education at Miss Elderberry's.

"Yes, yes." She made a dismissive gesture. "Your letter told me all that. What I'd like to know is why a pretty, young girl like yourself would want, or *need,* such a job? It will be rather dull, shut up here three days a week with a cantankerous old lady, writing thank you notes of various kinds, accepting invitations and turning them down."

She regarded me with a curious and penetrating gaze. "I have the strangest feeling I know you. I usually have no memory for names, though I never forget a face; yet, somehow your signature struck a chord. Challys Winthrop." She paused. "Is it possible? *Have* we met?"

I saw no reason to lie and no way to avoid the truth.

"Yes, my lady, we have met. Last October we were both passengers on the same stagecoach. Unfortunately, there was—"

"*Of course!* Why in the world didn't I place you at once? Now it's all coming back. You had a child with you, did you not? A little boy?"

"Yes, my brother."

"I recall he was very spunky about the whole deplorable affair. You were calm and resourceful. Not like *most* silly young girls would be. That ninny Thompson, my maid, never did get over the fright. She left me, can you imagine? Once we got home. Her nerves were shattered, she said. Stuff and nonsense. She felt some guilt that our belongings were never recovered, as though it were her fault, that I somehow blamed her."

At once, the picture of Lady Bethune's ruined alligator tea case in the Brindles' storage room flashed into my mind, and I suffered a pang of guilt at the knowledge. But Lady Bethune was rattling on, and I tried to focus my attention on her.

"Well, good-bye and good riddance, I say. I cannot abide people who let unforeseen circumstances overwhelm them." She pursed her lips. "Now it's all coming back. You did not go on with us the next day, did you? Something happened . . ." She broke off frowning as if annoyed at her faulty recall.

"Ty, my brother, suffered a bad chill. He became ill and was too sick to be moved. We had to stay and—"

That's as far as I got with my story because suddenly we heard men's voices from out in the hall.

"Is my aunt at home?" came a deep authoritative voice.

I felt myself tense. A moment later the morning room door opened, and there in the arched doorway stood Nicholas Seymour.

"Nicholas, dear boy! Come in!" Lady Bethune exclaimed delightedly. "The most marvelous coincidence has just occurred." She gestured toward me. "This young lady came in answer to my ad, and it turns out she and I had a previous meeting."

His gaze fell on me and lingered there. I felt warmth rise into my cheeks, and I experienced the same erratic heartbeat I'd felt at our first meeting. I'm not sure how long we stared at each other. Only a few seconds perhaps, surely no longer. I felt the planet spin under my feet, and somehow I knew nothing would ever be the same for me again.

Thank goodness, as Lady Bethune began explaining to Nicholas in detail the amazing coincidence, I had a few moments to regain my composure. During her recital, Nicholas walked into the room and stood by his aunt's chair, outwardly attentive to her, but looking at me. When she finished her tale, she asked, "Isn't that the most remarkable thing you've ever heard?"

He smiled slightly, his expression unreadable. "You mean the *very same stagecoach* that had the accident, the one I tried to talk you out of taking?"

"Oh, fiddle, Nicholas! Do you always have to prove yourself right?" Lady Bethune said impatiently. "But, yes, the very same. And as you can see, I'm paying for not taking your advice with this foot!"

She turned to me, touched her foot with the tip of her cane. "I twisted my ankle badly when we were struggling out of the overturned carriage that night. I didn't notice it too much at the time. It's given me a great deal of trouble ever since. That's one reason I need someone to help me do things."

"You mean fetch and carry for you, don't you, Aunt Isabel? I hope you don't plan to hire Miss Winthrop to take the unfortunate Thompson's place?"

"Of course not!" Lady Bethune said indignantly. "If she takes the position, which I'm certainly going to offer her, she'll be answering invitations, paying my bills, writing cheques, that sort of thing. She has very fine handwriting."

Again I felt his amused gaze on me, and again I blushed.

123

"Pay no attention to Nicholas, Miss Winthrop, he's a terrible tease." Lady Bethune gave him a severe look. "Sit down somewhere, Nicholas, and let Miss Winthrop and me get on with our business."

To me she said, "Just ignore him."

If that were only possible! I tried to follow her suggestion, but I could not forget his presence in the room, nor his gaze on me.

Lady Bethune made quick work of the rest of the interview and offered me the position at a wage far higher than I had expected. Stunned, I agreed.

"Good. Well, then, can you start right away, next week?"

"Yes, that will be fine." I got to my feet, pulling on my gloves, ready to depart.

Nicholas immediately rose and sauntered toward me. "I gather you live locally, Miss Winthrop?"

I hesitated, uncertain as to whether I should give my address as Briarwood Manor and reveal my connection with the Hazeltons.

"Yes, just a little past the village."

"Then I can give you a ride. I'm going in that direction."

I glanced at Lady Bethune, who had not been quick enough to conceal her surprise. Noting it, I asked him, "But haven't you just come to visit your aunt?"

Nicholas exchanged an enigmatic look with Lady Bethune, who took her cue and said, "Haven't you forgotten this is my afternoon to play whist, Nicholas? My friends are coming at three, and I must take my nap beforehand. Perhaps you can attend to whatever business you have in the village and join me for dinner this evening."

"Splendid idea, Aunt Isabel. I *did* forget. So, you see, Miss Winthrop, I will be killing two birds with the proverbial stone by giving you a ride into Meadowmead and transacting my business too."

I had planned, after my interview, to wait at the end of the road for the postman's return trip or the carrier cart going to the village. Since I did not want to divulge my true identity to Nicholas Seymour, I decided I would ask him to leave me off at the town square.

Accepting a ride with him meant I would have to walk back to Briarwood Manor in Auntie Evelyn's too small, French-heeled boots. A small price to pay, I decided, for the chance to ride beside Nicholas Seymour in his shiny, gold-trimmed phaeton pulled by a fine black horse.

In the weeks that followed my coming to work for Lady Bethune, I employed diverse ways of keeping my relationship with the Hazeltons a secret. With some self-reproach, I realized I had become quite adept at being covert. For a person who had hitherto prided herself on honesty, I was collecting quite a number of secrets and half-truths. I'd conspired with Nanny to take Ty away from his father. I'd concealed from the Brindles the true state of my financial situation when Ty became ill. I'd told neither Lady Bethune nor Nicholas Seymour about the stolen goods stored at the inn. The only person I'd confided that to was Francis Vaughn, who had advised me to keep quiet about it. Francis was also the only one who knew about my brief career as an artist's model, and no one knew about *him*.

For my short years I had racked up quite a series of less than honorable positions and activities.

At the end of each day's work, I walked out Elmhurst Hall's drive and concealed myself behind the high boxwood hedge at the gates. The road was one used by carriers, workmen, and farmers on their way to and from Meadowmead, and someone always gave me a ride home.

This became more and more difficult, however, as Nicholas began appearing at his aunt's house nearly every day I was there. He always had a viable reason—he happened to be a weekend guest at some friend's country place or had come down from London on some estate business or had just dropped by to see how his aunt was faring.

He would slip into the room where his aunt was dictating

replies to me or I was working at the desk. It was quite un-nerving. The minute he appeared I became acutely aware of his presence, though I tried to keep my attention on my work while he remained idly chatting with Lady Bethune about mutual friends or regaling her with the society gossip she loved to hear. If I attempted to leave quietly, he would be on his feet at once, purportedly with errands to do in the village, and offer to drive me home.

The game of keeping my background a secret became harder and harder to play.

As the Scottish poet Robert Burns so aptly wrote, "The best laid plans of mice and men often go astray." So did my intention of keeping my relationship with Lord and Lady Hazelton to myself.

With my first month's salary from Lady Bethune, I took Ty to town to buy him some badly needed clothes. He had out-grown the hand-me-downs the inn's cook had passed on to him, and he was badly in need of new boots.

We were just coming out of the village shoe store when we almost collided with Nicholas.

"Upon my word! What a happy coincidence!" A broad smile lighted his usually rather stern expression. "Miss Winthrop! And who is this fine little fellow?" he asked look-ing down at Ty.

"My brother, Tyrone," I stammered, taken completely off guard.

Ty, of course, had not been with me at our first meeting, that day I was on my way to kidnap him, and the day Nicholas had come to the inn, Ty had been nowhere in sight. Nor had I subsequently mentioned Ty.

"Ah, then this is the plucky lad my aunt told me about. From what I heard about you, young man, you were as brave a fellow as anyone could want in a disaster. My aunt was very impressed."

Nicholas then looked at me, raising his eyebrows. "I think

this calls for some kind of reward. On behalf of my aunt, I'd like to buy this fellow a treat. What do you say to that?"

I felt Ty tug my hand. His upturned face looked hopeful.

"That is very kind of you, Mr. Seymour, but not necessary."

"I never do things because they're *necessary*, Miss Winthrop, only when it pleases me to do them. Come along, then, shall we?"

16

We were soon seated at a corner table in the nearby cozy tea room and surrounded by delicious smells of roasting coffee, cinnamon, and chocolate. While Ty made a serious study of the pyramid of goodies on the tray the waitress presented for his selection, Nicholas addressed me.

"I really owe *you* a debt of gratitude, Miss Winthrop. My aunt's disposition has taken a decided turn for the better since your coming to Elmhurst Hall. I had been getting quite concerned about her. The injury she sustained in the accident was more serious than she led you to believe. It has confined her severely, limiting most of the activities she enjoys.

"It was unlike her to become morose and depressed, but at her age, I think she felt most of the joy of life was over. There has been a remarkable change in her now that she has a cheerful, young companion three days a week, even though I think she may be hard put finding enough for you to do each time. It is important that she has something to look forward to, and I am very grateful to you for offering your services."

Overwhelmed with such extravagant praise, it seemed less

than honest to allow him to think my answering the ad was the sort of thing an idle young lady with time on her hands might do for a lark. The time to lay my cards on the table, so to speak, had come.

"Mr. Seymour, I would not have you laboring under a false impression of me. I did not offer my services to Lady Bethune out of sympathy. In fact, I did not know of her injury until the day I came to apply for the position."

I paused, meeting his direct gaze. "While *you* may never do anything out of necessity, others are not so fortunate. I *needed* employment and had few qualifications other than the ones outlined in your aunt's advertisement."

I glanced at Ty. "I must earn my living and support my little brother."

"I understand," Nicholas replied. "I find you refreshingly honest, Miss Winthrop. It is a quality I hold in high regard. I would be disappointed if you were anything less."

Ty tapped my arm and in a loud whisper, asked, "Could I have the strawberry pie with cream *and* an apple tart?"

I was about to say, no, choose *one,* when Nicholas responded instead.

"Of course, you may have whatever you want." He smiled over Ty's head at me, chiding teasingly, "A growing boy, Miss Winthrop!"

After we'd finished our tea, there was no way I could refuse Nicholas's offer to drive us home. I was glad I had taken the chance to explain our true situation. Otherwise, Nicholas might have been startled when he drove up to Briarwood Manor. He would have had to be blind not to see the condition of the grounds, the forsaken look of the house itself.

As we came to a stop in front and Ty scrambled down, I turned to Nicholas. "My aunt and uncle are not receiving just now. My uncle is elderly and not well. I hope you understand why I cannot invite you in."

He held up one hand. "No apology, please, Miss Winthrop."

However, at that very moment, Aunt Evelyn, alerted by

the unusual sound of carriage wheels on the gravel drive when she had long since stopped entertaining or welcoming guests, came out onto the stone steps. At the sight of the splendid phaeton and my handsome escort, she looked abashed. I saw her hands flutter to her hair, then smooth down her skirt.

It was then, I believe, I came to admire Nicholas Seymour in a new way. He treated Auntie with elaborate courtesy, making the most gentle and tactful conversation with her. If aware of her discomfiture at her present circumstances, he seemed to consider them of no account and strove to put her at ease. I recognized then the gentleness and consideration under his urbane, confident facade, which might even be taken for arrogance.

Before he departed, he asked Aunt Evelyn if he might call on us next time he was down from London. She assured him he would be most welcome. When he turned to me, as if for confirmation, there was a look in his eyes that left me quite breathless.

I was glad the truth was out. In the days that followed, I felt more relaxed and able to enjoy going to Elmhurst Hall. Lady Bethune treated me kindly, the work was easy, and the surroundings were luxuriously pleasant.

The longer I lived at Briarwood Manor and worked for Lady Bethune, the further away the whole awful experience at the inn seemed. It got so that entire days passed when I didn't even think about it. But when I did, I felt cold shivers run up my spine. Sometimes I woke up at night terrified by dreams in which I was caught and accused of being the Brindles' accomplice. These dreams became less and less frequent, however, and I intentionally tried to put the memory of those dreadful times out of my mind.

I still worried about Muir tracing us, though. I wondered if my absence from Miss Elderberry's had been reported to him. Had he investigated my whereabouts or put Ty's disappearance together with that of my own? Or did he even care? Having depleted my mother's fortune, perhaps he had nothing to gain by finding us. Perhaps he remained in a drunken stupor unable to think or act.

On the days Uncle George seemed more alert, I approached him about consulting his lawyers about adopting Ty. He always agreed, but nothing was ever done. In two years I would be twenty-one, legally of age. Then I could adopt my brother myself. In the meantime, I lived from day to day, hoping for the best.

Almost a week to the day he had met Aunt Evelyn, Nicholas called on us. He arrived with a bouquet of flowers for Auntie, a box of fine cigars for Uncle George, a box of assorted French chocolates for me, and a large red ball for Ty. He conversed on many subjects, tactfully ignoring Uncle's vagueness. He revealed a fine mind as well as a sense of humor.

After he left, Auntie declared him charming. She told me she had often heard people speak highly of him. "However, he's thought to be a confirmed bachelor," she said with a slight twinkle in her eyes. "Many a debutante's mama has hoped to net him for her daughter. He's avoided capture—until now."

After that, whenever he was down from London, which was more and more often, Nicholas called at Briarwood Manor. On the days I worked for Lady Bethune, he drove me home from Elmhurst. These were always happy occasions. Nicholas was an interesting, well read, and amusing raconteur. His humor was never cruel; he had a tolerant way of looking at other people's foibles and laughing at his own.

Auntie's remarks about Nicholas's eligibility and his invulnerability to marriage-minded mamas made me curious. Even though I couldn't deny my attraction to Nicholas, I tried not to allow myself any fantasies about him. After all, he was a sophisticated, worldly gentleman, widely traveled, well educated, and at least ten years older than I. For all Auntie's insinuating comments, I doubted Nicholas had romantic feelings for me. Gratitude for my lifting his favorite aunt out of the doldrums was probably closer to the truth.

At Elmhurst Hall, the household staff became used to my presence, as did Lady Bethune's frequent visitors, so much so I often worked at the desk in her sitting room while she entertained guests. When her three special friends came to have tea and play whist with her, I was often amused and sometimes scandalized by the society gossip they exchanged.

One afternoon while addressing invitations to a party Lady Bethune was planning to give at Elmhurst when the gardens would be in full bloom and she would be rid of her cane, I overheard fragments of the ladies' animated discussion. In spite of myself I was drawn to listen.

"Indiscreet isn't the word for it!"

"Blatant, I'd say!"

"If they had only used some—"

"Discretion?"

"No one would have been the wiser."

"But Neville Cuthcart! Never!"

"Typical male."

"There's blame enough all around."

"She's always been headstrong."

"Wild as a March hare. I've known her all her life."

"Well, she's done it now."

"Lost everything, I heard."

"Not quite."

"What do you mean?"

"She managed to slip her portrait out and sold it."

"*Sold* it, to whom?"

"A commercial company that is using it—"

"*Using* it? How?

"On candy boxes, playing cards, powder tins, and soap wrappers."

Loud gasps all around.

"*No!*"

"Surely not?"

"Indeed. She got scads of money for it and—"

"You don't mean it."

"I do, and she's off to France."

"*France!* But the scandal of it—"

"In France it will be considered fashionable."

A spatter of laughter followed this remark, then I heard Lady Bethune's voice cut through the levity.

"That may be all well and good now, in France, as you say. But in *England* even the *whisper* of scandal is social death. No matter how long she stays abroad, she'll never be received here by anyone again."

A murmur of agreement went around the table.

Though I felt a small, undefined sensation at Lady Bethune's pronouncement, that bit of gossip about an unknown lady of quality who had lost her social standing soon faded from my mind.

I finished my work that day and slipped out, leaving the ladies still playing cards. I found Nicholas waiting outside in his phaeton.

"What are you doing here?" I asked, genuinely surprised. "I thought you were in London."

"Spur of the moment decision." His eyes were full of mischief. He helped me into the buggy, and we started off down the drive. "However, if you believe *that,* you must also believe in providence? Do you?"

"Do I what?"

"Believe in providence? Some call it fate, chance, or coincidence. Think back. Don't you believe it's a remarkable coincidence we have crossed each other's paths before and now you are my aunt's social secretary and the two of us have become friends and are driving along this country road in this particular part of England?"

I had to laugh. "Well, when you put it that way—"

"Aha! I'll tell you that even on that first morning, when I put Aunt Isabel on that stagecoach and saw you, I *knew* we were bound to meet again."

"Do you have such premonitions often?"

"No, not at all. That's what makes that one so remarkable."

I started to tell him about the second time our paths had crossed so strangely, that day at the inn when I was a scruffy maid, my arms full of laundry, and he, a fine gentleman, came striding in, demanding information from Mrs. Brindle. In fact, I was tempted to tell him the whole of my experience at the inn, but we were turning into the gate of Briarwood Manor, and as we came up to the front of the house, Ty came bounding down the steps to greet us. Later I fervently wished I had told Nicholas then about my experiences at the Brindles', but the opportunity was lost.

Nicholas, who had become quite a hero to my little brother, got out and spoke to Ty fondly, tousling his curly head. "Want to give Seneca a lump of sugar?" he asked.

He took a small rock of sugar out of his pocket, placed it in Ty's hand, lifted him up, and told him to open his palm and hold it out to the horse.

Seneca gobbled it up, and Ty shrieked happily. "It tickled!" he shouted. We all laughed.

After inviting us to go on a picnic with him down at the river the next afternoon, Nicholas said good-bye and rode off.

"I like him, don't you, Lyssa?" Ty asked me as we went hand in hand up the steps and into the house. I didn't have a chance to answer because Aunt Evelyn was waiting for us, holding a letter she had received that day from Nanny Grace.

The letter was in reply to the one I had sent to her at her sister's, telling of our safe arrival at Briarwood Manor. I read it eagerly, but its contents alarmed me and revived some of my old dread. Nanny wrote she'd heard from Lily, Mama's former maid who had left to get married.

When Muir sobered up and found us gone, he had gone into a wild rage, cursing and threatening everyone. He had summoned the sheriff to Crossfield Grange, ordered him to issue a warrant for my arrest and to send out men to track me down.

The local constabulary had reason to dislike Muir because of his frequent brawls in town taverns, his violence, and his brutal dealings with tenants on the farm. The sheriff had been heard to say that any child would be better off without a father like Muir, so it was possible the man had not followed Muir's directions regarding the matter.

Lily also reported that Muir was constantly drunk, shut up in the isolated house. He had sold most of the furniture, paintings, and silver, dismissed all the servants who had not left in disgust. The villagers assumed he would eventually drink himself to death.

Nanny concluded by saying she prayed every day we would remain happy and safe. I put aside Nanny's letter, echoing her heartfelt prayer.

It seemed to me that more than enough time had passed. If we'd not yet heard from Muir, maybe the villagers were right, maybe he'd already drunk himself to death. Was it safe to feel safe? I wondered. Perhaps it would all work out for us. Apprehension soon gave way to anticipation, however, for the next day Ty and I were to go on a picnic with Nicholas.

Nicholas's idea of a picnic, I discovered, was far different from the haphazard bun and apple sort on which Ty and I had gone during our time at the inn. Even the April day itself, full of sunshine and soft breezes, could not have been more perfect if Nicholas had ordered it himself.

Nicholas took us to a lovely spot on the parklike grounds of Elmhurst Hall, where swans glided gracefully on a placid pond, and from where, every now and then, a doe and fawn could be seen in the nearby grove of aspens.

With a great flourish he spread a linen cloth on the ground, brought out silver and plates, then lifted a large wicker hamper from his buggy. He dispensed its contents, an array of delicacies that would have delighted the most particular gourmet. Our feast consisted of rolls of thinly sliced ham stuffed with chicken salad, pâté spread on wedge-shaped wheat wafers, hothouse pears and chilled grapes, assorted

French pastries, lemonade served in crystal glasses, and hot tea sipped from porcelain cups.

Nicholas was a wonderful storyteller and kept Ty raptly listening to tales of derring-do. He also had a repertoire of limericks and jokes that made me laugh until tears came and had Ty rolling on the grass with irrepressible laughter. Nicholas, at play, was not the stern, rather arrogant person I had believed him to be at our first encounter. In fact, I could not have imagined a more delightful companion.

After we'd eaten, Nicholas produced a cribbage board and taught me to play while Ty sailed a toy boat at the edge of the water.

It was a day of simple relaxation and fun, and when it came to an end, I felt sorry. I realized it was the first such day I could remember having since I was a child. It was the first of many such happy days spent with Nicholas, more often than not with Ty, as well, who was forming a real affection for Nicholas. I appreciated Nicholas's interest in my brother, who had been sadly in need of a strong male figure in his life.

I had been Lady Bethune's secretary for over two months when one day Aunt Evelyn called me into her sitting room.

"We must have a serious talk, Challys. Sit down, my dear." She patted a place beside her on the cushioned window seat. The sun streaming in through the diamond panes behind her created a halo of light around my aunt's gray hair, giving her a slightly angelic aura. The expression on her face, however, sent a rush of alarm through me. She took my hand in both of hers and began.

"You have been here long enough to observe and understand the situation in which your uncle and I find ourselves. I'm sure I don't have to elaborate." She shook her head. "However, I have always been one to face things squarely and not indulge in self-pity. Things are as they are, and we must make the best of whatever circumstances in which providence sees fit to place us.

"I need to discuss Tyrone's future, and yours, Challys, as

they are irrevocably linked. What *you* do inevitably affects him. That's why we must plan your debut carefully."

"My *debut*, Auntie?" I wondered if my aunt had lost her senses. A debut in our dire financial condition? Debuts for young ladies involved a fortune in various expenses. Surely she couldn't mean a fancy ball to introduce me to society.

"Yes, of course. It is the only possible way for you to meet an eligible man to marry, one of prestige and wealth, the kind you *must* marry to insure Ty will have a proper education at Harrow or Eton and then at Cambridge or Oxford."

Auntie halted for a moment at what must have been my shocked expression, then went on. "All this takes a great deal of money, Challys. It would be different if George and I were able to provide you with a large dowry, as once we might have done. Now that is out of the question, so I've taken matters into my own hands."

I could think of nothing to say to all this, so I just waited for Auntie to proceed.

"Fortunately, we still have connections in society. I have given George's health as the reason we no longer go out or entertain. However, I have a dear friend, Lady Prudence Cahill—we were schoolgirls together and have remained in touch through the years—who is willing, in fact happy, to be your sponsor, to launch you into society by giving you a ball at the end of the summer and, if you make a good impression on her, of which I have no doubt you will, perhaps even a London season."

I stared at Auntie, protest ready, but I didn't have a chance to speak.

"No, don't interrupt, dear. Let me finish. We have corresponded, and she is enthusiastic about the plan. She has married off several granddaughters very successfully to men of rank and wealth. She loved doing it and is eager to do it again. She is coming to meet you and discuss her ideas with you as to the theme of the ball, the invitations, and all the details."

Auntie looked so pleased with herself I didn't have the heart to tell her how I felt about such an arrangement.

It was only later in my bedroom that I gave way to my true feelings. Ty, who now felt at home at Briarwood, had been moved to the small room next to the old nursery. I was glad for the privacy, as I was overcome with emotion. The fact that my debut was a *fait accompli,* arranged without my knowledge or consent, stunned me. For nearly seven months I had been on my own, making my own decisions, caring for my brother, working under the most trying conditions. It had given me strength and independence. I had lost touch with how things were done in the world of society, which Aunt Evelyn still inhabited, the one into which I'd been born as well.

An arranged marriage, based on the man's property and position, was the accepted custom in society. A girl of good family had only to be personable, socially graceful, and pliable. This had remained unchanged. It was I who had changed. A marriage based on achieving security was repugnant to me, but what Aunt Evelyn had pointed out was true—Ty's future depended on my entering into the proper marriage. But a loveless one?

Restlessness made sleep impossible for me that night. Everything Auntie said had sounded reasonable, even justifiable. Yet something within me recoiled. I didn't want to be traded for financial compensation. Somewhere in my girlish dreams, deep in my romantic heart, still dwelled the hope of one day knowing a forever love, a mutually spontaneous one, the kind I'd read about in novels and poetry. Was this hope to be denied me for my brother's future?

Without willing it, Nicholas Seymour came into my thoughts. For the first time, I allowed my true feelings about him to surface. I recalled how my pulse leapt when he walked into the room, how I relived our most casual conversations. I saw his face, those keen, gray eyes full of intelligence and humor, the mouth I had once thought so stern, smiling, its expression transformed. His gentleness with Ty especially touched me. I saw him lift my little brother up into the saddle and to Ty's delight lead him around the circular driveway several times. Nicholas Seymour may have entered my life by accident, but he had invaded my dreams, captured my heart. If only *he* . . .

Quickly I banished that possibility. It was wishful thinking and futile. By all accounts, Nicholas had had many opportunities to marry and yet remained a bachelor. I told myself it would be silly to think his interest in me was anything but platonic.

That night I wept foolish tears, relinquished my dreams. Marrying the *right* man to ensure Ty a good education, his rightful place in the world, was my duty. I could not refuse the means to accomplish that. Whatever they were. A debut ball was the accepted stepping-stone. I convinced myself I must take the opportunity Auntie and her friend offered.

When morning came I had resigned myself to my fate. At breakfast Auntie told me Lady Cahill would be coming for tea the following afternoon.

Shortly after my meeting with Lady Cahill, plans for my debut into society at a summer ball held at her country estate were initiated.

The weeks leading up to my debut ball were hectic. There had to be many fittings for the extravagantly beautiful dress Lady Cahill's dressmaker was making for me. Even though I tried my best, for Auntie's sake, to appear happy and grateful for all she and her friend were doing, a shadow hovered over what should have been a lighthearted time of gaiety and anticipation.

Until a week before the ball, I continued going to Elmhurst Hall three days a week. Lady Bethune was interested in hearing all the details of my debut. She wanted to know every person on the guest list and had comments to make on each one. Strangely enough, my final week at Lady Bethune's, Nicholas never appeared.

All summer he had come down from London each Friday and most often spent the weekend, visiting his aunt and calling on us at Briarwood Manor. It took every shred of willpower not to ask Lady Bethune about his absence. Fortunately, she volunteered the information. Nicholas had sent word that certain matters kept him in the city. I felt inordinately disappointed.

Then on my last day of work, Nicholas appeared.

In my sudden confusion, I blurted out the question I'd been determined *not* to ask—had he received an invitation to my ball and, more importantly, was he coming?

His smile was enigmatic as he replied, "Of course, I wouldn't miss it."

Afterward, I could have bitten my tongue. I wished I'd not given him the satisfaction of knowing it mattered to me at all whether or not he came. Of course, it *did*.

It mattered most dreadfully.

What hurt the most was that it did not seem to occur to him that my debut would change everything for me. For *us!* Even if our relationship was only a friendship, it had meant a great deal. However, if my ball accomplished what Auntie and Lady Cahill hoped it would and I attracted some eligible wealthy man and became engaged, well, then I could not spend time with Nicholas, even on the most casual basis.

How much I would miss that.

17

As the day of the ball neared, I tried to hide my increasing depression as I went through all the expected and necessary preparations. The night of the ball, Auntie fluttered around me as I dressed. *She* was thrilled and delighted.

My gown was a gorgeous creation, a divine shade of azure blue satin with an overskirt of Valenciennes lace. A Grecian bertha edged the neckline, setting off Mama's matching sapphire and diamond pendant and earrings. I was thankful I'd held on to them.

In spite of it all, I felt heavyhearted as Auntie and I left Briarwood in the carriage Lady Cahill had sent for us. I kept telling myself Ty's future was at stake. I must be witty, charming, and flirtatious.

Ironically, we had to pass Elmhurst Hall on the way to the Cahill's estate. For a moment I wondered if Nicholas would come to the ball as he'd promised, or if the bouquet he had sent was a substitute for his presence. The enclosed card contained a mysterious message, written in his bold, slanted handwriting: If you know the language of flowers, you will understand the meaning.

Nicholas loved riddles and conundrums. He was always trying them out on Ty and me. What was he saying with these flowers?

A debutante traditionally received many bouquets on the night of her debut. Among all I had received, I'd chosen his to carry, a single perfect white rose surrounded by mignonette.

Ignorant of the language of flowers to which he'd referred, I asked Auntie to explain the symbolic meaning of his bouquet.

"He praises your youthful beauty, offers you admiration and affection."

I was touched by the tenderness of his message, yet in my heart of hearts I wanted more than admiration and affection from Nicholas—I wanted deep passionate love, hopeless as my desire was.

When we reached the Cahills', for Auntie's sake I put on a bright face, my most radiant smile. Light shone out from the long windows, and as we mounted the steps into the house, I heard music playing.

We were greeted by Lady Cahill and her stout, jovial husband and led into the ballroom, aglitter with myriad candles in crystal chandeliers reflected in mirrors on the walls.

Almost at once I was surrounded by potential dance partners. One by one, Lady Cahill introduced me to young men, all of whom asked to write their names on my dance card. Lady Cahill looked so pleased, I assumed they were all on her list of eligible suitors.

Whirled onto the polished floor, I was soon caught up in a sense of excitement any girl would enjoy. I danced with one charming partner after another in a dizzying assortment of schottisches and waltzes.

At one short pause between sets, to my surprise, Nicholas appeared. In a black swallow-tailed jacket, white satin waistcoat, batwing collar and silk cravat, he looked more handsome than ever. With his usual assurance, he bowed slightly, then offered his arm to lead me out for the grand promenade.

As I looked up into his eyes, I saw something different in them and felt a ridiculous surge of happiness, a fantastic hope that something wonderful was about to happen.

When the promenade ended, Nicholas took my dance card and crossed out every other name, substituting his own. Until midnight, we danced every dance together. I was dizzy with delight, floating on a cloud.

When the other guests went into the dining room to partake of the sumptuous buffet supper, Nicholas took me into the conservatory, which adjoined the ballroom.

The abundance of ferns and tropical plants and the heavy perfumes of the exotic flowers Lord Cahill cultivated created an Eden-like atmosphere. The murmur of voices and music faded into the distance, and we were alone. We could have been on some enchanted island, the feeling of intimacy was so complete. Nicholas took both my hands, twirled me around in front of him, his gaze sweeping over me.

"In case I did not tell you, Challys, you look beautiful tonight. But, then, you have always seemed so to me." He smiled, then said more seriously, "I had not meant to speak so soon. I meant to let you have your moment in the sun, let you enjoy the experience of having these eager chaps buzzing about you like bees around the loveliest of flowers.

"However, I find myself gripped by the basest of emotions—jealousy. I cannot bear watching. I'm afraid someone else will somehow attract you, and I shall miss my chance."

Still holding my hands he drew me closer. His voice lowered and his eyes seemed to deepen in color as he searched my face. "I discovered I am unwilling to risk losing you to someone else, so I decided to throw caution to the winds and not wait any longer to tell you."

"Tell me what, Nicholas?" I asked breathlessly.

"*What?* Haven't you guessed? That I love you."

"Love me?"

"Yes. Of course. Madly, truly, completely. Couldn't you tell? I love everything about you—your sweetness, your strength, your sincerity, your loyalty, the sound of your laughter, *everything*. I adore you."

Then Nicholas drew me even closer and after an eternal moment, kissed me. It was a tender kiss that slowly deepened. It had in it the promise of passion that even my inexperience recognized and responded to; it was a kiss that forever made impossible my ever belonging to any other man.

When at last it ended, Nicholas held me at arm's length. "Now, do you believe what I said about our meeting being more than mere chance?"

I looked at him with wonder. "Yes, I do believe it, Nicholas." I felt my eyes mist with tears.

Immediately Nicholas whipped out an immaculate white handkerchief and dabbed my cheeks. "No tears. Not ever. If I have anything to do with it, there will never be any more tears for you." His smile was tender. "Oh, my darling, I am going to make you so happy there will never be a need for tears."

Suddenly I felt a marvelous warmth, as though a silken blanket had been thrown about me, protecting me from all the hardships and danger of the past, securing me from any possible harm in the future.

That night, which was supposed to be my introduction into society, was successful in a way no one could have predicted. Even though everyone, including Lady Prudence Cahill, declared delight at Nicholas's proposal, they all seemed shocked—the confirmed bachelor whisking out of circulation the newest debutante of the season. It was unheard of. Everyone was stunned. Nicholas wanted our engagement announced immediately, the wedding planned for three months hence. "Impossible!" Aunt Evelyn, Lady Bethune, and Lady Cahill protested in unison.

"December, then," conceded Nicholas reluctantly. "That is all the longer I am willing to wait," he declared adamantly.

Auntie Evelyn, and even the imperturbable Lady Bethune, were amazed, to say nothing of the circle of society that had written off Nicholas as impervious to the wiles of hopeful young ladies and their mamas.

I felt a passing sympathy for Lady Cahill, who had gone to so much trouble and expense to launch me. However, she dismissed my apologies, saying she had never married off one of her protégées so quickly, nor to someone of Nicholas's caliber. She assured me she was as happy as I was.

But she couldn't really be *that* happy. My happiness knew no bounds.

Now I could express all my pent-up longings and secret feelings for Nicholas that I had kept buried, thinking they were impossible. I could hardly believe I had won the love of such a man. I basked in his loving, protective attitude toward Ty and me. He was everything I could have asked for. He was generous and had a sense of humor, as well as having the qualities I most admired—integrity, intelligence, and kindness. For the first time since childhood, I felt completely loved, cared for, and protected.

A few weeks later we were strolling through the garden at Lady Bethune's when Nicholas presented me with an engagement ring. It was not the traditional diamond or birthstone gem often given as an engagement ring, but one especially crafted from Nicholas's own design. It was a gold, sculptured lily with a large, rosy pearl nestled in the center and tiny diamonds scattered on the opening petals like dew drops.

"Oh, Nicholas, it's beautiful," I murmured as he slipped it on my finger. "It's the loveliest ring I've ever seen."

"I wanted you to have something unique, a ring unlike anyone else's, a symbol of our love."

Our promise to each other was sealed that day with the ring and a kiss. I felt Nicholas's love enfold me like the petals of the lily, and I felt myself opening up to that love like a bud to the warmth of the sun.

Two things endeared Nicholas to me even more and made me realize further how fortunate I was. First was his determination to start legal proceedings to adopt Ty. Second, when I confided to him my reluctance to leave my aging relatives in their failing health and impoverished state, he promptly told me he had been considering offering to buy their estate, renovate the house to its former splendor, and make it *our* home.

I moved through those weeks before our scheduled wedding in a haze of happiness, not knowing just how fragile happiness can be.

18

Ours was to be a winter wedding, set for the first week in December. By then the renovations at Briarwood Manor would be finished, providing a perfect place for the reception following the ceremony. Auntie was in seventh heaven, consulting with decorators and drapers, picking out fabrics for curtains and new upholstery. Uncle George seemed to regain some of his old buoyancy with all the activity around him. Ty, who worshiped Nicholas, was wild with happiness that Nicholas was to become his brother and legal guardian. It all seemed too perfect.

Alas, it was.

Early in November I went to Lady Cahill's London town house, where she gave a reception to introduce me to some of her friends and Nicholas's London friends whom I had not yet met. It was a lavish affair and duly described in the society pages. Lady Cahill tried to persuade me to stay on with her and have some of my trousseau gowns made by the exclusive dress salon she herself patronized. Nicholas urged me to do so and thus what was to have been a weekend visit lengthened into a two-week stay.

Returning late one afternoon, I found an envelope addressed to me propped against the mirror of the dressing table in the guest room I was occupying. Curious, I picked it up, examining the London postmark and the special delivery notation at the bottom left-hand corner. The handwriting was lavishly decorative. Perhaps it was a congratulatory note from one of Nicholas's London friends whom I had not met.

I tore it open, and the moment I saw the signature, I felt my knees weaken. Francis Vaughn! I'd never in the world expected to hear from him again. In fact, I'd purposely tried to forget my experience with him along with that terrible time at the Brindles' inn. It was as if that whole episode had happened in another lifetime, to someone else. But at the sight of his name, it all came rushing back.

I sat down on the bed, took a deep breath, and began reading the letter.

My dear Lyssa,

When I recently read in the society news of the engagement of a Miss Challys Winthrop, niece of Lord and Lady Hazelton of Briarwood Manor, to the Honorable Nicholas Seymour, my first thought was how quickly fortunes can change! Yours for the better, and sadly, mine for the worse. Life is certainly full of odd turns and twists, peaks and valleys, is it not?

Reading of the marvelous shift in your future, I could not help but remember the thin, little barmaid with frightened eyes and a look of desperation whom I befriended little more than a year ago at the country inn. There was something appealing about your face that attracted my artist's eye, but more, I was moved to compassion by your plight. I'm sure you haven't forgotten how, out of the kindness of my heart, I offered you a way out of your misery.

Fate provided for both of us at that time. You were the model I was seeking for a special painting I had been commissioned to produce, and the fee I paid you for posing gave you the money you needed to escape from the den of iniquity in which you were trapped. And trapped you were. You knew of the criminal activities going on there and yet did not report them to the authorities for fear of being arrested as an accomplice. I remember how afraid you were when you told me of your knowledge of this. I suspect you never did report the Brindles. In that case, you are still in danger of being charged as an accessory to their crimes.

Fate has chosen to have our paths cross again. I hope, again, to our mutual benefit.

Much to my crushing disappointment, the painting for which you so willingly posed was not my key to fame after all. When I returned to London to present the finished painting to the man who had commissioned it, I found he had gone abroad, leaving no word as to the date of his return.

I had spent the last of the advance he had paid me on a magnificent frame befitting the subject matter and found myself financially depleted. I found myself without funds and without a place to stay.

In London, I could not afford a suitable studio or apartment. I have been reduced to living and working in a rat hole in one of the worst sections of London. I have written my sponsor numerous times, telling him that the painting is ready and I need to be compensated for this fine work of art, but so far there has been no response. Needless to say, I have reached a state of near despair.

So why should all this concern you? To put it simply, reciprocity. Did we not become friends at a time when you desperately needed a friend? Do not friends have concern and sympathy for one another, the willingness to aid each other in times of trouble?

Because I banked everything on the successful acceptance of the painting for which you posed, thinking it would provide a way into my sponsor's circle of wealthy friends, people who would admire the painting and offer other commissions, the failure of this man to live up to our agreement dealt me a devastating blow. I have been deeply depressed and unable to paint. My debts are piling up daily, and time is running out for me. I was at the point of self-destruction when fate stepped in once more.

Inspiration struck as my eyes fell again on the beautiful completed painting of you as the lady of the castle bidding farewell to her beloved knight. With a few deft strokes of my brush, I could make certain changes that would enable my selling it to a commercial enterprise! I could alter the medieval costume into a diaphanous Grecian-style robe and present the painting to a company that could use it to sell cosmetics. This has been done successfully before. Quite spectacularly so, as a matter of fact, although it was quite a scandal at the time. The portrait in question was of a well-known, albeit notorious, lady of society. It made her a financial fortune, which she needed badly at the time.

When this thought occurred to me, a second one followed. It would be unseemly to have the image of the bride of such a prestigious gentleman as Nicholas Seymour appear on soap wrappers, talcum tins, hairpin boxes, and cologne bottles used by shop girls, perhaps even by women of infamous character. Yet it would certainly save the day for me.

I am reluctant to confront you with this possibility, Lyssa, because you were such a nice little thing, and I grew quite fond of you during the time we spent together. I am sincerely glad you have found a wealthy protector, who possibly is ignorant of your past. However, as you once said yourself, desperate times require desperate actions, and I am desperate.

I am sure Nicholas Seymour would be shocked to see an image of his beloved fiancée, garbed as a woodland nymph, displayed throughout Britain, purchased for a few pennies.

To put it bluntly, I need money, enough so I can travel to France, and pursue my career without financial worry. I'm sure as the future Mrs. Nicholas Seymour you can secure 1,000 pounds, an amount that will eliminate the necessity of my selling the altered painting commercially.

If you ignore this letter and my request, I may be forced to go to Mr. Seymour himself, tell all, and secure from him sufficient reimbursement for my painting of you and for my silence concerning the things in which you were involved at the Brindles' inn. As they say, a word to the wise and all that. I feel sure you will agree the sooner this is arranged the better. I will give you until next Monday to deliver the money. Better you come in person with the money. I don't trust the post, or the people in this miserable slum where I'm now forced to stay. Come to the pub, Dauntless Dan's. I'm there every day at four. It is a neighborhood tavern where I go for my one daily meal and pint. The address is at the bottom of the letter. I will expect your response by return post at the same address.

Yours more in regret than retribution,
Francis Vaughn

My heart pounded. My fingertips tingled. A deep shudder left me weak. The letter slowly slipped from my hands. Within the minutes it had taken me to read the letter, I was transported back to those Sunday afternoons when I had posed for Francis Vaughn at his studio in the woods. I remembered all that he had told me about himself as he painted. So much of it had gone in one ear and out the other, preoccupied as I was by my own problems. Now fragments of those dark confidences came into my mind—his sad childhood, the tragedy of his father's experience in debtors' prison, his obsessive fear he might fail and suffer the same fate, his strange moods. I remembered that sometimes when depressed, he drank heavily, and I recalled how he confessed to taking chloral.

All this came flooding back to me as I sat on the bed shivering at the thought of what Francis threatened.

I leaned down and picked up the pages of the letter, looked at them again. The paper was filled with ink blots, many crossed out words and underlinings. It looked as if it had been written by someone in a chaotic state of mind, perhaps a mind under the influence of drink or drugs. He had told me that after some of those periods of induced oblivion, he could barely remember what he had done. He had added that such times were perhaps better forgotten.

Was this one of those times? Having posted this letter, would Vaughn have forgotten he had written it? Another shudder shook me. No, that would be too easy. This was real. His threat was real. A man I had thought merely an erratic artist had become a dangerous enemy.

I don't know how long I sat there, paralyzed by the contents of his letter. I knew the price of scandal. If something as sordid as this came out, it would mean the end of everything. How could a man of Nicholas's position marry someone rumored to be an artist's model, worse still, an accomplice of thieves? At the thought of losing Nicholas, I felt sick and trembly. Not only would I lose the man I loved, but with him would go my brother's future, my relatives' hope of a comfortable old age.

Something else came into my mind—the conversation I'd overheard among Lady Bethune and her friends, the story of the lady who had sold her portrait commercially and fled to escape the swirl of scandal. I didn't remember all the details. What I *did* remember was Lady Bethune's unequivocal statement: "In England even a whisper of scandal is social death. She will never be received by anyone here again."

I shuddered, remembering the tone of her voice. Nicholas was her nephew. Whatever scandal touched him would spill over onto his relatives. I thought of Lady Prudence Cahill, who had so graciously sponsored me, staking her own reputation by doing so.

I got to my feet and began pacing back and forth. I *should* have told Nicholas *everything*.

I had, of course, told Nicholas about my having to work as a maid to pay off my debt to the Brindles. After I recounted the daily humiliations, the heartless treatment I'd received, to say nothing of the physical toil, he had taken both my hands, turned them over, and kissed the palms and fingertips.

"My poor darling," he'd said, "how courageous you were! All that is now in the past, and we never need speak of it again. I plan to fill your life with so much happiness that those awful times will be forgotten."

Oh, if that could only be true! If only I could forget.

Nicholas had listened with such tender sympathy then; surely if I'd told him the rest, he would have understood how desperate I'd been. Now it was too late to expect either understanding or sympathy.

I put both hands to my throbbing temples.

If this horrible letter had accomplished one thing, it had proven that there were some things from which even Nicholas's love could not protect me. This unexpected threat had the power to ruin all my bright dreams.

Although my afternoons at Francis Vaughn's studio had been perfectly innocent, they could be made to sound shameful and incriminating. The other threat seemed almost worse—my knowledge about the stolen goods, among which were Lady Bethune's belongings. How could Nicholas ever trust me, knowing I'd withheld that information?

The more I thought about it, the worse my situation seemed.

There was no way out but to meet Francis Vaughn's outrageous demand. But how? Where could I get the kind of money he wanted? And in less than a week. All I owned of any value were the few pieces of sapphire and diamond jewelry my mother had left me. I had no idea what they were worth. Family heirlooms were not meant to be sold. Even if I knew where to sell them, I was sure I would not get what they were worth. They had belonged to my father's family, the Winthrops, before he gave them to Mama as a wedding gift. They were priceless, in one way, yet would they pay my ransom?

That's how I saw my situation. I was a hostage, a prisoner to Vaughn's sick mind, his desperate greed. There was no way out. There was no one in whom I could confide, no one to advise or help me. I would have to agree to Vaughn's terms. Maybe then I would be free.

Pleading a headache, I didn't go down to dinner that evening. Lady Cahill was going out to the theater and then to a supper party. She had a tray of soup and tea sent up to me and stopped in to check on me before she left, telling me she hoped I'd be better in the morning.

Of course, I wasn't. I was worse.

I had hardly slept at all. I had spent most of the night staring into the darkness, feeling the darkness was really an abyss opened up before me by Vaughn's threat.

I felt sick at having to give in to Vaughn but felt I had no alternative. Worse than my fear of the possible scandal that would blacken not only my name but that of my brother, my dear aunt and uncle, and Nicholas, was my anguish at keeping the whole situation from Nicholas. But, I asked myself, wouldn't it be worse if Vaughn carried out his ugly threat? I must at least try.

As painful as it was, I decided I must find some way to sell Mama's jewels. If it was for less than the amount Vaughn had asked for, I'd have to get the rest some other way.

I had to take advantage of my being in London. Surely in a big city I could find a discreet jeweler to whom I could sell my heirloom set, without becoming the focus of gossip. I didn't know how I would explain the missing set if anyone should ask. Likely, only Aunt Evelyn would notice they were gone. I would have to make up some story . . .

A chill went through me. I recalled something I'd learned in childhood. "Oh, what a tangled web we weave when first we practice to deceive." I was finding out just how true that saying was.

154

That afternoon I had to manufacture an excuse for my errand. "Another fitting?" Lady Cahill's eyebrows lifted. "I've never known Madame Sophie not to get measurements right at a single session. Perhaps she is getting on in years though."

Feeling guilty for maligning the poor seamstress to fit my purpose, I left the house, my jewels secreted in their velvet pouch in my muff.

The need for lies multiplied after my first foray into the city looking for a place to sell my jewelry proved unsuccessful. "In for a penny, in for a pound," Nanny used to say. Quoting my dear nurse made my face burn with shame. What would she say about this situation?

I remember little about the next few days. I moved in a trance, motivated by desperation, frantic with fear.

After another day spent vacillating in front of two fine jewelry stores, I lost heart and nerve. On the very threshold of one, I turned away. I could not bear parting with the only possessions I had from my beloved mother. My reluctance overcame desperation.

I dreaded the questioning looks any reputable jeweler would give me for wanting to dispose of such exquisite pieces of jewelry. What I needed was someone who would not ask embarrassing questions, someone who dealt with people in desperate circumstances. I needed a pawnbroker. A pawnbroker would give me cash and would hold my jewelry for a certain length of time without reselling it. Perhaps, somehow, I could find a way to buy it back myself.

Coming back into the house, I noticed Lord Cahill's study door was open. He and Lady Cahill had gone to a dinner party, and the evening paper he was reading before they left was on his desk. It struck me that I might find the name of a pawnbroker in the classified section. I darted in, folded the paper under my arm, and returned to my room. There I scanned the pages, searching desperately for the information I needed. I was amazed there were so many.

One particular advertisement caught my eye.

LADIES AND GENTLEMEN IN TEMPORARY FINANCIAL
DISTRESS will find prompt aid without embarrassment.
Courteous, confidential. Contact William P. Mossberger.

An address followed. I tore it out, put it in my purse, determined to contact Mr. Mossberger.

At dawn, I wrote a letter to Vaughn stating that I intended to meet his deadline but that I needed more time to collect the amount he had specified. I asked for two more days past the deadline. I signed only my initials. Using the address of the pub, I addressed the envelope, then slipped out of the house before anyone else was awake, scurried like a frightened mouse to the corner, and slipped the envelope inside the postbox.

Luckily, Lady Cahill, busy with her own social life, assumed I was happily occupied with various errands pertaining to my trousseau. She accepted all my explanations of visits to milliners, glovemakers, and shoe shops as plausible. She even excused my distracted air as that of a bride-to-be, her wedding only three weeks away.

I was very much aware of how little time I had to accomplish what must be done. With each passing day, the danger that Vaughn would grow impatient and contact Nicholas increased.

19

*G*iving one of my now well-practiced excuses, I went out, caught a hansom cab at the corner away from the house, and gave the driver Moss-berger's address.

When the carriage came to a stop and the driver hollered down to me, "Here you are, miss," I was shocked. This part of the city was a strong contrast to the streets of exclusive shops where I'd been shopping for my trousseau.

Timidly, I walked up to the door of the shop, identified as that of a pawnbroker by the three brass balls hanging over the entrance. The window was dusty, dead flies clustered in its corners. At the edges of a display of clocks, watches, musical instruments, and an assortment of jewelry were a heart-breaking number of wedding rings.

I hesitated. Would this kind of appraiser really know the value of my heirloom set? Well, I was here now. I might as well find out. If the price didn't seem right, I wouldn't have to proceed.

The day outside was overcast, and when I stepped inside I felt like I was entering a cavern. The interior of the shop was dingy, musty smelling. Slatted blinds on the tall rectangular windows at the back allowed little light to sneak in, leaving an overall gloom. Filled with self-disgust at my errand, the urge to turn around and leave was strong. Anger rose up in me at Vaughn's betrayal, which had brought me to this place. But there was no turning back.

The floor was bare and uneven, and my footsteps echoed hollowly as I walked toward the counter. There, visible behind a wire cage, I saw a bald man who looked up at my approach. "Yes, miss, what can I do for you?" His voice was oily and his eyes disappeared into slits as he squinted at me.

I stepped closer, swallowed, then said in a whispery voice, "I would like to have you appraise some jewelry."

"Well, let's see it."

Trying to conquer my distaste, I brought out the velvet bag, opened the drawstrings, and laid the beautiful sapphire and diamond earrings and pendant on the wooden surface. I watched his bony hands with their dirty nails reach for the set and draw it in. He fitted a cylindrical viewer to one eye and bent over to examine them.

The price the man quoted shocked me back to reality. "You must be joking! They are worth far more than that."

He shrugged. "Take it or leave it, miss." His mouth twisted in more of a smirk than a smile.

Indignantly, I scooped up the set, replaced it in the velvet bag, turned on my heel, and walked out, letting the door with its tinkly bell slam shut after me.

For about two hours I walked those grimy streets and went in at least three more such shops. Each time I had to gather my courage, swallow my pride. Each time the price offered was lower than the first had been. Finally, it was getting late, the day darkening quickly. Maybe I should have taken Mossberger's offer. Half-blinded by angry tears, I marched back down the street and into his shop.

To my sorrow, I received a harsh lesson in the ways of the world. The shrewd pawnbroker, guessing what had happened, what had brought me back, lowered the amount of his first offer.

I didn't trust myself to speak. I mumbled something about thinking it over and dashed out. I almost ran to the corner, where I hailed a passing cab. Inside I hunched in the corner, stared out at the dismal early evening. A day lost, I thought, a day closer to the danger of giving Vaughn reason to act. By the time I got back to Lady Cahill's I had a screaming headache.

Upon my return I found a bouquet of hothouse roses had been delivered from Nicholas. In it was a note saying he was sorry to have missed me. He was on his way down to the country. There he would stay with Lady Bethune while meeting with the architect who was overseeing the renovation and remodeling at Briarwood Manor. One wing was being built into a private apartment for us after we were married. Nicholas had spent a great deal of time in the country, busy with all the details of the construction.

I placed the beautiful roses in a vase and set it on my dressing table. Nicholas had been so generous to us all, so kind, so thoughtful. Bitter tears sprang into my eyes. I did not deserve Nicholas's trust and love.

I was to go home to Briarwood that weekend. I'd been gone two weeks and was anxious to see Ty and my aunt and uncle. Nicholas would still be at Elmhurst. I was both longing and dreading to see him. Nearly numb, I returned to Briarwood, uncertain about Vaughn and what he would do, but most uncertain about my future.

Auntie thought I looked tired, and she was right. "You probably overdid in London," she chided gently. "Do try to get proper rest. You don't want to be a pale bride on your wedding day."

My wedding day! Would that ever be?

Nicholas would be riding over from Elmhurst that evening, so I had to bathe and change. As I sat at my dressing table, brushing my hair, I became more and more nervous. The thought of what I was withholding from him made me so weak and dizzy I had to put my head down on my knees to keep from fainting. When I raised it, I saw myself in the mirror. My eyes looked shadowed. Nicholas had always complimented me on my clear, candid eyes. They were no longer so. "Liar!" I accused my reflection.

Later, when I went downstairs, I looked into the drawing room. Nicholas had arrived and was sitting on the floor with Ty, helping him build an enormous edifice of some kind with the marvelous set of blocks he had given him. Suddenly, a similar scene flashed into my mind—Ty playing with the old wooden Noah's ark Francis had found for him at that dark little cottage in the woods. The memory was so vivid, I swayed slightly and reached for the door frame to steady myself.

At that moment, Nicholas looked up and saw me. His smile was quickly replaced by a frown. "Lyssa, darling, what's the matter? You look as if you've seen a ghost." His tone was teasing, but he looked concerned.

For a moment, I could neither move nor speak.

Nicholas's frown deepened. "What's wrong?"

Auntie, too, glanced at me from where she sat working on her needlepoint. "What is it, dear?"

Quickly, I gathered myself together, forced a smile, and brushed aside their questions. "No, no. I'm fine. What a splendid building you two are constructing," I said, turning everyone's attention to Ty's project.

"Indeed," Nicholas agreed, laughingly. "In a few years I predict your brother may become another Christopher Wren."

Later that evening, when Auntie had taken Ty up to bed, Nicholas said seriously, "I think I'll encourage Ty to choose architecture for a career. He has the talent, an innate sense of proportion. He's such a—"

Nicholas stopped, looked at me quizzically. "You're not

160

listening, are you? There *is* something wrong. What is it, darling? You've seemed distracted all evening."

"Have I? I'm sorry. I guess there's so much to do right now, so much to plan . . ."

"I don't want you worrying and overdoing. I never wanted all this fuss of a big wedding. It was both our aunts' idea mostly, and I assumed, like most young ladies, that *you* had dreamed of one. I assure you, I'd be every bit as happy to have a small, private ceremony, just call everything off."

His words, meant to comfort me, chilled me. *Call everything off.* Maybe that's what we should do. Maybe, that's what *would* happen. Unless Vaughn was paid. Unless . . .

"Oh, of course not, Nicholas. Auntie would be terribly disappointed. She's enjoying every minute of all this. I am just tired. Shopping and so on."

He accepted my denial, but left earlier than usual, saying I should get a good night's rest.

On Monday, I went back up to London on the pretext of more fittings. In reality, I was determined to delay no longer, to swallow my pride, to pawn Mama's jewels.

The following morning I woke up in Lady Cahill's guest room to the sound of pelting rain. A sheet of gray veiled the windows, and a gusty wind bent bare-branched trees in the fenced square below. A morning to match my own depressed mood.

When I came down to breakfast dressed to go out, Lady Cahill exclaimed, "Surely you're not going out on a day like this?"

"Yes, I must," I replied, trying to get a sip of tea down my fear-constricted throat. I could not tell her that tomorrow was my new deadline to come through with the money. I couldn't put it off. I had to go to that dreadful pawnbroker, take what I could get for Mama's jewels, meet Vaughn at his pub, and beg his mercy for the amount I was short.

From Lady Cahill's expression, I'm sure she would have continued questioning the necessity of my going if it had not been for a minor domestic crisis in the kitchen with her new cook. After a whispered conference with the butler, she hurried out to settle it, leaving me free to leave without further explanation.

I knew Lady Cahill would offer me her carriage, but I couldn't allow that, knowing my destination. Outside I put up my umbrella and hurried to the end of the street. Passing all the impressive houses, I thought how shocked their residents would be if they knew my errand. At the end of the street, on the main thoroughfare, I hoped to hail a passing cab.

There were no cabs in sight. The drivers were probably busier than normal, due to the weather. With my umbrella tugged by the brisk wind, my skirts dampened by the driving rain, I walked several blocks in the shivering cold. I finally sighted a hansom and waved for it to stop. I gave the driver the address of Mossberger's pawnshop and settled back, feeling miserable and sick. I tried to convince myself I would not have to leave Mama's jewels in the keeping of that shifty-eyed pawnbroker for too long.

Somehow I would find the means to redeem them before they were resold. Maybe I should take Auntie into my confidence. Perhaps among all the valuables at Briarwood Manor there would be something of less sentimental value we could sell to buy back the sapphire and diamond set.

If only I'd had the courage to tell Nicholas the whole story.

As we bounced along the rain-slick cobblestone streets, another thought struck me. Maybe I should meet with Vaughn before taking the last step of pawning the jewels. If I met him face-to-face, reminded him of our friendship, the desperate situation I was in, and how much harm his threat promised to do to me, to Ty as well, maybe I could convince him to relent. It was worth trying, wasn't it?

Impulsively, I knocked on the ceiling of the cab. When the driver opened his little box and poked his head through, I raised my voice above the drumming of the rain and told him I'd changed my mind. I gave him the name of the tavern Vaughn frequented. Surely there was an enclosed side for ladies. There I could wait until Vaughn showed up.

"That's down on the waterfront, miss. You *shure* that's where ya wants to go?" The cabbie's voice was doubtful.

"Yes. Dauntless Dan's," I repeated, willing my voice not to shake.

"If you say so, miss." The cabbie still sounded uncertain, but he closed the box and we went on. I peered out the rain-spattered window. The streets we were now passing were meaner, more squalid. Dim figures huddled in doorways, shabby women, ragged children with old faces, drunks. I shrank back, frightened. I'd never been in this part of London nor seen such poverty, such degradation. No wonder the cabbie had seemed uncertain.

Then with a sudden jolt, the cab stopped. The driver opened the ceiling flap again. "This is the closest I can get, miss. There's sumpin a going on up front. A right crowd there is. You *shure* this is where you wanted to go?"

I sat forward. "What do you suppose is the trouble?"

"Can't say, miss. People runnin', jamming the way. Don't rightly know. There's always sumpin goin' on down in this part of town. I don't want to get messed up wi' it, I can tell you that. I'm goin' turn around, miss. You goin' get out or not?"

I pushed open the window, leaned my head out to see for myself. Clusters of people moved in groups, spilling out from the sidewalks onto the street directly ahead of us, ignoring the shouts of wagon and cab drivers. I caught sight of a helmeted policeman trying to stem the flow of the crowd.

Whatever was going on, I still had to meet Vaughn. I couldn't wait. "Will you wait for me?" I called up to the driver. "I've promised to meet someone. If he isn't there, if I can't find him, I'll come back."

The driver began shaking his head, but I rushed on. "It won't take long to just check. I'll pay extra. Please wait."

I got out, gingerly holding my skirt high. The street and

sidewalks were filthy. Above the huddled backs in the crowd, I saw the weathered sign of Dauntless Dan's swinging in the wind-driven rain. I moved cautiously forward. The stench was terrible—unwashed bodies, rotting garbage from over-flowing trash cans, the rank smell from the river just beyond. As I inched toward the tavern, I heard comments from the people crowded around the entrance, their thick cockney accents almost unintelligible to me. I strained to hear what was happening, what excitement had created this crowd. What I heard shocked me.

"Poor sod."

"'Ad it comin' to 'im, I'd sy."

"Reglar braggart him."

"Alus talkin' big. Jest t'other night he was buying drinks for the house, tellin' everone within earshot 'e'd come into some big money. Reglar windfall, 'e called it."

A murmur of anticipation and excited whispers rippled through the crowd. Someone close to me said, "They're bringin' the body up from the river now."

The crowd surged forward, creating a passage for me to slip through. It closed behind me almost immediately, and I was wedged tightly at the very edge of the pushing crowd.

"What's happened?" I asked breathlessly.

A shawled woman next to me shoved her wrinkled face right into mine. I could smell whiskey and onions. Opening a toothless mouth, she said, "They found some poor bloke a bobbin' in the water and dragged 'im out. Seems his throat's been cut."

I gasped, instinctively drawing back in horror, but I found I couldn't move. People were crowding ever closer, hoping to catch a glimpse of the action. There was nothing I could do but stand there horrified as a stretcher, carried by two hefty men, passed not two feet away from me.

A gray canvas sheet had been thrown over the body, but one arm had slipped off and dangled stiffly off the side clos-est to me. My eyes locked on that hand. Nausea overcame me. I clenched my teeth, trying to control it. With all my strength, I twisted around, elbowed and pushed my way through the thick wall of people until I managed to emerge on the other side, gasping hungrily for air.

I stumbled forward just as the strident clanging of a bell shrieked through the foggy air. A police ambulance clattered down the street. I looked around frantically for my cab, praying the driver hadn't left. Spotting him among other stalled vehicles at the next corner, I picked up my skirt and ran.

I was shaking violently as I yanked open the door, pulled myself inside, and closed the door shut behind me. Panting, I fell back against the shabby leather seat.

The driver looked down at me through his box. "Nasty bit, that wuz, eh? Now where to, miss?"

For a minute I was too shaken to reply. Where to, indeed. What now? I leaned my head back and closed my eyes. Weakly, I gave the driver Lady Cahill's address, and we started again. It was all such a nightmare. I hadn't seen Vaughn, nor had I taken the jewels to be pawned. Nothing had been accomplished. Another day had passed, bringing threatened disaster nearer.

20

I don't remember much about that long ride from the waterfront, with its grim streets and grinding poverty, to the elegant, treed, fenced square with stately Georgian houses. I felt drained of all feeling, except horror.

Lady Cahill was standing in the front hall, speaking with her maid, when I came in the front door. Her expression underwent a quick change when she saw me.

"My dear child! Whatever has happened? You look ghastly. Are you faint?" She came toward me, her taffeta train rustling behind her. Her hand on my head felt refreshingly cool. I closed my eyes, wishing I could erase the scene I'd just witnessed.

"Dora, take Miss Winthrop up to her room immediately. Help her out of these wet clothes. I'm afraid you're coming down with a chill," she said to me. "I told you you shouldn't go out in this frightful weather. I'll send up some hot water at once."

Within minutes I was upstairs, Lady Cahill fussing over me. I was wrapped in warm blankets, my feet soaked in steaming water, my damp hair dried. I was tucked into bed with a flannel-wrapped heated brick at my feet, quilts piled on top of me.

"Now, there you'll stay, young lady. Nicholas would be very cross with us if you came down with something so close to the wedding. I'll send up a hot toddy to take away the chill."

If only it were that easy to take away the deep chill within me. I shuddered. Nothing could reach that.

The hot toddy made me drowsy, and I slept fitfully off and on that afternoon. Later, waking from dreams haunted by the scene at the waterfront, the unresolved threat still hovered. I had to find a way to contact Vaughn, to keep him from going to Nicholas. But making another trip down to Dauntless Dan's was too much to contemplate.

As I lay there in the darkened room, slowly the graphic picture of the murdered man on the stretcher passed through my mind's eye. As if I were standing there at the edge of the crowd again, I saw the gray, bloated hand swinging from the stretcher.

A scream caught in my throat. I sat bolt upright in bed, clutching the covers to my chin. I knew that hand! I recognized it! Many times I'd seen it holding a brush, raised in a flamboyant gesture, covered with paint. On the little finger was the onyx signet ring he wore. The man they'd dragged from the river was Francis Vaughn!

Every nerve in my body quivered and twitched as over and over I saw the image of the shrouded figure on the swaying stretcher. I huddled under the blankets, unable to stop shivering. Strangely, the realization that his death meant I was free from his threat was slow in coming. Neither did I feel immediate relief. Who could rejoice over such a savage death? Who could have murdered him? Was it premeditated, or had Francis simply been in the wrong place at the wrong time? Even mistakenly killed?

I shuddered. I knew I couldn't be mistaken. The ring I could not forget. Unless someone had stolen it from him. Unless robbery had been the motive for his murder. But

Francis, by his own admission, was without means. Why would anyone think differently? Was he the victim of a random assault?

Endless questions pounded in my mind. I had to find out. Surely a brutal murder like this would be in the newspapers. I would have to get hold of a paper, though that would take some doing. Ladies were not supposed to read newspapers. Ladies were considered too delicate to be exposed to the harsh facts of life printed in their pages. Fathers or husbands usually removed the society and household sections for them.

Just then Lady Cahill peeked in to check on me. "Feeling better, my dear? Nicholas sent word he is coming up to London tomorrow afternoon."

I assured her I would be fine by then, and she went away, leaving me to my own dark thoughts.

Nicholas! I had hardly thought of him for hours. I had been too distraught over my experience at the waterfront. Now, however, I realized that Nicholas might never have to know *anything!* The threat was gone. Yet, something lurked in my heart and peace eluded me.

The next morning, when Dora brought up a breakfast tray, I risked asking her if she would fetch me the morning paper, if Lord Cahill had left his.

She gave me a surprised look, then said in a low voice, "Oh, miss, there's been the most horrible murder! I seen the headlines when I placed the paper on his lordship's desk. It's enuf to give you the creeps, miss."

Dora didn't seem to think it odd I wanted to read the account. She soon returned with the paper tucked under her apron and produced it with a conspiratorial flourish.

I didn't have to search for the article. It was right there on the front page.

POLICE FIND BODY OF MURDER VICTIM
A body found floating in the river near the waterfront early yesterday, and first thought to be that of a drowning victim,

was in fact that of a murder victim. Examination revealed death was caused by a knife wound to the throat. Police assume the victim was then thrown into the water. Although there was no identification found on the body, persons at the scene identified the man as a regular patron of Dauntless Dan's, a local tavern. Witnesses testified the victim had been drinking heavily the night before, buying drinks for other customers, and flashing a large sum of money. Further questioning of these same witnesses indicated the man was a sign painter who called himself an artist. He was known to have taken jobs in exchange for meals and drinks. It was discovered he rented a flat, which he used as a studio, under the name Francis Vaughn. Police are asking for information as to next of kin or any other help in locating persons who may know the victim or any motive for his killing.

It *was* Francis Vaughn. But how could I go to the police? I had no information other than the ring I recognized. I had no idea where Francis came from, who his family might be, or even if he had any relatives.

For the rest of the morning, I fluctuated between elation and despair. To be free of the shadow of scandal that had hung so heavily over me the last week was wonderful. But at what cost? A man's murder? There was still the question of the painting. What had Vaughn done with it? Where was it? Had the police found it among his belongings when they went to his flat? Had he already altered it? Was it possible the painting would surface at some later date?

As I changed and dressed for Nicholas's visit, I debated whether I should tell him everything. I had been through so much since I last saw him. I had held our future precariously at the brink of a disaster that could have destroyed everything for us, including his reputation, our families' honor, my brother's welfare. Miraculously, it had not happened.

Although I had not been forced to lie to Nicholas, I'd withheld the truth. Could I go into a marriage with someone I loved and respected carrying the weight of such a dark secret?

The thing I was most ashamed of was how far I had been willing to go to keep him from knowing the truth about me, willing even to give in to Vaughn's evil plan.

Deep down I knew I had to tell Nicholas everything. There was no use trying to justify doing anything else. I had to lay it all before him. Whether he could forgive me, I didn't know.

When Dora came to tell me Nicholas had arrived and was downstairs waiting for me, I had a moment of weakness. Did I really have to risk it all? Risk losing the man I loved? I knew that's what was at stake. How could he love me if he knew my shameful secret?

As I reached the landing of the stairs, I felt faint. I reached out one hand, grasped the newel post to steady myself, and whispered a prayer for the strength to be courageous enough to be truthful.

I might have been Marie Antoinette going to the guillotine as I went down the remaining stairs to Lady Cahill's drawing room. Each step I took led me closer and closer to the inevitable. I imagined Nicholas's anger, his bitterness at my deceit. When I came to the last step, I could see him through the open door to the parlor. He was standing at the fireplace, his back to the hall, looking into the cheerful blaze. He must have sensed my coming or heard my footsteps, for he looked up into the gold-framed mirror above the mantel, and seeing me, his whole face lit up. Smiling, he turned around.

With a few quick strides he crossed the carpet, hands extended to me. "Lyssa, darling."

At his loving tone, I felt my heart clutch painfully. I longed to rush into his embrace, yet I dared not. I tried to speak normally, but my voice sounded tight as I forced it over the hard lump rising in my throat. "Good afternoon, Nicholas."

"Why so formal?" he teased. "We're betrothed, remember? I could at least have a kiss, couldn't I?"

I passed him instead, stepped around the marble-topped table in the center of the room and went to stand behind the curved rosewood sofa.

Nicholas looked puzzled. "What is it, darling?"

He started toward me, but stopped when I held up my hand.

"Nicholas, I have something—something very important—I must discuss with you."

He regarded me with tender amusement. "Of course, darling, but does it have to be discussed at such a great distance? Why don't we sit down together where we can be comfortable?"

From his lighthearted manner, I knew he thought the something important was something trivial, such as some difficulty with the caterers for our reception. Could they provide fresh salmon sandwiches or should the icing on the petit fours be pale green or pink? I wished with all my heart it *was* something so insignificant.

"No, I'd rather not." I shook my head. "Please just listen and don't interrupt." I spoke more rapidly than usual, and I saw both concern and curiosity in Nicholas's eyes.

I slipped off the beautiful lily engagement ring and held it enclosed in my palm. I recalled the symbolism of its design, the pristine pearl, the sparkling diamonds, representing purity and truth, the virtues Nicholas believed I possessed. I didn't deserve to wear it. I would give it back to him before he asked to be released from our engagement. I was convinced that once he knew the truth about me, he would not want me.

But I wanted to hold on to it a little longer, to give me the courage and strength I needed. It represented the pledge of our love and mutual respect, the promise of fidelity. It was a symbol of our belief that from the beginning we were meant for each other and would belong to each other for the rest of our lives.

I gripped the ring as, haltingly, I began my story.

Nicholas listened gravely to all I had to say. I could not tell from his expression what he was thinking or feeling as I stumblingly told him all I'd left out before. How I'd met Vaughn in the Brindles' taproom, agreeing to pose for him in my desperation, of my escape after discovering the stolen goods, the jolt of receiving Vaughn's threatening letter, how I'd planned to pawn my mother's jewels and pay Vaughn the blackmail.

When I came to the part of standing in the crowd watching the stretcher with its tragic burden pass in front of me, seeing the ring, I nearly broke down. But I struggled on to the end. It was the most difficult thing I had ever done.

I could not bear to look at Nicholas to see his reaction. I put my head down, held out the hand with the engagement ring, and opened my palm.

The silence that stretched between us in the room seemed endless. Then I felt Nicholas's hand on mine, felt him pick up the ring from my palm, turn my hand over, and place the ring back on my finger.

I opened my eyes, and slowly he drew me by my hand around from the back of the sofa and into his arms. He smoothed back my hair, and with a sigh that was a half sob, I leaned against him and felt his arms around me. I clung to him, tears running down my cheeks. His lips touched my temples, moved slowly down my cheeks, kissing my tears. I heard such caressing words as "dearest one," "my love." Then his mouth covered mine in a long, tender kiss.

I leaned my head back and looked up at him through tear-blurred eyes. "Oh, Nicholas, you're not disgusted with me or angry? You don't despise me after all I've told you?"

"Challys, my darling, don't you know that nothing you could tell me would change my love for you? I have promised you my heart, my love, my protection—forever. I would never take that back."

Speechless, I gazed at him. "But, Nicholas, how can you accept me after—"

"I love the bravest, loveliest, most truthful person in the

world. I am proud and honored not only to know you but to have you as my wife." He kissed me again.

"The only thing that troubles me," he said then, "is that you have suffered so needlessly. If you'd come to me in the first place, I would have settled it at once without you having to go through all this anguish."

He pulled me again gently into his arms, and a sweet, comforting warmth spread through me.

"Now, listen, my darling, and I hope we never have to discuss this again. It seems Vaughn had a penchant for writing threatening letters, not only to you, but to me and to others as well. A man with that sort of a mind would not bank on simply frightening an innocent young lady.

"He anticipated you might have trouble securing enough money to pay him off. He wrote to me, assuming I would fear a scandal and give in to his demands. He didn't foresee that I would not play his dirty game, that I would take his letter directly to the police, providing them with evidence of his criminal act.

"He also wrote to the Brindles. The information you had given him about the stolen property was a weapon he thought he could use there. He hadn't the sense to know that the Brindles, who were not too bright themselves, were hooked into some clever, experienced thieves and smugglers who would stop at nothing to insure their own safety. I have no doubt they were the ones who did the fellow in.

"The police informed my bank of the blackmail threat. They gave me marked bills to use that could be traced. I then sent the money by messenger to Vaughn at the tavern he frequented, along with the message that I would meet him at his flat to pick up the painting. He never came. In the meantime, he had foolishly flashed his ill-gotten gains in public view, so there were plenty of witnesses who saw he had come into some unexpected cash. The thieves working with the Brindles, already alerted to Vaughn's talkativeness, proba-

173

bly took matters into their own hands and silenced him before the police could catch up with him."

I looked at Nicholas aghast. "Then, you knew all this!"

"Except that he had threatened you, darling. I had hoped to keep all this unpleasantness from you."

New tears rushed into my eyes. "Oh, Nicholas, let us promise never to have any more secrets between us."

"I agree. If we've learned anything from this experience, it is that trying to keep the truth from someone can hurt rather than help. If we had both told each other the truth from the beginning, we could have prevented the agony caused by Vaughn's threats. The truth would not have endangered our love. Nothing could do that." He pulled me close, so close I could feel his heart pounding against mine. "No more secrets."

After a few seconds in which I enjoyed the lovely security of Nicholas's embrace, I drew back and asked, "But what about the painting?"

Nicholas made a grimace. "Dreadful, my dear! As the newspaper article about him stated, Francis Vaughn was a *sign painter* not an artist, although the poor fellow had grand illusions, or perhaps I should say delusions, about his talent. No wonder his mentor turned the painting down flat. Refused to pay for it. Certainly no one would have recognized *you* as the subject."

"But how do you know? Did you see it?"

"I was notified by the police when his body was recovered. They had found my address in his flat. I went with them to the place." Nicholas shook his head as if to rid himself of the memory.

I recalled Vaughn's secretiveness. "He would never let me see it while he was working on it. What about the Brindles?"

"It seems they and that whole operation had been under surveillance for some time. When I went there myself, shortly after the stagecoach accident in which you and Aunt Isabel were victims, I had my doubts as to whether the Brindle woman was telling the truth. There had been reports of other such mishaps, and it's suspected that some were not accidents at all but were deviously planned. Fallen trees *placed* in the road, perhaps. They'll serve long terms in prison."

Nicholas's arms tightened around me. "To think, my poor darling, you were caught up in that web. From now on, as long as I have anything to do with it, nothing will ever harm you, frighten you, or threaten you again."

My favorite stories as a child had been fairy tales with happy endings, though often over the past years I had doubted such things existed outside of books. Now every wish I had ever dreamed was coming true.

Also in fairy tales, the "dragon" always comes to a deserved end. When Nanny Grace accepted our invitation to come to the wedding and live with us afterward at Briarwood Manor, she came with the news of Muir's demise. Riding home one cold, snowy night from an evening of imbibing at the village pub, his horse slipped on a slick bridge, throwing the inebriated Muir into the rushing stream below. His half-frozen body was found the following morning.

Few could mourn the death of such a cruel rogue. For my brother and me it was the lifting of the shadow that had hovered over us since running away from Crossfields. Gone forever was the possibility that Ty might be taken back by his father. He was safe and happy now, the center of the lives of our elderly relatives, and he was looking forward to the protection and love of Nicholas, once we were wed.

I was never so aware of God's gracious mercy as I was during those happy days prior to my wedding. He had protected me through everything leading up to this moment in my life, through the dangerous valleys and dark places, to bring me safely to the desires of my heart.

Nicholas and I were married in Meadowmead's centuries-old, gray stone church on a December morning newly blanketed with snow. My gown was white satin, trimmed at the rounded neck and wrists with narrow bands of ermine. I wore a veil of antique lace that Lady Bethune had worn as a bride. Mama's sapphire and diamond jewelry caught the light from the flames of the six ivory tapers on the altar as I reached the end of the aisle on Uncle George's arm.

When Nicholas and I said our vows, we exchanged matching rings of twisted gold on which two clasped hands were carved.

Our honeymoon was the reverse of most newly wed couples. Nicholas and I spent ours at Briarwood Manor in the recently renovated, newly furnished wing. Instead of going on a wedding trip ourselves, Nicholas had arranged for Aunt Evelyn and Uncle George to spend the rest of the winter in the warm, sunny climate of Italy, and Ty was to stay at Lady Bethune's for a fortnight. Nicholas's aunt had taken quite a fancy to my little brother, saying he reminded her of Nicholas, her favorite nephew, when he was the same age.

My heart was full of thanksgiving for all my unexpected blessings following the time of trouble and trial.

The early winter dusk cast purple shadows across the snow as Nicholas and I entered our home together. As I turned to look at my new husband, I saw in his eyes the love I had always longed to know.

A Perilous Bargain

Jane Peart is a prolific author of romantic fiction who lives in Fortuna, California. She is the author of the Orphan Train West series and the International Romance series.

A Perilous Bargain

Jane Peart

Fleming H. Revell
A Division of Baker Book House Co
Grand Rapids, Michigan 49516

1

The Ocean Liner Mesalina, en route
from New York to England

March 1895

O riel had been standing alone at the ship's rail, deep in her own troubling thoughts, when through gauzy shreds of fog, the tall figure of a man emerged.

As he took a place beside her, the man nodded. "Looks like we might be in for a rough crossing. Temperamental, the Atlantic, this time of year."

His comment needed no response. The ocean, smooth as glass upon leaving New York harbor three days before, now churned in choppy waves. Strong wind rocked the large ship as if it were a small fishing boat, sending most of the passengers below to seek refuge in one of the many lounges or to huddle miserably in their stateroom bunks.

"We seem to be the only ones braving the storm."

Oriel glanced over her shoulder to confirm he was speaking to her. Indeed, they were the only two on deck.

"Perhaps I should introduce myself. I'm Morgan Drummond."

The introduction was unnecessary. Oriel had recognized him at once. He was the grandson of Brendan Drummond, millionaire industrialist and well-known philanthropist. Morgan Drummond had been the subject of shipboard gossip from the first day out, the target of romantic speculation among many hopeful women on board—that is, until they learned he was engaged to an English debutante, Edwina Parker.

Oriel took a discreet glance at the man standing beside her. He *was* impressively handsome—over six feet tall, wearing a tweed Norfolk jacket. His profile, outlined against the fog, was classically sculptured with a high-bridged nose and a strong chin.

"And you are . . . ?" he asked.

"Oriel Banning." She gave her name reluctantly.

"Not many of our fellow passengers seem to have sea legs. You must be a good sailor."

"I'm fortunate to come from a long line of New England seafarers." At once she regretted her reply. It seemed to invite further comment. She did not want to enter into an idle conversation with a stranger. She had too much on her mind. She moved slightly down the rail, distancing herself from him. Besides, what could they possibly have in common? Their paths would never have crossed if she had not been traveling with her wealthy employers. She would not have been among his affluent fellow passengers in the first-class section of this luxury liner.

Although her passport listed her occupation as social secretary and companion, it would be easy for Morgan Drummond to assume Oriel belonged on the A deck. Her appearance warranted that. But appearances can be deceiving. She had often been told she resembled the popular British royal, Princess Alexandra of Denmark, whose hairstyle and dress were widely copied in both Britain and the States. Tall, slender, with a graceful carriage and confident manner, Oriel had an understated elegance that seemed aristocratic. However, her situation and that of the princess could not have been more different. While the popular princess, married to Edward, Prince of Wales, heir to the British throne, lived a luxurious life, Oriel's had been a precarious existence.

Oriel gazed down into the pewter-colored sea, picking up the thread of her thoughts. Being hired by the McPhails was one of the many strange coincidences that had marked her life. After her father's financial ruin and death, Oriel had obtained a position at the fashionable boarding school she had once attended. When Berenice McPhail enrolled, Oriel had been assigned the thankless task of tutoring her to bring up her grades to passing. Neecy was an indolent student at best. Her mother, Mrs. Clarence McPhail, widow of a manufacturing tycoon, approached Oriel to take on an unusual job—to groom Berenice for her debut into society. The salary Mrs. McPhail offered far exceeded Oriel's pay as a teacher, so she had accepted.

Oriel felt she had earned every cent of the salary that had at first seemed so generous—was *still* earning it. The flighty, pampered girl was a handful. Looking after her had proved a round-the-clock chore.

Now, two years later, they were on their way to England, where Berenice was to be married to an English aristocrat, Valmont Thorndyke. Berenice was what the yellow journals of the day vulgarly called a "dollar princess," meaning an American girl from a rich family who made a mutually beneficial European marriage. The Americans gained titles, the British, fortunes to save ancestral estates.

The relief Oriel might have felt once the wedding took place was overshadowed by a problem—Oriel's job would be finished. What next? That need had prompted her to escape from the confines of her adjoining cabin to Neecy's. After a late night, her charge had chosen to spend the day in bed, eating chocolates and reading a romantic novel. Mrs. McPhail, feeling unwell, was also closeted in her stateroom. Oriel had jumped at the rare opportunity of being by herself.

It wasn't the first time Oriel had faced an unknown future. After her mother's death, when Oriel was only a child of eleven, she had become her indulgent father's companion. They had traveled the world, stayed in the finest hotels, visited the best European resorts. Then, when she was seventeen, a series of bad investments coupled with a national financial panic had swept away her father's fortune. Shortly afterward, her father had suffered a fatal heart attack. In a matter of weeks, Oriel's life had changed drastically. She had faced the unexpected challenge of making her own living with only her courage, energy, and intelligence to help her make her way in the world.

Her privileged background had been her only asset, and she used it. Thanks to her father, she had received an excellent education, a cultured background. These qualifications served her well but did not pay adequately. Penny-pinching had become a way of life.

The hardships Oriel had endured, however, had developed qualities she had not dreamed she would ever need. She had tasted poverty and it was bitter. The job with the McPhails had shown her the kind of life she herself might have enjoyed if things had been different.

She had made her own living for the last six years, and she would continue to do so. She needed to think, to plan. When they returned to the States, should she apply again at Miss Porter's Academy or seek some other kind of employment? At the moment, her future seemed as dense as the fog that surrounded the ship.

The muffled blast of the foghorn cut through the damp, clinging air, jolting her. There was an eerie loneliness in the sound. Darting a quick look around, she saw that the man who had stood beside her was gone—gone just as he had come, in a drift of fog.

Contrary to Oriel's assumption that meeting Morgan Drummond had been a single, random encounter, she had several other such chance meetings as their ship moved toward England. The weather continued to be bad. Oriel soon discovered that Morgan Drummond was among the few hardy passengers like herself who took an early morning stroll on the deck regardless of the weather. Neecy and Mrs. McPhail preferred to stay snug in their cabins and have their breakfast brought in by the stewards. A brisk walk in the misty morning air eased Oriel's anxiety and enabled her to better face the day. Whenever they passed each other, Mr. Drummond always nodded, saying, "Good morning, Miss Banning." Sometimes he even slowed his long stride to murmur some remark on the weather or make a casual comment.

One evening at the dinner table, Mrs. McPhail complained of an annoying draft on her shoulders and sent Oriel back to her stateroom to fetch her shawl. In the passageway, Oriel ran straight into Morgan Drummond, looking splendid in his evening clothes, on his way to a predinner party in the captain's quarters.

Oriel was wearing one of Neecy's castoffs that she had altered and remodeled, a claret-colored taffeta, more becoming to her olive complexion and mahogany brown hair than it had been to Neecy's bland coloring.

"How charming you look this evening, Miss Banning." Morgan bowed, adding with an amused smile, "I don't believe I've ever seen you except wrapped in scarves or muffled in a mackintosh."

Oriel felt foolishly pleased by his compliment. She had followed in Neecy's social shadow so long she realized she wasn't used to attention, especially from an attractive man.

The next time Oriel encountered Morgan it was an excruciatingly embarrassing moment. Constant friction existed between Mrs. McPhail and her daughter, with frequent eruptions over Neecy's behavior. Even though engaged, Berenice flirted openly with every male on board. Oriel often found herself acting as a buffer or, more often, as a silent bystander during fierce arguments. This particular one took place one evening at the entrance to the dining room. Forgetful that other passengers were within hearing, both voices were raised. Oriel was trying to think of some tactful way to intervene without infuriating the combatants further, when Morgan Drummond suddenly appeared. Oblivious of being observed, the McPhails continued their dispute. For a single second, Morgan's gaze met Oriel's. In that look was shared mutual disgust.

Realizing that her own thoughts were being read, Oriel lowered her eyes. It would never do to show, even by so much as a flicker of an eyelash, the contempt she felt for her employers' display of bad manners. Without a word, Morgan passed by, pretending not to have seen or heard anything.

Five days later, docking in Southampton, Oriel was sent up on deck to stand guard over the McPhails' mountains of luggage while they bid leisurely good-byes to shipboard acquaintances.

Oriel was glad to see the ocean voyage over. It had been, as Morgan Drummond predicted, a rough passage, but it was not just the stormy weather that had made the journey unpleasant. The relative confinement of the accommodations had subjected Oriel to the peevish demands of the mother and the irresponsible selfishness of the daughter. Her relief at the journey's end was short-lived, however, since there was still the wedding to get through. She would be expected to deal with its myriad details.

Trying to distract herself, Oriel glanced around at her fellow passengers. Eager now to start their travels on foreign soil, they crowded to the rails to wave at their welcomers. She saw Morgan Drummond come up on deck.

He nodded and walked over to her. "Good morning, Miss Banning. Ready to put your feet on solid ground?"

"Yes, it will be a nice change, although I've not minded the weather all that much."

"So you said. From a long line of seafarers, right?" He smiled. "Well, I wish you a pleasant stay in England." Then, as an apparent afterthought, he asked, "Where are you staying?"

"We have reservations at the Claridge Hotel."

"So do I. Perhaps our paths will cross again." With that, he tipped his hat and moved away to join others at the ship's rail.

Oriel watched him lean forward over the rail, as though searching into the sea of people waiting to meet passengers. Then she saw him wave.

At last, the giant ship was docked and the gangplank let down. Passengers began to throng ashore. Curious to see who Morgan Drummond had been so eager to find, Oriel moved over to the rail and followed his tall figure until she saw him greeted by an exquisite blonde. Her royal blue cape, lavishly furred in silver fox, flowed out behind her as she embraced him. She must be his fiancée, Edwina Parker.

Next Morgan turned to greet a well-dressed couple, who evidently had accompanied her. The older woman, a stout fading blonde, might be a forecast of Edwina twenty years hence. Did men notice such things? Oriel wondered ruefully.

The McPhails arrived just then, flurried and fussing. Oriel was caught up in the ensuing confusion of getting a porter to trundle their baggage down the gangplank and securing a coach to take them to the train station for their trip to London. By then, Morgan Drummond and his party had long since departed.

2

London, England

Two Weeks Later

The newlyweds had hardly left for their honeymoon when the mother of the bride disappeared into her hotel room. Oriel was left to settle all the bills, to pay the caterers, wine merchants, musicians, and others who had provided their services for the reception. It was her task to tie up all the loose ends after Neecy's windswept departure.

Soon after this was accomplished, Oriel was summoned to Mrs. McPhail's suite. Eunice McPhail, in a peach satin jacket, was still in bed, propped up on pillows, her breakfast tray on her lap. The morning papers were scattered over the quilted coverlet.

She listened with pursed lips and narrowed eyes to Oriel's accounting of the financial responsibilities she had completed. Then, flourishing one diamond-ringed hand, she said, "Well, that's the end of your duties, Miss Banning. Now that Neecy's settled, we will, of course, no longer need your services. You will need to find other lodgings."

At first, Oriel wasn't sure she'd heard correctly. Puzzled, she asked, "You mean until we return to the States?"

Mrs. McPhail's eyebrows arched, as if she was astonished at the question. "*We?* I thought you understood. I am not going back home right away—not until Neecy returns from her honeymoon. Naturally *you* are free to make any arrangements you choose."

For a moment Oriel was speechless. Slowly, the meaning of Mrs. McPhail's announcement began to sink in. Still she needed to clarify the statement. "Then my passage back to the States will not be paid?"

Mrs. McPhail looked outraged at such a suggestion. "Certainly not! We made no such guarantee. With Neecy's marriage, your employment ended."

Stunned, but too proud to plead or protest, Oriel managed to say, "I will need a letter of reference, Mrs. McPhail."

Mrs. McPhail seemed startled, maybe at the calm way Oriel seemed to be taking her announcement. Perhaps she had expected some kind of outburst. Shrugging her plump shoulders, Mrs. McPhail said impatiently, "Yes, of course. I'll leave it with your check for this month's wages. You can pick them up at the desk."

Not trusting herself to say more, Oriel turned to leave.

Mrs. McPhail's shrill voice followed. "It's not that you were unsatisfactory, Miss Banning. I'm sure Neecy benefited a great deal from her association with you. You're a clever girl—I'm sure you'll have no problem finding a new position."

Oriel felt her face flush. Her hand already on the doorknob, she did not turn around. Quick, hot anger rushed through her, but she refused to give Mrs. McPhail's throwaway compliment the dignity of a reply. She stepped into the hallway and closed the door behind her.

Mrs. McPhail's lame comment rang in her ears. Oriel recalled having to drum even the simplest formalities into Neecy's empty head. What she *could* have retorted to Mrs.

McPhail was, "Indeed your daughter *did* benefit from my training. I taught her how to conduct herself in society. Until I'd coached her, she didn't even know how to enter a room properly or which spoon or fork to use at a formal dinner! If it weren't for *me*, your daughter would not at this moment be honeymooning on the Riviera with the son of one of England's most prominent families!"

There was plenty Oriel could have said, but she knew it would have been useless. Mrs. McPhail was worse than her daughter, unaware of her shortcomings. She blundered her way with only her money making her acceptable. Any rational self-justification would have only been self-defeating. It would have fallen on deaf ears; more likely, it would have brought down Mrs. McPhail's wrath, possibly even vindictive retribution. Oriel needed her reference letter if she was to explain the two years spent with the McPhails to any prospective employer.

Outside Mrs. McPhail's hotel room, Oriel's knees nearly buckled. She steadied herself against the door frame. A waiter wheeling a cart rattling with a load of dishes gave her a curious glance as he went past. Oriel drew a long shaky breath, straightened her shoulders, and walked stiffly down the corridor to her own room.

Once there, she closed the door behind her. Feeling weak and dizzy, she sat down on the edge of the bed. She had, of course, expected it—but not this soon. Not like this.

I should have known better, she thought, *should have found out about my return ticket before leaving New York.* It had simply not occurred to her that she would receive such shabby treatment. *Dismissed!* She'd had no notice, and worse, no severance pay.

Gradually Oriel's righteous indignation subsided and her practical nature emerged. She had not been on her own since she was seventeen for nothing. It was useless to expect anything from Mrs. McPhail. The woman was not only without conscience but without gentility. Oriel should not have been surprised at her shoddy behavior.

Oriel's first thought was What shall I do? The second one came as naturally as breathing. Pray. At an early age, she had been taught to seek God's help in an emergency. This situation certainly qualified as that.

Next she drew a long breath. She knew she needed to take one thing at a time. Obviously she could no longer stay in this luxury hotel, where the daily rate would probably pay for a week's rent in more modest accommodations. How was she to go about finding one? She did not know London. Her time, so far, had been limited to the details of Neecy's wedding, dealing with tradesmen, shopkeepers, and the hotel staff.

She would not panic. She would be sensible, practical, use her brains. Her gaze fell on the morning paper, which had been delivered with her breakfast tray. It was still folded. She had not had time to read it before being called into Mrs. McPhail's suite. Turning to the ad section, she checked several smaller hotels. The rates still seemed too high for the small amount of money she had. Perhaps a rooming house would be better. She would probably only need a place for a few days. As soon as she received the check for her salary, she would buy passage back to the States. She marked three ads that specified "Gentlewomen Only." After all, Oriel *was* alone in a large city where everything was unfamiliar and she knew no one. It would be wise to be careful.

Oriel quickly packed her belongings, then tucked that section of the newspaper into her handbag. At the concierge's desk she left word that she would need her luggage brought out to her cab. Then, holding her head high, she walked across the lobby to the entrance.

The doorman, looking like a gold-braided general, tipped his hat and greeted Oriel courteously as she came out onto the steps. She had arrived here with the McPhails in all their ostentatiousness. They had been given the awed respect such obvious affluence brings. Now everything had changed.

She had been ignominiously dismissed, treated like a no-body. Oriel lifted her chin defiantly. If she was to be thrown out, she was going in style. She asked the doorman to whistle for a cab for her. In a short time, one arrived and Oriel's luggage was stowed inside.

After giving the cabbie the first address she had marked, Oriel took one last look at the entrance of the elegant hotel before entering the carriage and settling back against the worn leather seat. Her stomach tightened painfully, but she refused to indulge in self-pity. This was simply another challenge to be met.

The cabbie moved the hansom out of the line of splendid carriages arriving at the hotel and into the street. Peering out the window, Oriel began to notice a gradual change in the neighborhoods through which they passed. The farther they got from the Claridge, the dingier things got. The buildings on either side were drab and soot-stained, the sidewalks more crowded, the people's clothes shabbier. Ragged little boys swept horse droppings or sold newspapers. Vendors peddled meat pies and roasted chestnuts.

The first place Oriel stopped, the room advertised had already been taken. At the second, however, she had more success. This turned out to be a tall brick house with a tiny fenced front, scrubbed doorstep, and dark green painted door. A cardboard Vacancy sign was placed in front of starched lace curtains in one of the narrow downstairs windows.

Oriel asked the cabbie to wait, although she knew it would add to his fare. A small plaque under the doorbell read, "E. M. Pettigrew." Oriel twisted the metal bell and heard it echo inside. A thin, spectacled woman with graying hair opened the door.

"Mrs. Pettigrew?"

"The same," the woman replied, folding her arms and surveying Oriel critically.

"I'd like to see the room you have for rent if it is still available," Oriel said pleasantly.

The sharp eyes moved over Oriel, not missing an inch of her simple yet stylish blue suit and feathered bonnet. Evidently Oriel passed whatever criteria the woman had because she opened the door wider and said, "It is. Come in. I'll show it to you."

Oriel followed her into a dark hallway, up a long stairway, past one landing, and up another flight of stairs. At the top of the steps, the woman opened a door. "This is it. Step inside and have a look."

The room was high-ceilinged and sparse in furnishings— a far cry from the luxurious hotel room Oriel had just left. Still, it was neat and clean. There was an iron bed, a table, one straight chair, an armchair, a wardrobe, and a small stove.

"The bathroom is down the hall, shared with other tenants. Each roomer has a scheduled day of use for hot bathwater. I require a week's rent in advance and then paid weekly for as long as you stay."

The rental price she stated seemed reasonable. "I'll take it," Oriel said. "Since the room is available, I suppose it's all right if I move in today?"

"It is, and you may," the woman said briskly.

Oriel opened her purse and counted out the money.

"Come down to my parlor and I'll give you a receipt. What's your name?"

"Oriel Banning."

As they started down the steps, Mrs. Pettigrew asked, "How long do you plan to keep the room?"

"A week, possibly two. It depends on how soon I can book passage back to the States." That was as close to the truth as Oriel could manage.

"So you *are* American." The woman paused, turning to look back at her. "I thought I recognized the accent."

"Yes." Oriel was not able to discern interest or disapproval in Mrs. Pettigrew's voice.

Their transaction was quickly done. Oriel went out to the cab, paid the driver, and tipped him for his help in bringing in her two large suitcases. He dropped them just inside the door and left. *Better get used to fending for myself again,* Oriel thought as she struggled back up the steep staircase with her bags.

Once alone in the spartan room, the enormity of her situation struck with full force. She had been reacting on a practical level, doing what needed to be done. Now the emotional impact hit. Here she was in an unfamiliar place among strangers. There was no one to whom she could turn for advice or help, no one to depend on but herself.

She must keep her wits about her and not give way to despair. First, she must decide what to do. The small amount of money she had would not last long. Perhaps the best thing to do would be to buy the cheapest passage back to the States on one of the smaller ocean liners. Mrs. McPhail had handled the arrangements for their tickets to England. Oriel had no idea what even a second-class ticket back to the United States might cost. She might not be able to afford even *that!* She certainly hoped she wouldn't have to travel steerage.

Nonsense! She was imagining all sorts of horrible possibilities when the whole thing would be settled tomorrow after she went to the Claridge and picked up her check and letter of reference. Things would fall into proper perspective. There was no use in worrying needlessly.

She had the whole day ahead of her. At last rid of both the McPhails, she could do as she pleased and go where she wanted, with no one to answer to, no one to accommodate but herself. A wonderful feeling of freedom replaced the downward spiral her spirits had been taking. She would explore London on her own, something she had been longing to do.

Putting on her jacket and hat again, Oriel set out. If she had known what the next day would bring, her step would not have been quite so jaunty nor her spirits so high.

3

Oriel awakened after a restless night. Although she had not slept all that well, she had made a decision, and having made it, felt positive. After she picked up her check from Mrs. McPhail she would go directly to a shipping office, find out how much a second-class ticket would cost, and book passage on a ship leaving for America as soon as possible. She would feel more secure once she was back in the States. She was almost certain she could get a teaching job again at Miss Porter's. If not there, some other school would take her.

Having a definite plan of action, Oriel set out for the Claridge Hotel. This time she chose a more economical mode of transportation, the horse-drawn omnibus, which carried up to sixteen passengers. Two blocks from the hotel, she got off and walked the rest of the way. Ahead of her the large structure rose majestically, overlooking the busy street. A continuous parade of shiny carriages drew up in front of the impressive entrance and discharged fashionably dressed people. Only the day before *she* had gone in and out, a part of it all. Now it seemed rather intimidating.

At the registration desk, the clerk looked at Oriel without recognition. She had spoken to him every day when she came to pick up or leave messages for Mrs. McPhail, yet he regarded her now as if he had never seen her before. His attitude lit sparks of indignation in Oriel. With elaborate politeness, she asked for her letter.

"A *letter?*" His brow wrinkled as if she had asked for a rare jewel of some sort.

"Yes, for Miss Oriel Banning. Mrs. McPhail was supposed to leave one for me." The man looked baffled, so Oriel was forced to explain. Checking her irritation, she said, "I was a guest here with the McPhail party."

"The McPhails?" His nose wrinkled slightly. Then, lifting his eyebrows, he said, "The Americans?"

"Yes, Mrs. Clarence McPhail and Miss Berenice McPhail. We had a suite." Oriel gritted her teeth, wanting to add that the suite had been one of the hotel's most expensive and lavish ones. She would not, however, give the clerk the satisfaction of seeing her lose her temper. "Will you please check? Miss Oriel Banning," she repeated evenly.

He turned, briefly surveyed the boxes on the wall behind him, then shook his head. "No, miss. There is nothing here under that name. The McPhail party checked out yesterday," he added coldly.

Startled, Oriel stared at him. "*Checked out?* But she couldn't have—I mean, Mrs. McPhail didn't say anything about leaving. Are you sure?"

Looking offended, the clerk said, "Quite sure, miss. Mrs. McPhail left to take the boat train. I assume she was going to France. Left no forwarding address."

"And *nothing* else—no letter? You're sure?"

"Nothing, miss. I'm *quite* sure." His tone was icy. "Now if you'll excuse me." He glanced past her, over her head. Oriel realized there were people standing behind her, hotel guests whom he obviously considered far more important than she.

Oriel stepped away from the counter in disbelief. Would Mrs. McPhail really have gone off without leaving her final check? And no letter of reference? Surely she couldn't have. There must be an explanation of some sort. Perhaps Mrs. McPhail intended to mail it from France. Oriel could not believe the woman would do anything so blatantly dishonest. Thoughtless, selfish, inconsiderate—Eunice McPhail was all those things, but *dishonest?*

Oriel moved a little distance from the reception desk. This was an entirely unexpected blow. No forwarding address had been left. How could she contact her former employer? What should she do now?

As she stood there trying to get hold of herself, she became aware of the activity around her. It was the luncheon hour and the lobby was full. Well-dressed men and women moved toward the dining room. All at once, Oriel's unfocused gaze picked out a familiar figure. It was Morgan Drummond, accompanied by the same exquisite creature who had met him the day the ship docked. Once again, the woman was dressed in the height of fashion. This time she wore a cinnamon velvet jacket with sable collar and cuffs. Her extravagant hat was of black velvet, lined with turquoise satin and trimmed with black ostrich tips, its curved brim framing her lovely face. That day at the docks in Southampton, she had looked excited and happy. Today she looked flushed, petulant. Morgan, too, looked upset. They hardly presented the picture of a blissful couple.

Shielded behind one of the marble pillars, Oriel was hidden from sight. However, Morgan and Edwina paused just on the other side of where she stood. Since Edwina made no effort to lower her voice, Oriel heard every word she spoke.

"I'm *not* going to change my mind, Morgan. It's out of the question. How could you possibly expect me to agree to such a thing?"

What had he asked that was so impossible? Oriel knew about the trivial concerns of people of wealth. She had heard the McPhails argue endlessly about the simplest matters. What could someone like Edwina Parker, with her beauty, her wealth, her future, have to complain about? Possibly Morgan's choice of play or musicale tickets.

Then Oriel heard Morgan's voice, edged with annoyance, say, "You're being completely unreasonable, Edwina. You haven't even seen—"

"I don't have to *see* to know I'd hate it!" she interrupted. "No, Morgan, you can't persuade me. *Never!*"

Oriel watched as they left the hotel, Edwina sweeping ahead of a grim-faced Morgan. It was a lover's quarrel, a silly tiff that would be over in a few hours. Oriel shrugged and walked back across the lobby, consumed by her own immediate problem.

Remembering her former employer's tendency to procrastinate, Oriel hoped the promised check and letter of reference would come soon—maybe even tomorrow. She would have to wait to buy her steamship ticket. She didn't want to use up her available cash should Mrs. McPhail delay sending the check.

Oriel pushed out through the front doors of the hotel just in time to see Morgan Drummond and Miss Parker get into a shiny black carriage and drive off.

It had begun to rain, and Oriel had no umbrella. Catching the doorman eyeing her suspiciously, Oriel drew on her gloves, went down the steps, and hurried to where she could catch the omnibus back to the rooming house.

As she waited under a store awning for the bus, the scene she had witnessed between Morgan Drummond and his fiancée played through her mind. How strange to see Morgan Drummond again and to overhear that snatch of argument. *So even the wealthy have problems,* she thought. Her own, however, were more urgent.

Maybe she should try to find work of some kind to supplement the wages due her. She would have to look in the employment ads in the newspaper. She hailed a paperboy and bought the evening *Times*. The omnibus appeared and she boarded, seated herself, and opened the paper to the employment columns. As her eyes tracked her finger down the list of available positions, her heart began to sink. Governess, companion, lady clerk, milliner's assistant—why would anyone hire an American for these positions when there were probably many qualified English ladies ready to fill them?

She stopped reading the list when she realized that the bus was nearing her stop. She warded off her creeping depression by assuring herself that her dilemma was only temporary. The promised check and reference would surely arrive tomorrow. Tomorrow she would return to the Claridge to pick them up. Tomorrow things would look different.

It was still raining when she got off the omnibus. To avoid getting drenched, she ran the few blocks to the rooming house, using the folded newspaper as a makeshift umbrella.

She reached the steps almost the same time as another young woman, who then stood on the stoop closing her umbrella before entering the house. With a glance at Oriel and a quick motion, she pushed open the door and together they both rushed into the entry hall.

Vigorously shaking the rain from her umbrella, she turned to Oriel, laughing. "That was close, I'd say! No umbrella, dearie? You ought to carry one always. Doesn't pay to take chances this time of year. Never know when you'll get caught in a downpour."

The woman had a round, friendly face, with a sprinkle of freckles across an upturned nose. Regarding Oriel with curious eyes, she said, "I'm Nola Cooper. I live upstairs in the third floor front flat. You must be the new roomer."

Oriel introduced herself.

"Pleased to meet you, I'm sure." Nola smiled. "Mrs. Pettigrew tells me you're an American. I have a cousin who lives in Boston. Do you know it?"

"Yes, as a matter of fact, I lived quite close when I was growing up—in Lynwood."

"Well, I'd say that was a coincidence, wouldn't you?"

"Yes, I suppose it is."

"Well, I'm off to get out of these wet duds. My intended is taking me out to the music hall tonight." She smiled. "Be seeing you, I'm sure. Ta-ta!"

With a wave of her hand, Nola ran up the stairs, leaving Oriel to follow more slowly. Suddenly her day seemed wasted—the long bus ride, the futile errand. As she plodded wearily up the stairs, she felt discouraged and lonely.

4

Oriel awoke to another gray London day. A full week had passed since Mrs. McPhail had sailed for France. Oriel had gone every day to check if her money and reference had come. Although she did not always have to deal with the same clerk to make her inquiry, Oriel always received the same answer—no letter, no nothing.

Today was Friday. If the check and letter didn't come, Oriel faced a weekend of worry. Her money was dwindling fast. She tried to economize by eating only one meal a day at a restaurant near the rooming house. If there was nothing from Mrs. McPhail today, Oriel would have to find work, even if only temporary, to tide her over. Maybe she would stop by the employment agency she had seen advertised in the newspaper and fill out an application. With her education and qualifications, she should be able to get some type of teaching or tutoring job. Even better would be a position as a traveling companion, perhaps even back to the States.

Bolstered by a determination not to be defeated by her circumstances, Oriel got up and got dressed. Conscious of the importance of making a good impression, Oriel chose a walking suit of Prussian blue wool, its jacket edged with darker blue braid. Her bonnet was trimmed with matching ribbon. It was one of the outfits she had made for herself, not one that had once belonged to Neecy. Over the years, out of necessity, Oriel had become quite a skilled seamstress.

Satisfied with her appearance, Oriel set out with high hopes. She was just leaving her room as Nola came down the steps.

"G'morning. You're off, then? I take the omnibus at the corner. Want to walk together?"

Glad for Nola's cheerful company, Oriel agreed. Together they went the rest of the way downstairs, with Nola merrily recounting her evening out with Will. On the way to the bus stop, Nola kept up a running chatter, telling Oriel she was a tailor's apprentice, an orphan, that Will was her steady beau and they were saving their money so they could get married within the year. At the bus stop, Nola asked, "Where are you off to?"

Oriel hesitated for a moment before saying, "The Claridge Hotel."

Nola looked surprised. "You work there?"

"Well, not exactly. Actually, I'm looking for work."

Nola gave her a searching, sympathetic look. She seemed about to say something when they heard the sound of horses' hooves and the heavy wheels of the omnibus.

"Here comes mine," Nola said as the bus pulled to a stop. She hopped on board and waved her hand, calling back, "Well, good luck."

At the hotel, Oriel received the same negative answer to her inquiry. She turned away, shaken, discouraged. All her brave optimism disappeared. She had to face the truth. Mrs. McPhail was not going to come through. There was no point in hoping. She was stranded in London, with little money.

She didn't want to go back to the rooming house, to her curious landlady and cold room, where the small stove emitted meager heat. Besides, she had to take action. If she got a job, perhaps within a few weeks she could earn enough money to buy the cheapest steamship ticket back to the States. She had noticed while riding the omnibus that the employment office was only a few blocks away from the hotel. She walked toward it resolutely.

The small brass plate identified the severe-looking woman behind the desk as Miss Ellerbee. Frowning, she studied the questionnaire Oriel had filled out, put it aside, then gave Oriel the bad news. The world economy that winter was on a slow downturn; the employment picture, even for those most qualified, was bleak. She looked over her nose glasses at Oriel and sighed.

"I must be quite honest with you, Miss Banning. I don't know any place I could send you where you might be employed. To be truthful, you have two major disadvantages. First, you are an American seeking employment in England at a time when many native gentlewomen are also doing so. Second, you are young and quite attractive. I'm afraid any woman who might interview you as a social secretary or a governess would have some reservations—especially if she had a husband with a wandering eye, or an attractive son."

Oriel's astonishment must have shown. She started to protest, but Miss Ellerbee interrupted. "I hate to be so brutally frank, but there it is."

"Even as a domestic?" Oriel asked desperately.

Miss Ellerbee shook her head. "You have no such training, Miss Banning, nor any references, I might add. The servant system in England is a very regimented one. Girls go out into service at twelve or thirteen, work themselves up from scullery or cook's assistant to parlor or lady's maid. It is also a very closed system. I doubt you would ever be admitted."

That brought the interview to an end. In a bewildered frame of mind, Oriel left. Weary and downhearted beyond belief, she caught the omnibus. Preoccupied by her own disturbing thoughts, she missed her stop. She then had to walk three blocks back. Her head and her feet ached. Oriel was just rounding the corner in sight of the shabby rooming house when she saw Nola hurrying along just ahead of her.

At the doorway, Nola asked, "Any luck yet, dearie?"

"Not yet."

Something in Oriel's tone of voice caused Nola to give her a sharp glance. They went inside. "Why not come up to my room. We'll have a cup of tea."

"That's very kind of you."

"Not at all. I like a bit of company and a good chat. Come along up."

Nola's room was furnished much the same as Oriel's. However, Nola had made it distinctly her own with special touches. There were several ruffled throw pillows with satin-stitched quotations in swirling script, artificial flowers in painted vases, and large bows for curtain swags.

Nola got a fire going right away and set on the kettle. She kicked off her shoes and put on a pair of purple house slippers.

"There, that's better!" She sighed, then said to Oriel, "Take off your hat, dearie, and get comfy. You look tired. Job hunting's no fun. Not a nibble, eh?"

Oriel shook her head. "It seems I'm overqualified for some and underqualified for most."

Nola pursed her lips. "Don't American girls learn a trade?"

"Some do," Oriel began, wondering how much of her background she could share with this nice girl without alienating her. They had grown up not only in different countries but in different social worlds.

The hissing of the kettle halted any revelations. Nola busied herself making their tea. She handed Oriel a cup decorated with seashells.

"Well, don't worry, dearie. You're pretty and smart," Nola said comfortingly. "Something's bound to turn up sooner or later."

It better be sooner, Oriel thought, sipping her tea. It was the *later* that was depressing. She dreaded to think how long *later* could be.

Nola held her cup with both hands thoughtfully for a moment. Then she leaned forward and said, "Want a bit of advice, dearie?"

"Of course."

Nola hesitated a second or two. "If I were you, dearie, I wouldn't say nothin' to Mrs. Pettigrew about being unemployed. She's a nosy old biddy and, well—just a word to the wise." She gave Oriel a wink.

A word to the wise, indeed. The truth of Nola's statement confirmed Oriel's own intuition about their landlady. Although pleasant enough, Mrs. Pettigrew had shown a growing curiosity about her. What was Oriel actually doing in London? Where did Oriel go when she went out each day? Oriel had seen her peeking out the parlor window when she returned from her futile errands. Mrs. Pettigrew always seemed to have some reason to come to the door of her downstairs apartment or to the row of mailboxes in the hallway to engage Oriel in probing conversations. Her narrowed eyes asked the questions her nimble mind was thinking. Why was Oriel, an American, apparently without a job or friends, staying in London?

With a great deal of trepidation, Oriel paid another week's rent, then began a relentless job search.

She dredged up the courage to go into stores and shops of all kinds and ask if there was any available work. She had hoped her neat appearance and manner would overcome her lack of references. That had not been the case. She had been consistently turned down. For the most part, Oriel withstood the cold looks and the suspicious questions, but by the end of a week of tramping the bleak London streets, she was exhausted and discouraged.

She was almost at the end of her rope. Next week her rent would be due again—then what? Could she go to the American embassy as a last resort and plead destitution? She shuddered. Not yet. She wasn't giving up.

One gray morning, chilled and depressed, Oriel started to return to the rooming house after another failed job search. She halted at the thought of a possible grilling by Mrs. Pettigrew. She decided as long as she was already out, she would walk to the Claridge. By some chance, a very slim one, just maybe . . . Oriel whirled around and went in the other direction.

A few blocks from the hotel, it began to drizzle. Oriel hurried along, trying to stay close to the buildings to protect herself from a sharp wind that penetrated her light wool suit. She turned up her jacket collar, hoping she could get to the hotel before the leaden clouds opened up and poured down sheets of rain. Resentful thoughts of Mrs. McPhail spurred her to walk faster. Her former employer was probably basking in the sunshine at some European resort!

Stopping at the curb across the street from the Claridge, Oriel paused as a carriage clattered past. Its wheels hit a puddle, sending a spray of dirty water onto Oriel's skirt and soaking her shoes.

Oriel let out a gasp and looked helplessly after the offender. All she could do, really, was hurry on. She hoped the dampened edge of her hem wouldn't show as she entered the luxurious lobby. She didn't want to look as bedraggled and poverty-stricken as she felt.

At the top of the hotel steps, Oriel came under the appraisal of the uniformed doorman. She suspected he was considering whether he should run down with his large umbrella to escort her into the lobby. While he debated, Oriel lifted her head and started up the steps, trying to look as much as possible like a returning guest.

Concentrating on maintaining her poise, she was startled to hear a deep, masculine voice behind her say, "Miss Banning?"

5

*O*riel turned. *Morgan Drummond!* She stared at
him, astonished that he remembered her name.
Then he was towering over her, sheltering her with
his large umbrella, looking as surprised as she felt.

"Miss Banning, what on earth are you doing here?" he
asked. "I thought you'd left with Mrs. McPhail. I saw her leaving and I naturally assumed that since you were with her on
board our ship—"

"I'm no longer in her employ," Oriel replied, cutting off
any further speculation on his part.

"Ah, I see," he said, still puzzled. "But you are still staying
here at the hotel?"

Uncomfortably aware of his scrutiny, Oriel said, "It's rather
a long story." Just then, a strong gust of wind tugged her hat
brim, blowing it up from where she had fastened it to her
hair.

"Well, let's not stand out here in this wind. You can tell me
about it inside. Let's get out of this storm." He smiled. "We
always seem to be meeting in inclement weather, don't we?"

He took her arm and escorted her up the steps through
the entrance. Inside the lobby, Oriel straightened her hat,

tucked back a stray strand of hair, and smoothed down her jacket collar.

"To answer your question," she said, "I returned today to see if my letter of reference and my—" She stopped herself before blurting that she also awaited her badly needed funds. "Mrs. McPhail promised . . ." Her words trailed off, leaving her thought dangling. Did Morgan guess what she was hoping that letter contained?

If he did, he brushed it off easily. "No matter. Now that we have encountered each other again, might I suggest you join me for tea? I've been out all this miserable morning on a dreary round of business appointments. I'm badly in need of some cheerful company. Would you accommodate me?" A smile softened his face.

Oriel considered whether it would be proper to accept his invitation. Under ordinary circumstances, no. She hardly knew Morgan Drummond. However, the fact that they had been fellow passengers might bend protocol a little. More importantly, the emptiness in her stomach reminded her she had had only a scant cup of tea and single slice of bread for breakfast. She *was* very hungry. Practicality overtook propriety. With just the right amount of ladylike hesitation, Oriel accepted. "How very kind. Yes, thank you."

"Fine. Come along, then. You can check for your mail afterwards."

Oriel had had enough experience with the affluent to realize they could not imagine her urgent need for money or understand anything about being unemployed and impoverished. Morgan Drummond had no idea how desperate checking her mail was for her. Still, Oriel decided to put her anxieties aside and enjoy this unexpected meeting and the opportunity for a comforting tea. She had not the least premonition of the importance of this chance encounter.

At the door of the dining room, the head waiter greeted Morgan by name, bowed deferentially, and led them to a table near a window. A waiter appeared and Morgan ordered.

Soon a large pot of tea and a covered plate were placed before Oriel. When the waiter lifted the silver dome, a delicious aroma of grilled chops, bacon, and sausage rose tantalizingly. There were also tomatoes, mushrooms, and a mound of creamy scrambled eggs. A dish holding toasted crumpets dripping with butter and currant-studded buns was set between them, along with an assortment of jams, jellies, and marmalades. Oriel had not had such a meal for quite a while. With great effort, she tried to eat daintily and not appear too hungry.

With her second cup of tea, Oriel felt revived. Sitting across from him, Oriel realized again how good-looking Morgan Drummond was. He was kept from being entirely handsome by a nose that was slightly crooked. He had black wavy hair and a keen, intelligent face with defined features. Heavy dark brows met over penetrating eyes, which gave his face a discontented, brooding expression. It seemed strange that anyone with his wealth, power, and physical attributes should be unhappy, but Oriel knew everyone had secret problems. Morgan Drummond was probably no exception. Even as she considered this possibility, she became aware that Morgan Drummond was regarding *her* thoughtfully.

At first, their conversation had been polite small talk about the crossing, some of the events on board, the English climate. Nothing personal was discussed until he signaled the waiter for a fresh pot of tea. Then, leaning forward, he asked, "So, Miss Banning, now that you are no longer with the McPhails, do you intend to stay in London? Or do you have other plans?"

"I have no special plans at present. I've been waiting—" Oriel halted. Ordinarily a truthful person, she felt reluctant to tell him about her financial dilemma. Nor did she want to appear to be seeking sympathy. One didn't pour out one's heart to a stranger.

If he noticed her delay in answering, he did not show it. He simply waited, keeping her in his steady gaze.

Oriel improvised. "I'm considering several possibilities." That, at least, was true. "And you, Mr. Drummond, are you enjoying your stay in London?"

The frown between his brows deepened. "Actually, it's become more business than pleasure, and somewhat unpleasant, I'm afraid. I've been meeting with my grandfather's lawyers." His mouth straightened. "I have received some bad news." He paused. "It seems I've inherited a castle."

"A castle? That doesn't sound like bad news! It sounds very exciting."

He looked glum. "In *Ireland*."

Oriel had to laugh. "Wherever! When I was a little girl, I used to pretend I had a fairy godmother who would one day appear and give me three wishes. One wish was always to live in a castle."

Morgan looked half-amused, half-doubtful. "Sounds like you've an active imagination, Miss Banning. Is it possible you're a bit Irish yourself?"

Oriel smiled. "My great-grandmother was, I think. At least partly." She mimicked a brogue. "Name of O'Meara."

Morgan laughed. "Ah, Miss Banning, I do think you have the famous Irish sense of humor. I wish I had more of that in my nature. I'm afraid along with the castle I've inherited the dark side of Irish character. Somehow the thought of the long, gloomy Irish winters always depresses me." He sighed and frowned again. "The castle comes with a requirement. I have to take possession within a month."

"Oh, so you'll be going to Ireland to see your inherited castle? That should be interesting."

"I shall have to," he said grimly. "Actually, Miss Banning, it isn't the great gift you seem to think. It is very complicated. I hadn't planned on *living* in Ireland."

"I see," Oriel said quietly.

Morgan shook his head. "No, you don't. You couldn't really see unless you knew the whole story."

His tone was dismissing and Oriel felt rebuffed. "I'm sorry."

"No, I'm the one who's sorry. I shouldn't have brought the matter up." He signaled the waiter for the check. "Other people's burdens are a bore. I don't intend to spoil this delightful interlude we've had by doing that."

He rose and came around to help Oriel from her chair. "I am taking the night boat to Dublin and then will journey to Kilmara to inspect my new property. My grandfather has paid a large sum of money to maintain a staff there all these years in the hope that he could return himself. The castle became his hobby, actually. He dispatched agents to buy furnishings, rugs, paintings, and other artifacts to further glorify his boyhood dream of one day living there at Drummond Castle."

Morgan gave a derisive laugh. "One man's folly, and I am supposed to appreciate all that has gone into it and live out Grandfather's dream. A family legacy, and I am the only one left to see to it. Do you have any such family legacy to uphold, Miss Banning, or are you more fortunate?"

"I don't know whether I would call myself *fortunate,* Mr. Drummond. Both my parents are dead, and I have no brothers or sisters—a fact I've often regretted."

"Forgive me, I spoke facetiously. I did not mean to offend you."

Oriel shook her head. "No offense taken."

They walked out to the lobby. Although Oriel felt uncomfortable, Morgan accompanied her up to the reception desk while she asked if there was any mail for her. It did not escape the haughty clerk's notice that this time Morgan Drummond was standing beside Oriel. He was a little less hasty in his negative reply that the hoped-for letter had not come. Disappointed, Oriel turned away, trying to hide her dismay as best she could.

"Why don't you leave an address where you can be reached?" Morgan suggested. "If your mail comes in the afternoon post, the hotel can send it to you and save you another trip."

Of course. It was the sensible thing to do. Oriel wondered why she had not thought of it herself before this. She was a little hesitant to give the address to the haughty clerk, sure he would recognize the neighborhood in which it was located, but there was nothing else to do. As coolly as she could, she gave the address, noting the slight rise of the clerk's eyebrows. However, with Morgan beside her, the clerk was politeness itself, and he assured Oriel that anything bearing her name would be forwarded.

"You can't go traipsing around in this dreadful weather. I insist on calling you a cab." Morgan gestured to the long, satin-draped windows through which they could see a steady downpour. He pulled a comic face. "Pity me. They say weather in Ireland is much worse!"

"Well, I wish you the best." Oriel smiled. "I've always heard Ireland is a fascinating country, full of beauty and mystery."

Morgan walked her to the hotel entrance. When Oriel thanked him for the tea, he shook his head slightly. "It is I who should thank you, Miss Banning, for the company. I was in a foul mood when we met. You gave me a most enjoyable distraction from what had been a bad day with depressing news. I'm grateful." He then handed Oriel over to the doorman, who took her carefully down to the waiting hansom.

As it drove off, Oriel peered through the rain-splattered window to wave at Morgan, who was still on the top step. It was quite a coincidence, their meeting again like this. It was then that Oriel realized he had not mentioned his wedding or Edwina Parker. In a way, it was like having read a few random chapters of a story, not knowing how it began or how it would end. Now she would never know. She certainly never expected to see Morgan Drummond again.

6

*The London Law Offices of Tredwell,
Loring, and Sommerville*

April 1895

urwin Tredwell regarded his client with narrowed eyes. Although he had known and liked the grandfather, his opinion of the grandson was—not to put too fine a point on it—suspect. He held the view that heirs to great fortunes were usually not worth the trust they were given by their benefactors. There was always the danger of them going rapidly through the hard-earned money they inherited, no matter what their lawyers did to prevent it. A favorite saying of his own grandfather, the eminent lawyer who had founded the prestigious law firm of Tredwell, Loring, and Sommerville had been, "From shirtsleeves to shirtsleeves in three generations."

The third generation of the Drummond fortune was sitting opposite him at the present moment, reading over a copy of his grandfather's lengthy will. Durwin was wary. In the first place, the man was an American. Durwin had had few dealings with Americans. Further, although the firm had carried on an extensive correspondence with Morgan Drummond, Durwin had never met him before he'd come to London a few weeks ago. When Durwin had been given the case to handle by his father, Morgan had been described by him as being "too good-looking, too rich, and too clever for his own good." Durwin studied him. In person, Morgan Drummond validated the description; he was tall, magnificently built, dark-haired—too handsome by far.

When Morgan finished turning the last page, he tossed the document back on Durwin's desk, saying grimly, "That's it, then. No loopholes, no escape clauses. This is unbreakable, right?"

"It has been legally signed, witnessed, and officially filed. The only reason it would not be upheld is if *you* decided you did not wish to fulfill the requirements of the inheritance. In that case, your grandfather signed a codicil, giving us the authority to assign the full amount of the estate to the various charities and institutions he listed."

Morgan muttered something under his breath, sprang up from his chair, and began to pace the room in long strides. "There must be another way."

Durwin placed his hands in an arch, fingertips touching, and slowly shook his head. "Not, I'm afraid, unless the young lady in question changes her mind."

"That won't happen." Morgan's jaw clenched.

For a moment, a tense silence hung in the high-ceilinged, wood-paneled room. From beyond the windows, draped heavily in green velvet, the muffled sound of London traffic could be heard.

After a long while, Morgan said slowly, "There might be a solution. That is—" He turned to the lawyer, pulled the chair closer to his desk, and leaned forward to outline his idea.

Durwin leaned back in his high-backed leather chair and listened. It was a bizarre plan, but it might work. There was nothing illegal about it, although some might find that it rather stretched the limits of the intention of the will. He would have to check to see if there were any unforeseen traps before drawing up such an agreement.

"So what do you think?" Morgan demanded.

Durwin surveyed his client curiously. "And you say this young woman is—"

"Yes, without financial resources—no parents, no family. It couldn't be better. An only child *and* an orphan!"

A sardonic smile lifted the corners of Morgan's mouth slightly, hardening the expression. For a moment, Durwin felt a chill at the cold-bloodedness of the scheme.

On the other side of London, late that afternoon, Oriel dragged herself up the steps of the rooming house, opened the door, and wearily mounted the stairs to her room. Without taking off her hat or coat, she sank down on the chair by the window. Outside it was getting dark, and rain was beading on the glass.

It had been a long, discouraging day. She had checked out two promising job ads, one at a stationery firm, where someone was wanted to copy legal documents and address envelopes, and the other at a bookstore, where a clerk was needed. Knowing she wrote a fine hand, she thought she could qualify for the first job. Since she was well-read, she could certainly suggest titles for browsers, which should make her a good choice for the second job. She had started out feeling fairly optimistic. However, after a tedious bus ride and an almost frantic search for the small, out-of-the-way bookstore, she found both positions had already been filled—by *men.*

Oriel took stock. Her situation was becoming desperate. After paying another week's rent, she would barely have enough to last two weeks—if she were extra careful. That meant making the allotment of coal for the stove stretch for two days and limiting her food to one full meal a day. If Mrs.

41

McPhail failed to pay her, there was only one week's rent left between Oriel and the poorhouse.

Oriel chided herself for being melodramatic. Maybe this was the worst crisis she had faced in her life, but she still wasn't ready to give up. On the bus, she had picked up a newspaper another rider had discarded. She unfolded it and began to scrutinize the employment section. She sat up late going over the Help Wanted ads in the newspaper. Maybe she had overlooked something, a job she had not considered possible before. Then she saw it: "WANTED IM-MEDIATELY: Piecework women to do plain sewing. Fast workers needed. Earn good pay. Apply Mr. Jarman." An address followed.

Sewing! At least she knew she could do that. It didn't sound too difficult.

She left the rooming house early the next morning, not wanting to miss the opportunity for a job as she had the day before. She also did not want to run into either Mrs. Pettigrew or Nola. Nola had begun to look at her cautiously, as though not sure whether to ask how the job search was going. As for Mrs. Pettigrew—well, who knew what the landlady was thinking. As long as she could still pay the rent, Oriel did not want to have to deal with her.

After a long bus ride, Oriel found herself in a drab street with dark, soot-stained buildings rising on either side. It was an industrial section of London. Clutching the ad with the address of a possible workplace, Oriel hurried down the dirty sidewalk.

When she saw a line of shawled women hurrying toward a wide wooden door, she quickened her step. Touching the arm of one of them, she asked, "Are they hiring today?" The woman jerked a thumb. "Jarman's the one to see," she told Oriel in a hoarse voice, then hurried on.

Oriel joined the end of the line that was moving slowly toward the entrance, then followed the last woman through the door. The interior was so dim, she halted to let her eyes become accustomed to it. Just a few feet away stood a man slouched against the wall.

She advanced cautiously. "Mr. Jarman?"

"That's me." He had a blotched face with small, curious eyes, a bulbous nose, and slack mouth. "What do you want?"

"A job. I mean, I saw your advertisement and I—"

The man's eyes roved over her skeptically, boldly challenging. "Can you make buttonholes, take out basting stitches?" he asked.

"Yes, of course," Oriel answered.

"You get paid by the piece. Understand?" he demanded, moving a toothpick from one side of his mouth to the other. "The more you can do in a day, the more's your pay. Get it?"

"Yes."

"Well, come on, then. Meg's the supervisor in the workroom. You've got to see her. She'll find you a place and assign your work."

Oriel followed him down a narrow hall. He opened a door and barked, "Meg, come here!"

A large woman with a coarse complexion and a pinched expression walked over to him. He jerked his thumb toward Oriel. "New worker. Find her a place and get her started." Then, with one more evaluating look at Oriel, he sauntered off.

"Hang your coat and hat over there," Meg said sharply, "then come with me."

The workroom was narrow. Hazy light from grimy windows was augmented only slightly by smoky oil lamps hanging from the ceiling. Women were seated on either side of long tables bent over great piles of material, their shoulders hunched forward as they squinted over their work.

Oriel was directed to a table where there was an empty chair at one end. As she took her place, she nodded and smiled tentatively at her fellow workers, but received only blank stares in return.

43

A pile of material was dumped in front of her, and a tin container holding scissors, thread, a thimble, and a needle was put down beside it. "See you take care—if you lose or break a needle, another one is docked from your pay, understand?" Meg said harshly. It wasn't really a question.

The hours ticked by in endless monotony. No one spoke; everyone worked steadily, hardly glancing up at one another. Oriel's neck began to ache painfully and her shoulders stiffened. She tried to shift her position in the hard chair, but it was almost impossible. The chairs were placed so close together that if she tried to move, she bumped into her neighbor.

Her eyes began to water from strain. The light was so dim it was difficult to work on the dark material. By the time a shrill bell rang announcing the end of the day, Oriel could barely move. Every bone and muscle protested. Her fingers were sore; her back and arms ached.

As she gingerly stood up, she discovered one foot had gone to sleep and tingled painfully. When she glanced around at the other women, she had a horrible realization. Their pale faces, red-rimmed eyes, and rounded shoulders told a tragic story. Who knew what circumstances had forced them into this grinding, unrewarding work? How long had they worked here under these conditions? Again, no one spoke as they wearily reached for hats and jackets and filed out of the workroom into the crowded London street. It was nearly dark when Oriel emerged from the building. She was as close to despairing tears as she had been in all these anxious weeks.

That night, she was too tired even to stop and get something to eat. She could hardly undress before she fell across the bed, pulling the quilt over her and falling into a deep sleep. It was morning before she could believe it. The jangle of her alarm clock jolted her upright, and she stumbled out of bed. It was still dark as she hurried to the bus stop, wondering how she could possibly get through another day in the workroom. She had to earn at least enough to pay another week's rent; surely by then Mrs. McPhail's check would come. She dared not think what the alternative would be.

The days of that week ground by slowly. The work was not only mindlessly boring but wearying. The silence of the workroom was oppressive. No one seemed inclined to relieve the heavy atmosphere with any sort of conversation. The watchful presence of Meg and Jarman, who periodically stalked the aisles between the tables, was enough to discourage anyone inclined to converse. Every time Oriel raised her head from her work when Jarman was in the workroom, she met his speculative glance. She had to suppress the uneasy feeling it gave her. She told herself she would wait until the end of the week and see if working here was worth it. She *was* a quick worker and found the work simple. She never got to the end of it, though. The minute she finished her allotment, another pile was dumped before her.

She managed to get through the tedious hours by using her imagination. After her mother's death, Oriel had discovered she could live in another world peopled by imaginary characters. In the dreary workroom, she told herself stories and thought of her beloved father, who had given her everything to make her happy. What would he think of her present situation, the circumstances in which she now found herself?

On Friday morning, Oriel woke up with a sense of relief. She had survived the awful week. She was sure her fast work had added up to a good sum, at least enough to make next week's rent. On Saturday, she planned to go to the Claridge and check her mail just in case the clerk had not forwarded her letter as she had requested.

Taking the last stitch, Oriel knotted her thread and snipped it with the scissors. She replaced her needle into the pincushion, placed it with the scissors and thimble back into the small tin container, and folded her last piece just as the bell rang. Today was payday, and even among the quiet workers there was a sense of anticipation. They lined up to get the envelopes containing their wages, given to them by Jarman, who sat at a desk near the building entrance. As the last hired, Oriel was last in line. As she approached the table, Jarman looked up.

"So you made it, Miss Banning." His mouth twitched in his version of a smile, one that looked more like a sneer. "I had a wager you wouldn't. Made me lose my bet, didn't you?"

Oriel did not answer. She waited. He must have her check. Why didn't he just hand it to her? Finally, she said, "My pay, please?"

"Meg says you're a fast worker. Did more than your quota." Stubby fingers with dirt under the nails flipped over the file cards. "Did you expect a little bonus, Miss Banning?"

A queer sort of alert quivered through Oriel. She was the only one left in the workroom. She had heard the outer door slam after the last two workers had gotten their pay envelopes and gone. She felt a tingling along her scalp, a warning of danger. She felt her breath rise, become shallow. She wanted to get out of there. She held out her hand. "No bonus, just what's coming to me, Mr. Jarman."

He shoved back his chair. It made a grating noise on the cement floor. He stood, picked up a pay envelope, and came around the desk. His bulky height loomed over her. He pushed his face close to Oriel's, and she could smell liquor on his breath as he said, "Then how about a little bonus for *me*, Miss Banning? That is, *if* you want your pay."

She stepped away from him, but he reached out and grabbed her upper arm. She struggled, trying to shake loose, but his fingers tightened. "Ah, no you don't, Miss High and Mighty."

Panic swept through her, gave her strength. Oriel pulled away from him, and with her free arm, brought her handbag up and smashed it full in his face. The bag had an ornamental metal clasp that scraped his forehead. He groaned and dropped her arm. His hand went to his face and Oriel saw that the blow had drawn blood. Taking advantage of his momentary incapacity, she ran for the exit and pushed through the wide doors into the street.

She kept running, not looking back until ahead she saw her omnibus slowing at the corner. She picked up her skirts and ran faster. Breathless, she mounted the steps and sank into a seat, weak with relief. The vehicle moved forward. She felt faint from the hideous episode and her narrow escape.

It was only a few minutes later that she realized she had not received her pay. A sickening sensation washed over her. That terrible week and nothing to show for it. The thought of going back to claim her wages made her shudder. Jarman would probably deny everything. He might not even admit she had ever worked there.

Oriel felt drained. She slumped against the bus seat. Her futile attempt to survive had ended in a grotesque nightmare. She stared out the window, then wearily pulled the bell at her stop. She got off the bus and with great effort, doggedly headed toward the rooming house.

Oriel felt the rise of panic and fought it. She had known the soul-wrenching anxiety of poverty, always a step away from calamity, teetering on the yawning abyss of illness, accident. Trusting God was the only security. The job with the McPhails had proved that. As a child, Oriel had been taught to pray. However, she had also been told not to expect miracles. A good mind, imagination, and strength of character were given to a person to find her way out of difficulties. With God's help, she would get through this.

Letting herself into her room, Oriel shivered. It felt dank, chilly. There was no more coal in the bucket. She picked up her purse, emptied the contents, and counted out enough coins for a scuttle of coal. At least she could be warm while she figured a way out of her dilemma.

She marched downstairs and knocked at her landlady's door. Oriel had avoided Mrs. Pettigrew all week, but getting the coal was now a necessity.

"Oh, it's *you*, Miss Banning!" the landlady said as she opened the door. "I was just thinking about you. I must've missed you coming in. I kept an eye out, but then I went to fix my tea. You must've come in while I was in the kitchen. I have something for you—come this afternoon by special messenger."

Mrs. Pettigrew turned, bustled back into her cluttered parlor, then hurried back, holding out an envelope to Oriel.

Puzzled, Oriel took it, examining the fine quality of the paper. Then, seeing the gold-embossed lettering of the Claridge Hotel on the back flap, she felt a wave of relief. It must be the check and letter of reference from Mrs. McPhail.

Though Mrs. Pettigrew was quivering with curiosity, Oriel was not about to open it in front of her. "Thank you," Oriel said, tucking the letter into her sweater pocket. She handed the landlady her coins and said, "Could I have my ration of coal, please?"

Mrs. Pettigrew looked disgruntled as she accepted the coins and filled the scuttle for Oriel. Unable to contain her curiosity, she remarked pointedly, "I hope it's not bad news."

"Oh, I'm sure it isn't. Thank you, Mrs. Pettigrew." Oriel went back upstairs, trying not to appear to be hurrying.

7

*I*n her room, Oriel set down the coal scuttle and tore open the envelope. Inside were several pages written in a bold, slanted hand—but it wasn't from Mrs. McPhail, and there was no check enclosed. She quickly turned to the last page and read the signature. Oriel blinked with astonishment. It was from Morgan Drummond. It contained the most bizarre offer Oriel had ever received.

My dear Miss Banning,

Although our meeting the other day might have seemed the slightest of chance, in retrospect I believe it to have been one of those rare opportunities fate places in our paths.

If you have not made other plans that will take you back to the States and have no other commitments in England, I would like to present a suggestion for a year's employment of a rather unusual kind. It comes with generous financial compensation and future security.

If this interests you, would you please meet me Tuesday next at the offices of my lawyers—Tredwell, Loring, and Sommerville. I sincerely hope you will come. I believe when you learn the details of this plan, you will find that it not only solves your present uncertain position, but also appeals to your obvious sense of adventure.

With all good wishes and the sincere hope that you will agree to come to discuss the possibilities of mutual benefit in this arrangement.

Yours very truly,
Morgan Drummond

A business card was enclosed with the engraved name of the law firm and the address.

Oriel's first question was why? Something vaguely disturbing hovered in her mind. Why would Morgan Drummond contact her in such a mysterious way? Chance and casual gallantry might have explained the invitation to tea the other afternoon, but they did not begin to explain this. Her curiosity was piqued, however. Though Oriel did have some vague misgivings, she put them aside. What did she have to lose at this point? Could this possibly be the miracle she had been taught not to expect?

The Tuesday of Oriel's appointment to meet Morgan Drummond at his lawyer's office, she awoke early. Peering out the window, she saw the sky was leaden, the streets were once again wet. She chose her outfit carefully. Having no idea what type of position Morgan planned to suggest, she decided to wear her best—a persimmon wool dress under a gray fitted coat with a short shoulder cape. Her hat was a black velvet pancake shape with shiny black feathers curled over the small brim. Before she set out, she checked her well-worn map of London for the location of the lawyers' office.

As the bus rattled through the streets, the scene outside the window became more and more impressive. Oriel got off at the entrance to a tree-lined square. A parkway divided tall stone buildings on either side. All the buildings seemed identical, with dark shiny doors and discreet brass plates bearing the names of the firms doing business within.

At last Oriel found the one marked Tredwell, Loring, and Sommerville. The polished door outside opened into a thickly carpeted foyer. A clerk took her name and asked her to follow him down the hall to another office.

"I will let Mr. Tredwell know of your arrival." The clerk bowed slightly.

Oriel glanced around at the handsome furnishings. Leather chairs were placed in front of a marble fireplace, above which hung a gold-framed portrait of a gentleman in a judge's wig and robes.

A moment later, a tall, well-dressed middle-aged man walked toward her. "Good afternoon, Miss Banning. I'm Durwin Tredwell. Mr. Drummond is waiting in the inner office. Later, I will be available to answer any questions you may have—anything you would like clarified about the proposal we have drawn up at Mr. Drummond's request."

"Thank you," Oriel responded.

Mr. Tredwell led the way back to an equally well-furnished room. Floor-to-ceiling bookcases lined the walls, filled with maroon leather-bound law books. The tall windows were curtained in green velvet.

Morgan Drummond rose from one of the leather armchairs. Seeing Oriel again in her simple, yet stylish outfit and becoming hat, he decided his judgment had been right. Oriel Banning had a definite air of understated refinement. She would fit in anywhere. Certainly she could not be called beautiful; however, the slight irregularity of features gave her face a distinctive individuality. Besides, hadn't he discovered, to his recent disillusionment, that flawless physical beauty did not guarantee other qualities he also considered important? Instinctively, he felt that Oriel Banning might possess other characteristics he would find admirable and valuable—certainly ones essential for carrying out the plan he was about to present to her.

"Good afternoon, Miss Banning. Thank you for coming." After greeting her, Morgan again sat down in the leather chair opposite the one Tredwell had indicated for her.

Once seated, Oriel studied Morgan Drummond. She was still puzzled as to the motive behind this meeting. His letter had indicated "mutual benefit." What could that possibly be?

Tredwell took his seat behind a massive desk, and a short silence followed. Oriel wondered which of the two men would broach the subject of this meeting. Tredwell seemed in no particular hurry; perhaps he was waiting for his client to begin. That seemed to be the case, because Morgan then came directly to the point.

"Miss Banning, I want you to know I appreciate your coming on such brief notice and under such ambiguous circumstances. However, I could not be more explicit in my letter. The plan I am about to unfold needed to be explained to you in person. You are obviously an intelligent young woman and must be puzzled at the method I have used. I am sure you have even questioned the propriety of coming here. After all, most shipboard acquaintances end at docking." He smiled slightly.

Oriel gave him her complete attention.

"You may remember I told you I had been meeting with my grandfather's lawyers about my inheritance. You may also recall I said it was quite complicated. Grandfather left some strange conditions to his will, conditions I found not only difficult, but nearly impossible to meet."

He broke off, his mouth tightening into a stern line. "Actually, I have been trying with the lawyers to work out some way to modify or alter the terms." He sighed and shook his head. "However, it has finally been concluded that I must comply with them or lose all of the inheritance. This would affect not only me personally, but also many of the institutions—charitable and altruistic foundations—that my grandfather expected me to continue to support. Out of loyalty to him, I feel I must do this.

He paused and then began again. "Let me explain. Grandfather came to America as a poverty-stricken boy from Ireland during the devastating potato famine in 1840. He was the only one of his family to leave Ireland. All the others had died when they were forced off their farms by absentee landlords. My grandfather had brains, courage, and luck; he prospered, married, raised a family, and gradually became very successful. Unfortunately, his three sons, one of whom was my father, all died young. I'm the only remaining Drummond, so I became my grandfather's heir."

Morgan glanced at Tredwell as if for confirmation. The lawyer nodded solemnly. Morgan continued, "Grandfather never forgot his humble beginnings, even though he had become a very rich man. He felt great nostalgia for the land he'd been forced to leave and for all things Irish. On a trip to Ireland, he went back to the village where he had often walked past the great manor house the villagers called the castle. As a barefoot lad, he'd peer through the gates. Now it had fallen into a bad state of disrepair, for the English aristocracy had departed once the land no longer provided them the wherewithal to live luxurious lives. On impulse, Grandfather bought the castle of his youth, intending to retire there and bring it back to its original splendor. Sadly, when he went back to the States, he became ill and was never able to return and carry out his plan."

Morgan's voice had a bitter edge as he said, "Strange, isn't it, that the dead are at peace and their survivors are left with the trials and tribulations of the world?" He shrugged. "So now the castle belongs to me—that is, *if* I decide to carry out Grandfather's plan and fulfill the conditions of his will. With that comes all his other wealth and the responsibilities that go with it. However, this is not my decision alone." He paused.

"I'll be quite blunt, Miss Banning. You may have heard I was engaged to Miss Edwina Parker. I believe it was common knowledge on board ship." He seemed to be quite used to the idea of being the subject of gossip. "Our plan was to be married here in London, where she has been staying. When I found out the conditions of my inheritance—that I must live with my bride for a full year in the castle in Ireland—and told Edwina . . ." He gave a harsh laugh. "Well, I can only leave it to your imagination when I say she did not go along with such an idea."

His expression changed. A shadow fell across it, hardening the line of his mouth, setting his jaw. "Maybe I could have handled it more diplomatically. Or maybe that wouldn't have mattered—maybe nothing would have mattered. You see, my fiancée absolutely refused to marry me under those conditions. Her exact words were, 'What? Stay in a drafty old castle in an isolated village through a wretched Irish winter? You must be out of your mind!'" Quoting Edwina, Morgan's voice shook with anger. He continued, "The result is our engagement has been broken."

Not knowing what else to say, Oriel murmured, "I'm sorry."

Morgan held up his hand. "I didn't tell you this to gain your sympathy, Miss Banning, but rather to explain why I am seeking your help."

"My help?" Oriel was still confused.

"I wouldn't have thought to involve you with my personal problems if I didn't suspect you have your own crisis at the moment—one that is far more crucial in some ways. That's why I want to make you an offer—a legal proposition, actually—that might solve both our dilemmas."

"And what is that, Mr. Drummond? How does this concern me?"

Morgan's gaze riveted on her. "This is what I propose. It must be clear to you by now that Mrs. McPhail is not going to live up to her promise to send you your pay. I am also assuming you have not been able to secure a job since I last saw you. I am suggesting an alternative for you to consider."

Oriel clasped her hands tightly in her lap as Morgan explained. She would enter into an "in name only" marriage with him and live at the castle in Kilmara for one year, legally fulfilling the requirements of his grandfather's will. At the end of the year, they could obtain a quiet annulment, claiming an unconsummated marriage. At that time, Oriel would collect the large amount of money placed in a trust fund for her in return for her agreement to stay the year.

"This has been discussed thoroughly with my lawyers, as Tredwell here can assure you," Morgan stated. "Everything will be spelled out legally, duly witnessed, and signed. The lawyers will make sure everything is done with utmost legality." Morgan's mouth twisted upward as he glanced at Tredwell. "This is a well-known firm of unquestioned integrity and propriety. The contract we sign will be valid and carried out to the letter. Even if you have doubts about me, you would be guaranteed complete protection by this document."

Speechless, Oriel looked from Morgan to Tredwell, then back to Morgan.

"Naturally, we expect you would want to think it over carefully, consult someone you trust, ask advice," Tredwell said.

"Naturally," concurred Morgan, not taking his gaze off Oriel, weighing her reaction. Oriel's candid eyes met his. She did not seem so much shocked as interested. This confirmed his impression of her intellectual curiosity. It was, however, impossible to tell what she would decide. He waited.

The silence seemed to lengthen interminably. Then, drawing a long breath, Oriel said, "You have been quite frank with me, Mr. Drummond. I shall be equally honest with you. I *am* in desperate financial straits. My plans have not worked out as I had hoped. Giving my former employer the benefit of the doubt, there is still a chance I may receive my salary check and reference. In that case, it would be best for me to return to America, where my chances of employment are better than they are here."

Oriel paused. "I have no immediate family, no one whose advice I could seek in regard to this matter. Although agreeing to your plan would help me over my present difficulties, whether in the long run it would be a good thing to do, I am not sure."

"At least you haven't completely rejected my idea, nor do you seem offended," Morgan said, a glint of amusement—and admiration—in his eyes.

"I have lived on the edge of poverty most of my adult life, Mr. Drummond, so the possibility of financial security is tempting, whatever the conditions. However, my position with the McPhails was supposed to have offered me that and it has turned out quite differently. Naturally, I am cautious. My situation has grown more urgent every day, so I am forced to make a decision quickly. That is why you might understand how your proposal—I should say offer of *employment*—seems less shocking than it otherwise might. Of course, I would need time to consider."

She met Morgan's intense gaze. To think of spending a year with this man under the oddest of circumstances seemed bizarre, indeed. And yet . . .

"As long as we are being frank with each other, Miss Banning, there is one more thing," Morgan said, squinting a little. "I must ask you a question that would seem intrusively personal if we were not discussing a *business* proposition. I must assume there is no *romantic* interest in your life at present who would object to your making such a contract, who might at some later date cause a problem?"

Taken aback, Oriel did not answer at once.

"You see, I wouldn't want any old attachments coming up. Someone from your past suddenly appearing on the scene would be very awkward. Although our association would be strictly a *business* arrangement, there *are* appearances to be kept up, especially in a small village like Kilmara, where all eyes will be upon the residents of the castle. You understand, I'm sure, the importance of the public image of a happily married couple, spending their first year together on the idyllic Irish seacoast, as was my grandfather's hope." Morgan's mouth moved into a wry smile; then he went on. "You can understand how awkward someone with a romantic interest suddenly showing up would be."

How ironic the question seemed to Oriel. When, in the poverty-driven past few years, would she have had time for a romantic relationship? But a man used to moving in high-society circles, where shallow flirtations and casual romances were commonplace, would not understand that. In other circumstances, she might have considered Morgan's probing inappropriate, but that was before she had come to such desperate straits.

Returning his calculating look, Oriel simply shook her head and replied coolly, "No, there is no one."

Morgan nodded as if satisfied and did not question her further. "I sincerely hope you will accept this proposal, Miss Banning. The castle *is* isolated, and I don't care much for entertaining. Still, there is much to enjoy for a person not given to social life. I believe someone with your education and background will find much to appreciate at Kilmara. My grandfather's estate has a hundred acres overlooking the ocean on the southern coast of Ireland. There is a well-stocked library, and you will certainly be free to go up to Dublin, a half-day's journey, to shop or attend the theater."

"How soon must I let you know?" Oriel inquired.

"The sooner the better as far as I'm concerned, so that my year at Kilmara can begin. But I certainly want to give you adequate time to think over the matter and consider your answer. A week? Perhaps ten days at the latest." His voice deepened as if to emphasize his next words, "I can promise you I will carry out my end of our bargain in every way. You will have no regrets if you agree."

"I will give it my fullest consideration. Now I think I must go."

Tredwell got to his feet at once. "Of course. Let me see you out."

Morgan rose also. "Good day, Miss Banning. I will be waiting for your answer."

Tredwell escorted her to the firm's carriage, which had been brought around to the front of the building to take her home. As he handed her in, the lawyer said courteously, "I am at your disposal, Miss Banning, for any assistance you might need to reach your decision. You need only send me a note."

"Thank you. You have been most kind," Oriel replied.

As the carriage moved off, Oriel let out a long sigh. What a curious turn of events. It was all rather overwhelming. She might indeed call upon Mr. Tredwell for answers to her myriad questions. First she had a great deal of soul-searching to do.

8

For the next few days, all Oriel could think about was Morgan Drummond's startling proposal. She paced around her small room and went for long walks, considering the advantages and disadvantages of accepting. She vacillated between disregarding the whole thing and wondering if it was some sort of miracle.

She had so many questions. For example, the startling information that Morgan's marriage to the beautiful Edwina had been called off—what was *she* thinking? Her engagement was broken, her plans in shambles. Oriel recalled all the planning Neecy's wedding had required. Edwina must have been planning the same kind of society affair. How upset and angry Edwina must have been to call all that off at the last minute. She must have been dead-set against spending a year in Ireland to break her engagement. Perhaps that was what the quarrel was about the day Oriel saw them in the lobby of the hotel. How would Edwina feel about their arrangement?

To live a year in an Irish castle sounded like a fantasy come true, especially considering her current situation. On the other hand, there must be pitfalls Oriel could not foresee.

She searched for hidden hazards, unknown perils. She hardly knew Morgan Drummond. Could she trust him? What kind of year would it be, spent with a man wounded by the woman he loved? What repercussions from his own unhappiness would fall upon her?

Yet deep within Oriel was the longing for a richer life, a life protected and safe. The horror of her experience with Jarman was still vivid. His was the kind of world in which most women fending for themselves were forced to live. She had struggled to support herself for so long that the idea of having her future so well secured was tempting. Still, Oriel wavered.

She knew her own nature, her faults as well as her strengths. She had survived the hardships of these past years determined that things would get better for her if she took advantage of the opportunities God sent her way. She was also a romantic, clinging to the hope that one day she would find a true love. If she accepted Morgan Drummond's offer, would she be forfeiting that kind of love for herself? Would entering into a loveless marriage ruin her own chances later on?

After two days of debate and heartfelt prayer, Oriel woke to gray skies, still unresolved, soon another week's rent due. She knew she would not be able to force herself to go back to the workshop and demand her rightful pay from that wretch, Jarman. Common sense and practicality began to win over all the arguments to the contrary. Perhaps this *was* God's way of providing for her. She decided to go to the offices of Tredwell, Loring, and Sommerville and see Morgan's lawyer once more. Only then could she make her final decision.

Seated again in Mr. Tredwell's office that afternoon, Oriel listened intently as Mr. Tredwell began to explain. It was a repetition of everything Morgan had already told her. Everything would be handled with extreme confidentiality, including the ultimate deed—the annulment at the end of the year. When Mr. Tredwell named the amount Morgan would place in the trust fund to be paid to Oriel at the end of the year in Ireland, she had to control a gasp. Her mind whirled.

With that much money, Oriel could buy what she desired most—freedom. She'd have freedom from constant anxiety, from the never-ending search for a position with adequate wages, from the fear of poverty in old age. If she were careful, the money could provide her with lifetime security. She could travel, maybe even buy a little house. For years Oriel had lived in a series of rented flats, teacher's quarters, and other people's houses. Now, something she had thought was forever beyond her means, a home of her own, was within the realm of possibility.

With a stroke of the pen, all this could be a reality. All that remained was her signature. Was the risk of signing this strange bargain worth the rewards?

Tredwell's discerning gaze rested upon Oriel Banning as she read over the document he had handed her. Morgan's judgment of her character seemed to be correct. If Morgan was determined to go through with the strange scheme, he may have chosen the best candidate for the bizarre arrangement. She was taking long enough to go over the agreement paper, reading the fine print. Tredwell silently congratulated her caution. Unobtrusively, he took out his watch and checked the time.

Just then, Oriel raised her head and looked at him. Her eyes—her best feature, large, hazel, and long-lashed—met his in a look both intelligent and candid. Would Oriel Banning sign or wouldn't she?

Oriel packed feverishly. Since she had signed the agreement, she had kept herself constantly busy. Having made up her mind, she dared not look back. Second thoughts were now out of the question. It was too late. As she rushed through the preparations, she kept reminding herself that it would be only for a year. Maybe it would be the greatest adventure of her life.

She was to meet Morgan Drummond at the Registry Office later that morning. The terms of the agreement were very clear and seemed reasonable. Oriel had stopped worrying about the right or wrong of it. Her own motives were simply survival. God had sent her an opportunity and she had grabbed it.

But Morgan? His reasons seemed far more complicated. Even without fulfilling the terms of his grandfather's will, he would still have been wealthy. Was it some kind of distorted revenge? Oriel wondered. There was no mistaking the strong emotions under that sophisticated surface. His broken engagement must have been a blow to his pride. Resentment, anger, and bitterness might seethe beneath his outer calm. Would those volatile feelings ever be turned against her? No, she decided. Emotion did not enter into their relationship. Theirs was strictly a business agreement, nothing more. She had to believe that. They were practically strangers; partners for the length of a year's contract—nothing more.

Oriel buttoned the jacket of her blue suit. As she anchored her bonnet with a pin and adjusted the polka-dot veil, she took a brief glance in the mirror. Hardly a bridal outfit, but then she was hardly a typical bride. She thought ruefully of her childhood dreams of weddings. This would not be like those fantasies—just an impersonal Registry Office ceremony, with Mr. Tredwell and one other court-appointed witness. After the signing of a legal document, it would be over. She would be married to Morgan Drummond, at least for a year.

Her suitcases opened, Oriel made a quick survey to be sure she had not forgotten to pack anything. The rented room where she had spent some of the most worried nights of her life was now empty, stripped of even the most basic personal belongings. Leaving here, she would leave not a trace of herself.

She shut her suitcases and fastened them, then glanced at her lapel watch. It was time to go, time to begin the next phase of her life. Morgan was sending a carriage for her and she wanted to be ready when it came.

Just as she stepped out into the hallway with her suitcases, Nola, leaving for work, came down the steps. "Oh, my, aren't you looking chipper this morning!" Her gaze went to the suitcases. "You're leaving? Did you find work, then?"

Oriel hesitated. What would Nola think of her strange bargain with Morgan Drummond? Quickly she juggled the facts. "Well, yes, in a way. I'm going to Ireland."

"*Ireland!* Oh, my! That's a long way off. I hope they're paying you well. What kind of work will you be doing?"

Realizing Nola assumed she'd secured a job, Oriel replied, "A sort of companion."

"Well, I do wish you luck, dearie. I was getting worried about you—looking so long and hard with nothing turning up."

"Thank you. That was very kind of you."

"Well, is there anything I can do for you? Here, let me take one of them bags." They started down the stairs together.

Nola's sincerity touched Oriel. She suddenly realized Nola was the only person in London that knew her or cared the slightest bit about what happened to her. When they came down into the entry hall, Nola put her finger to her lips, winking at Oriel as they slipped by their landlady's door. Once outside, she set down the suitcase and adjusted her hat, saying, "I've got to be on my way or I'll be late for work, and old Snyder, my boss, don't like that one bit. You sure there's nothing I can do? Maybe you could give me your address, just in case it don't work out or you get some mail?"

Oriel considered that. Even at this late date, Mrs. McPhail *might* come through with the check and letter of reference. Since she'd given the clerk at the Claridge this address, it would be sent here.

"Oh, would you? That would be very kind. I am rather expecting a letter—from my last employer. It would have my last month's wages in it as well." Nola, a working girl herself, would certainly understand the importance of such a letter.

Addresses exchanged, Nola started down the steps. Halfway she stopped, then ran back up and gave Oriel a hug. "Good luck, dearie, and the Lord bless!" she said. Then with a wave, she hurried back down the steps and along the street toward the bus stop.

Oriel, looking after her, felt quick tears. Why this impulsive gesture by someone she had known only a few weeks? Had Nola seen some vulnerability in her, some of the anxiety in her eyes? Whatever the reason, Nola's show of concern warmed her heart.

A few minutes later, the splendid carriage Morgan had hired to pick her up arrived. Oriel was glad Nola wasn't there to see it. She surely might have drawn the wrong conclusions about Oriel's job as a companion. With a mixture of apprehension and excitement, Oriel got into the carriage. It started off, carrying her inexorably to her destiny.

9

The Steamer Donnegal, en route from Liverpool to Dublin

April 1895

*I*t was with an eerie sense of déjà vu that Oriel again stood in swirling fog at the ship's rail. This time it was on the steamer *Donnegal* departing for Ireland. She nestled her chin into the mink collar of the short black Persian lamb cape, relishing its warmth. Morgan had given it to her after they left the Registry Office. As she opened the box from the famous furrier, he had said offhandedly, "Irish weather is miserable."

The wedding gift was as practical and unsentimental as the civil ceremony itself had been. Oriel had not expected to feel emotional about it, so she had not been prepared for her own reaction. In the short time since she had signed the agreement, she had been reassuring herself that it was simply a contract and *not* a real marriage. Yet, when the moment came to give her responses, she had felt dizzy. She had always regarded marriage as a sacred step taken by two deeply committed people. To regard it as a temporary contract suddenly seemed wrong.

As she hesitated, Oriel had looked at Morgan, wondering what he was feeling. Was he thinking of another ceremony, another bride? Conscious that both the magistrate and Morgan were staring at her, she had breathlessly responded, "Yes, I will."

Then it was over.

From the Registry Office, they had gone to collect Morgan's luggage at the Claridge. They had had a quiet lunch before catching the train to Liverpool. On the train, Morgan had read the *Times* while Oriel gazed out at the passing landscape, trying not to dwell on the strange circumstances.

In Liverpool, they had boarded the overnight boat to Dublin. Upon boarding, Oriel had been shown to her small but nicely appointed single cabin. She wondered if the steward thought it strange that the Drummonds had separate accommodations.

She had come back up on deck, where she now stood in the fog. Within a few minutes, Morgan joined her at the rail. The salt-scented air and thin mist brought back Oriel's vivid memory of their first encounter on board the ocean liner *Mesalina*. At that time, she could never have imagined the strange turn of events that had brought them to this moment.

Watching the lights of Liverpool recede as the boat slid into the sea, neither of them spoke. Eventually Morgan said, "Good night," and went below.

When the steamer docked the next morning, Morgan and Oriel were met by a coachman in a dark green uniform trimmed with gilt braid. He greeted Morgan respectfully and led the way to a handsome black carriage with bronze trim hitched to two coal-black horses. The interior was lined and cushioned with a velvety plush. This, Oriel thought, was the kind of comfort the rich took for granted. After her days of riding rickety trolleys, omnibuses, and other plebeian means of transportation, traveling in style might be very easy to get used to—maybe too easy.

After their luggage was loaded, they rolled through the city streets and out into the surrounding countryside. At first, Oriel was too busy looking out the window to note that Morgan had slipped into a moody silence. When he failed to respond to several of her comments, she observed that he was slumped in one corner, his chin resting on his doubled fist, elbow propped on the ledge, staring morosely out the window on his side of the carriage.

Was this his reaction to returning to Ireland? Was it *that* depressing to him? Of course, Oriel realized he was not with the companion of his choice. He had hoped to be bringing Edwina here as his bride. Oriel felt that tact was appropriate and after that was silent. Soon the rocking motion of the carriage made her drowsy and she drifted off to sleep.

She awoke with a jerk at a sudden jolting of the carriage wheels. Peering out the window, Oriel saw dark clouds overhead. Strong, gusty winds blew against the swaying carriage. They were no longer traveling on the main road but had turned off onto a rutted narrow one. Oriel turned toward Morgan, who evidently anticipated her question.

"We're almost there," he said. "Another twenty minutes or so and we'll be in the village of Kilmara. Then it's only a short distance to Drummond Castle." His voice held an edge. His expression was unreadable, and Oriel was left to interpret it on her own. Was Morgan already regretting their arrangement?

As for herself, Oriel had mixed feelings at their approach to Drummond Castle, the place where she would be spending the next year of her life. She determined to make the best of things.

When Morgan spoke again, it was to say, "There it is, straight ahead."

Oriel would never forget her first sight of the castle. On the crest of the hillside stood a majestic stone structure silhouetted against the purple-gray sky. It was so amazingly like every castle Oriel had ever imagined that she almost expected to see a moat and hear the creaking of chains as a drawbridge was let down for them to cross and armored knights rode out to greet them.

Nothing so dramatic happened, however. In another few minutes, they rumbled through scrolled iron gates and up the long, curving driveway.

As the carriage came to a stop, Morgan announced, "Well, here we are. Drummond Castle."

The massive carved front door opened and two men hurried down the stone steps. One opened the door while the other, a bald, dour-faced fellow wearing a dark coat, bowed formally. "Good evening, sir."

"Good evening, Finnegan. May I present Mrs. Drummond."

"Madam." Finnegan extended his hand to assist Oriel out of the carriage. As she stepped down, he spoke words Oriel could not understand, *"Cead mai failte."*

Morgan placed his hand under her elbow and they mounted the steps leading into the house. Curious, Oriel whispered, "What did he say?"

"It was a traditional Gaelic welcome. We are wished a long and happy life together here."

Oriel did not miss the hint of irony in his voice. Ironic, indeed. Their agreement was for only a year, and happiness? Happiness was not in the bargain she had made with Morgan Drummond.

Escorted by Finnegan, they walked through a massive carved door into the vast front hall. Tapestries hung from the vaulted ceiling and suits of armor stood in shadowed alcoves.

"May I introduce Mrs. Nesbitt," Finnegan said with obvious deference in his tone. Oriel knew the housekeeper was always next to the butler in the pecking order of household staff.

At Oriel's greeting, the woman inclined her head but did not extend her hand nor curtsey. Instead, she met Oriel's friendly smile with a chilling reserve.

The housekeeper's appearance was formidable. Her iron-gray hair was pulled back severely from a face with a prominent nose and narrow mouth. Her extreme pallor emphasized the brilliance of her small dark eyes, which regarded Oriel with suspicion. Perhaps it was only natural for someone who had been in charge to be wary, even suspicious, of a new mistress, Oriel decided. Then a second thought struck. Did Mrs. Nesbitt expect someone else—Edwina Parker, perhaps? There had probably been a picture of her in the society papers when the engagement was announced. Maybe the change of plans had not been made known to the staff.

Oriel thrust those questions aside and moved on to face the curious eyes of the stout, red-faced cook, Mrs. Mills, then the two rosy-cheeked maids, Molly and Carleen, and the two footmen, Conan and William.

These formalities over, Morgan said to Oriel, "Since it's been a long day, you must be weary from travel. I suggest we both make it an early night." He then said a few words to the housekeeper and turned again to Oriel. "Mrs. Nesbitt will show you to your room and have a supper tray brought up to you."

Before Oriel could respond, Morgan turned abruptly and walked away, leaving her standing in the great hall alone. Although she had not prepared herself for what to expect when they reached the castle, it was a shock to be left so completely on her own.

"Mrs. Drummond . . ." The housekeeper's use of her unfamiliar title brought Oriel sharply back to attention. "If you'll come this way." Mrs. Nesbitt gestured toward the shadowy staircase.

Oriel nodded. Conscious of being under the servants' surveillance, she followed the thin figure to the stairway. She wondered if the servants thought it unusual that the newlyweds were not sharing the master suite, then reminded herself that household staff in such manor houses as this one simply accepted the way of the gentry even if they did think them strange.

Oriel had to hurry to keep up with the housekeeper's swift pace up the winding steps. Reaching the top, she moved along a dark, drafty corridor to the end, where Mrs. Nesbitt opened a door.

Oriel stepped into a huge bedroom, dominated by a poster bed canopied in heavy damask. In a windowed alcove was a dressing table and a chaise lounge. Two wing chairs were placed on either side of the fireplace, where a fire had been laid but not yet lit. The room felt cold and had a damp, unused smell. Involuntarily, Oriel shivered.

"I'll send Molly up to get the fire started, ma'am," Mrs. Nesbitt said. "We weren't sure what time you'd get here. Didn't want to burn a fire for nothing." She moved to the door, saying, "I'll send up a tray for you, ma'am. If you need anything else, just ring." She pointed toward the tapestry bell pull by the massive stone fireplace.

As the door closed behind the housekeeper, Oriel stood in the middle of the room looking about her. Rubbing her arms to warm herself, she walked over to the windows. The wind moaned and she shivered again.

Edwina Parker's words as quoted by Morgan echoed in her mind: "What? Stay in a drafty old castle in an isolated village through a wretched Irish winter? You must be out of your mind!"

Just then, a gust of wind blew open one of the windows, crashing it against the outside wall. Startled, Oriel ran over to drag it shut. An icy blast of cold air swept over her.

Shuddering, Oriel wondered if Edwina had been right. Was it *she,* Oriel Banning, who had been out of her mind to agree to stay a year at Drummond Castle?

10

$\mathcal{A}$lthough tired from all the traveling and tension, Oriel did not sleep well her first night at Drummond Castle. Her room was cavernous, filled with grotesque shadows cast onto the walls from the firelight. The storm that had threatened for the last few hours of their journey finally broke. The wind whistled down the chimney, sending sparks flying from the fireplace. Rain pounded on the slate roof with a staccato clattering sound. A clap of thunder rattled the windows. Oriel sat up in bed, clutching the covers. After that, it seemed hours before she could settle into a sound sleep. The last thing Oriel heard before drifting off was the pelting of rain against the windows.

What next woke her Oriel wasn't sure, nor was she sure how long she had been asleep. A murky, gray light filtered in between the folds of the draperies Oriel had drawn across the windows before she went to bed. The fire had gone out, and the room felt chilly and damp. As Oriel came fully awake, she heard a persistent clicking noise. One of the latches must have come loose. She threw aside the satin-covered quilt, got gingerly out of bed, and ran in her bare feet over to shut the casement.

Pushing aside the curtain, she reached out for the handle when she saw something. Just below, a hooded figure moved rapidly through the mist, a cape billowing behind it like a huge sail. The form seemed to glide across the grounds before disappearing at the stone wall. The morning fog hid what lay beyond the wall. Who or what was it? Could it be some kind of optical illusion of fog and gray dawn light? It had passed so swiftly Oriel wasn't even sure she'd actually seen it. She closed the window and fastened it. Hurrying back to bed, she dove under the quilt and burrowed her head in the pillows.

Some time later, she woke to the sound of crackling wood as a fire was being lit. Oriel sat up and saw Molly, the maid, sitting on her heels on the hearth, using a hand bellows to get the blaze going.

Hearing the movement behind her, Molly turned and gave Oriel a smile. "Good morning, ma'am. I brought up your tea. Will you have it in bed or would you like to sit in front of the fireplace?"

"I'll get up. Thank you."

Being waited on was such a novel experience, Oriel could only wonder what the maid would think if she knew what her situation had been only a few days ago.

As she took her first sip of the hearty tea and buttered a slice of soda bread, Oriel remembered what she had seen from her window earlier. In the light of day, with a snapping fire brightening the room and the solid presence of the cheerful maid, the eerie sight seemed unreal. Had it been simply her own sleepy state, a fragment of a dream? Last night she had been exhausted from her travels and the tension of her new role. She could have imagined it.

Finishing her breakfast, Oriel went to the window and looked out. The storm's wind that had blown rain against the windows and wakened her during the restless night had stopped. The sky showed signs of turning blue, and the soft green of the hills emerged in the distance. As Oriel stood there, she saw in the distance the outline of a building.

"Come here for a minute, Molly," Oriel called over her shoulder. "What is that building?"

"Which one, ma'am?" Molly came over to stand behind her.

"Over there." She pointed.

"Oh, that's just a pile of rubble, ma'am—what's left of an old monastery from many years ago."

"It looks interesting. Is there no one there anymore?"

"Oh, no, ma'am, for sure." There was a tiny pause before the girl said, "But some folks say . . ."

Whatever Molly was about to add was interrupted by a sharp rap on the bedroom door. It was Mrs. Nesbitt, the housekeeper. She gave Molly a pointed look, and the maid hurried out.

"Good morning, Mrs. Drummond."

Oriel cloaked her sense of surprise at being so addressed. "Good morning, Mrs. Nesbitt. Won't you sit down?"

"No, thank you, madam." Mrs. Nesbitt drew herself up coldly, as if Oriel had crossed some invisible threshold of proper decorum. "I just came to inquire if you want the cook to come up to discuss the menu or if you would prefer I do it?"

Feeling rebuffed by the housekeeper's condescending tone of voice, Oriel said quickly, "Oh, I think it best for you to carry on as usual, Mrs. Nesbitt—until I'm more settled."

The housekeeper gave a curt nod and departed, leaving Oriel feeling somewhat unnerved. It was almost as if Mrs. Nesbitt was trying to intimidate her. No, that was foolish, Oriel told herself. It would take time to establish herself with the staff. The housekeeper and Finnegan had been running the household without supervision for several years. The staff was probably apprehensive about how things were going to be with a new mistress.

In the meantime, Oriel had plenty to do. She spent most of the day unpacking, and with Molly's help, got her wardrobe sorted and hung in the huge armoire. She could tell the maid was impressed by her clothes, not knowing most of them were secondhand items.

Once during the afternoon, Oriel looked out her window and saw Morgan stride out across the stone terrace and push through the wrought-iron gate in the stone wall at the end of the wide lawn. "Where does that lead to?" Oriel asked Molly, pointing in the direction Morgan had disappeared.

Molly peered over her shoulder. "Oh, that's the path down to the beach, ma'am. It goes along the cliffs and down to the cove."

Oriel said nothing more, but made a mental note of it. She would like to explore all the surroundings of Drummond Castle in time. Before Molly left again, she told Oriel dinner would be at seven.

At five minutes to seven, Oriel went downstairs. She wore a dress Neecy had considered too plain, a simply cut blue velvet, with a deep neckline and long tapered sleeves. Morgan was just crossing the wide hall. He greeted Oriel rather absently, and they entered the dining room together. His expression was much the same as it had been last evening upon their arrival. Oriel was determined to ignore Morgan's moodiness and make the dinner hour as pleasant as possible.

The huge dining room was lighted by candles in wall sconces, a wrought-iron chandelier, and flickering tapers in a branched silver candelabra on the long table. Several dark tapestries depicting hunting scenes hung on the walls and over the huge fireplace at the far end of the room.

"Good evening, madam," Finnegan greeted her as he drew back a high-backed, richly carved chair for her. Morgan seated himself at the other end. It was only then Oriel noticed a third place was set.

Surprised, she remarked, "I didn't know we were expecting a dinner guest."

Morgan lifted his head and glanced at the other place setting. A fierce frown drew his heavy brows together. "We're not." Motioning to the footman standing at the sideboard, he ordered, "Take that away."

The footman looked startled. He turned beet red and glanced at Finnegan, who was overseeing the serving. Tension crackled in the air. Oriel felt it, but did not understand what had caused it. For a full minute, Finnegan did not move, nor did the footman.

Then Morgan banged his fist on the table and roared, "I said take that plate away. I don't want to see that done again, do you hear?"

The anger in his voice set Oriel's heart pounding.

Finnegan gave an imperceptible nod to Conan the footman, who moved forward quickly, swept up the setting, and left the room with it.

Soon the footman came back and began to serve the meal. After such an upsetting scene, Oriel found she had little appetite. She expected some sort of apology or explanation for the outburst, but none was forthcoming. Morgan made no effort to engage in conversation during the rest of dinner. Course after course was brought and removed, hardly touched.

Not wishing to offend the cook, Oriel took a few bites of the dessert pudding, then placed her spoon on the plate. She folded her hands in her lap, awaiting the signal from Morgan that he was finished and Oriel could excuse herself. Oriel longed to escape to the privacy of her room. Her first dinner at Drummond Castle had been completely ruined.

At length, Morgan drained his glass and stood. They left the dining room together. In the hall, he said a brief "Good night," turned on his heel, and walked down the hall to his own suite.

That was it. He was making it clear that as far as he was concerned, their marriage was an arrangement that needed neither courtesy nor accommodation to social amenities. Oriel mounted the broad stairway and went slowly down the shadowy corridor to her bedroom. The scene at dinner had been deeply disturbing.

75

Since their arrival in Ireland, Morgan Drummond had undergone a significant change. Gone was the sophisticated man Oriel had thought attractive, interesting, and intelligent. This moody, morose, rageful man who had taken his place was a frightening stranger. It was obvious he was desperately unhappy—not only about being in Ireland and at Drummond Castle—but also about being with the wrong woman.

When Molly came to turn down the bed, Oriel noticed the maid seemed more subdued than she had in the morning. Oriel presumed all the servants had heard about the uproar at the dinner table. Whatever was going on, the household servants knew. Oriel decided to ask Molly about the third place setting.

Given the opening, Molly was more than anxious to tell her the story behind the ruckus. It seemed, like many old houses, Drummond Castle had a legend.

"'Tis a story I've heard ever since I was a wee child," Molly began. "My own granny swears it's true and that once, as a little girl, she saw Shaleen herself!"

"Shaleen who?"

"Shaleen O'Connor, ma'am." Molly's eyes widened at her ignorance. "'Tis said she walks along the beach looking for lost ships and comes up to check the castle gates at night to see that they're not locked."

"I don't think I understand."

"Well, ma'am, if you like, I'll tell you about it." Molly warmed to her task of enlightening Oriel. "In the days of Queen Elizabeth when the English were fighting for lordship of the seas and battling the threat of the Spanish Armada, Shaleen O'Connor was a legendary pirate queen. The O'Connors were a powerful tribe, and Shaleen was the undisputed mistress of the many hundred islands and inlets about the bay. Her fame spread to London and to the court itself, where she was received by the queen. The queen welcomed her since Shaleen's band had destroyed many of the Spanish ships and plundered others shipwrecked on the treacherous Irish coast.

"However, on Shaleen's return trip to Ireland, her ship ran short of supplies and put into the harbor just below the land of Drummond Castle. In those days, this house and land were owned by Sir Tristam Lawrence. While Shaleen's men were stowing provisions on board, she knocked at the gates of the castle seeking hospitality.

"'Tis said the family was at dinner and she was refused admittance. This put Shaleen into a fury, and later she kidnapped the infant son and heir of the master and sailed off with him. Legend has it that part of the ransom paid for the child was the sworn agreement that the gates of the castle would always remain open and a place at the table always be set for the head of the O'Connor clan.

"And that was always done, ma'am, even up to the time the last of the Lawrence family left here, before Mr. Drummond's grandfather bought the castle," Molly said in a whispery voice. "Terrible things would happen if it wasn't done—at least, that's what people always said."

In spite of herself, Oriel shivered.

"Begging your pardon, ma'am, but if I was you and had any influence over the master, I'd persuade him to continue the practice of setting a place for Shaleen."

"Mr. Drummond must know about this legend, doesn't he?"

Molly pursed her mouth thoughtfully before answering. "Well, ma'am, Mr. Drummond's only been here twice before this. He stayed at the hotel in town the last time, come up here during the day to check out everything and make sure provisions were ordered, the wine cellar filled, and the beds made fresh."

Molly hesitated. "It's common talk in the village he don't care for Ireland nor living here at the castle." Molly gave her head a little toss. "Perhaps that's why he dislikes our traditions as well."

Something warned Oriel she had best drop the subject at this point. Did Molly know the only reason Morgan was here now was to insure his inheritance? While she had no intention of discussing the matter further, it bothered Oriel that she sensed a real resentment in Molly for Morgan. Did the rest of the staff feel the same way? If they believed what Molly had reported, that he had no love for the land or the country, it could mean nothing but trouble during this year.

Was accepting Morgan Drummond's bargain the worst mistake Oriel had ever made?

11

$\mathcal{B}$y the time Oriel had been at Drummond Castle a full week, she had reached the conclusion that her time here would be solitary indeed if she depended on Morgan for company. After a week of days left to her own devices, silent dinners, and long evenings alone, that had become clear. But then, what had she expected—for Morgan to see that she was constantly occupied and amused? Oriel had learned early in life to make the best of whatever circumstances in which she found herself. She would do the same here. What this year was like would be up to her.

This part of Ireland was beautiful, as she had already discovered. Although the spring weather had been stormy, signs of life and growth were everywhere. The terraced lawns were a rich velvety green, with trees and shrubs in various shades of emerald and jade. Giant rhododendron bushes lined the driveway with heavy blooms of rich pink, magenta, and purple.

So far, Oriel had only explored the castle grounds, but she had every intention of venturing farther. She had thought that would be something she and Morgan could enjoy together. After the strange incident at dinner her second night at Drummond Castle, however, she realized Morgan did not share her enthusiasm for the land.

One morning of her second week at Drummond Castle, Oriel went to her bedroom window to check the weather. For the first time, the heavy mist did not obscure her view. It would be a good day to take a walk to the cliffs, see the ocean. Just then something caught her attention—a small stone building with a pointed roof just beyond the terraced hedge of the gardens.

Oriel was eager to explore the sea, the cliffs, the lush green countryside, and the quaint little town of Kilmara. She would have to investigate the intriguing little building too.

She ate breakfast, then dressed in a tweed walking skirt and sturdy boots before going downstairs. Carleen, the other maid, was dusting, and Oriel stopped to ask, "How far is it to the village?"

"About three miles, ma'am."

"An easy walk, then?"

The girl's bright eyes widened in surprise. "Sure—that is if you're used to walking."

"Oh, I'm used to walking." Oriel smiled, remembering the miles of city streets she had walked in her job search in London.

Oriel was at the door when Carleen's voice halted her. "Shall I tell the cook you'll be back for luncheon?"

Oriel paused. Why should she hurry back to another meal eaten alone or opposite a glum Morgan. "No, Carleen, I won't be back until tea." She said good-bye and left the house.

Oriel walked down the drive, stopping here and there to examine a clump of white narcissus coming into bloom or touch the delicate petals of pink and lavender wood violets half-hidden under the trees. As she straightened up and began walking again, she noticed a ruddy-faced gardener, a short distance away. He had been observing her with some curiosity. "Good morning," she called, waving. "The flowers are lovely!"

He looked startled.

"I'm Mrs. Drummond," Oriel said, and the name sounded odd and unfamiliar even to her. "The new mistress here."

The man quickly took off his cap, mumbled, "Patrick's me name, ma'am," then head averted, he moved away.

Oriel stood there for a moment feeling rebuffed. Then, with a slight shrug, she walked on. The gardener was probably just shy or maybe just not used to American informality. It would take time for the people at Drummond Castle to warm up to her.

When she got to the wrought-iron gates, Oriel recalled the legend of Shaleen O'Connor, and as she pushed through the gates, she wondered if they were always kept unlocked—in spite of Morgan's violent objection. Was there someone at Drummond Castle who dared not risk the disaster promised if the gates were locked? They clanged behind her and she stood for a minute wondering which way to go. Then, spotting a path that looked well-worn at the edge of the road, she took that.

The path wound downward and crossed over a small curved stone bridge. Soon, Oriel found herself on the edge of the town of Kilmara. Kilmara looked picturesque and serene, a place far removed from the dense, crowded city of London with all its filth and noise. Of course, Oriel had no idea what lay beneath the placid surface of this little town. Proceeding slowly, she passed clusters of small houses with thatched roofs. Children at play stopped to stare at her, shyly returning her smile; women came to their doorways and watched her curiously. Some nodded, but a few turned their heads or frowned. Oriel had planned to stroll along the winding cobbled streets, perhaps stop at some cozy tearoom. However, she became aware of an indefinable tension.

Women holding shopping baskets and chatting on a corner turned away suddenly as she approached; others ducked quickly into a nearby store. Upon opening the door of the general store, Oriel saw something in the face of the man behind the counter that caused her to hesitate. She turned around and left the shop. Her sense of discomfort was strong, so Oriel quickened her pace and was soon out of the village, heading back to the castle.

Was Kilmara an unfriendly place, unwelcoming to strangers? Oriel remembered what Molly had told her, how the people were offended by Morgan's attitude. Knowing *she* was from the castle, were they including her in their resentment?

Oriel turned all this over in her mind as she walked. If something wasn't done, this kind of hostility would take all the pleasure out of her time at Drummond Castle. She didn't want to be a prisoner there. She must find her own place in Kilmara, show people she wasn't like Morgan. Realizing it was still quite early to return to the castle, Oriel slowed her steps. Then she remembered the ruins of the old monastery she had seen from her bedroom. Maybe this would be a good time to find it.

At the top of the hill, she saw a line of arching trees that led to the ruins, forming a cathedral-like ceiling. The wind moved through the trees above her, and her footsteps slowed as if she were approaching a sacred spot.

Oriel knew most of these ancient monasteries had been thriving hubs of activity in the past—housing busy monks who provided food and shelter for the poor, cared for the sick, and chanted prayers and praise to the glory of God. A pervasive, mysterious quality hovered over the ruined abbey. Almost overwhelmed by the sensation, Oriel turned to go, but something caught her attention.

A blurred figure came toward her through the broken arches. Instinctively, she drew back. Her heart jumped. Remembering the hooded figure she had seen from her window in the eerie dawn, her first thought was that she was observing a monastic ghost. Then, realizing that was silly, she stood still. Slowly, fear gave way to relief. She let out the breath she had been holding.

As the figure approached, she saw it was not the ghost of a monk, but a live man. His jacket, with its wide collar turned up, and his brown corduroy hiking outfit had given her the impression of a monk's garb.

A few feet away, the man stopped and raised a hand in a friendly wave. As he came closer, she saw he had a wide smile, very blue eyes in a sunburned face, and a thatch of brown windblown hair. "Ah, a kindred spirit!" he called. "You must love old haunted places too." He smiled. "I'm Bryan Moore."

"I'm Oriel Ban—" she started to say, then quickly corrected herself, "Oriel Drummond."

He looked at her with interest and amusement. "Ah, then I believe we must be neighbors. I rent a cottage just this side of Drummond Castle." He paused. "You've just arrived then? There was no one living at the castle when I first came and I haven't seen anyone about. I would have. I roam these hills and the cliffs above the ocean daily."

"We've been here a little over a week."

"We?"

"My husband, Morgan Drummond, and I."

He nodded. "Yes, I heard he was coming." He smiled again. "Village gossip. You'll find little goes on here that isn't discussed, mulled over, and given opinions about. I've been here before, you see. Every so often, I rent a cottage for a few months at a time. This time I'll be here for a year."

"I'll be here for a year too," Oriel said without thinking. Immediately she was sorry she'd blurted that out. What would Bryan Moore make of that? He hadn't *seemed* to mark it with any special significance. He was gazing about the ruins.

"What stories these rocks would tell if they could speak, right? I'm very keen on history—exploring and digging for the bits and pieces historians sometimes overlook, the human drama. Ireland is a wealth of such stories."

The late spring wind stirring the trees overhead became sharper, colder. Oriel began to feel somewhat awkward, standing in this lonely spot with a stranger. "Well, I must be on my way," she said and turned to retrace her steps.

"Wait, I'll go along with you. I'm headed for the village to lunch at the Shamrock. I go there at least twice a week to buy a *Times* and catch up on local news. You never know what you'll hear or learn. Otherwise I might find myself getting a bit daft living alone."

He lives alone, then, Oriel mused. *What is an attractive man in the prime of life doing in this isolated coastal Irish village, renting a cottage for a year?*

As they fell into step, Bryan answered her unspoken question. "Writing is a solitary business. A poet's life demands times of absolute aloneness, but the social part of my nature demands that I get out and about regularly."

They had reached the bottom of the path and were standing on the road again.

"Well, Mrs. Drummond, it's been delightful to meet you— one of those rare chances that gives life unexpected moments of pleasure." Bryan Moore gave her a little salute and started walking in the direction of the village.

A few steps farther, he turned. "Do give my regards to Mr. Drummond," he called with a slight smile. Then he continued down the road.

Oriel watched him for a minute longer, wondering if he knew Morgan. There was something in the way he had spoken that made her curious. She would have to mention meeting him to Morgan.

12

*B*efore she had the opportunity to bring up the subject of Bryan Moore that evening at dinner, Morgan announced that he was thinking of going up to Dublin for a few weeks. He would be looking at some horses, he told her.

Morgan glanced at Oriel to see her reaction to his statement, but her expression revealed nothing. He shifted uneasily in his chair, discomfited by her silence. "I thought I'd look for a good riding horse for you." He paused. "You do ride, don't you?"

He was rewarded by how her eyes brightened and by a smile that transformed her face.

"Yes, I do! And I'd very much enjoy having a horse to ride."

"Good! I'll see to it then," Morgan said, satisfied that his afterthought had given her such pleasure.

He'd not done much for Oriel since their arrival, and he'd been feeling somewhat guilty about her. Not that he should. After all, Oriel was a smart woman. She had accepted their arrangement when it was offered, must have considered what it meant.

However, to be truthful, neither of them had *really* known what this year would be like, nor what its outcome would be either.

At first, the thought of several weeks alone at the castle was daunting to Oriel. But then, what real difference would it make if Morgan were gone? So far he had kept to his own rooms and library, gone on solitary walks around the estate. In a way, it might be a relief to have him gone—better than having to force polite conversation as they did in the presence of the servants. The truth was their dinner hours were becoming more and more a strain.

The following morning, Oriel came downstairs and found Morgan standing at the front door, his suitcases piled in the hall. Oriel was not too disturbed at his departure. She wished him good-bye and good luck selecting the horses and went on into the dining room to have her breakfast.

Oriel considered that with Morgan gone this might be a good time to make her presence felt by the household staff. She felt sure the staff was puzzled by the relationship between her and Morgan. Still, since she was to be mistress here, if only for the year, it was important for her to assume the traditional role.

First, she would make a complete tour of the house, something she had been hesitant to do before. She felt awkward about opening the many doors that lined the great hall, thinking she should ask Morgan about them. Now it dawned on her, that as Morgan's *wife*, she could open any door she chose.

Oriel knew it was important to get to know the cook, to let Mrs. Mills know she was interested in how she ran her establishment. If meals were to be well cooked and presented with style, it was necessary to recognize that in the kitchen the cook reigned as queen. After finishing her breakfast, Oriel decided to begin her tour at the kitchen.

The kitchen at Drummond Castle was much more modern than Oriel had thought it might be. Morgan's grandfather, coming from his American mansion, must have made that a priority when he started restoring the place. There was a large cast-iron range, and its jet-black shine told Oriel the cook took great pride in her main working tool. In the center of the room was a rectangular wooden table, its surface scrubbed almost white. There was a sandstone sink with running water. Hanging from racks were copper pans, skillets, and pots of all sizes. Against one wall was a tall pine hutch with rows of pottery bowls, mugs, and platters. On one side off the kitchen was the scullery, where vegetables brought in from the garden were washed and prepared. A door on the other side led into the pantry, Finnegan's realm, where the fine china and silver were kept.

At first Mrs. Mills greeted Oriel warily, as though skeptical of why the lady of the house had come into *her* territory. Little by little, under Oriel's tactful questioning, the cook let down her reserve and recited her complaints.

"'Tis not much reward cookin' for them that don't enjoy their food. I never get so much as a word one way or t' other from t' master. I don't know what he likes or what he don't." She shrugged.

Oriel gave her a sympathetic smile. "That is hard, I'm sure, Mrs. Mills. I hope to change all that. I like simple food, but well cooked. You do a fine job with the local produce and the game and meat available here. There is a kitchen garden, isn't there?"

"Indeed there is, madam." Mrs. Mills launched into a description of some of the tasty dishes she liked to concoct with the vegetables grown on the property.

Warming to her subject, Mrs. Mills continued, "And there's no entertainin' whatsoever. I am a light hand with pastry, madam, and no one ever bested me on pudding or trifle."

"Perhaps we'll have occasion to put those skills to use," Oriel said warmly.

When Oriel left, the cook was all smiles, proof that a good rapport had been achieved.

Oriel mounted the broad staircase to the upper floor. So far she had not explored any of the other wings. Upstairs, a web of corridors fanned out from the broad stairway into wings consisting of six large bedroom suites. At the end of one wing was a room for the lady's maid to attend to the wardrobe of the mistress. It contained a pressing closet, an ironing board, and cabinets stocked with everything needed to keep the clothes cleaned, mended, and in order.

At the end of another corridor, the one to the right of the top of the steps, a door opened onto a balcony that overlooked the downstairs ballroom. Oriel knew from her historical reading that this was called the minstrels' gallery, the place where the musicians who played for the dancing that took place below were seated.

There was still another door within the minstrels' gallery, and Oriel cautiously opened it and peered in. Portraits heavily framed in gold lined the walls. Oriel stepped inside, looking about her. She circled the room slowly, stopping every so often to study individual pictures. There were soldiers in uniform, rows of medals on their chests, swords at their hips. The women were all quite elegant. Their gowns, painted with exquisite detail, were of lush velvet and shimmering satin. Standing in front of a particularly lovely lady's portrait, Oriel wondered if this might be the unfortunate young woman whose baby was kidnapped by Shaleen O'Connor.

Slowly an eerie shiver ran down Oriel's spine. All at once, she felt claustrophobic. The room felt cold, heavy with the weight of time and people who had lived in centuries past. Suddenly she was anxious to get out, to escape. She spun around and hurried to the door, pushing on the carved metal handle.

It wouldn't budge; the door wouldn't open. It was stuck—or locked. Oriel began to breathe hard. This was silly. Could it have latched behind her? Frantically, she pushed on it. After pressing hard on it, Oriel was finally able to push the door open and stumble through the minstrels' gallery out into the hall.

Just then, she saw the formidable figure of Mrs. Nesbitt approaching, her keys rattling at her waist. Upon seeing Oriel, the housekeeper stopped short. Looking both surprised and annoyed, she asked coldly, "May I help you, madam?" She regarded Oriel suspiciously, as if she were an unwelcome intruder, someone who had no business roaming around the house.

For a split second, Oriel felt intimidated. Did Mrs. Nesbitt suspect that her position here was temporary? In the mysterious way of servants, did she know the truth about her agreement with Morgan? Whatever the facts were, Oriel knew this was a critical moment, one that could go either way. Either she or the housekeeper would be the victor. It was important for the rest of her time at Drummond Castle that she be in control. The other servants' attitudes toward her depended on the housekeeper's. Oriel had learned in various situations to use tact. She decided to choose that now.

She smiled and said, "Good morning, Mrs. Nesbitt. I've just been acquainting myself with the house. It must be difficult to keep a large place in such fine order."

Mrs. Nesbitt ignored the obvious compliment. A muscle in her thin cheek moved slightly, but she did not respond.

Oriel rushed in to fill the awkward pause. Gesturing to the door, she said, "I have just discovered the minstrels' gallery."

"Viewing the family portraits, were you?"

Oriel stepped back inside. "Yes. I found them absolutely fascinating. I had no idea there were so many Drummond ancestors."

"They're *not* Drummonds," Mrs. Nesbitt said sharply, following Oriel into the portrait room. "They're of the Lawrence family. It was they who built this castle." Mrs. Nesbitt came in and stood behind Oriel. "They were a fine, honorable family, the Lawrences, with a proud heritage. They fought for their land, their faith, their honor." She moved along the line of paintings. "This has not always been Drummond Castle."

Mrs. Nesbitt stopped in front of the portrait Oriel had earlier admired. "Lady Lavinia Lawrence," she said softly, almost tenderly. "Now there was a *real* lady. In spite of all she had to endure, she put family first. It was her children who inherited this castle after her husband was betrayed and murdered." Mrs. Nesbitt spoke as if the eighteenth century event had happened only yesterday. "He had sent her away out of danger. But she came back and brought her children to live here in this castle—just as they were meant to do." Mrs. Nesbitt shook her head sadly. Oriel had not thought the housekeeper capable of such deep emotion. "She died of a broken heart . . ." The woman's stern expression relaxed. There was a noticeable softening of the straight-lipped mouth.

"This is certainly an interesting house with quite a history," Oriel said. She was about to broach the subject of the Shaleen O'Connor legend when Mrs. Nesbitt suddenly turned and walked swiftly away, seeming to disappear into the shadows of the far wing.

Oriel looked after her, bewildered by the abrupt end to their conversation. The woman was certainly caught up in the history of this place, as if it were her own. Oriel hoped by showing her interest, she had made a good impression on the housekeeper.

That night, for the first time since coming to Drummond Castle, Oriel slept through the night without once waking up. She knew her efforts had been worth it. She had taken a first step toward making a place for herself at Drummond Castle. The maids, the footmen, and even Finnegan now seemed willing to accept her as mistress. All the servants accepted her—except Mrs. Nesbitt. That lady would need a great deal more winning over.

13

With Morgan away, the castle felt larger and gloomier. Not that he provided much companionship, but there was some comfort in knowing he was there. For the past few weeks there had been rain, and Oriel had become restless, longing to get out to walk. She was happy to see that the morning looked clear. Possibly the sun would break through the mist and it would be a fair day—a good day to take the cliff path overlooking the ocean.

After breakfast, Oriel noted the clear weather and eagerly left the house. As she started out, she remembered the small stone building she'd been curious about and decided this would be a good time to find it and figure out what it was. She went out through the garden looking for it, turning into several paths that simply circled into an intricate bordered design. Had she mistaken its position?

She halted, looked up at the house to locate her bedroom window and the angle from which she had noticed the little structure. Following that line of direction, she passed through a twist of hedges. She came upon it suddenly, the stone structure almost obscured by a heavy growth of ivy vines. Coming closer, she saw it had narrow windows and an arched wooden door. Curious, she tried the latch, but it seemed to be bolted; at least it was too hard for her to open. She cupped her eyes with her hands and peered in through one of the windows. The glass was too murky for her to tell what it was like inside.

Instead of being a trysting place for lovers or a children's playhouse, it was probably used for storage or tools, or some other mundane purpose, not at all what her romantic fantasy imagined. From her reading, Oriel knew such structures were called "follies," a rather strange name for a building, evoking all sorts of mysterious connotations.

Her curiosity satisfied, Oriel went back the way she'd come. Outside the gates, she took the path opposite the one to the village. She had not gone far when she began to smell the tang of salt in the damp air. The climb was gradual, and she soon found herself near the top of the cliff. Stopping to catch her breath, she looked back and saw the castle. It looked like an illustration in a fairy-tale book, with its gray stones gilded by the morning sun, its diamond-paned windows shining like colored gems. Oriel felt a strange, soft warmth within her. It was a beautiful place, worthy to be cherished. Ireland was weaving its magic spell on her. She had come to love the hills, the sea, the rocky coast, the fields dotted with grazing sheep. Given a chance, Oriel felt she would also love the village of Kilmara with its whitewashed cottages and slanted thatch roofs—once she met its people and they got to know her. That might take time, but she had a year. It was time enough if she really tried. There was always time for the things you wanted, for love to grow if you cared enough.

Drawing a long breath, she continued walking. The climb was difficult but well worth it when she caught a glimpse of the sea, crashing against the jutting rocks, glistening with silver light from the sun breaking through the clouds. She halted, taking in the magnificent sight.

A few minutes later, she saw three people coming along the path from the other direction. It was Bryan Moore, accompanied by a man and woman whom she didn't recognize.

Bryan waved and shouted something she could not hear, his words carried away on the brisk wind. As they came closer, Bryan smiled and hailed her. "Another hardy soul! We should form a walking club. Mrs. Drummond, how nice to see you again. Let me introduce my friends, Mr. and Mrs. Wicklow. Michael and Suzanne are neighbors of yours at Bracken Hall, just over the hill from Drummond Castle."

The couple he introduced were both tall and fair-skinned, with aristocratic features. They were both bundled up warmly; Mrs. Wicklow in a bulky knit sweater. From under her woolly tam, tendrils of blond hair escaped, blowing in the sharp ocean wind. She had an engaging smile and bright blue eyes. The man's eyes were shaded by the beak of his deerstalker cap, and he was wearing a gray tweed Inverness cape.

The woman spoke first. "I'm delighted to meet you, Mrs. Drummond. We heard the castle was going to have occupants again. It's been empty so long."

"Indeed," Michael agreed. "For years it was crawling with workmen of every sort, renovating, restoring, rebuilding—whatever in the world Drummond was doing over there."

Oriel detected a sarcastic note in his tone and wondered why. His wife gave an embarrassed laugh. Putting her hand on his arm, she said in a playfully reproachful tone, "Darling, *really!*" She then turned to Oriel. "Don't mind Michael, Mrs. Drummond. He is one of those purists who thinks that an artifact, be it a Roman urn or a house built in the seventeenth century, should remain unaltered—nothing touched." She rolled her eyes in mocking amusement. "He'd still rather have maids trundling up with boiling water for his bath every morning than be able to turn the faucet and have it pour out nice and hot."

"I'm not *that* reactionary," Michael protested good-naturedly.

They all laughed.

"Mrs. Drummond is an American," Bryan told them.

"An American! How exciting! I'd love to visit the States, but Michael hates to travel and won't budge. Thinks Ireland's the world, don't you?" her voice was teasing.

"And it is, at least to *me*," he replied edgily.

Bryan stamped his feet. "It's getting cold standing here. You'll find Irish summers are unpredictable, Mrs. Drummond. Rarely the kind of summer days you find in the States. Misty mornings, short sunny afternoons, then the fog rolls in about five."

"The fog is tricky. Sneaks up on you sometimes before you know it," Suzanne commented.

"How far are you planning to walk, Mrs. Drummond?"

"I've heard there's a beautiful little cove around here somewhere. I thought I'd look for it."

Bryan frowned. "It's a treacherous climb down to it."

"But well worth it," Michael interjected.

"There is a ladder," Suzanne said. "It's makeshift, but usable."

"Just be careful going down. Watch that the tide doesn't surprise you," Bryan warned.

"We ought to be moving on." Michael put an arm protectively around his wife's shoulders. "Nice to have met you, Mrs. Drummond."

"You must come to tea some day soon, won't you?" Suzanne suggested. "You can't miss the house. It's very visible from the road."

"There's a shortcut through the woods from Drummond Castle," Michael told her. "It's a little dense, but there should still be a visible path winding through. I used to play there as a boy."

"Come along, Michael." Suzanne took his hand. "Good day, Mrs. Drummond. Remember, we'd love to have you for tea. When you come, I'd love to hear all about America. I'll send a note."

"Thank you, I'd like that very much," Oriel responded.

The couple hurried past, but Bryan lingered a moment. "So, do you always take solitary walks? Doesn't your husband enjoy tramping through our beautiful countryside?"

Oriel felt her cheeks flush. "He's away just now. Gone up to Dublin for the horse fair. He's planning to stock the stables." Why did she feel she had to explain Morgan's absence? How could she explain that whether he was here or not, he would not think of taking a walk with her?

"So he intends to stay, then?" Bryan's eyebrows lifted. "It was wagered in the village he wouldn't."

Oriel felt the heat in her face deepen. "Why, yes. His grandfather left him the castle."

"Well, then, so much for rumors, eh? I've never placed much credence in them anyway." He shrugged. "Have a nice walk and do be careful if you decide to check on the cove. Remember what I said about the tide."

They said good-bye and Bryan hurried to catch up with the Wicklows. Oriel resumed her walk along the path in the opposite direction. She felt happy for the first time in a long time. It had been a nice encounter. She had liked the Wicklows right away and she hoped Suzanne would follow up on her invitation to tea. Oriel had a feeling that Suzanne was someone with whom she could be friends.

Suddenly the year ahead at Drummond Castle did not seem so bleak. She loved the countryside, and she had just met some cordial people who might become friends. She had an intuitive feeling meeting the Wicklows would change her life in Ireland.

A week passed and Morgan still had not returned. Soon after meeting the Wicklows, Oriel found herself confined to the house as the weather had turned rainy once more. Oriel soon tired of reading, playing solitary card games, and eating meals alone in the large dining room. When a note was delivered from Suzanne Wicklow inviting her to tea at

Bracken Hall, she was inordinately pleased. She sent a note back accepting the invitation and saying she was very much looking forward to coming.

Happily, the next afternoon a sudden break came in the weather. The rain stopped and the fog evaporated, so Oriel decided to walk the short distance over to the Wicklows' home. Having been without exercise most of the week, she knew the fresh air and brisk walk would be good for her.

She kept to the road, not wanting to miss the way. However, she did see a path not far from the gates of the castle that was possibly the shortcut Michael Wicklow had mentioned. It was heavily overgrown with ferns and almost invisible. Oriel was afraid she might get lost if she tried that way.

At Bracken Hall, Suzanne opened the door herself. "Your cheeks are like roses!" she greeted Oriel. "Aren't we lucky to see some sunshine for a change? But don't get too happy, my dear, Irish summer being what it is." She laughed. "Some say it's like the Irish character—all smiles and laughter one moment, glower and gloom the next! I don't know if Mr. Drummond suits that description, but Michael certainly does. Come along, let's have our tea."

Suzanne led Oriel to the library, where the furnishings were unpretentious but in good taste. Draperies with overblown flowers and trailing vines were pulled across the windows, giving the room a more intimate feel. There was a large sofa piled with pillows. Several comfortable chairs were scattered around the room. In front of the fireplace was a table with a silver tray, on which a plate of sandwiches, two cups, and a silver teapot had been placed.

"I'm so delighted you could come." Suzanne gestured to one of the chairs. "Do sit down and I'll pour our tea. Michael's out on one of his rambles, so it will just be us."

Without the sweater she had worn on the day they'd met on the cliffs, Suzanne seemed thin, although attractive in a rather ethereal way. Her features were delicate, her skin like white marble. Her pale blonde hair was deeply waved and so thick it seemed almost too heavy for her slender neck. She was wearing a fitted coral dress, its severity softened by a fine Italian cameo.

When Suzanne poured the tea and handed Oriel a cup, Oriel noticed Suzanne wore a narrow gold wedding band much the same as her own. However, Oriel assumed Suzanne had received hers in a ceremony very different from the brief, impersonal one she had gone through in the London Registry Office.

Suzanne was animated and seemed happy to have company. Oriel herself had been starved for female companionship and found Suzanne charming and spontaneous. Suzanne was eager to learn about Oriel's American background. Her warmth and interest made it easy for Oriel to answer her questions. It was only when Suzanne asked about Morgan that Oriel decided she had better be more discreet. It would be unwise to reveal too much about their relationship. Suzanne would certainly never understand their strange bargain. When the conversation became too personal, Oriel changed the subject as subtly as she could by asking Suzanne about her delicate white china cups.

"It's an original design. Very rare because it's not made anymore, although the molds probably exist somewhere. It used to be made right here in Kilmara. It was a thriving village industry, exporting all over the world. The firing kilns and buildings are all boarded up now. It's very sad. It makes Michael livid." She broke off, as though she had said too much. "Of course, that was before—" she halted again as if uncertain whether to continue. "That was before everything got so bad. I'm sure you know of all that—the failure of the potato crop that caused such terrible famine. The factory was closed, and the men who worked in it had to emigrate or go to England to work."

"Have you lived here long?" Oriel asked.

"Only a few years. Michael's mother grew up here and he wanted to come back." A thoughtful expression came over Suzanne's face for a moment. "Houses have histories, you know. They say the past can influence the lives of later occupants of a house."

Oriel started to say she was sure Drummond Castle had a history. She might have gone on to ask Suzanne if she had ever heard of the legend of Shaleen O'Connor, but just then they heard the slam of the front door and footsteps in the hall. A moment later, the door opened and Michael stepped into the library.

Michael's entrance somehow shifted the mood between the two women, his presence subtly changing the intimate atmosphere. Suzanne darted several anxious looks in his direction, and Oriel got the impression that something was on Michael's mind he didn't feel free to discuss in front of company. He was, however, affable enough to Oriel, and both he and Suzanne walked her to the door.

"Not too far for you, is it?" Michael asked. "We can easily have one of the servants take you back in the trap."

"No, thanks. I love walking."

"Well, then, you'll enjoy it. It's still fair, so I suggest you take the cliff path. I just came that way and the ocean is really lovely—a sight to behold." He smiled ruefully. "That is, if you have the soul of an Irish poet."

Oriel laughed. "I guess I'll leave that to Bryan Moore, but I'm sure I'll enjoy the view." She thanked Suzanne for the tea and said good-bye.

"Do come again soon. I feel we're going to be great friends!"

"Thank you. I'd like that. You've been most kind."

Oriel set out from Bracken Hall with a lighter heart than she had had in weeks. The Wicklows were a friendly pair, and their home had a warmth that was sadly missing at Drummond Castle. Oriel suppressed a sigh. Taking Michael's advice, she took the road that led to the cliffs.

She walked briskly, and her breath was coming fast when she reached the path that overlooked the ocean. Mist had begun to rise quickly, and as she stopped to stand on the cliff's edge, she could hear the pounding of the surf against the rocks below. She swayed slightly in the strong wind blowing in from the sea.

Suddenly she felt frightened. A strange sensation of malevolence crept over her, as if someone or something was watching her, wishing her harm. She felt an urgency to get away from the cliffs. She turned and began to walk fast, then faster. Finally, she began to run. Ahead of her loomed the castle—stark, foreboding. Instead of reassuring her, the sight filled her with dread.

14

That evening, Oriel felt peculiarly restless. Suzanne's animated company had accentuated her alone-ness at Drummond Castle. With Morgan still in Dublin, the castle seemed cavernous. After eating a solitary meal in the dining room, Oriel went up to her own rooms. She felt lonely and anxious. It was a different kind of anxiety than she had experienced those weeks in London. Then she had lived on the hope that her situation was only temporary; here the year stretched gloomily ahead. It was an odd para-dox. Even though Ireland itself had captured her, life at Drummond Castle was far from what she had imagined it might be.

It struck her more than ever what a reckless thing she had done, agreeing to Morgan's bizarre proposition. If she had waited longer, possibly Mrs. McPhail would have come through. Even the day she left London there had still been that chance. That's why she had given her address to Nola. Perhaps something *had* come to her at the rooming house. Maybe she should write to Nola, remind her to forward any mail that might have come.

Oriel sat down at the desk in her sitting room and got out some stationery. It was engraved with the Drummond Castle crest. She hesitated. Would Nola think it too grand, be put off by the rich-looking heading? Oriel had told Nola she had a job as a companion. What would Nola think if she knew the truth of Oriel's situation at Drummond Castle? Oriel searched the desk drawer further and found some plain sheets to use instead.

Dipping her pen into the inkwell, Oriel began to write, "Dear Nola, I think of you often and of your kindness to me when I was in London looking for a job."

She paused. What to write next? Nola would not possibly comprehend Oriel's strange existence at Drummond Castle. There was no way to explain it. The important thing was to let Nola know she had arrived at her destination and was still hoping for a letter from her former employer.

Oriel started to write again when something—she was not sure quite what it was—halted her. She felt a quiver at the base of her neck, trailing like an icy finger down her spine.

She put the pen down and sat back in the chair, listening—for what? Then, drawn by some uncanny compulsion, she got up and moved over to the window. Her heart pulsing in her throat, she twisted the handle on the window and slowly pushed it open.

The night was clear. No mist or swirling fog obscured her view. There it was—moving, or rather *gliding* across the terrace toward the gates—an ethereal cloaked figure. As Oriel watched breathlessly, the figure seemed to float through the closed gates! Or had they been left *unlocked* for the spectral visit of Shaleen O'Connor?

Oriel slammed the window and fastened it. She was trembling. Was what she had seen real or imaginary? She moved over to the fireplace, hugging her arms and shivering. Was being alone in this ancient castle getting to her? Was she losing her good sense listening to old ghost stories? What she had seen was probably the movement of trees along the drive, she told herself firmly.

In a few minutes, Oriel went over to the window and made herself stare out into the night. There was nothing there. She drew the curtains shut and turned back into the warmth of the room. She refused to be trapped into believing the ghost of Shaleen O'Connòr haunted Drummond Castle.

Sleep didn't come easily that night, and Oriel woke up the next morning feeling unrested. She decided that being alone and confined to the castle was unhealthy. She determined that whatever the weather, she would get out every day and walk.

Right after breakfast, she set out. Once outside, she felt her spirits rise. The sea breeze had blown away the fog and it looked as though it was going to be a clear summer day. As she turned up the path that led to the ocean cliffs, she heard the distant drum of the surf. Reaching the top, she saw the wide expanse of the sea. Moving along the edge, she looked down. The tide was out and the beach had been swept clean.

Oriel peered down at the cove. It looked inviting. Foamy ripples of blue water curled on the edge of the little beach. She very much wanted to go down there. However, when she tried the posts at the top, they felt unstable. The makeshift ladder was made of wooden boards, and it dropped steeply down the precipice. Oriel stood there for a few minutes debating. It would be a definite challenge. She recalled Bryan's caution, Michael's challenging glance. Both seemed to doubt her ability to climb down the steep hill. If only to be able to tell them both she had done it, she had to try.

Oriel hiked up her skirt, tucked it into her belt, and swung around backwards. Holding on to the two posts, she took the first step downward. The ladder shook with her weight, and she felt it sway. The last few rungs of the ladder were broken. Timidly, she turned her head and looked down. There was still quite a long way down to the beach. Oriel paused there for a minute, wondering how to proceed. Her feet fought for footholds. She held on to the side of the ladder with one hand, then gradually let go. Rocks rolled under her boots, causing her feet to slip. She clutched for something to break her downward slide. It was useless; she had to go with the shifting sand until she reached the bottom. She landed in a sitting position, scrambled to her feet, and looked around.

The sun sparkled on the deep blue of the ocean, flecked with dancing whitecaps. Above her, seagulls dove and screeched. The wind mingled with the roar of the surf. Oriel straightened her skirt and dusted off the sand. She found a smooth rock to sit on, hidden beneath the jutting cliffs. Michael had been right. It *had* been well worth the treacherous climb down. A wonderful, soothing peace came over her. This was surely a special place, a place that could be a refuge. Here she could find a private haven to escape from the oppressive atmosphere of Drummond Castle.

Nothing happened by chance. Oriel knew she had been given this opportunity, this year, as a learning experience. "Every good gift comes from above." Oriel had learned that Scripture as a child. A gift from God should be appreciated, used well. That's what she intended to do with the rest of her year in Ireland—despite Morgan's poor attitude and the myth-haunted castle. If she used this gift well, she might find something in it, something within herself, for which she'd been searching—a sense of God's purpose for her life.

After enjoying her surroundings for a while, Oriel was ready to leave. It was hard going scrambling back up the ladder. The unstable wooden structure swayed and shuddered with every foot placed on the rungs. Oriel was panting when she finally pulled herself up the last step and onto the top of the cliff.

"So, you did it!" a familiar voice exclaimed.

Surprised, Oriel turned to see Bryan Moore coming up the path. "Yes! And you were right—it was glorious!" she said breathlessly.

His blue eyes were amused. "Well, good for you! I wasn't sure you would make it. That shows you've got pluck, something I admire greatly in a woman, in anyone for that matter. Would you let me give you tea for a reward? My cottage is just down the beach a little."

Noting her hesitation, he said, "Oh, we'll be well chaperoned. Suzanne and Michael are coming too. They're on their way."

"Thank you, I'd like to," she responded. As a single woman it would have been improper for Oriel to go unaccompanied to a bachelor's home, but as a *married* woman, it was acceptable, and with the Wicklows also there it would be silly to turn down this generous offer of hospitality and friendship.

"Fine, come along." He held out his arm for her to take. "It's almost as treacherous a path to my place, but that keeps me snug and unbothered by visitors—*uninvited* ones, of course."

He laughed, and Oriel thought it was a good, hearty laugh. It had been a long time since she'd heard a man's laugh. Certainly she had not at Drummond Castle.

As he opened the door for her, he said, "We'll just have a country tea. Nothing fancy. I live very simply here, as a bachelor should." His blue eyes twinkled merrily.

Bryan's cottage, a whitewashed stucco with a thatched roof, was typical of those along the Irish coast. Inside it was small, but cozy. There was a fireplace, shelves of books, a desk in front of a window that looked out over an ocean view.

"What a charming cottage," Oriel remarked as she looked around, thinking it such a contrast to the large, gloomy castle. She almost added, "Just the sort of place I'd like myself." She caught herself in time, but not before Bryan gave her a glance as if he knew what she was thinking.

To cover her sudden discomfort, she went over to examine the painting over the mantel of a small stone church nestled among misty green hills. "You have everything anyone would need or want here. Didn't a poet write, 'May I a small house and a large garden have, and a few friends and many books both true, both wise, and both delightful too'?"

"Good heavens! You're not only a good climber but *literate* as well! As I live and breathe, quoting Abraham Cowley, one of my own favorites." Bryan looked at Oriel with admiration. "Do you like poetry, then?"

"I do. I'd love to borrow some of your books. I've not read much poetry lately."

"Isn't there a library at Drummond Castle?"

"Yes, but I haven't really explored the contents." She did not like to say that Morgan spent a great deal of time there and she did not like to intrude.

Bryan fixed her with his thoughtful gaze. "Why is it I have the feeling that you and Mr. Drummond do not share the same interests? If I had a beautiful bride, I would certainly not spend a day longer than I had to in Dublin."

Oriel could think of nothing to say. The gentle questioning in his eyes made her uncomfortable. Before she was forced to answer, there was a rousing knock at the cottage door.

"My other guests!" Bryan declared. "Another time you and I will have to discuss poetry."

Tea was enjoyable. Oriel could not remember when she had had such a good time. Bryan and Michael had a jovial yet adversarial friendship. There was a great deal of joking and mutual joshing. When Michael stood, saying it was time for them to leave, he offered to walk Oriel home.

"No need," Bryan said quickly. "I'll escort Mrs. Drummond home. It will soon be dark and you two will have to hurry to get home yourselves."

"Don't worry about us, Bryan. Michael knows a shortcut through the woods. He can see in the dark like some kind of woodland creature," Suzanne assured him.

After the Wicklows left, Bryan handed Oriel two slim volumes. "Here, take these. You can return them on your next visit, which I hope will be soon."

Bryan looked out one of the small windows. "The fog's already rolling in. We'd better be on our way."

It was fast growing dark. Large clouds moved overhead and wisps of fog were creeping in from the ocean. When they came in sight of Drummond Castle, Oriel saw lights blazing from most of the windows.

"Morgan must be back!" Oriel exclaimed. "You needn't come any farther. Thank you so much for a lovely afternoon, for tea and for these books! I know I shall enjoy them."

"You're sure you don't want me to see you to the door?"

"No, thanks. I'll be fine—really."

"You don't think your husband would approve of your being brought home by a stranger?"

"Oh, it's not that." Oriel felt flustered. The truth was she wasn't sure just *how* Morgan would react.

"Never mind," Bryan said amiably. "I enjoyed our time together. Good evening, Mrs. Drummond."

"Good evening," she said, pushing through the gate and hurrying up the driveway.

15

Oriel had hardly stepped inside the front hall when Morgan appeared at the door of the library and demanded, "Where have you been? No one—not Finnegan, Mrs. Nesbitt, or Molly—knew where you were. Don't you realize it's dangerous to go wandering past the grounds? The ocean cliffs quickly get masked in fog. It's easy for someone to get disoriented and fall. Those cliffs are—" He broke off, frowning. "It's a long way down to the beach."

Oriel stood there open-mouthed as he raved on. "See that you are more careful in the future," he finished. Then, just as abruptly, he spun around and stalked off to his suite. A part of Oriel was pleased at his obvious concern. On the other hand, to be reprimanded like some naughty child come home late for supper made her furious.

That evening at dinner, Oriel expected Morgan to apologize for the way he had behaved, but he never did. Acting as if the scene had never taken place, he asked her, "So what have you been doing to amuse yourself while I've been gone?"

Still miffed by his high-handed treatment earlier, but forced by the presence of Finnegan and Conan to carry on some kind of civil conversation, Oriel told him about the

Wicklows and Bryan Moore. "Well, I've met some very nice people. I think you'd like them, especially Bryan, who is a published poet and scholar. Michael knows a great deal about Irish history—Kilmara, in particular."

"I'm afraid neither interests me a great deal," Morgan said flatly.

"They have been most cordial. I should like to return their kindness by having them to tea some afternoon, unless you have some objection."

"I *do* object," Morgan said. "I don't want a lot of strangers coming in, asking a lot of questions, involving me in shallow conversation." He halted, realizing his reaction was too strong. "If you want to invite these new friends of yours on your own, that would be fine, I suppose."

"I wouldn't think of doing that. This is, after all, *your* home. Please, forget I said anything."

A strained silence followed. Morgan noted the tight line of Oriel's jaw and her flushed cheeks and was struck with the desire to smooth things over. After a minute or two, he said, "I've bought you a very fine saddle horse, a mare with a gentle nature and sensitive mouth. The dealer originally bought her for his daughter, but the young lady has gone in for jumping and this is strictly a riding horse."

Still smarting from the abrupt way he had dismissed her request, Oriel replied tightly, "Thank you, Morgan. That was very kind of you."

"Not kind at all," he said, smiling. "It will give you something else to do besides having tea with dreamy-eyed poets and amateur historians and wandering about in the mist."

Indignation flared up in her again. Was that remark Morgan's attempt at humor? If so, she did not appreciate it. Before she could utter a protest or defend her new friends, Morgan rose from the table. "They're bringing your horse down tomorrow or the next day. If you'll excuse me, I'm tired from my journey." After bowing slightly, he left the room.

Oriel sat there for a minute quietly fuming. Why did Morgan seem so intent on being difficult? Was there no common point of interest they could share? Was he truly satisfied with the isolated manner in which they were living? Oriel realized, somewhat to her surprise, how important it was to her that Morgan be happy, that they be friends.

"Your dessert, madam," Conan said, setting a dish of lemon custard before her. For Mrs. Mills's sake, Oriel ate every spoonful. Then she left the dining room. On her way upstairs past the library, she gave the closed door a furious look.

Two mornings later, Oriel woke to the sound of heavy rain. It was coming down in sheets. There was no chance of getting out today. More and more she looked forward to her walks and the chance of running into Bryan or the Wicklows. Morgan's reaction to her suggestion of inviting them to tea still rankled her, but she was hardly in a position to insist.

After breakfast, Oriel wandered into the empty library. She stood for a few moments at the long windows, watching the rain run in crooked rivulets down the diamond-paned glass.

The sound of male voices in the entrance hall and the clatter of heavy footsteps startled her. The library door was flung open and Morgan stood there. "The mare I bought for you has come," he said, his eyes beaming.

"In this weather?" she asked, surprised.

"Yes, yes, I know, it's one devil of a day for them to have arrived, but there it is. You can never tell about the Irish temperament or the weather. I was clever enough to give the man only half when I was in Dublin, to make sure he'd carry through his end of the bargain. Anyhow, would you like to take a look?"

"Of course!" Oriel said, pleased with the uncharacteristic eagerness Morgan displayed.

"Well, come along then. We'll go down to the stables together."

She hurried toward the door to the hall. "I won't be a minute."

She ran upstairs to get her jacket and then followed Morgan out to the stables.

The horse Morgan had bought for her use was a roan-colored mare, sleek and sweet-tempered. Mavourneen was her name. Oriel loved her the minute she saw her and stroked her velvety nose.

"Oh, I hope the weather clears soon so I can start riding," she said. Then, turning to Morgan, she smiled. "Thank you."

He was disconcerted by her obvious delight. He said an awkward "You're welcome," and quickly started talking to the groom.

Oriel realized Morgan wasn't the sort of man who wanted or needed excess gratitude. She should just accept Morgan's kind gesture and enjoy it. Perhaps, with a mount of his own, they might ride together and find a way to live in a more harmonious manner.

Over the next few weeks, Oriel began to ride daily. The horse was gentle and sensitive to her slightest touch on the reins, a real joy to ride. So began the happiest period in Oriel's life at Drummond Castle.

To Oriel's surprise and without her effort, as the summer progressed, Morgan's manner gradually changed. He was less gruff, more amiable. Sometimes at dinner, he initiated conversation and even seemed to enjoy talking as they lingered over their coffee.

Occasionally, after an unusually pleasant dinner hour, Oriel once again saw the man she had thought Morgan to be. She allowed herself to wonder what their relationship might be like if they were here under different circumstances. She imagined what might have happened if she and Morgan had met on the ocean liner as fellow passengers and been attracted to one another. They could have had one of those shipboard romances novelists are so fond of writing about. Sometimes her thoughts even went so far as to picture Morgan bringing her to Drummond Castle as his true bride.

At this point Oriel usually cut off her wild imaginings. Daydreams were one thing, but reality was something else entirely. When she tried to share her own growing love for Ireland with him, she found that line of conversation seemed to bore Morgan. She decided that his new congeniality was probably only because he had grown tired of his reclusiveness. Most likely, her company was tolerable because there was no alternative.

For Oriel, however, the days of that summer would have been long and lonely had it not been for Bryan. He seemed to genuinely enjoy her company. They shared many common interests—an appreciation of the beauty of this part of Ireland, a love of literature, especially poetry, and they both relished a good discussion, even if they did not agree on every topic.

"You're very American, you know, Bryan," Oriel teased him one day as they walked along the cliffs overlooking the ocean.

"And *you* are quite *Irish!*" he retorted mischievously. Then his voice softened. "Besides, you have the soul of a poet."

"I'll take that as a compliment." She smiled.

"That's what it was." He paused. "Alas, I have the feeling it is wasted at the castle."

For a moment something hovered between them, so seemingly natural, yet dangerous. The slightest word, gesture, movement would change their relationship. Oriel was starved for companionship. Bryan was warm, amusing, interesting, fun to be with, and she needed and longed for that.

However, both valued too much what they had found in each other to jeopardize it. Bryan was a gentleman of honor. Oriel had too much integrity even to hint at breaking the contract, bizarre as it was, she had made to Morgan.

She was not free to be anything more to Bryan than a friend. Neither would ever cross that line. That was understood, if never spoken.

16

*T*he summer months passed all too quickly. Fall seemed to come overnight. With it came a nagging feeling about the hospitality Bryan and the Wicklows had often extended to Oriel. Not to reciprocate seemed unspeakably bad manners. She felt she could not let their kindness be unreturned any longer. While she waited for the right opportunity to bring up the subject to Morgan, something happened that made it inevitable.

The local hunt season opened, and one afternoon, quite unexpectedly, Michael arrived with the gift of a brace of pheasant. As a result, Oriel impulsively invited him and Suzanne to dinner. When he accepted at once, she knew she must proceed to inform Morgan no matter the consequences.

That evening at dinner, Oriel knew she had to speak of her impromptu invitation. She waited until Conan had poured their coffee and removed their dessert plates. Then, taking a deep breath, she said, "Morgan, I know you may not like it, but I have invited the Wicklows to dinner next week and will include Bryan Moore too. It seems the only polite thing to do. I felt we must reciprocate. They have been so friendly and hospitable to me—especially when you were gone. Then, of course, with Michael bringing the pheasant—"

"Probably poached from Drummond land," Morgan sneered.

"You don't know that," Oriel said, her indignation rising. "Besides, doesn't it ever occur to you that I might long for more company?"

Morgan's expression underwent a change. His eyes softened and he looked at her intently. There was a flicker of uncertainty in his eyes, but when he spoke, his voice was firm.

"I thought you understood being here was temporary. I have no interest in establishing myself as a genial host among the local gentry."

Oriel stood up and flung her napkin down beside her plate. "Have it your own way, Morgan. Come or don't come—I don't care. I have issued an invitation to some very gracious people who have been kind to me, and I don't intend to cancel it."

With that, Oriel turned and walked out of the dining room. She was almost to the stairway when Morgan called, "Wait, Oriel." She turned to face him. He regarded her with something like respect.

"Look, I apologize," Morgan said. "You have every right to invite anyone you wish here, have a dinner party, whatever." He paused, biting his lower lip before going on. "I am an antisocial creature, as you may have noticed. I have a great deal on my mind. My grandfather laid many rather heavy and complicated responsibilities on me. I don't mean to make things unpleasant for you." He broke off, as if he didn't know what else to say.

There was something in his expression, a plea for understanding in his eyes that immediately struck a responsive chord in Oriel. Her natural inclination was to reach out, touch him, say something to comfort him. Knowing he might resent any such gesture, she restrained herself. She did nothing, allowing him his pride.

"Of course, Morgan. I understand," she said quietly. "I still think you would find the Wicklows and Mr. Moore interesting and enjoyable guests."

Morgan's conciliatory manner vanished. "Don't count on it," he said curtly. "Now, if you'll excuse me, I'll bid you good night."

With that, he turned on his heel and walked down the hall, leaving Oriel standing there, frustrated. She had more to say, things that Morgan should hear—like how unhealthy it was for him to let regret, remorse, or resentment eat at him, to turn inward, mourning a love he could not have.

Then, suddenly, Oriel felt drained. What was the use? Why did she even care? She turned and started up the stairs. A movement caught her attention, and she looked up just in time to see a shape leaning over the banister. Startled, she halted. As she glanced upward, it backed away, disappearing as quickly as a shadow, but not before she had caught a glimpse of the face and its smugly satisfied expression. It was Mrs. Nesbitt. Had the housekeeper been eavesdropping and found Oriel's argument with Morgan somehow satisfying?

In the days leading up to the dinner party with the Wicklows and Bryan Moore, Oriel was busy with preparations. She was anxious for her first entertaining at Drummond Castle to go well. Maybe that would impress Morgan. If he found it enjoyable, it might be the beginning of other such evenings. That, she knew, was a far-fetched hope, but it was still worth making the effort.

Oriel went over the menu in detail with Mrs. Mills, soliciting her suggestions, trying to include some of what she considered her specialties. The cook was excited about the chance to show her skills at this first social dinner. Oriel also consulted with Finnegan on which china, silverware, and table linens to use. She asked Morgan to select the wines, but he referred her to Finnegan, making his disinterest in their dinner party apparent. Oriel spent time with Patrick, the gardener, to see what flowers were available in the garden and greenhouse for the table centerpiece and for arrangements to be placed in vases in the drawing room.

To her surprise, Oriel enjoyed seeing to all these various details. Her natural talent and good taste made her suited to just such a role. Her only regret was Morgan's lack of interest and involvement.

Sometimes she imagined again how lovely it would be if this were real, if they were at Drummond Castle because they wanted to be here together. What if Morgan had remained the charming, considerate man she knew he could be—the kind of man it would be easy to fall in love with? Quickly, Oriel reminded herself that she was here in a business arrangement, playing a role. Still, there was no harm in enjoying what she could.

The evening of the dinner party, Oriel was nervous. Regardless of Morgan's attitude, she was determined to act the part of the charming hostess. By doing so, she might shame Morgan into doing his part. Certainly he would rise to the occasion, if only for pride's sake.

Molly helped Oriel dress and arrange her hair. "Oh, madam, you look ever so elegant!" Molly declared, carefully placing a high-backed comb into Oriel's chignon. Oriel's gown, a cinnamon satin, had been altered so skillfully even the original owner would not have recognized it. Daily rides and walks in the moist Irish sea air had enhanced Oriel's coloring, making the dress even more becoming.

When the Wicklows arrived, Oriel welcomed them and introduced them to Morgan. Bryan followed soon after. They gathered in the drawing room, where a selection of hors d'oeuvres had been laid out. To Oriel's increasing irritation, Morgan made no effort to engage anyone in conversation after the introductions. She tried to draw her guests out on various subjects. In an attempt to start a lively discussion, Bryan brought up the subject of how the pottery factory might be started again, reviving the economy of the village. This comment seemed to make Morgan belligerent.

"People seem to think all that's needed is money," Morgan snapped. "It takes more than that to revive an industry, to give people incentive."

"I agree," Bryan said quickly. "But someone with money *and* enthusiasm could give the community reason to get involved."

"That would take years," Morgan countered.

Bryan struggled valiantly on. "Perhaps, but . . ."

"I don't have years," Morgan said shortly.

A silence fell. After that and even before Finnegan announced dinner, glasses were emptied and the conversation languished.

Oriel led the way into the dining room, thinking the good food she and Mrs. Mills had planned would restore energy and brighten the talk at the dinner table.

Her hopes were quickly dashed. Instead of being the success she had hoped for, dinner was a disaster. She watched helplessly as the courses she had so carefully planned were presented in reverse order. The salad came before the fish course; the soup followed the meat and vegetables. Oriel felt herself grow more tense every minute. She could only imagine what must be going on in the kitchen. Desperately, she tried to keep up some conversation, avoiding the bewildered faces of Conan and the unflappable Finnegan as they stoically continued service.

At one point, Oriel thought Morgan might come to the rescue, but he seemed to be unaware of the awful drama of the ruined dinner. He failed to exercise the charming social skills she knew he possessed.

The dessert was brought in. The well-mannered guests, whatever they might have been thinking, tried several topics of conversation. Suzanne made a feeble comment on the weather and Michael asked Bryan if he had read a recently published book on the history of this part of Ireland. Morgan did not add anything to the discussion.

At last the final course had been taken away and they all went into the drawing room, where Finnegan served the coffee.

Oriel took this brief opportunity to dash into the kitchen, where she found a distraught Mrs. Mills weeping copiously.

"Oh, madam," she wailed, wiping her red eyes on her apron. "I don't know what happened. The dessert was near spoilt, so I had to make a soufflé instead, and Mrs. Nesbitt come into the kitchen slammin' the door and it fell! Then I forgot to ladle the soup out for Conan to carry in and—oh, madam, should I give notice?"

"No, no, Mrs. Mills, don't cry. It's all done now. I don't think anyone but I noticed. Just get a good night's sleep and we'll sort it all out tomorrow."

Oriel went back to her guests feeling like an early Christian going into the lions' den. What an evening it had been. *And no help from Morgan at all,* she thought furiously. By this time, Oriel wished the terrible evening was over. So must have the guests, for soon afterwards they declared they must be leaving. Bryan accompanied the Wicklows.

Too angry to trust herself to say anything to Morgan, Oriel bade him a cool good night and went immediately upstairs.

17

The next morning, Oriel awakened with a headache. Thinking that maybe a brisk canter in the crisp fall air would help, she put on her riding habit before going downstairs for breakfast.

She was still angry about Morgan's behavior the evening before. Why couldn't he have at least made an effort? Bryan had been a real help, bringing up every possible subject that might draw Morgan into friendly conversation. Finally, even he was exhausted. Michael had fallen into a resentful silence. Who could blame him with a host like Morgan? Even Suzanne and Oriel had run out of small talk. The evening had petered out to a dismal close. Oriel had to admit her first attempt at entertaining at Drummond Castle had been a miserable failure.

When she came into the dining room, she was surprised to find Morgan sitting at the table, reading the newspaper. With only a cool glance at him, Oriel helped herself to toast and eggs, then sat down at the other end of the table.

Realizing once again he had made Oriel unhappy, Morgan awkwardly apologized for being poor company the night before, mumbling something about having a great deal on his mind.

Carefully keeping her voice even and her expression composed, Oriel said, "It's more than that—something I think we should talk about, Morgan. Perhaps we should redefine my position here. Perhaps I misunderstood. Perhaps I am only a paid tenant at Drummond Castle. Perhaps I should not offer an opinion, speak only when spoken to, and not do anything to make life here more pleasant for either of us."

Not daring to linger, Oriel rose from the table and left the dining room. She walked toward the stables, trying vainly to control her disappointment. She had nearly reached the stables before she realized she was grasping her riding crop so tightly that there was a band of red across her palm.

Then she heard steps on the cobbled apron of the stable yard. Turning her head, she saw Morgan running toward her.

"Oriel, I apologize. I always seem to be doing that. If I seemed rude to your guests, I apologize, but, it's *you* I'm most sorry about." His voice softened. "I never meant to hurt you or offend you. Sometimes I think this whole thing's been a mistake. If you're not happy here, then—"

"Whether I'm happy or not is irrelevant," Oriel interrupted him. "A bargain is a bargain." She walked away, not wanting him to see the tears stinging her eyes. The pain of disappointment was keen, even though a part of her was touched by his concern. She had been optimistic about last evening, but had been horribly wrong. Why couldn't Morgan have behaved decently in the first place and spared her the apology later?

At least the weather was wonderful. The sun was shining, the sky a clear blue. Oriel prayed the ride in the brisk autumn air would clear her head and restore her spirits.

Tim, the groom, was waiting at the mounting block, holding Mavourneen's bridle. Oriel greeted him as cheerfully as she could manage. "What a glorious morning," she said.

"Now 'tis fine enough. But if I was you, madam, I'd not go far or stay out too long. Fog's going to roll in before too long."

"You're sure?" Oriel asked doubtfully. "There's certainly no sign of it now."

"It's in the air. I can smell it." He nodded his head.

Oriel had observed Irishmen came in two categories. Some were eternally optimistic; others, like the dour Tim, were given to dark predictions and warnings. Oriel had learned to enjoy the one and ignore the other. With a determinedly cheery good-bye, Oriel mounted and trotted out of the stable yard toward the hills.

Oriel should have listened to Tim's warning. Not twenty minutes later, she suddenly seemed to be immersed in fog. Turning Mavourneen around, she started back in the direction she had come. The horse seemed hesitant, and Oriel herself began to feel confused.

She was surrounded in a swirling mist, which was growing ever more dense. The horse would take a few steps and then stop. Oriel dared not urge her on, fearing she might be dangerously close to the cliffs. One false step and they would both go hurtling over, crashing onto the beach below. Holding tightly to the reins, Oriel dismounted. Perhaps it would be better to go on foot, leading the horse slowly, step by cautious step, back to Drummond Castle.

She squinted through the fog, hoping for some familiar sign to show her she was on the right path. Suddenly, Oriel thought she discerned the outline of the curved arch of the castle's wrought-iron gates. *Thank God*, she breathed a silent prayer of relief.

Almost there, she became aware of movement just ahead. A shadowy figure sprang out of the depths, coming toward her. A hooded figure, its cape was unfurled behind it like a huge fan. Oriel's heart began racing wildly; cold perspiration washed over her. Her hands became sweaty in her leather riding gloves. Her breath was caught in her throat, where a scream was trapped with fear. One terrified thought raced through her mind—*the ghost of Shaleen O'Connor!*

With a gasp, she turned, hiding her head against Mavourneen's neck, squeezing her eyes shut. She heard the horse whinny softly, shifting her feet to one side. She felt a swish of air, as if the figure had passed so close it left an icy breath on her cheek. Shuddering, Oriel clung to the horse's bridle.

She didn't know how long she stood there shivering, afraid to open her eyes. It could have been a minute or longer before she forced herself to pull away from the horse, to look forward. Thin swirls of gray obscured the house, but the gates were in plain sight. There was nothing else.

She moved her head, peering in each direction, but saw nothing. She felt faint. What had she *really* seen? She had certainly *felt* something. Someone—or some*thing*—had passed her as she stood rooted in place. But *who? What?* Her breath was still shallow and the urgency to get through the gates, back to the castle and safety, was strong. Dragging on her horse's reins, she started walking, stumbling at times because her legs were so shaky.

Finally, she left Mavourneen with a worried-looking Tim, who gave her a curious glance before taking the horse away. Unable to speak rationally, Oriel mumbled something and then hurried up to the house.

Breathlessly she struggled up the steps and was about to open the front door when it was yanked open by Morgan. His face was flushed and angry. "Where have you been? Tim was up here with all kinds of dire predictions about your getting lost and falling over the cliffs, or—"

"Morgan, I saw her!" Oriel gasped, shaken out of her gripping fear.

"Saw who? What are you talking about?"

"At the gates, just as I was coming in—she floated. It was Shaleen O'Connor."

"Are you crazy?" Morgan demanded. "Have you been thrown and hit your head?"

"No, listen! Morgan, I know I saw—"

Morgan's eyes flashed furiously. "Whatever you saw it *wasn't* that. I thought you had better sense than to be taken in by the superstitious tales of uneducated servants," he said furiously. "It's clear you've had a bad scare of some sort. Just don't ever mention Shaleen O'Connor, or any other silly Irish legend to me again." He turned around and stalked off toward his rooms. The slam of the door echoed in the hall.

Oriel stood there, stunned by his angry response to the incident. There was no use. He'd never believe that she had seen anything. He seemed unwilling to believe any Irish myth—especially one that concerned his castle. Wearily, she started toward the stairway. She needed a hot bath, a cup of tea.

As she reached the first step, she looked up and saw Molly standing on the landing, a strange, knowing expression on her round face. She knew Molly was curious about what she had overheard her tell Morgan, but she didn't feel free to bring up the subject again with the maid. It would just support the village contention that Drummond Castle was haunted and the wild rumors among the servants. No matter how much she wanted to discuss the apparition she'd seen, Oriel knew it was better to say nothing.

She did decide, however, to borrow some of Bryan's books about the old Irish castles and the families who had built them and lived in them. Maybe there'd be some factual information to give credence or disprove the Shaleen O'Connor story.

After that explosive scene with Morgan, Oriel made a decision. She could not change the situation nor Morgan. To expect anything more would only lead to disappointment. Still, a bargain was a bargain. It was October—six months more and this whole farce would be over. She would be free, independent, and richer than she could ever have imagined. And yet a part of her knew it would be difficult to leave the castle, to leave Morgan.

She knew her feelings for Morgan were dangerous. She had never dreamed she would feel anything but a kind of detached interest in the man with whom she had made such a perilous bargain. Realizing the impossibility of such feelings was one thing, but dreams and emotions had a life of their own. Sometimes she couldn't seem to control them, often drifting into thoughts of what might have been, if only . . .

More and more, the cove became Oriel's special place. One particular day after breakfast, she bundled up, put an apple and some biscuits in a small basket, and set out for the hidden beach. Morgan was nowhere in sight when she left. She knew he had taken to early morning rides by himself, sometimes not returning until late in the afternoon. In the current state of their relationship, what did it matter?

Oriel walked briskly up the cliff path, then went down the rickety ladder to the sheltered place hidden under the cliffs. The sea was slate gray and angry looking. As she stared out at the breaking waves, they seemed as turbulent as her own mood.

Sighing, she opened her book—*Wuthering Heights*. She had read it before, but its romantic plot about two star-crossed lovers appealed to her just now. She was soon lost in its compelling story, so much so that she was oblivious to the changing tide. All at once, the foamy edge of a wave washing up on the sand wet the hem of her dress. Startled, she looked up and saw she was surrounded by ripples of water. Remembering Bryan's earlier warning about the tide, she jumped to her feet, grabbed her basket, and hurried toward the ladder.

The quickly rising water was already lapping at her feet, the surf rapidly eating up the circles of remaining sand. Slipping the handle of her basket over one arm, Oriel grabbed hold of the side of the ladder with her free hand. As she did, she felt it sway back from the rock. She looked up and saw the top was leaning forward. Somehow it had come loose from where it was anchored at the top of the cliff. As unstable as it seemed, she would have to climb it, hoping she could manage to reach the top before it gave way entirely. She had to force herself to put her foot on the lowest rung. Since the bottom few rungs were missing, it was quite a way up to the first rung. She had done it before, but not with the top posts so unstable. There was no alternative. She had to try.

She started up. The flimsy ladder wobbled with her weight. Her fingers tightened on the rung above; moving slowly, she took the next step up. Two, then three steps. The ladder shuddered in the wind. She dared not look up, knowing how far she had to go to reach safety.

Suddenly, she heard a horrible snapping sound as the old wood cracked and splintered. The ladder swung precariously. Frozen with fear, Oriel looked up and saw that the upper part had been loosened entirely from the posts. Try as she might to hold on, her weight pulled the ladder away from the rocky cliff. Her hands lost their grasp, the basket fell, and she hurtled back toward the beach below.

18

$\mathcal{S}$he fell backwards, landing on the wet sand with one leg twisted under her. Her breath was knocked out of her and the pain was intense. For a moment she lay there, stunned and immobilized from the shock of the fall. Slowly, the awareness of the danger she was in came back. Conscious of the oncoming tide swirling around her, she struggled painfully to a sitting position and dragged herself to her knees. Her skirt was soaked and her shoes were heavy with sand.

With tremendous effort, she got to her feet. An agonizing pain seared through her ankle, but there was no time to waste. The tide was coming in faster and faster. She had to get up the cliff or she would be trapped by the tide and drown. She slogged back toward the cliff, her sodden skirt and water-soaked boots impeding her progress. Ignoring the painful ankle, she hobbled to the side of the cliff. It seemed impossibly steep and high. Her legs felt weak. Behind her, the water level grew higher with each wave.

She started to climb. The jagged rocks scraped her bare hands as she searched for a hold. She pulled herself painfully up, then slipped back. A terrified sob caught in her throat. *Oh, dear God, help me,* she prayed. Desperately, she clawed her way up again, inch by inch. She must make it. She must! The fear of falling again down to the roaring water below kept her going, pulling herself with all her strength, panting and groaning with each movement.

Then, from far off, she heard shouts. *Oh, could it be— please God—maybe someone is coming,* Oriel thought.

"Hold on, Oriel, I'm here. Catch hold of this rope, and I'll pull you up." It was Bryan. He must have been out on one of his rambles and somehow seen her plight.

He gripped her upper arms and pulled her up over the edge of the cliff. His hands went around her waist, dragging her to her feet. As soon as she put weight on her foot, a wrenching pain stabbed her ankle and she collapsed against Bryan, crying out.

"What is it, Oriel? Are you hurt?"

"My foot," she gasped. "I think I twisted my ankle when I fell. I'm not sure I can walk."

Gingerly she tried, but the pain was too intense. Shaking her head, she said, "I can't. I'm sorry . . ."

"Don't," Bryan said firmly. "You'll injure it more if you try. Lean on me. Michael should be along in a few minutes. He was coming to my cottage, and I decided to walk up and meet him. As soon as he gets here, we'll carry you. Don't worry. It will be all right."

Oriel was feeling too shaky to object. It seemed like a miracle Bryan had happened by. If he hadn't, she didn't know how she would ever have made it back to the castle.

Within minutes, Michael Wicklow appeared walking jauntily from the woods. Michael looked startled when he saw Oriel clinging to Bryan.

"Michael, come here!" Bryan called. "Oriel's been hurt. That blasted ladder. Someone should have fixed it or taken it completely away. It's a death trap."

Oriel shuddered at his choice of words. It made her realize how horribly close her escape had been.

The two men crossed arms, making a seat. Then Oriel put an arm around each man's shoulder and was lifted up. As they approached Drummond Castle, Oriel whispered a prayer of thanksgiving that Bryan had happened along when he did. Another hour and she would have been clinging to the cliff alone, her strength waning and finally giving out. She would surely have fallen to her death.

A startled Finnegan opened the door. His expression rapidly changed to alarm.

"Your mistress has had an accident," Bryan said. "Best you inform your master at once and get someone to help her."

The two men carried Oriel into the great hall. By now her foot was throbbing fiercely and she was shuddering from the cold. All at once, the hall was filled with people hovering around her. Molly hurried to Oriel's side, murmuring expressions of distress and sympathy. Mrs. Nesbitt came down the stairway and glanced at the men, then asked Michael, "What's happened?"

"The ladder near the sea cove gave way and Mrs. Drummond fell," Michael replied.

Then Morgan came storming from his wing of the house, demanding explanation, barely listening to what Bryan tried to tell him.

Before Oriel could protest, Morgan swept her up in his arms. Barking orders for Molly to follow, he carried her up to her bedroom. Molly was right on his heels, all the while speaking words of comfort as he laid Oriel gently on her bed.

"See to your mistress," Morgan said before striding out of the room.

"Oh, ma'am, you're soaked! We must get these off before you catch your death," Molly proclaimed as she helped Oriel out of her wet clothes. "How ever did you get so drenched?"

Oriel's teeth were chattering too hard to answer.

"My, oh my!" Molly clucked her tongue as she wrapped blankets around Oriel's shivering body.

A few minutes later, after a brief knock at the door, Morgan returned. He handed Oriel a tumbler of brandy. "Here, drink this," he ordered. He turned to the maid. "Does she have a fever, Molly?"

"No, sir—not that I can tell. She will if we don't get her right into bed."

"Well, do it then," Morgan snapped. He turned to Oriel, anger belying the visible concern in his expression. "What were you doing down in that cove anyway? Didn't you know it was dangerous?"

Oriel was too upset to try to explain. Her head was aching and she couldn't seem to stop shivering. Morgan took the empty glass from her shaking hands and turned to leave.

"Wait, Morgan," Oriel said, and he halted. "Do thank Bryan and Michael. I don't know what would have happened if they hadn't come along."

He nodded curtly and left the room.

Molly wrapped Oriel's swollen ankle with strips of flannel, then helped her into her nightdress, which had been warmed by the fireplace. As she eased Oriel back into the bed piled high with comforters, Molly gave a puzzled frown. "I still don't see how it could have happened, madam—the beach ladder breaking apart like that. There should've been a sign or something, don't you think, ma'am? To warn people it wasn't safe. That is, unless—"

"Unless what, Molly?" There was something in the maid's voice that sent a nervous jolt through Oriel.

"Well, ma'am, it does seem like someone might have done it on purpose." She turned her head, busily tucking in the covers, avoiding Oriel's surprised gaze.

"Why should anyone do that?"

Molly turned back, her face flushed but determined. "To scare you off, maybe—you and the master both. It's no secret folks around here resent Mr. Drummond, hold grudges against him for all sorts of things, real and imagined. Now that he's come back with a wife, well, some people don't want him to stay."

Before Oriel could question Molly further, a sharp tap came on the bedroom door and Mrs. Nesbitt came in, carrying a small tray. She set it down on the table beside Oriel's bed. It held a pitcher of water, a glass, and a small envelope, which was propped against the glass on the lace doily. "I've brought you a sleeping powder, madam. I keep some in my supplies for emergencies and for when I cannot sleep myself. It will relax you and help you to rest after your frightening experience."

"That's very kind of you, Mrs. Nesbitt," Oriel said, but there was no kindness in the housekeeper's eyes nor compassion in her expression. The thought passed through Oriel's mind, *Why does Mrs. Nesbitt dislike me?* She quickly thrust it away. It was just the woman's stiff, reserved manner, she told herself.

Mrs. Nesbitt turned to the maid, who was still standing nearby. "Molly, I think you should leave Mrs. Drummond now. Don't tire her out with your talk."

"Yes, ma'am," Molly said hesitantly, darting a quick look at Oriel as if checking that she agreed.

"I'm fine, Molly," Oriel assured her. "Thank you for all your help."

"If you need anything in the night, just ring the bell," Mrs. Nesbitt said. She took a few steps toward the door, then stood waiting for Molly to obey her direction. With another anxious look at Oriel, Molly left. The housekeeper followed.

For some reason Oriel did not want to take the sleeping powder Mrs. Nesbitt had brought, even though the effect of the brandy had worn off. The one lamp left burning in the room cast strange shadows. Molly's scary explanation for what had happened kept Oriel wakeful. Could it possibly be true? Would anyone want them to leave Drummond Castle so badly as to risk endangering Oriel's life? Or was it all Molly's imagination?

The next morning, Oriel felt stiff and sore and her ankle was quite swollen. Her shallow sleep had been disturbed with nightmares of her ordeal.

"A day in bed is what's best, ma'am," Molly advised. "Don't even try to stand on that ankle. There's no need for you to stir yourself at all."

After Molly took her breakfast tray away, Oriel leaned back against the pillows. She was still mulling over what Molly had said the night before. Were there people in Kilmara who hated Morgan, resented the rich American who had come, flaunting his wealth? Were there those vicious enough to use her to get to him? Whether it was true or not, Oriel felt she should talk to Morgan about it. Even Bryan had hinted at possible retribution. Did Morgan know his grandfather had been threatened? She should at least suggest the possibility to Morgan.

Molly returned to announce that Dr. O'Toole had arrived.

"But I don't need a doctor," Oriel protested.

Molly raised her eyebrows. "Well, the master thought you did, ma'am. He sent for him first thing this morning."

"Oh, well," Oriel shrugged resignedly.

The doctor, a ruddy-faced man with grizzled gray whiskers and merry eyes, examined her ankle. "It's a nasty sprain. You were lucky it wasn't broken. Stay off it until the swelling goes down. And stay away from those cliffs, young lady. They've been responsible for a few deaths, not all of them accidental."

Oriel hardly had time to absorb that statement when Molly was back. "The master asked if he could come up, ma'am." Molly helped Oriel into her pink quilted robe and assisted her over to the chaise lounge.

When Morgan came in, he rushed to Oriel's side. "You're sure you're all right? No serious injuries?"

"Yes, just fine. I'm a little sore, but the doctor says my ankle will be fine with some rest." Oriel looked around the room and lowered her voice. "There is something else we should talk about."

He frowned, a flicker of alarm in his eyes. "What is it? Is there something you need or want? Just name it." Morgan seemed anxious to please her, to make her happy.

Oriel saw something in Morgan's reaction she had never seen in him before. He really *had* been worried about her. Still, she knew she would have to tread carefully in laying out her theory about the accident. Slowly, she began, watching him closely as she spoke.

Disbelief, skepticism, and anger all flashed through his eyes. His jaw clenched several times and Oriel thought he might interrupt her, but he listened until she had finished.

He got up from the chair and began pacing, his hands clasped behind his back. He went over to the window and stood there for a long minute staring out. Then he whirled around and said angrily, "But why *you?* Why *now?* All that stuff happened centuries ago. It has nothing to do with now. We're in the late nineteenth century. And besides, Shaleen's vengeance was against the Lawrence family, *not* the Drummonds. We had nothing to do with it. Why would anyone want to harm you?"

"Memories are long in Ireland," she replied softly. "At least that's what Bryan Moore contends."

"What does *he* know about it?" Morgan demanded.

"He's a student of history—*Irish* history. You should talk to him sometime—especially since you are now a property owner here."

Morgan glowered, his handsome face a contradiction of emotions. "Sometimes I wish I'd never come here!" he said, pounding his clenched fist into his open palm. He gave Oriel a quick glance. "And I'm sure you do as well. I should never have brought you here, exposed you to this."

Impulsively, Oriel reached out her hand. "I don't feel that way, Morgan. Maybe I'm wrong. Maybe this is all wild speculation. I'm sorry."

"No, I'm the one who's sorry." He pressed her hand. Then slowly, as a smile broke across his face, Oriel realized once again how handsome he was.

"Well, I won't be scared off and I won't let you be either. They'll have to deal with me if they try anything else. I'll tell you what, as soon as you're up and about, we'll go up to Dublin—get away from this gloomy castle with all its old wives' tales and ghost stories. I just got a letter from my cousin, Paige. Her husband is Freddy Redmon. His family has a chain of stores in England and they're opening a new one in Dublin. They've rented a house there and have invited us to dine with them and go to the theater. A change of scenery might be the best thing for both of us. How does that sound?"

Oriel could hardly believe her ears or the change in Morgan toward her. "It sounds marvelous! I'd love it."

"Done! I'll write her immediately."

After Morgan left, Oriel smiled to herself. Maybe her accident had been worth it after all.

19

$\mathscr{A}$ few weeks later, Oriel's ankle had fully healed. The date for departure on the promised trip to Dublin had been set and Morgan had made all the arrangements for their stay.

When Oriel came down to breakfast a few days before they were to leave, Morgan held up a note that had come in the morning post. "It's from my cousin, Paige, inviting us to stay at their townhouse. I've already written her back that we have reservations at a hotel. I thought that would avoid any awkward explanations about separate rooms." Although Morgan's tone was matter-of-fact, his face reddened slightly and he avoided looking directly at Oriel by glancing through the rest of the mail.

So, Oriel thought, Morgan had not shared the secret of their strange marriage with his relatives. That might make being with them difficult—to play the part of a newly married couple yet not act overtly affectionate toward one another. Oriel hoped Morgan didn't regret his impulsive suggestion that they take this trip. She was looking forward to it. The long days while her ankle was healing had been particularly tedious. She missed her daily horseback rides and brisk walks and felt very confined indeed. She was longing for some diversion.

Not that she could complain. Everything had been done to make her convalescence comfortable and pleasant. Bryan had sent over books for her to read; the Wicklows sent flowers and fruit. Morgan had been particularly considerate. He began having his dessert and coffee served upstairs in her sitting room each evening. Oriel felt that during this time, they had somehow gotten past the barriers of the first few months at Drummond Castle and become companionable friends.

The afternoon before their departure, Oriel was busy packing. She had sent Molly to the laundry room to get her freshly ironed clothes when a tap came on her bedroom door and Mrs. Nesbitt entered. She stood stiffly on the threshold, glancing disapprovingly around the cluttered room. An array of jackets, skirts, and blouses were spread out on the bed. Conscious of the disarray, Oriel laughingly apologized, "Don't worry, Mrs. Nesbitt, we'll soon make order out of chaos."

There was no answering smile. Mrs. Nesbitt clasped her hands together over her belt with the ever-present keys and said coldly, "A proper lady's maid would make short work of this. That is precisely why I wanted to speak to you before you left, Mrs. Drummond. I wondered if you intend, while you are in Dublin, to interview young women to hire for your personal maid? There is a very good domestic employment agency in Dublin. They require the best references and recommend only the most highly qualified people." She added disdainfully, "Most of the local girls are hopeless."

Puzzled, Oriel looked at her blankly for a minute. "No, Mrs. Nesbitt, I have no such intention. It never crossed my mind."

"You must realize, Mrs. Drummond, that Molly has not been trained as a lady's maid. She is a housemaid." Then, as if Oriel did not know the difference, she added, "The duties of each are totally different."

Oriel bit her lower lip to refrain from the indignant response that rushed to her mind. The nerve of the woman! For all her veneer of respect, it was obvious Mrs. Nesbitt was trying to embarrass her. Determined not to give the woman the satisfaction of upsetting her, Oriel replied calmly, "Molly suits me perfectly, Mrs. Nesbitt. I have no intention of replacing her."

This did not seem to deter the housekeeper, because Mrs. Nesbitt continued, "I just thought I should suggest it, madam. We were all rather surprised when you arrived unaccompanied by your own maid."

By this time, Oriel's temper was rising. Who did Mrs. Nesbitt think she was? "I understand that, Mrs. Nesbitt," Oriel replied with icy calm. "However, Molly is quick and smart and teachable. I'm entirely satisfied with her and do not intend to make a change."

Mrs. Nesbitt drew herself up with frigid dignity. "Very well, madam."

In a gesture of dismissal, Oriel turned her back and went over to the bed as if contemplating the choice of her dresses. She stood there waiting until she heard the rustle of the housekeeper's skirt and the click of the bedroom door as Mrs. Nesbitt went out. Then she let out a long sigh of relief.

Perhaps when she returned from Dublin she would have to deal more firmly with the housekeeper, establish herself in a more direct way as mistress at Drummond Castle. For now, however, she wasn't going to let this incident spoil her holiday.

Molly returned with a pile of starched clothes, remarking with a bit of a chuckle, "Mrs. Nesbitt just sailed by me looking like a thunderstorm."

Oriel knew better than to share Mrs. Nesbitt's comments with Molly. It would only serve to increase the friction that already existed between the two. Still, Mrs. Nesbitt's hostility bothered her. From the beginning, the woman had seemed to resent Oriel. Why? It was hard to figure. Had she known Edwina Parker? Perhaps the woman had expected Edwina to be her mistress and was disappointed when Morgan arrived with Oriel.

Oriel dismissed the worrisome problem. Tomorrow she would be away from both the castle and its resident "dragon," as she privately dubbed the housekeeper.

Dublin

November 1895

Upon their arrival in Dublin, Oriel knew Morgan had been right. A change of scene was just what she had needed. The busy streets, the bright store windows, and the well-dressed people were stimulating after her long time in the isolated country.

They checked in at the Shelbourne Hotel. Its red and white exterior led into an interior just as elegant. A uniformed bellhop showed Oriel to her room. Oriel looked around with delight. It was spacious yet very feminine, with cabbage roses on the wallpaper, a tall brass bed piled with pillows, a ruffle-skirted dressing table, and the luxury of an adjoining bath.

After freshening up, she was to meet Morgan back in the lobby, then do some shopping. Oriel felt excited. She hadn't realized how deprived of activity her life had been lately, especially when laid up with her sprained ankle. This trip was more than a welcome change, it was a lifesaver. She felt happier, more lighthearted than she had in months.

Oriel wasted no time washing up and fixing her hair. Soon she hurried back downstairs. Entering the lobby, she saw Morgan before he was aware of her coming. He was talking with a balding, red-whiskered man in a frock coat and striped trousers whom she guessed was the hotel manager.

At a discreet distance, she stood for a minute observing Morgan. In his belted tweed suit, he looked the epitome of a country squire. The role suited him—if only he would accept it. He was also extremely handsome, Oriel noted anew, with his black wavy hair, strongly molded features, and vivid blue eyes. She allowed herself to wonder what it might be like if the two of them were up from the country for a festive weekend holiday together, if things between them were different. Without realizing it, she sighed.

Just then, Morgan turned his head and saw her. He nodded to the manager, then strode across the lobby toward her.

"I thought you would enjoy doing the shops without a male tagging along." He smiled. "I know most women do. I want you to take all the time you need, then meet me back here in a few hours. There'll be plenty of time for you to rest before our evening out. Paige and Freddy will pick us up at seven. Paige said she has the theater tickets and we'll dine together beforehand." He paused, enjoying the pleasure in her eyes. "Does that suit you?"

"Oh, yes," she said, beaming.

"You have your letter of credit with you, don't you? I made a deposit with the manager here at the hotel in case you want to draw more."

Oriel blushed. "That isn't necessary. I have more than enough." As part of their marital agreement, Morgan's lawyer had opened an account for Oriel at a Dublin bank from which she could write checks.

"I know it isn't necessary," he said quietly. "I very much want you to enjoy yourself, Oriel. You deserve it. If you see something you want, I want you to get it. Understand?" His tone was decisive.

Feeling a little embarrassed by his making such a point of it, Oriel simply nodded. Did the fact she had had to scrimp and save for so many years show? It was certainly a glorious feeling to have money in her purse and be given license to spend it.

"See you later, then," Morgan said, smiling.

Oriel left the hotel and strolled along, gazing into the store windows. She stopped to look at a glittering display of cut glass. As she stared, the idea of buying a gift for Nola came to mind—something small, perhaps, as a gesture of gratitude for her friend's cheerful kindness.

Inside the store, all different patterns of beautiful china were presented in several table arrangements. As Oriel wandered up and down the aisles, she remembered the Wicklows talking about the factory in Kilmara that had once produced its own lovely dinnerware. She had seen examples of it in Suzanne's teacups. Now, however, Oriel saw nothing even similar. It was sad that the original designs had been lost when the factory shut down. If only Morgan were interested, if he wanted to stay in Kilmara and help bring the factory back to life . . . Well, it had nothing to do with her, not really. She was only going to be here a year, actually only another five months.

Oriel continued wandering through the store. She saw a gracefully shaped crystal vase and bought it at once. She knew Nola would be thrilled to receive it. She'd probably give it a place of honor in her keepsake-filled room.

After purchasing the vase, Oriel went down the street where there was a large women's clothing store. The minute she went through the etched glass doors of the fashionable store, Oriel felt she had stepped into the past. Its deep carpets and faintly perfumed air brought vague memories of accompanying her mother to similar exclusive Boston stores.

Slowly, Oriel walked around, surrounded by lavishly furred cloaks, hats adorned with exotic feathers, dresses gleaming with sequins, beaded handbags, silk scarves, and pearl-buttoned gloves. It was dizzying and seductive. Yet despite the letter of credit and Morgan's reminder that she was to buy whatever caught her fancy, Oriel felt hesitant.

"May I help you find something, madam?" a saleswoman asked.

"Oh, I'm not sure . . . perhaps—I'm going to the theater tonight."

"And what did madam have in mind? A gown, perhaps?"

"No, I have that." She had brought one of the most extravagant of Neecy's hand-me-downs, a jade taffeta with balloon sleeves and a pleated neckline. Oriel's wandering gaze stopped and she pointed to a flowing black panne velvet cape lined in pale green satin. "I think I'd like to try on that."

"The very thing, madam."

The next minute Oriel was standing before a full-length mirror in the dressing room while the saleswoman draped the cape over her shoulders. The ruffled collar framed her face like a fan.

"Ah, perfect!" the saleswoman declared. "It could have been made for you."

Oriel sighed. She could not possibly have walked out of the store without it. "I'll take it!"

Oriel was soon back out on the street with her packages, on her way back to the hotel. However, she could not resist pausing before a jeweler's shop window. As she halted there, she was startled by Morgan's voice just behind her. "Anything you like in there?"

She whirled around to meet his laughing eyes.

"Oh, indeed—half the window!"

"Anything particular?"

Still in a playful mode, she pointed to a jade and pearl pendant. "That for starters."

"Then you shall have it." Morgan took her arm and brought her along as he opened the store's door. They went inside together.

"Morgan," she whispered, trembling at his closeness, "I was only—"

He didn't let her finish. At the counter, Morgan spoke directly to the benignly smiling clerk, who came right up to wait on them. "We'd like to see the jade and pearl necklace in the window, if you please."

"Certainly, sir, at once. One minute while I get it."

"Morgan, no, please," she whispered. "I was only joking."

"Now, Oriel, don't fuss. You want it, and I want to give it to you. It will be a memento of a happy day in Dublin."

His voice was firm and she realized that to argue would be to cause an unnecessary scene. The clerk laid the necklace carefully on a cushion on the counter for them to view. The pale green jade stone was circled in tiny pearls. The pendant hung on a delicate gold chain.

"There are matching earrings," encouraged the clerk.

"We'll have them too," Morgan declared, and the transaction was quickly made.

The clerk handed the long, narrow box to Oriel, saying, "You have made an excellent choice. May you wear it with joy, madam."

Outside in the street again, Oriel said shyly, "Thank you, Morgan."

He smiled down at her. "I'm glad you've found something in Ireland that pleases you."

"Oh, but I've found much that pleases me! I thought you knew that."

He looked somewhat rueful. "I'm afraid I haven't noticed much that's been going on since we've been here." He drew her hand through his arm, saying, "But that's going to change."

20

*B*efore she went down to the lobby, Oriel gave
herself a critical appraisal, trying to imagine
how she would be seen by Morgan's relatives.
The cape *was* perfect and it went beautifully with the dress.
The jade pendant was an added touch. Morgan should be
pleased at the effect. Certainly he would not be ashamed to
introduce his bride to his cousins.

Oriel felt very glamorous in the flowing cape with its flat-
tering ruff as she swept down the hotel stairs. At the turn of
the stairway overlooking the lobby, she paused. She saw Morgan chatting with a well-dressed couple; his cousins, she assumed. At that moment, Morgan turned and looked up and
his expression caused her heart to give a little leap. It was a
look of genuine admiration.

She halted, wanting to seem poised. Morgan said something to the couple and they both glanced at her as she came
the rest of the way down the steps into the lobby. Meeting
her at the bottom of the stairs, Morgan took her arm and introduced her. "Oriel, I'd like you to meet my cousins, Paige
and Freddy Redmon."

Paige was a tall, handsome woman, bearing a strong family resemblance to Morgan, with her dark wavy hair and eyes the same deep blue. She wore a beautiful gown of dusty rose satin, a garnet and pearl necklace, and a short mink cape draped over her shoulders.

Paige extended both hands to Oriel. "This is too marvelous! We never dreamed we'd have a family reunion in Dublin! I'm so happy to meet Morgan's bride."

Oriel controlled the urge to look at Morgan. After this enthusiastic greeting, Oriel was certain he had not informed his cousin that their marriage was a business contract. She returned Paige's greeting cordially and turned to meet her husband.

Freddy was two or three inches shorter than his wife; he was balding, but had a rosy face and a cherubic expression. He wasn't at all what Oriel had expected as the scion of a prosperous family business, the successful chain of Redmon stores throughout Great Britain. His mild manner was in sharp contrast to his wife's ebullient one, but Oriel found his shyness rather endearing.

As Morgan escorted Oriel out of the lobby to the carriage waiting to take them to the restaurant, he glanced at her. She was glowing, her eyes shining with excitement. Suddenly Morgan realized Oriel was more than attractive, she was appealingly lovely. Impulsively, he leaned toward her and said, "You look absolutely stunning."

Surprised but pleased at his unexpected compliment, Oriel murmured, "Thank you, Morgan."

At the candlelit restaurant, the headwaiter seemed to know the Redmons, greeting them with friendly deference. They were seated at a round table covered with crisp Irish damask cloths, gleaming crystal, and fine china. Menus were brought immediately and the first few minutes were spent choosing their entrées.

146

When the waiter departed, Paige turned to Oriel and asked, "So how do you like Ireland thus far? And of course I want to know all about Drummond Castle." Not waiting for Oriel's answer, she went on, "I've heard about the castle all my life. Morgan's father and my father were brothers, you see, and they were both brought up hearing tales of Ireland—the village where Grandpa had been a barefoot boy, the whole family legend! I suppose Grandpa wanted to start his own dynasty here. He claimed we were all descendants from the kings of Ireland." She laughed. "I've never seen the castle, you know. I know Grandpa spent hundreds of thousands on restoring and modernizing it. I do hope to see it while we're here."

"Of course you must," Oriel said impulsively, then darted a quick look at Morgan.

His expression was unreadable, but he said, "Yes, of course. A weekend soon?"

"We'd love it, wouldn't we, Freddy?"

"We might have to bring Madame Tamsin along," Freddy said rather hesitantly. "We expect she will be arriving in Dublin within a week or so to be our guest."

Morgan frowned. "Who is Madame Tamsin?"

"Do tell them, Freddy," Paige urged. "It's totally fascinating."

"Madame Tamsin is a remarkable woman," Freddy explained. "She is a certified graphologist from Italy. My brothers, who head our stores in England, learned about her through a scientist friend of theirs. They actually met her later at a country weekend affair. It's not a fad or something totally on the fringe, such as the phrenology phase everyone was going through for a while. This is bona fide."

"Bona fide *what?*" Morgan asked.

"She analyzes people's handwriting," Freddy said.

"Now don't look like that, Morgan," Paige interjected. "Wait until you hear the rest."

"It's been proven to be quite authentic, Morgan," Freddy continued. "It seems character traits cannot be concealed in handwriting. It's very revealing as to traits of honesty, dishonesty, responsibility, dependability—just the sort of things you are looking for in managers. She has been hired to screen employees as well as potential customers, to determine whether they are good credit risks."

Morgan's raised eyebrows indicated skepticism.

"I admit it's a new profession, but it's being given credence by several eminent scientists," Freddy continued. "My brothers have found it to be a reliable way of hiring people for responsible positions. I've decided to try it as we set up our staff for the Dublin store."

"All this on hearsay?" Morgan said incredulously.

"It's more than that, Morgan. I've met the lady myself—both of us have."

Paige nodded vigorously. "We both found her very credible."

"Well, I have to hand it to you, Freddy. You're always willing to take a chance on something new." Morgan smiled. "And this is the lady you want to bring to Drummond Castle with you, is it?"

"If it's all right with you and Oriel."

Morgan laughed. "Indeed it is! It should make for a very interesting weekend."

The waiter arrived with their orders—delicate, tender filet of sole, saffron mushrooms, and fresh vegetables. As they began to enjoy their delicious food, conversation turned to other things. Paige was lively and amusing and kept the table talk interesting. As time was getting short—the theater curtain was scheduled for eight o'clock—they decided to pass on dessert and go somewhere after the performance.

The theater lobby was extravagantly decorated, hung with glistening crystal chandeliers. Women in gorgeous gowns and brilliant jewels and men in evening clothes added to the elegant scene. The Redmons had reserved box seats in the mezzanine with a great view of the stage. Oriel had not had many chances to attend the theater in this style. A few minutes after they settled into their places, the curtain parted and for the next hour Oriel became completely immersed in the play.

When Paige touched her arm at intermission, Oriel was still caught up in the drama. In the mezzanine, people began flowing toward the stairway to go downstairs in search of refreshment. Morgan and Freddy excused themselves, telling the ladies they would brave the crowd and return with a cool drink.

"Thank goodness!" sighed Paige, relieved. "It's always such a crush down there during intermission." She unfurled her fan. "You always bump into people you'd rather avoid, then are forced to carry on some inane conversation when all you actually want is to get some refreshment!" Her light laughter took the sting out of her remark.

As if on cue, a woman's high-pitched, imperious voice hailed, "Paige Redmon! My dear, I had no idea you were in Dublin."

Oriel and Paige turned to see a large, florid-faced woman, her silver hair magnificently coiffed, moving toward them. She wore a mauve lace gown.

Paige seemed a bit flustered at her approach. "Why, Lady Soames, how nice to see you. Freddy and I have only just arrived a few weeks ago. Freddy's opening a new store, and—"

"Yes, yes, I've heard that," the woman interrupted. "He's here with you, I presume?" Her gaze turned to Oriel, barely skimming her with a cursory glance.

"Yes," Paige said quickly. "We're here with our cousin and his bride." She turned to Oriel and introduced her, mumbling her name. She hastened on to explain, "We're still settling in—there's so much to be done. I haven't called on anyone yet—" Paige faltered.

Lady Soames nodded. "Of course, I assure you I quite understand. Life can be terribly trying and upsetting. Just let me tell you what I'm enduring. I'm just back from Italy, and what do you suppose? My niece is coming for a visit! Unexpected, to say the least. At the height of the season in

149

London, I could not understand it. Of course, my sister tells me the poor dear has had an emotional setback—a broken engagement, I think. Anyway, she suddenly decided she wants to come to Ireland. I shall have to find some way to entertain her, and I'm sure I haven't a clue. I don't have many young friends. That's why I'm delighted to see *you,* my dear."

Lady Soames went on, hardly stopping for breath. "I'm sure by the time she comes, you and Freddy will be entertaining within your Dublin circle and could see that she is invited to some of the more festive events . . ." Lady Soames seemed to have an endless source of topics to chat about. She did not slow down until a passing couple spoke to her and she suddenly sailed off to bend a new set of ears.

Paige seemed visibly relieved at Lady Soames's departure. Looking embarrassed, she said, "I hope it won't bother you to know that Lady Soames is Edwina Parker's aunt."

Edwina Parker. The name dropped like a leaden weight on Oriel's euphoric mood. She had been so happy all day, happier than she had been in months and months, then suddenly—that name.

Nothing more was said, and soon Morgan and Freddy were back, handing the women glasses of chilled Perrier to sip before the warning chimes sounded, announcing that the next act was about to begin. They went back to their box. Somehow Oriel couldn't get back her earlier interest in the unfolding drama.

During their after-theater dessert following the end of the play, Paige didn't mention the encounter with Lady Soames. Oriel was curious as to why she didn't. Did she think it would upset Morgan? Did Paige know how devastating the broken engagement had been for him? Whatever the reason, Oriel was grateful. Even so, the incident had left a bitter taste in an otherwise enjoyable evening.

Later, parting with the Redmons at their hotel entrance, Morgan and Oriel entered the lobby.

"Did you enjoy yourself, Oriel?" Morgan asked.

"Oh, very much. Your cousins are so nice."

"They liked you." Morgan smiled. "I could tell."

"I'm glad." Oriel felt her cheeks warm with pleasure. Afraid she might reveal too much, she thanked him and quickly said good night.

In her room as she took off the beautiful cape, Oriel thought that in spite of that one unfortunate moment, it had been a wonderful evening. Oriel wondered again why Paige had avoided mentioning that Edwina was coming to Ireland for a visit. Had she feared Morgan's reaction? Or had she tactfully not wanted to bring up the past and ruin what seemed, on the surface at least, to be a happy new marriage? If she knew the truth, would Paige still have refrained from mentioning Edwina Parker?

That name, Oriel thought, had been like a pebble dropped into a quiet pond, disturbing the surface, spreading ever-widening circles, ending who knew where.

It was late the following day when they arrived back at Drummond Castle. Although Morgan did not magically become a jovial fellow traveler, his attitude was decidedly changed. In comparison to their first trip to Kilmara, this journey home was most pleasant.

Finnegan came out to greet them. He opened the carriage door and assisted them out. As they started into the house, Morgan paused. "Wait a minute," he said. He walked over to the stone steps where a late-blooming rose bush boasted one lovely yellow flower. He snapped the stem, and with a smile, brought it over and presented it to Oriel. "Welcome back to Drummond Castle."

Touched by this unexpected gesture, Oriel felt a stirring within that was the whisper of hope. "Thank you, Morgan," she murmured, bringing it to the tip of her nose, inhaling its fragrance. As she did so, she happened to raise her eyes and see a shadowy figure at an upstairs window. Whoever it was stepped back from view, dropping the curtain quickly. With an involuntary shiver, Oriel felt the discomfort of having been observed. Instantly, she experienced a startling conviction. Whoever had witnessed the small scene between her and Morgan did not wish them well—did not want them to be happy at Drummond Castle.

21

*T*he days following their return from Dublin were marked by a changed atmosphere at Drummond Castle. Most visible was the change in Morgan's attitude toward her. His new regard for her gave Oriel confidence to take a more active role as mistress of the castle. Her involvement in the household seemed to motivate the staff. The house took on a new shine. Fresh flowers from the greenhouse appeared in vases in the occupied rooms. Meals became more varied.

The only person who remained aloof, in spite of all Oriel's efforts, was Mrs. Nesbitt. She seemed to take Oriel's interest as interference. She resisted any changes Oriel suggested, either failing to inform the other servants or ignoring the suggestions altogether. It was obvious the woman resented Oriel. It seemed there was nothing Oriel could do to make a difference in the housekeeper's jaundiced manner toward her.

Two incidents that happened shortly after the Dublin trip made Oriel realize that trying to win over Mrs. Nesbitt was futile. The first one occurred the day after their return. Just as Oriel was about to leave for her daily ride on Mavourneen, Mrs. Nesbitt came into Oriel's sitting room.

"I believe this is for you, madam," she said disdainfully, holding between her thumb and index finger a pink envelope.

Puzzled, Oriel repeated, "For *me?*"

"I believe so, madam. It is addressed to *Miss* Oriel *Banning.*" The housekeeper's gaze was cold.

Oriel took it, and seeing the crooked, childish handwriting recognized at once that it was from Nola. Of course it would be addressed to her *real* name. Nola thought Oriel was single, at Drummond Castle as a companion. Oriel realized Mrs. Nesbitt was trying to fluster her. "Thank you, Mrs. Nesbitt," Oriel said coolly. She could have explained that it was from a friend who did not know of her marriage, but she refused to give the woman the satisfaction of an explanation.

The letter from Nola was short, and it carried the news that a letter for Oriel had come. Enclosed was a battered-looking envelope addressed to her in care of the Claridge Hotel. It was the long overdue check and letter of reference from Mrs. McPhail, with no explanation, no excuse as to why the delay. The reference stated simply that Oriel had been in her employ for two years and had been "most satisfactory." Nola also wrote that she and Will had nearly reached their financial goals and planned to be married within a few months. That reminded Oriel that the bud vase in which she had placed the rose from Morgan was actually meant as a gift for Nola. It had been the perfect repository for the exquisite flower, which Oriel had taken much pleasure in seeing on her dressing table. Now she must wrap it and mail it to Nola. It would make a lovely wedding present.

The second incident with Mrs. Nesbitt occurred when Oriel returned from riding later that same day. Her vase was nowhere in sight. She made a cursory search of the room, then rather absently opened the top drawer of her dressing table. Inside, to her dismay, she found the vase broken and the rose crumbled, its petals among the shattered pieces of glass. Impulsively, Oriel tugged the tapestry bell pull, summoning Molly. Instead, Mrs. Nesbitt appeared.

"Molly is polishing the silver, madam, one of her *regular* duties that she has neglected of late." Mrs. Nesbitt spoke with excessive emphasis. "Is there something I can do for you?"

Oriel was trembling. Instinctively, she felt Molly was not responsible for the broken vase. She tried to control her anger, asking as calmly as possible, "Has anyone been in my room while I've been out?"

Mrs. Nesbitt looked affronted. "Only Molly, I should think, madam. To bring down your tea tray and make your bed."

Oriel pointed to the broken vase, the crumpled rose. "How did this happen, then?"

Mrs. Nesbitt looked shocked, a look Oriel suspected was pretense. Then the housekeeper's face twisted scornfully. "I told you, madam, Molly is not used to being a lady's maid, to being around delicate objects such as your vase. It is a common thing with ignorant help. They break something valuable and then, in a panic, try to hide it." She paused significantly. "Why don't you question Molly, madam? Or would you rather I did? I could discipline her."

"No, thank you, Mrs. Nesbitt. I'll attend to this myself." Oriel knew she could not openly accuse the housekeeper, even though she felt instinctively that she had something to do with the broken vase. It looked like a deliberate act.

Oriel decided to say nothing to Molly about the vase. It would only upset the girl and cause dissension among the staff. She would simply get Nola something else. Peace at any price seemed the better choice. Oriel had no premonition her decision was wrong.

During the next few weeks, Oriel felt more and more comfortable at Drummond Castle. With her new confidence, Oriel embarked on an even more ambitious project. The idea came about quite casually on a day when she encountered Bryan Moore on the cliff path. Though the late autumn winds were sharp, she still enjoyed her daily walks.

"So, Oriel, you're looking blooming. Things must be going well at Drummond Castle. The trip to Dublin seems to have done you a world of good," Bryan commented.

"I think it did. I shopped and we saw a play. I met some of Morgan's relatives, a delightful couple who will be coming down for a weekend soon. I should like you and Suzanne and Michael to meet them when they come."

"Entertaining then? You should put on the kind of show they used to hold at Drummond Castle. From what I've read, those were fantastic times."

"How so?"

"I have a book all about the balls, parties, and festivities that used to be held at the castle. The whole village was invited to them."

"I'm not planning anything as grand as that," Oriel said, laughing, "but I'd like to read about the entertainment they had in the olden days."

"I'll lend you the book," Bryan said.

True to his word, he did, and Oriel found the reading fascinating. The book was lavish with illustrations and detail. Oriel read that every autumn, the manor house gave a huge party in celebration of a good harvest and to reward the farm workers and the villagers for their loyalty. Another was held at Christmas. It was then, while looking through the book of Irish lore, that the idea of a medieval ball came to her.

One evening after an especially pleasant dinner, Oriel outlined her plan for a costume ball. She watched Morgan's expression pass from astonishment, to doubt, to guarded caution.

"Good grief, Oriel. That would take an enormous amount of planning, preparation, and work. Are you sure you want to tackle something like that on such a grand scale?"

"Yes, I'd love it. It would be fun, and besides—" She halted before adding, "It would most certainly break the monotony of the days here."

A look of amusement crossed Morgan's face, almost as if he read her unspoken thought. "Well, then go ahead. If you're game to do it, I won't stand in your way."

Given Morgan's agreement, Oriel's imagination took off and the ball began to take on reality. As she began to make lists of things to do and ideas for entertainment, music, and games, Oriel's excitement rose. She knew Suzanne would help. Bryan would have suggestions, maybe Michael as well. Oriel wrote to Paige about her plans and received a letter by return post almost immediately.

"I love it!" Paige responded. "The weekend we come with Madame Tamsin, you and I can toss all sorts of ideas around. It will be the society affair of the season—what a brilliant idea."

Oriel researched the menu possibilities with Mrs. Mills. The cook was at her best, she told Oriel, with large dinner parties and feeding many guests. "Of course, we'd have to hire extra help, with all t' baking to be done beforehand. I know several of t' village women who would welcome t' work," she assured Oriel.

Suzanne entered into every phase of the planning. The two young women exchanged notes almost daily, listing new ideas about the party. Oriel became preoccupied with what kind of costume she would wear. She and Suzanne discussed sources to research authentic costumes. Oriel invited Suzanne over to look at the portraits in the castle gallery and study some of the ladies' outfits. Since Oriel was a skilled seamstress, she thought she might copy one of the gowns.

"Oh, I'm not that clever," Suzanne sighed. "I think I'll just order costumes for me and Michael from a Dublin firm that specializes in theatrical costumes."

Oriel lingered in front of a particularly splendid looking gentleman's portrait. She could just picture Morgan in a velvet tunic, a starched ruff, and a lined cape. He would make a fantastically handsome lord of the castle. She knew she could make one of those Elizabethan doublets for Morgan—that is, if he'd let her.

The date for the ball was finally set for the first week in December. Oriel got Bryan to help with the wording of the invitation, then sent the copy to a professional calligrapher to be penned onto parchment.

She had decided on her costume, ordered the velvet fabric, and begun tracing the pattern from the gown worn by Lady Lavinia Lawrence in the portrait gallery. Her coup was persuading Morgan to let her make his doublet.

At first he had adamantly refused.

"It will only take a few minutes," she argued. "I'll get your measurements then. One fitting should do it. I can make the ruff, and we can order tights and boots from the Dublin costume shop."

With her gentle urging, he finally gave in.

Molly was present in Oriel's sitting room the morning Morgan showed up for Oriel to take his measurements. The maid seemed highly amused at the sight of Morgan standing tall and stiff while Oriel, tape measure in hand, solemnly measured the breadth of his shoulders, chest, and waist and recorded the numbers in her small notebook.

"Taking my measure, are you?" Morgan said with gruff humor.

"Oh, I already have that, sir!" Oriel retorted.

"Indeed? And what, pray tell, is it?"

"All bark and no bite, perhaps. Or like a chestnut—hard shell and soft within." She put her head to one side and looked up at him with a mischievous smile.

They looked at each other as if for the first time. It was an electrifying moment, a moment of recognition. Oriel felt her breath taken away with its intensity. She lowered her eyes and made some meaningless scribbles on the paper. "That's all, Morgan," she said briskly. "That will do nicely. Thank you."

"You're sure?" His voice seemed to hold an underlying question.

"Quite," she replied, turning away so he wouldn't see the warm color flooding into her face.

Molly, observing the two, pressed her mouth tightly together so as not to break into the wide smile puckering the corners of her mouth.

On the weekend Paige, Freddy, and Madame Tamsin were expected, Oriel made one last round of their rooms and the rest of the house. She was determined this party would not be a repeat of her first attempt at entertaining. She wanted everything to go smoothly. If this visit went well, she knew the ball would also be a success.

She still wondered if Paige and Freddy knew of the bargain she and Morgan had made. In Dublin there had been no mention of what appeared to have been a whirlwind courtship and hasty marriage. Perhaps people like the Redmons were too well-mannered to bring up sensitive subjects or ones that might cause embarrassment. However, Paige obviously knew about Edwina Parker and had assumed that Oriel also knew of the broken engagement.

As she went through the entire house one last time, Oriel complimented herself, knowing everything was in perfect readiness. She was confident that she had anticipated every possibility. She couldn't have been more wrong. She was totally unprepared for the one possibility she had never imagined.

When she heard carriage wheels on the drive, she looked out from her bedroom window and saw not one, but two carriages coming toward the house. Hurrying downstairs, she stopped at the library door to alert Morgan their guests were arriving.

He followed her to meet the visitors at the front door just as the occupants of the second coach were emerging. To Oriel's stunned amazement they were Lady Soames and her niece, *Edwina Parker.*

22

*P*aige, looking embarrassed and flustered, skimmed up the steps and took Oriel's suddenly cold hands. She leaned forward to kiss her cheek and whispered, "I'm sorry, Oriel. I had no way out. We met them in the village. They are on their way to a house party at the Mosgraves of Linden Wood. When we told them where we were going, Edwina insisted on coming along!"

Oriel did not dare glance at Morgan for his reaction.

It was Edwina who broke the awful awkwardness of the moment. With infinite confidence and grace, she came up the steps. Under a short cape bordered with silver fox fur, she wore a scarlet traveling suit. Her feathered pancake hat was coquettishly tipped to one side. She seemed not the least conscious that her unexpected appearance might be upsetting. And if she knew, she did not seem to care.

Holding out both hands to Morgan, Edwina said, "I couldn't resist the temptation of seeing the king in his castle—or should I say the dragon in his lair!" She laughed.

Oriel thought it was the loveliest laugh she had ever heard—musical as crystal being tapped with a silver spoon—

but with as brittle an edge as cut glass. It stabbed like a jagged shard into her heart.

From some unknown, unplumbed source within, she gathered herself together. She welcomed Madame Tamsin and greeted Lady Soames, who at least had the grace to look somewhat uncomfortable.

"How nice to see you again. You will of course, stay to tea," Oriel said to Edwina's aunt, even while out of the corner of her eye she noted Edwina speaking to Morgan.

"Thank you very much, but the Mosgraves are expecting us. We should be there now." Lady Soames's voice was raised, Oriel was sure, to warn her niece. "Edwina just took it into her head to stop by here first." She shifted her mink collar and gave her gold-headed cane an impatient tap on the stone steps. "We really must be on our way."

"Well, perhaps another time?" Oriel heard herself suggest, then could have bitten her tongue for having put herself in such a position.

"That's very kind of you. But it is up to—well, we shall see." Lady Soames frowned, then raised her voice again, "Edwina, my dear!"

Edwina gave her aunt a quick glance. "Coming, Auntie!" She said something to Morgan, then came down the steps and flashed a smile at Oriel and Paige, saying, "I know I've displayed frightfully bad manners, but it was too good a chance to pass up as I'm *sure* you can both understand!" She turned to Madame Tamsin. "I am totally intrigued by your work, Madame. I would *so* like to know more about it. I do hope to see you again while we're here in Kilmara."

There seemed nothing polite to do but repeat the invitation Oriel had already issued to Lady Soames. "I've asked your aunt if you might join us for tea—"

"Oh, lovely! Of course, we'd adore it, but Morgan suggested dinner tonight." Edwina looked wide-eyed and innocent.

"Of course. Do join us then," Oriel replied evenly. If Morgan wanted her to come, who was she to argue?

"Well, good-bye for now," Edwina said with a flourishing gesture of one hand. She got gracefully into the carriage, leaving her aunt still standing outside.

Flushed and irritated, Lady Soames mumbled, "I do apologize." Then, assisted by Finnegan, she reentered the carriage. The door closed upon them, but not before Lady Soames was heard to say, "That was disgraceful of you, Edwina."

Paige gave a sympathetic look to Oriel, but Oriel did not need sympathy. She needed composure. She exerted all she had to give her other *expected* guests her full attention.

Madame Tamsin was a large woman with salt-and-pepper hair arranged in a most unusual way. Instead of a bonnet, she wore a long, multicolored chiffon scarf wound around her head in a sort of turban, the ends trailing, and she wore a long, velvet cape embroidered lavishly with colorful scrolls and flowers.

"I'll show you to your room, or would you like some tea first?" Oriel floundered, feeling distracted by what had happened. She looked around. Morgan was still standing at the top of the steps, staring down the drive in the direction the Soames carriage had disappeared. He looked white, tense.

"I find I am fatigued." Madame Tamsin spoke with a slight accent. "If I might have something in my room, perhaps, and a rest, I should be much better company this evening."

"Certainly, come this way." Oriel cast a searching look at Morgan, then took both Madame Tamsin and Paige upstairs. By the time she had shown both ladies to their rooms and Morgan had taken Freddy on a tour of the grounds, Oriel felt emotionally spent. She was stunned by this turn of events. What was Edwina trying to do—bait Morgan or beguile him back?

As if to suit her own depressing mood, the day darkened ominously. Heavy clouds moved across the sky, and late in the afternoon, rain began to fall. The guests were served tea in their rooms and Oriel took the opportunity to assess her situation. There was nothing she could do to prevent Edwina's coming or to offset whatever her purpose was. All Oriel could do was to meet her on her own terms, be as gracious a hostess as she could and, in so doing, contrast the rudeness Edwina had displayed in inviting herself for the evening.

After all, two could play at this game. Oriel had what Edwina had turned down—the role of mistress of this magnificent castle and, at least ostensibly, the master as well. She would take particular care with her appearance, look her best. She decided to wear the green taffeta she had worn in Dublin, the one Morgan had admired. With it, of course, she would wear the jade pendant and earrings. If anyone admired the set, she would mention that Morgan had given it to her.

She brushed her hair until it shone. Then she got her dress and hung it up on the door of the armoire. It was lovely, and she knew it was becoming. She went to bathe, pouring nearly half a jar of scented salts into the water before slipping into the fragrant warmth. Relaxed, her anxiety about the evening ahead seemed to float away.

At length, she got out, wrapped herself in her robe, and went back into the bedroom. A terrible sight met her shocked eyes. The casement windows were open and rain and wind were blowing in on her beautiful gown. The dress swung from the knob of the armoire as wildly as a ship's sail caught in a storm. The taffeta was wet and stained. With a cry of dismay, Oriel rushed over to the windows and slammed them shut. She turned with horror to examine her dress.

A low moan escaped her. Oriel knew enough about fabric to know the dress was ruined. There was nothing she could do to save it—at least to wear tonight. The taffeta had already begun to wrinkle and the material was soaked through.

How could this have happened? The storm was heavy, yes, but the windows had been securely fastened when she went in to take her bath. All at once, a sickening certainty washed over her. Someone had purposely unlocked the windows, knowing the gusty wind would send the driving rain onto her dress. Someone had deliberately done this mean-spirited thing. Someone wanted to ruin her gown. Oriel shuddered. Someone at Drummond Castle hated her.

23

*U*pset as she was, Oriel determined not to let the ruined dress become an omen. She refused to accept it as a premonition of a disastrous evening ahead. Later, she would deal with the full implication of it all. Right now there was no time to waste. She had guests, a dinner party to conduct.

Her first task was to find something else to wear. She made a quick survey of the possibilities, and within a few minutes, she had put together a charming outfit. With a white silk blouse trimmed lavishly in Irish lace, she wore a short black velvet jacket and a flaring skirt of green satin. Her jade and pearl jewelry provided the perfect accents. Pleased with her improvisation, she hurried downstairs and into the drawing room for a final check.

Draperies had been drawn against the dreary, rainy night. The pungent scent of purple asters and golden chrysanthemums mingled with the smell of logs burning in the fireplace. Everything was in perfect readiness. Except, Oriel thought ironically, for the hostess, who dreaded the arrival of guests she did not want to receive.

Oriel tried to tell herself it should not bother her if Morgan's feelings for Edwina had been rekindled. After all, they *had* been engaged. They must have been in love, and one doesn't get over love that easily. Even though they had quarreled, time had passed. Maybe Edwina's distorted image of the castle as an isolated, run-down building on the dreary coast had changed. Perhaps she felt she'd made a mistake letting Morgan go and wanted him back.

Whatever it was, there was nothing Oriel could do about it. Nor could she do anything about her own feelings except hide them. At least her friends, the Wicklows and Bryan, would be here this evening to support her. Madame Tamsin had agreed to give a demonstration of her craft, which would also make the evening interesting. All Oriel could hope for was to get through it.

Soon, Suzanne and Michael arrived with Bryan. Suzanne was excited, brimming with new ideas for the ball. Oriel introduced the Wicklows to Paige and Freddy. Madame Tamsin soon joined them, looking as eccentric as ever in a flowing gown that resembled an Arabian tent. Several colorful chiffon scarves were wound into a turban on her head.

Leaving her guests in a congenial conversation, Oriel went into the kitchen for a last-minute consultation with Mrs. Mills. She did not want a repetition of that first dinner party, which had been such a shambles.

Mrs. Mills seemed to have everything under control with Molly and Carleen helping her. Oriel was coming back from the kitchen when she saw Lady Soames and Edwina arrive at the front door. She slipped quietly into the drawing room to watch Edwina make her entrance.

Ushered by Finnegan, Edwina stood on the threshold for a moment, pausing dramatically. She looked stunning, tall and graceful, gowned in an elegant royal blue dress with a portrait neckline that revealed her gleaming white shoulders. Everyone turned to look at her. Her entrance had been brilliantly staged. Oriel glanced at Morgan, who was stand-

168

ing at the fireplace. When Edwina walked in, the only change in his expression was a visible clenching of his jaw. He set down the wine glass he was holding and took a step toward her. Edwina turned her back, however, sweeping into the center of the room.

Paige stepped up beside Oriel and whispered, "Everything is always a performance with Edwina." Her remark did nothing to reassure Oriel.

Edwina, smiling, glanced around the room, her gaze settling on Morgan, who remained standing, as though rooted to his spot in front of the fireplace. *Is he so stunned by Edwina's presence he can't function?* Oriel wondered. She realized it was up to her to do the honors as hostess and went forward to greet Edwina and her aunt.

Oriel gave Morgan a sharp glance. *Isn't he even going to introduce her to the rest of the guests?* she thought with dismay. He looked distracted, so Oriel was forced into doing it. Bryan seemed both amused and enchanted by this glorious, vibrant creature. Michael was a little more remote, but still fascinated. Suzanne was bedazzled by all the glamour.

Since Morgan continued to be distracted, Oriel saw to it that everyone had something to drink. She seated Lady Soames, resplendent in shimmering gray satin and rubies, beside Madame Tamsin. It was a relief when Finnegan came to announce dinner.

At dinner, Edwina shone. Oriel was sure she had never been more vivacious. She flirted with Freddy, surely aware of Morgan's glowering gaze on her. She tossed her golden head, laughed her lilting laughter, and gaily told anecdotes that showed off her wit and charm. In fact, Edwina took center stage, something she seemed to do naturally and easily, as if *she* belonged here at Drummond Castle.

While trying to carry on a sensible conversation with Freddy, who was seated at her right, Oriel watched Edwina with growing dismay. The excellent dinner she and Mrs. Mills had planned could have been cardboard for all she could taste of it. Course after course—clear mushroom soup, the saddle of lamb, baby carrots, onions in cream sauce, endive salad—came and went without Oriel's appreciation.

She felt her fork grow heavy in her right hand. She was aware of a new sensation, one she recognized as wounded pride, crushed hope. It hit her with its impact. Never in her wildest imagination had she imagined that she would one day feel any emotion—attraction, rage, certainly not jealousy or passion—for Morgan Drummond, worst of all, grief over the possibility of losing him.

It was ridiculous, her own fault. She should never have allowed herself to hope. But it was too late. She had let down her protective reserve, allowed herself to feel, to imagine, to dream. Oriel felt gradually diminished by Edwina, pushed into an ignominious shadow by the woman's electric brilliance.

Paige appeared miserable. Once in a while she attempted to catch Oriel's eye, with understanding and sympathy in her glance. Oriel knew Paige felt sorry about what she had inadvertently brought about.

Oriel would not have met Morgan's gaze even if he had been looking at her. All she wanted was for this dreadful evening to be over so she could escape to her room, where she could weep out her splintered dreams.

In one of those sudden lulls that occur sometimes even during the liveliest dinner parties, Freddy's comment addressed to Morgan was heard by all. "So, Morgan, have you gotten used to being an *Irish* country gentleman by now?"

Morgan replied, "Oh, I'm finding Ireland much to my liking in many unexpected ways."

"But what on earth do you find to do here?" Edwina asked.

Oriel felt herself stiffen. She glanced uneasily down the length of the table at Morgan. Edwina set her glass down and looked directly at Oriel. Her eyes glittered with malice, and there was something about the saccharine smile that lifted the corners of her perfectly shaped mouth that chilled Oriel.

To Oriel's immense relief, Finnegan and Conan entered just then with the chocolate mousse and cherry sorbet, and the moment passed as dessert was served. From the other end of the table, Oriel heard Edwina's crystalline laughter ring out again and she saw one of Morgan's rare smiles. In a reactive spasm of anger, Oriel crumpled her napkin in her lap.

After dinner, they all returned to the drawing room. Finnegan brought in trays bearing cups of coffee, which he solemnly passed among the seated guests. Oriel found herself sitting a little apart from the group. Voices faded into a background hum, underpinning the farce playing out in front of her. It was, after all, the stuff of high drama—the return of the intended bride to the scene where another holds her place.

Oriel looked at Morgan across the room and studied his expression as though he had been a portrait. It was animated in a way she had not seen it before. Was it because of Edwina's presence? she wondered. Was he trying to impress her by giving the role of perfect host a try? Oriel was sure the Wicklows must be surprised, especially after Morgan's morose, taciturn performance the night they had come to dinner before.

Eventually, the conversation turned to Madame Tamsin's reason for being in Dublin. Oriel's focus came back as Madame explained a little about graphology.

"It sounds like some sort of hocus-pocus to me," Lady Soames declared with a sniff. "If we all learned to write the same way, how can a few differences in loops and curlicues reveal a person's character?"

Madame Tamsin did not lose her temper, as Oriel thought she had every right to. Instead, she focused her direct gaze on Lady Soames and said, "Oh, but that's just it. It's in those very differences, those small insignificant twists an uninformed person might discount, that a trained eye can find meaning. The thief, the liar, the manipulator, the dishonest person—it all comes through. Handwriting comes directly from the heart, down the arm, into the hand gripping the pen, and out onto the paper. In a person's handwriting much can be revealed."

"It's true, Lady Soames. We've already used it most effectively in our London store and we are convinced it works." Freddy gestured to Madame Tamsin. "This lady is a genius at ferreting out a person's hidden character flaws, as well as revealing attributes. We have Madame Tamsin analyze the applications of our employees and she has been dead-on in all the choices we have made through her advice."

"It sounds logical to me," Bryan commented.

Michael chimed in. "A man's signature was extremely important in the days when only the aristocracy could write. Even an uneducated person felt it necessary to learn to sign his own name. The strength or weakness of his writing was there for all to see."

"What fun!" Edwina clapped her hands. "Why don't we all let Madame Tamsin analyze our handwriting?"

Madame Tamsin turned cool eyes on Edwina. "It is not a parlor game, Miss Parker," she said coldly. "I am not a fortune-teller or a soothsayer. I have studied for years to make this my profession."

Oriel felt the atmosphere fill with tension. Freddy and Paige exchanged a glance. Michael stared straight ahead, while Suzanne twisted her hands in her lap, looking embarrassed. Edwina seemed completely undaunted by Madame Tamsin's rejoinder.

"I'm sure Miss Parker meant no offense," Morgan said and was rewarded with one of Edwina's loveliest smiles.

Then Edwina, all eagerness, said, "Oh, do let's get on with it! What shall we write?"

Madame Tamsin turned to Oriel. "Could we have slips of paper for each one, please? And pencils or pens?"

Oriel, in turn, looked at Morgan. He waited a single second as if reluctant to take part in this. Then he got to his feet and left the room. He returned a moment later with paper and pencils, which he proceeded to pass out to the guests. Oriel looked down at hers, noticing the Drummond Castle crest at the top, embossed in gold lettering.

"It is very simple, actually," Madame Tamsin said. "Choose a sentence—it can be your own thought, a favorite quotation, a line from a poem, or whatever. The important thing for us tonight, in this small a group, is not to sign your name. You can give the source of your quote, if you like. What I need is enough letters of the alphabet used in ordinary writing. The main thing, and I emphasize this for those who think this is not scientific, is that what I do here tonight has very little similarity to the type of in-depth analysis I do with an employment application. Is that understood by everyone?" Madame Tamsin looked directly at Lady Soames, who seemed oblivious to her.

For the next five minutes, only the scratching of pencils on paper could be heard. Oriel hesitated. She couldn't think of anything to write down. Everything that came into her mind seemed too revealing in content. She lifted her head and looked across the room at Morgan. What would he choose to write? Her gaze passed to Edwina, who was tapping the end of her pencil on her perfect teeth as if she, too, was struggling to find something to write.

Just then, Oriel was aware of Morgan's gaze on her. She felt the warmth climbing up into her cheeks. For what seemed like a minute, their gaze held. Her heart twisted. *Oh, Morgan, if you only knew* . . . she thought desperately.

Oriel ducked her head and began to write.

A few minutes more went by, then Madame Tamsin spoke. "If everyone has finished, fold your piece of paper once. Will someone please collect them? Do we have some kind of bowl or dish to put them in so that I can pick one at random?"

Oriel gestured to a brass bowl. This time, not needing any prompting, Morgan went around the room for each guest to drop in the folded slip of paper.

One by one, Madame Tamsin took each slip of paper in her two hands. Her eyebrows met over closed eyes, as if she were meditating over it. Then, in her distinctive voice, she rapidly began the analyses. She explained how the slant of letters, the loop of an *l*, and the way a *t* was crossed all revealed something significant about the person writing.

Oriel only half-listened. Only one or two of the remarks struck a responsive chord in Oriel. "A tendency toward jealousy, vindictiveness," Madame Tamsin said. And about another sample, she declared, "It shows uncertainty, insecurity, indecisiveness." Her conscience pricked sharply. If she were truthful, tonight especially, either of those analytic statements could be about her. Was it *her* handwriting Madame Tamsin was analyzing? She glanced around the room. Was anyone else reacting like this, or was she the only one Madame's analysis fit?

With each slip, Madame's analysis was getting longer and more and more questions were asked. If she had not been so consumed with her own inner turmoil, Oriel was sure she would have found Madame Tamsin's talk interesting and informative.

As it was getting late, Oriel thought she should have some refreshment served. It had been a long evening. Quietly she excused herself, and went to find Finnegan. She told him the guests were playing a game that might go very late. She suggested that after bringing in a tray of biscuits, sparkling water, and teas, he needn't wait up.

On her way back to the drawing room, Oriel heard two voices from the cloakroom off the main hall, unmistakably Edwina's and her aunt's. "But just *who* is she?" Lady Soames asked.

"I'm sure I don't know." This was Edwina. "Except she's extremely attractive."

"You know what I mean—what is her background, her family? Where did Morgan meet her?" Lady Soames sounded impatient. "He certainly didn't pick her out of thin air!"

There was a laugh, a sharp one with a cutting edge, and Edwina replied, "On board ship coming from America! Isn't that ironic? On his way to marry *me*."

"Oh, one of those shipboard romances, then," her aunt remarked dismissively.

Oriel started to hurry past, but not quickly enough. Edwina emerged into the hall. She had her fur cape over one arm. With a malicious smile, she stepped in front of Oriel, blocking her way.

The beautiful eyes were shooting sparks, and the lovely face was swiftly transformed into a hate-filled mask. "I hope you don't fantasize Morgan feels anything real for you. He only married you to spite me!"

Oriel attempted to pass by, but Edwina reached out and caught her arm, jerking her back. Her face was very close. "He acted out of anger because I refused to come to this drafty, godforsaken place for a year. But he's never stopped wanting me and he wants me still. Don't delude yourself into thinking you can prolong this ridiculous charade." She released Oriel's arm with a flinging motion. Tossing her fur cape over her shoulders, she swept off down the hall, the train of her dress sliding on the stone floor behind her.

Oriel stood staring after her, speechless. She heard voices coming from the drawing room. People were getting ready to leave. She had to pull herself enough together to go back to her guests. Everyone was talking and laughing as Oriel reentered the room. Edwina avoided eye contact and chatted amiably with Freddy as everyone moved toward the hall.

Oriel stood beside Morgan as they saw their guests out to the carriages. Busy accepting the enthusiastic thanks of Bryan and Suzanne, Oriel was still aware of Edwina. She noticed that Morgan took her and her aunt out to their carriage. Before getting in, Edwina put her graceful gloved hand on his arm and said a lingering good-bye.

While Oriel saw to her houseguests, she heard Morgan ask Freddy to join him for a nightcap in his study. After a worried glance at Oriel, Paige escorted Madame Tamsin upstairs. At the top of the stairs, Oriel bade them all good night, and without another word, went quickly to the haven of her own room. Of all the nights Oriel had been at Drummond Castle, this one seemed to her the worst of all.

24

*I*n her bedroom, Oriel undressed. She sat down at the dressing table and started to remove her jewelry. She unfastened the earrings and dropped them into the velvet case. As Oriel started to undo the clasp of her jade and pearl pendant, her fingers touched it lovingly. She recalled that afternoon in the Dublin shop when Morgan had declared that she should have it. He had halted her protests, saying, "You want it, and I want to give it to you. It will be a memento of a happy day in Dublin."

She stared at herself in the mirror, searching to see what she was really thinking and feeling. Did it show? The muscles around her mouth ached from smiling, but the drawn look in her eyes showed the strain of the evening. Had anyone guessed how unhappy she was?

She stretched out on the bed, knowing sleep would not come easily. The year was only half over, but now that Edwina had come and Morgan showed every inclination of succumbing to her charm, would he want to break their contract? Could he not see through that facade to a woman not only less than perfect, but deeply flawed, even spiteful?

Could a man like Morgan really be in love with Edwina, who seemed to have nothing to offer but her beauty?

Oriel knew her unexpressed feelings for Morgan made her vulnerable. She relived the humiliating encounter with Edwina, her cutting words. If they were true, maybe she should offer Morgan his freedom, break the contract. Finally, she fell into a sleep, disturbed by dreams.

She awoke with a start just as daylight was breaking. She was terribly thirsty. Her throat felt raw and dry. She decided to go downstairs, slip into the kitchen, and make some tea.

She drew on her robe and went down the steps in her bare feet. As she passed the drawing room, something compelled her to go in. She was drawn irresistibly to the brass bowl into which Madame Tamsin had tossed the slips of paper after she had done the analysis. Curious if she could find Morgan's and read what he had written, Oriel unfolded each one.

She recognized his bold, slanted handwriting at once. Morgan had written, "There is a tide in the affairs of men, which, taken at the flood, leads on to fortune; Omitted, all the voyage of their life is bound in shallows and miseries.— W. Shakespeare."

Were those Morgan's real sentiments—that he had not acted when he should have, missed the tide? That he now was spending his life "bound in shallows and miseries"? Oriel dropped the slip back into the bowl. She stayed another minute, looking for her own paper, but it wasn't there. She counted the slips. There had been nine people—the Wicklows, Freddy and Paige, Lady Soames, Edwina, Bryan, Morgan, and herself—but there were only *eight* slips left in the bowl. Hers was missing! How strange. Why would anyone take hers?

Still musing, she headed for the kitchen. After making a cup of tea, she returned to her room.

Later that morning at breakfast, Morgan suggested taking Freddy on a tour of the stables for a look at his new horses. Since Madame Tamsin had asked for a tray sent up to her room, this left Paige and Oriel alone at the table.

Immediately after the men left, Paige leaned forward to Oriel, saying, "I must apologize again, Oriel, for letting Edwina manipulate herself into the weekend. I don't know what she's up to, but I'm guessing it's not good. What she can't have, she wants. Goes after it." She raised her eyebrows. "I never thought she was right for Morgan from the first minute I met her, but she is clever. Before anyone knew it, she had him wound around her little finger. Last night she was up to her same old tricks—anyone could see that. It was outrageous. I felt terrible and so did Freddy. For her to do that right under your nose!"

"Hold on a minute, Paige," Oriel interrupted. "I have to tell you something. First, there's no need for you to apologize. I knew about Edwina before I was married. Morgan was very forthright, and—"

Conan came in with a silver pot of fresh coffee, and conversation was suspended while he refilled both of their cups. Oriel waited until he left before continuing. "You see, Paige, Morgan's and my marriage is not what you think it is."

Paige looked puzzled. "Well, I know it was rather sudden, coming soon after Edwina broke the engagement, but that's what makes it all the more romantic. You met on the ship coming over, didn't you?"

"Paige, that's what I'm trying to tell you. It's not romantic at all. It's—well, if it weren't for me, I'm sure Morgan and Edwina would patch things up, and—"

Paige rolled her eyes in mock horror. "Heaven forbid! She's all wrong for him—that's what I'm trying to tell you."

"No, Paige, what I'm trying to tell you is if I were not in the picture—"

"Good morning." Madame Tamsin's dramatic voice greeted them, and they both turned to see her standing in the doorway. She had on a caftan with chiffon scarves in blue, purple, and mauve floating in all directions. "What a glorious morning! I could no longer stay in bed on such a beautiful day."

Oriel rang for Conan to bring more coffee, and Madame Tamsin helped herself to a currant scone and joined them at the table. "What a curious session we had last night," she said. "It is always hard to analyze handwriting seriously when there are skeptics in the group. They rank this new science along with card reading or fortune-telling!" She shook her head disgustedly, causing her long, looped earrings to chime.

"I'm sorry you were put in such an awkward position, Madame," Oriel said apologetically.

"It's not you, my dear, I have a quarrel with. It's the other woman and her niece. They were so—so *unsimpatico*—criticizing things they do not understand. Not like you others." She looked at both of them approvingly. "The rest of you seemed eager to explore new ideas, most enthusiastic."

The men came back in from inspecting the stables and soon Paige, Freddy, and Madame Tamsin were ready to begin the return trip to Dublin.

Just before she got into the carriage, Paige came over to Oriel and kissed her cheek. "I am so sorry I inadvertently made this a difficult weekend for you, Oriel. I want you to know how much I admire your quiet courage, your graciousness in this most trying circumstance. You're the best thing that could possibly have happened to Morgan. I hope he's wise enough to realize—"

Whatever Paige hoped Morgan was wise enough to realize was cut off by Freddy's joining them to offer his thanks. "Jolly good time. Never saw Morgan in better form."

Oriel forced a smile. As the carriage pulled away from the house and went down the drive, Oriel realized she had never had the opportunity to explain to Paige the real circumstances of her relationship to Morgan.

Instead of going back inside, Oriel left Morgan standing on the steps and headed for the path to the cliffs. Though it was cold walking weather, she wasn't ready to be alone with him, to discuss the weekend and Edwina's surprise appearance. She needed time to deal with feelings she had only just admitted having. There were only five more months until the term of the contract would be fulfilled. She would be free to leave. The trouble was, she did not want to leave.

She had not counted on feeling this way. She assumed when the time came, she could walk away, forget Kilmara, forget Morgan. Now she knew that was no longer possible. Morgan still loved Edwina, wanted her back. Any thoughts Oriel had entertained of a future here with him were just fantasy.

But what could she do in the meantime? She bent her head against the wind, walking faster to the top of the hill. At length, the fuzziness of her thoughts cleared, like evaporating fog. She would go on with the medieval ball. Plans had gone too far to change them now. Invitations were being printed, musicians had been engaged, elaborate menus planned, extra help hired, decorations ordered. No, there was no way to cancel it. Besides, it would keep her busy.

Yes, if she *had* to leave Drummond Castle forever, she would leave in a blaze of glory.

25

The next afternoon, Oriel set out for Bracken Hall to see Suzanne. She longed for the comfort of being with her friend after the tension of the weekend.

She was in the front hall just ready to leave when Morgan came to the door of his study. "Oriel, would you come in here, please? I want to talk to you."

She hesitated. She was feeling very vulnerable and did not want to expose herself to Morgan's nearness. "Will it take long? I'm just off to see Suzanne."

"No, not long," he said, holding the door open for her to enter.

A small fluttering began in her stomach. Suddenly filled with dread, she wondered what he wanted to talk to her about. Nervously, she went into the room and took the chair he indicated. He stood by the fireplace, his hands behind his back.

"I wanted to commend you. You handled the unexpected company remarkably well. It must have been quite a strain."

"No, not really," she kept her voice crisp, light.

He waited, as if expecting her to say something else. When she didn't, he went on. "Oriel, I've been doing a great deal of thinking recently and more and more I've come to realize how unfair I have been to you. My lawyers tried to tell me that before I had them draw up the contract, but I insisted. I know now my motivation was—well, not of the highest. I was acting in anger—a state not conducive to rational action."

Oriel started to say something, but he held up a hand to halt her. "It was completely wrong to pressure you—knowing you were in desperate financial circumstances—into signing an agreement that must have been odious to a woman of your refinement, sensitivity, and high morals. In retrospect, it was a despicable thing to do."

"Oh, no, Morgan, I—"

He again raised his hand to ward off her protest. "Please, Oriel, let me finish." He went on. "If you are unhappy—and I wouldn't blame you if you are—I have been of little or no help in making your time here pleasant or enjoyable." He paused. "Anyway, if you are unhappy, I would be willing to release you from our agreement with no penalty. I'll send word to my lawyers, and you will receive what you've been promised." His voice roughened. "You've earned it—every penny."

Oriel felt the blood draining from her head and she was suddenly dizzy. She felt cold, as if someone had opened a window and let in a blast of icy air. She stared at Morgan. So! *He* wanted out of the contract—that must be it. Edwina's coming had made him realize his terrible mistake! In some moment, they must have had a chance to talk, to reconcile. If they could get rid of the impediment, they could get back together. *She* was the impediment. How easy for Morgan with his millions to pay off the obstacle in his way. How he would get around the rest of the requirements of the will, she couldn't guess. Maybe he didn't care anymore. He would let Drummond Castle go, let it deteriorate again, let all his grandfather's efforts come to nothing!

Something inside Oriel knotted with determination. Something in her said, *I won't let that happen.* Oriel realized how much she loved the castle, Kilmara, Ireland. Drawing herself up, she replied, "No, Morgan, a contract is a contract. I intend to keep my part of the bargain. But, let us be truthful to each other. Let's not pretend. Let us frankly admit what is at stake here. Edwina's coming upset you. However, we both signed our agreement in good faith. No matter what the motivation on each of our parts, it is a legal, binding contract."

Morgan regarded her somberly for a full minute. When he spoke, his voice softened and he seemed confused by her reaction. "I did not intend to hurt you by what I'm suggesting. I wanted to be fair in offering you a release from the contract. I didn't mean to offend you."

"You didn't," Oriel said evenly. *But neither did you deny you are still in love with Edwina,* she added silently.

"I just wanted to be fair, and—"

"You were. And I want to be fair too." Oriel stood up, took a few steps toward the door, and said, "Let us just go on as before."

"As you like," Morgan said formally.

Oriel, her back straight, walked to the door. Her hand ready to twist the knob, she turned back. Deliberately keeping her voice steady, she added, "Plans for the ball have progressed too far to cancel. Besides, it will create a more friendly feeling about Drummond Castle."

He looked startled, as though he had just remembered the ball. "Good," he said brusquely. Then, "I appreciate all you're doing, Oriel."

She nodded, opened the door, and went out. What had been building up in her over the last weeks suddenly came forth. She realized how deeply she cared for Morgan, had wanted him to care for her. It was insane, she knew. It was not part of the bargain. She could just be thankful that Morgan could not read her mind, look into her heart.

By the time Oriel got to Bracken Hall, her outer composure was shattered. All her vague hopes about a possible future were gone. Morgan could not wait to be free but was too honorable to break their contract. Somehow she would have to brave out the rest of her time at Drummond Castle.

Suzanne, her usual effervescent self, welcomed Oriel. For a few minutes she chattered happily about her ideas for the medieval ball. Then, noticing Oriel's lack of enthusiasm, she stopped mid-sentence. "Is something wrong? You look— what's the matter, Oriel?"

"Oh, forgive me, Suzanne. I guess I'm just not in the right mood."

Suzanne was instantly understanding. "Too much company over the weekend! I told Michael I thought you looked strained Saturday evening, not yourself at all."

Suzanne paused, then asked more tentatively, "Did you and Morgan quarrel? I know when Michael and I have an argument, it's usually when I'm worn out physically, or have a headache . . ."

Oriel gave a harsh little laugh. "Morgan and I *never* quarrel, Suzanne. He doesn't care enough to quarrel."

Suzanne looked shocked, then sympathetic. "Oh, I'm so sorry, Oriel."

"It doesn't matter. It's not like you and Michael—ours is not a love match." She shook her head, then shrugged. "Morgan's in love with someone else, someone he knew before he met me, before we were married."

Suzanne put her hand on Oriel's. "Oh, Oriel, I'm truly sorry."

Their conversation might have gone further, but just then the front door slammed and they heard male voices. A minute later, Michael and Bryan came into the room.

Upon seeing the open scrapbook in which they had been compiling ideas, pictures, and other material about the ball, Michael struck his forehead in dismay and exclaimed, "Not that ridiculous party again!" He turned to Bryan and said,

"These two ladies do nothing but eat, drink, and sleep that gaudy affair to be held at Drummond Castle."

"I think it's a capital idea myself." Bryan smiled encouragement. He sauntered over to the table where the scrapbook was spread out.

Oriel stood up. She didn't want to stay longer now; her emotions were too near the surface. "Oh, we've done enough for today." She glanced at Suzanne, knowing she would understand. "I'll come by tomorrow, perhaps, and we'll go over some of the ideas then."

Soon Oriel was on her way again. The fog had thickened considerably, wrapping itself around her as she walked, like a heavy, soggy blanket. Her mood was also heavy. She dreaded returning to Drummond Castle, having dinner with Morgan, pretending nothing had changed.

Morgan had never promised her anything. It was she who had let her feelings get out of hand, to imagine possibilities. *It's my own fault*, she told herself mercilessly as she hurried on.

At length, she saw the outline of the castle eerily shrouded in fog. Lights shone out like fuzzy slits through the gloom. It was only a little farther to the gates. That's when she saw it, floating toward her menacingly—the hooded figure. *Shaleen O'Connor*. Instinctively the name formed on her lips. She drew back in horror. The billowing cape and stealthy glide were familiar as it approached. A prayer for protection rose from her heart. She squeezed her eyes shut tight. When she opened them, the figure had disappeared.

Her heart was beating in her throat. She *had* seen it. This time there was no mistake. It wasn't a wisp of fog. Something *real* had passed by her in the swirling mist.

She ran toward the gates. They were closed. She jangled the handles and finally pushed through. She shoved them wider. If she had anything to do with it, Shaleen O'Connor would not find them closed again and bring disaster upon Drummond Castle.

She started running up the driveway toward the house, when all at once, she stopped short. What had come over her? She realized what a superstitious thing she had done. Was she silly enough to believe the story of the ghostly vengeance against the castle residents? Yet she had seen that same figure several times since she'd come here. A ghost? Her common sense told her there must be some other explanation. She slowed her steps as she neared the front entrance. She certainly didn't intend to tell Morgan about this, suffer his scorn. Still, Oriel knew she had seen something. If it wasn't a ghost, what was it?

26

*O*riel plunged herself into weeks of meticulous planning and preparation for the ball. She had hoped such immersion would soothe her troubled emotions, her aching heart. It worked to some extent.

Her preoccupation in all this activity had proved enough of a distraction that she had not had much time to dwell on her relationship with Morgan. She had wondered, however, how long Edwina and her aunt had remained houseguests at Linden Wood. Had Morgan ridden over to visit his former fiancée there? Had he kept in contact with Edwina after she had returned with Lady Soames to Dublin? At her lowest times, Oriel could imagine they were counting the days until this farce of a marriage could be annulled and they could pick up their lives as if this year had never happened.

At last it was the night of the ball, and Oriel was getting dressed. Molly helped with the tiny hooks and eyes of the velvet bodice and the layers of crinoline that went underneath the bouffant taffeta skirt.

"Oh, ma'am, you look a fair picture!" the maid declared as she placed an ornamental comb in Oriel's hair. Oriel had gone countless times into the portrait gallery, studying the portrait of Lady Lavinia Lawrence. She had studied the painting so often—the details of the elaborate dress, her hairstyle—that she felt as if she knew her.

"It did turn out much better than I could have hoped," Oriel said with satisfaction, looking at the costume in the mirror. The color, a rich deep emerald, and the seventeenth-century style were surprisingly becoming. She could believe she looked just like a mistress of a manor might have in those olden days, about to welcome her guests to a gala ball.

Before she went downstairs, she picked up each of the two masks she had made, trying both in turn. Deciding upon the green satin one with beaded sequins along the edges, she put it on. It hid her eyes and the shape of her nose; a ruffle of gilt lace also covered her mouth. It was a perfect disguise. She wondered if she'd be able to guess which of her lady guests was Suzanne. Since they had decided to have the guests wear masks until midnight, Oriel and Suzanne thought it would be more fun not to divulge to each other what they would be wearing.

The great hall had been opened for the party, transformed into medieval splendor. Colorful banners hung from the rafters, along with red, gold, blue, and green streamers. Some of the banners bore appliquéd heraldic shields, copied from a book Bryan had lent Oriel. The music playing in the background might have been from ancient instruments. It all had the authentic look and feel of the kind of festive event that might have taken place in this very room long ago.

Carriage after carriage rolled through the gates and up the driveway, dispensing extravagantly costumed guests. Oriel had sent out over a hundred invitations. She had compiled lists with Suzanne of the landed gentry around Kilmara. She had also asked Paige for names of people in Dublin she would like to have invited. Morgan rather reluctantly had added a few of his own friends to be sent the calligraphy invitation.

As she received the dozens of guests flowing through the main entrance, Oriel decided she had been right. Costumes put partygoers in a certain mood, ready to have a special time. Everyone was in high spirits. As she moved about, Oriel heard such comments as, "There hasn't been a party like this in Kilmara for decades." "What a splendid idea this was." "Drummond Castle has become the center of social life here once again."

Oriel kept glancing at Morgan to see how he was responding to all of this. He looked handsome in his gentleman's black velvet doublet trimmed with gilt braid. The high starched ruff and a gold medallion swinging from a heavy chain perfectly set off his aristocratic good looks. He seemed to be enjoying himself.

After she had greeted and shaken hands with group after group of masked guests, Oriel looked around. Where were Suzanne and Michael? Had they come and she somehow missed them? Then, at last, she thought she spotted them. There was something about the tall couple who had just entered the hall arm in arm. Oriel was startled, however, when she saw the woman's costume. It was the dress worn in the portrait of Lady Lavinia Lawrence—exactly the same as the one Oriel had made for herself! What a coincidence—if that *was* Suzanne.

Oriel started toward them, ready to have a good laugh with them over the duplication, but just as she was near enough to speak, the couple turned away. Oriel felt a little taken aback. Had they not seen her, not recognized her? Surely Suzanne would have noticed they were wearing the same dress. But if it was not Suzanne, Oriel wanted to find out who else would have known about Lady Lavinia's portrait. She started to follow the couple, but they were swallowed up by the crowd and seemed to disappear. Bewildered, Oriel halted.

Someone touched her arm. "Oriel, what a success! Aren't you pleased?" It was Bryan. Even with the mask, she could tell. He was dressed as a medieval scholar in a dark robe and tasseled hat. "You've outdone yourself. I'm sure Morgan is very proud of you."

That remark brought her up short. As a matter of fact, Morgan had not said anything to show he was. She almost said as much, but bit her tongue. She was saved from having to reply when her attention was caught by the arrival of a group of four. She recognized Paige and Freddy's voices. Then she heard an unmistakable laugh—*Edwina!* On whose list had she been? The invitations had been addressed by a professional calligrapher, but Oriel had not seen Morgan's list. A chill went through her. Was her one moment of glory in her time at Drummond Castle going to be ruined by Edwina?

A mixture of feelings rushed up within Oriel at the sight of Edwina. Inexcusably rude though it was, she couldn't bring herself to greet the new arrivals. She would have to explain to Paige later. But it was impossible for her to welcome Edwina, especially after their unforgettable encounter when she had seen Edwina's malice toward her.

Edwina had come as Queen Elizabeth, bejeweled and bedecked in a gilt embroidered gown, a sparkling tiara set upon a curled auburn wig. She had not worn a mask but carried an ornate one on a small stick. She waved the mask flirtatiously as she chatted with Morgan.

Oriel's hands clenched. She suppressed a shudder and looked away. But not fast enough. She knew Bryan had witnessed her reaction. She tried to pick up their conversation but was too distracted. Her mind wandered hopelessly. When she chanced another look in their direction, it was just in time to see Morgan lead Edwina onto the dance floor.

Rigid with indignation, Oriel knew in order to face the rest of the evening she had to find a few minutes alone to compose herself. "Excuse me," she said to Bryan and moved, as in a trance, across the room in the opposite direction. She was stopped now and then by guests complimenting her on the party. Smiling, she murmured some appropriate response and went on. Minute by minute her need to escape became more desperate.

At length the chance came. She saw a path open up between the dancing couples and slipped out the door at the far side of the ballroom, into the hall, and up the stairs. The sound of music and voices, of dancing feet and laughter, all continued behind her. On the second floor, she moved along the darkened corridors to her room.

For some reason, she noticed the door leading to the minstrels' gallery was ajar. A faint light shone out. The musicians for the ball were in the great hall, so Oriel knew the room was not in use. She paused and heard voices—a man's and a woman's.

Although she could not make out the words, there was an intensity in their tone. Oriel felt a kind of furtive excitement tremble through her. Some dark instinct told her to stay where she was, to listen. Torn between what she knew was right and an urgency to hear what was being said, she hesitated. Then she heard her name. Morgan was the one who was using it.

Oriel stopped dead still.

She heard Edwina's voice, clearly wistful, pleading, seductive. "So, I was wrong. Are you never going to forgive me? What am I supposed to do? Be a penitent like in the medieval days? Wear sackcloth and ashes and come up the steps on my knees and beg you?"

Frozen, Oriel remained rooted to the spot, straining to hear Morgan's reply. Her heart was pounding. Part of her wanted to know, another part dreaded knowing it. There was a silence following Edwina's plaintive question. Were they embracing? Had Morgan *shown* her instead of *telling* her? Were they kissing?

Oriel felt stricken, knew it was ridiculous. She tiptoed away from the door, feeling weak and dizzy. She stopped, steadying herself by leaning against the wall. Gradually, the faintness passed.

She drew a long breath and started again on her way to her room. The hall was dark except for the dim glow of an old-fashioned globe lamp at the far end. She became aware of stealthy movement. Had someone followed her?

She twisted her head to look down the hall. It was empty, full of shadows. She saw no one. As she began walking again, she heard furtive footsteps moving swiftly, coming up behind her.

Before she could turn around to see who it was, she felt a hard thrusting shove on both shoulders that knocked her off balance. At the same time, she heard the sliding sound of something heavy being pushed aside. Before she could try to defend herself, there was a second shove, this time sending her stumbling on her knees into sudden darkness.

27

*H*er scream, strangled and incoherent, ended shrilly as the opening through which she'd been thrust slid shut again and impenetrable darkness closed around her. Her mind reeled. She felt shock, disbelief, fear. Where was she? Who had attacked her? Why?

At the hard shove, she had thrown out her hands to break her fall. The floor felt cold to her palms. It had uneven ridges. Stone? She fought the panic of being sealed away in some deep, dark place. The air was dank and moldy. She felt suffocated, and she fought for self-control. She tensed, listening for some sound. The stillness was unearthly. She could hear nothing—no voices, no music, no echoes of merriment from the party she had left only a short time ago. That meant she could not be heard either—no matter how long or loud she cried for help.

Oriel had heard a dying person sees their whole life flash before them—all the sins, errors, mistakes, regrets, remorse, the things done and undone. Something like that happened to her now. *I never should have signed that agreement,* she thought. *It was wrong to go through a false ceremony, to come here, live a lie. I am a liar, an impostor! This is my punish-*

ment! All kinds of terrible thoughts crowded in upon her, making Oriel cower against the wall and bury her face in her hands.

A choking fear gripped her. She battled it, telling herself not to lose control. There had to be a way out; she simply had to find it. She clasped her hands together in a desperate prayer. She tried to remember a fitting Scripture, perhaps David's cry to be saved from Saul's wicked plans. But all she could recall was part of something from the Old Testament, and not all of it. *Lord, show me thy way.* She fervently prayed it over and over. Gradually, she began to feel calmer. Assurance came. Surely God would show her a way out.

First, she had to try and figure out where she was. A secret room perhaps? A dungeon from the old days of the rack and other tortures? This was a nightmare, but she had to think her way out of it. She staggered up to a standing position, slowly reaching out with her arms to ascertain how wide a space she was in. She felt a wall to her right and moved over flat against it. She moved one foot, stretching her toe farther and farther. She felt an edge and moved cautiously forward. A step?

With her back against the wall, she took a step down. The wall seemed to curve. It must be a circular stair. Leading where? Her eyes were becoming somewhat used to the dark. She could just barely make out a slit farther down, one of those small alcoved windows she had noticed on the outside of the house. Why hadn't she investigated it, seen if there was a tower or a door?

Inching herself along, Oriel took another step and another, slowly, carefully, going down the steps. She became aware of the damp smell of old stones. The steps had to lead somewhere. If she kept going, she would come out somewhere. She counted the steps to herself in case she had to go up them again—in case there was nothing at the bottom of this stairway, or if what she found there was even more distressing.

Anxiety made her throat dry. Fear tightened her muscles. She couldn't be trapped in here! Would anyone even miss her, wonder where she was? But no, who would? Masks were not to be removed until midnight—hours from now. *Did someone want her to disappear, never be found? Did someone wish her dead? Who would benefit most from her disappearance?* she wondered. The name that immediately flashed into her mind horrified her. Could it be true? Edwina, of course. Then she would be free to have Morgan.

Suddenly there were no more steps. Oriel tested the space before her with her foot, then stretched out an arm. She seemed to be in a narrow corridor of some sort, a hallway. She drew a long, shaky breath. She couldn't stay here, and there was no use going back up the stairs. As she hesitated, she heard a scuttling noise along the passageway. Rats? Her stomach lurched. She had to get out of here, simply had to or she would go mad!

Like a blind person, she guided herself step by step by holding on to the slimy stone walls on either side. Then her toe hit a ridge. She ran her foot back and forth—another set of steps. This time they seemed to lead up. Still balancing herself with palms spread on each side, Oriel mounted the uneven steps.

These steps seemed to end at a blank wall. She reached out and felt the cold moisture of stone, the smell of mold prickling her nostrils. Was she still trapped? Was there no way out of this horrible tunnel through which she had just passed? Swallowing back a scream, she felt along the wall. Her hands met the roughness of wood—a makeshift ladder! It must lead somewhere. She lifted her arms and explored above her head. A door—leading up, out? She let out a small cry. Moving rapidly, her hands searched frantically. Splinters jagged her soft palms. Then she felt metal. It was some kind of handle, but there was a bar through it wedging it shut. She tugged at the bar, trying to loosen it. She pushed, wrenching it as hard as she could. Rusted with age, it didn't budge.

Despairingly, she began to claw at it, painfully breaking her fingernails in the attempt.

Tears of desperate frustration streamed down her face. Sobbing, she banged her fists against the unrelenting wood. *Oh, dear God, help me find a way out of here!*

I must not panic, she commanded herself. She took two deep breaths and then pulled at the bar with all her might. Finally, she felt it move. Again and again, using all her strength, she managed to slide it out. She pushed the latch back. Above her she felt the wood sag as it shifted.

Sobbing with relief, she pushed upward, heard the creaking of old wood. With a last great effort, she pushed hard with both hands and the door fell back with a crash onto a stone floor. A glimmer of light filtered into the darkness. With a groan that was also a prayer of thanksgiving, she realized she was free. Her breath coming in agonizing gasps, she managed to climb up the ladder and pull herself up through the door. She twisted into a sitting position, then staggered to her feet.

Her knees were so weak they were trembling. Dazed, she looked around her. She was in some sort of enclosure. Through mullioned windows, she could see the lights shining out from the castle. She took a few faltering steps. What had she come out of that awful place into? She was in some sort of circular structure.

All at once, Oriel realized it was the small stone folly. Still shivering, she glanced around. There was a wooden bench circling under the windows and some sort of round table in the center. She shuddered. Whatever its original use had been, she wanted to get out of it. There was a door. To her surprise, the knob turned easily and her hand came away feeling somewhat oily.

As she stepped out, she gulped the cold air gratefully. She looked at the house, saw the lighted windows, and felt an enormous sense of relief. She had escaped whatever danger lurked behind her. She became aware that snow was falling, and she quickened her step. She must get inside and up to her bedroom without anyone seeing her. Whoever had pushed her into that—whatever it was—was dangerous. But who could she tell? Who would believe her? Who was her enemy? Whoever it was wanted her out of the way—permanently. She had to get through the rest of the evening—somehow. There would be time enough later to sort through it all, to come to some conclusion and do whatever she must.

The party was going full force, so it was easy enough to slip unnoticed up the stairway. In her bedroom, Oriel quickly washed her face and hands and smoothed on some rose lotion to cool the stinging of her scratches. She filed the edges of her broken fingernails. Still, the condition of her hands would be noticeable. She yanked open a drawer and rummaged for a pair of suitable gloves. A pair of cream-colored ones would have to do. She winced a little as she worked them over her sore hands and buttoned them. Her dress had miraculously survived. Frantically, she brushed off dust and clinging cobwebs.

She had to do something with her hair, so she picked up her brush and tried to repair the damage. As she did, she realized she had lost the ornamental comb. It must have fallen out when she was pushed in that terrible cell. Well, if she needed it, it would be proof of her ordeal. Should she tell Morgan? No, that might not be best if—she dared not finish the thought. Her hand holding the hairbrush began to shake. "Later, later," she mumbled nervously to herself. When she could think rationally, she would figure everything out.

She knew she must still be in some kind of shock. She was unnaturally calm considering what she had just been through, yet she moved with energy, fueled by powerful twin emotions, fear and rage. Some evil force was afoot tonight in Drummond Castle.

Her mask, too, was gone. She must have dropped it somewhere in the passage when she was attacked. Involuntarily, she shuddered. It was all so horrible. But she mustn't think of it now. Luckily, she had made two masks, undecided as to which one to wear. She had another one she would be able to use. She had to get back downstairs and mingle among the guests. Perhaps she could attempt to discern who might be startled, even disappointed to see her alive and well. Then what? Should she confront her attacker or simply flee? She could pack her things tonight and escape Drummond Castle, with all its dark shadows and hovering danger.

She could decide that later. Right now she was going to make her appearance and watch for reactions. The culprit could, in surprise, tip his or her hand.

The party was still in full swing when Oriel descended the staircase. To her surprise, it was fifteen minutes before midnight—almost unmasking time. She had been gone longer than she thought. Oriel's gaze searched the room of dancing couples, looking for the dashing cavalier in a black velvet doublet. Ah, there he was, circling with a lady in an elaborate costume. Was it Edwina? She couldn't be sure. So many other couples were blocking her view. Could Edwina or Morgan have had time to follow her? Could either of them have been her attacker? No, there couldn't have been enough time for either of them to do it. Unless Oriel had been so stunned by what she had overheard in the minstrels' gallery that she had remained longer than she thought.

Oriel's glance swept the ballroom, looking for the lady wearing the same costume she wore. As long as that woman was still here, no one would have missed Oriel. She caught sight of the jade green dress. Ah, there she was. With whom was she dancing? A cavalier in a velvet cape and plumed hat. Michael? No one was to reveal his or her identity until the clock struck twelve. Oriel paused on the bottom of the steps.

"May I have this dance, m'lady?" A scholar bowed low and held out his hand to her. She recognized Bryan's voice. At least she felt safe with him. She inclined her head in acceptance, and putting her hand in his, allowed him to lead her onto the polished floor.

"You've done a magnificent job of recreating a medieval manor house party," he said admiringly. "It will go down in the annals of Kilmara society as the grandest ball given at the castle since the days of the ill-fated Lawrences."

Oriel's ears pricked up at his choice of descriptive words. "Why do you say ill-fated?"

"What else can you say about a family that over the years gradually lost everything—fortune, land, members of their family, those they had counted on to carry on their name and heritage."

"Yes, I suppose it is all very sad."

"It's almost like this castle was cursed. That is, until—"

"Until—?" Oriel prompted.

"I suppose some people—at least most in Kilmara—had hopes that the Drummonds would bring it all back to its former glory. And then—"

"Then what?" Oriel encouraged.

"It's common knowledge Morgan has no real interest in staying here, becoming part of this, building it into a thriving community with his grandfather's wealth."

Bryan had never spoken to her so frankly. Oriel started to ask him more when there was a roll of drums and the lead jester of the group of jugglers and performers leapt up on the platform. "Almost midnight, ladies and gentlemen. Time to find your favorite partners and unmask!"

"Excuse me," Oriel mumbled, disengaging herself from Bryan. Not waiting to explain, she moved quickly away, losing herself in the merry crowd. She wanted to find Suzanne. She would post herself where she could watch the unmasking. As soon as she saw Suzanne, she would go to her, seek her advice.

She found a place in one of the alcoved windows. Where was Morgan? Not that she would go to him—she wasn't sure she trusted him now. Everyone began removing their masks and there were shrieks of surprise as people made startling discoveries. Voices were raised and the whole place reverberated with laughter and fun. Where was Suzanne? Could she and Michael have left somehow without Oriel ever seeing them? She needed to get Suzanne alone. She must tell her what had happened and seek her help in getting away from Drummond Castle.

28

*N*ot long after the unmasking, the party began to wind up. It was agony for Oriel to stand beside Morgan as their departing guests expressed their thanks and compliments for the wonderful evening. Every time she glanced at him, she remembered his rendezvous with Edwina in the minstrels' gallery. What had been said? What had been planned between the two of them?

She shook hands and smiled without knowing to whom she was speaking or what she was saying. She kept looking for Suzanne and Michael to come through the line. She wanted to get some kind of message to her friend, maybe even make some excuse to go home with them or have Suzanne stay overnight.

Her nerves were tangled into agonizing knots. While she forced herself to smile, all she could think of was the moment she could escape. She found it hard to believe that Morgan would be involved in shoving her into that awful place, but she couldn't be sure. Enamored with Edwina again, perhaps he had been persuaded to try and frighten her into leaving. Aware of Morgan's nearness, Oriel felt threatened, vulnerable.

At last the final guest said good night and the last carriage drove away. Neither Suzanne, Michael, nor Bryan Moore had been among those last to depart. However, Oriel waited no longer. She was seized with a panic-driven need to get away. Without a word to Morgan, she turned and ran swiftly up the steps, down the corridor to her bedroom. She dismissed Molly, who was eager to discuss the party. Disappointed and miffed, the maid left and Oriel bolted the door behind her.

She felt weak and shaky. She took off her costume and cast it aside like her false hopes about this party bringing her and Morgan closer, allowing him to see her in a different light. It had all been for nothing. Or maybe not—maybe it had awakened her to the danger she had been in from the very beginning.

Oriel thought of all the things that had happened to her since coming to Drummond Castle—all the narrow escapes from injury, the accidents, the frightening episodes—and this one tonight! Were they all planned? And by whom?

Slowly, the fragments of her mind began to clear, like a lifting fog. Piece by piece, she tried to put the puzzle together. She knew for sure she had been shoved into that place by someone who meant her harm. How had they known about that room? It had to be someone familiar with Drummond Castle, or at least with a similar house.

With a gasp of sudden remembrance, she thought of the book Bryan had lent her about ancient homes and castles of Ireland. There had been floor plans and pictures of the rooms on page after page. Suddenly, Oriel remembered something she had read there. She found the book and read the passage.

In a time of severe religious persecution, many of the old families remained faithful to the Catholic religion. Although the practice of their religion was forbidden and punishable by death and the confiscation of their property, many broke the law. They built "priest's holes," secret rooms where they harbored fugitive priests and where they could hold mass and receive the sacrament according to their rite. This was a highly dangerous thing to do, and if caught, imprisonment or beheading was the fate of the master of such a household. That is why these hidden rooms do not show up in some of the floor plans.

Of course, that was it! It was a secret "priest's hole" into which she had been shoved. The steps down, the narrow hall, and the ladder led through the door into the folly, where the fugitive priests could escape in case the authorities came to search the house.

One thing was for certain, Oriel would not wait to be killed or injured. No, she would take matters into her own hands. Since sleep was out of the question, escape was her only choice. She would go to Bracken Hall, confide in Suzanne and Michael. They would help her.

Oriel packed a few things into her small valise, then waited for the first glimmer of dawn. She put on her coat with the shoulder cape, wrapped a light scarf over her head, and tiptoed out of her room into the upstairs hall. She did not take the Persian lamb, mink-collared cape Morgan had bought her as a wedding present nor the jade earrings and pendant. She wanted no reminders of times when there had been the hope of happiness here at Drummond Castle.

On the dressing table, she left a note for Molly to pack the rest of her belongings, telling her she would let her know later where to send them. Where would that be? In her distraught state of mind, Oriel had no idea. At least the check from Mrs. McPhail had finally come, giving her enough money to buy a steamship ticket to America. Perhaps one day she would be far enough away to forget all that had happened to her.

She crept quietly down the darkened staircase, carefully opened the front door, and slipped outside. Early morning fog blurred everything in sight. However, she knew her way and would have no trouble getting to the Wicklows' home, the place where she'd known warmth and friendship.

She hurried through the gardens. As she passed the stone folly, she shuddered. Down the driveway, almost to the gates, she began to have the feeling she was being followed. *It's my nerves,* she thought, quickening her step. *It's gotten to the point where I don't know reality from illusion.*

When she reached the gates, she put down her valise to free both hands to pull back the bolt, undo the chain. However, to her amazement the gates were unlocked and opened easily.

Just at that moment, she heard footsteps on the gravel. It *wasn't* her imagination. Whirling around, she saw a hooded figure approaching. A strangled cry rose in her throat. Not waiting to grab her valise, she spun back around, picked up her skirt, and started to run. Fear gave strength to her legs, and she ran as she had never done before, not stopping to look back, not taking even a moment to check to see if the harrowing figure was gaining on her.

It isn't my imagination. The words kept drumming into her. *I don't care what anyone says. It's real! I'm not going crazy—I'm not!* Someone *was* following her. Phantom or human—it wished her harm.

She was out of breath and panic-stricken, when she at last saw the fence surrounding Bracken Hall and knew safety was only a few yards away.

She stumbled up the driveway and onto the porch. There didn't seem to be any sign that anyone was up this early, but Oriel didn't care if she had to disturb them. Suzanne would understand—Michael too. Once she told them the danger she was in, her friends would give her protection.

She knocked furiously on the door even as she kept glancing fearfully over her shoulder. Surely Shaleen O'Connor would not pursue her here. *Please, please, answer,* Oriel thought frantically. *Somebody come to the door. Let me in!* Surely the servants would hear her and come to investigate.

She was panting painfully from running so hard and fast. At last, through the etched-glass panel of the front door, she saw the outline of a figure approaching. The door opened, and Oriel looked into the startled face of Nell, Suzanne's maid.

"Why, Mrs. Drummond," she sputtered. "It's ever so early—"

"I know, I know," Oriel said, ignoring the inference that it was a highly improper time to be calling. She brushed by the maid standing in the doorway, saying, "Please, Nell, I had to come. Something's happened. I must see Suzanne."

"Miss Suzanne's still asleep, ma'am. I haven't yet taken up her tea. It was a late night, you know," Nell said reproachfully.

"Yes, I know. That's why I must see her." Oriel was agitatedly rubbing her cold hands, glancing up the stairs to the upper floor. "It's important. Can't you wake her?"

"Well, ma'am, I dunno." Nell seemed very hesitant.

It was then Oriel noticed the dress hanging over the maid's arm. It was jade green velvet. It was exactly the same as *her* costume for the ball. She reached out and tentatively fingered the material, then looked at Nell in astonishment. "Is this Miss Suzanne's costume, the one she wore to the ball?"

"Yes, and 'tis a real pity. It's stained something terrible. The hem's ruined—looks as though it was dragged through the mud. Don't know if I can do anything about it." The maid looked worried.

Oriel frowned. Nothing made sense. "Well, she probably won't be wearing it again," she said vaguely. She had more urgent things on her mind. "Please, Nell, do take Miss Suzanne her tea and tell her I'm here. It's very important."

"If you say so, ma'am," Nell agreed reluctantly. "You can wait in the parlor."

Preoccupied, Oriel followed her. Nell opened the door for her and Oriel went in. There was no fire lit, and the room felt cold. Since Oriel was already so chilled, it hardly made any difference.

Nell, however, noticed it at once. She looked at Oriel anxiously. "This room is rarely used, ma'am," she said in explanation. "I'll send in someone to get a fire going."

"No, don't bother." Oriel's voice was tense. "Please, just get Suzanne's tea and tell her I'm here."

Oriel was so distracted by her own thoughts, it was a few minutes before she became aware of two things. First, she had never been in this room before. She and Suzanne had always met in her upstairs sitting room or in the library. This was a more formally furnished room. The second thing she noticed was the portrait hanging over the mantel. It took another second or two to make the connection. Oriel took a step closer. It was—yes, she was almost sure—Lady Lavinia Lawrence!

The portrait was smaller than the one at Drummond Castle, but the features, the hairstyle, and the dress were all the same! She was wearing a jade green velvet dress, the same costume Oriel *and* Suzanne had worn.

As these realizations came into Oriel's mind, a compelling question begged an answer. Why was a portrait of Lavinia Lawrence hanging in the Wicklows' parlor. *Why?* Unless . . . *unless* . . . Oriel's heart began thudding.

A door slammed hard in the hall and Oriel jumped. She whirled around. Swiftly, she moved across the room and to the closed parlor door. Listening to the voices, she felt relieved. It was Michael and Nell.

"I'm just taking up Miss Suzanne's tea, sir. Mrs. Drummond is here to see her and is waiting in the parlor."

"The *parlor?*" he repeated, sounding annoyed. "Why not the library?"

"I dunno, sir. I didn't think. She was so upset—"

"Never mind," he said curtly. "Bring us some coffee in the library. I'll take care of Mrs. Drummond. Just hurry."

Oriel quickly took a seat away from the fireplace, not facing the portrait. She tried to quiet her tingling nerves and appear calm when Michael opened the parlor door.

"Well, well, Oriel. Good morning!" he greeted her jovially. "What brings you out and about so early?" He glanced past her over to the empty fireplace. "It's colder than the arctic in here. Let's go into the library. I'll get the fire started. It will be much cozier in there." He motioned with his arm. "Come along."

Oriel felt prickles along her scalp. Michael's cheeks were ruddy, as if he had been out in the morning air. All through her body, warning signals coursed. She didn't want to have to explain to Michael why she was here, what she suspected about Edwina and Morgan. Michael had always struck her as being cynical and somewhat unfeeling. But there was no rational reason for her to feel such hesitancy about going into the other room with him. He had always been polite and cordial. Maybe there was even a simple explanation about Lady Lavinia's portrait being in the Wicklows' possession. Michael was an avid collector of Celtic artifacts and Irish antiques. He might well have seen it at an estate auction, liked it, and bought it. All she had to do was remark on it and ask him. Why did she feel that would be a mistake?

"Come along, Oriel. I'll have a fire going in a minute," he called over his shoulder as he went out the door.

Oriel got up from the chair and stiffly walked to the doorway. Then she turned again and looked at the painting of Lady Lavinia Lawrence, who had once been mistress at Drummond Castle. Why was it hung in a place of honor at Bracken Hall? A chill shuddered through her, a cold feeling of apprehension. She could hear Michael moving about in the library, the sound of brass hearth tools, the crackling of kindling as he coaxed the fire into a blaze.

The kitchen door swung open and Nell came down the hall carrying a tray with a coffeepot and cups. She went into the library and set down the tray on a low table before the fireplace. Nell passed Oriel again, gave her a curious glance, then proceeded up the stairs.

Oriel took a few steps into the hall and stopped. Through the open door, she saw Michael emptying the contents of a small envelope into one of the cups. She watched as if viewing a scene in a play. She was unable to move. Then she felt a surge of fear sweep over her entire body.

"Oriel!" The sound of her name being called in a hoarse whisper jolted her. Oriel spun around and saw Suzanne in her nightgown, hair streaming loosely over her shoulders, standing at the top of the stairs. Suzanne leaned over the banister, her eyes wide and frightened. "Oriel, don't—" Her words were cut off when suddenly a woman in a dark dress came up behind her and clapped a hand over her mouth.

Startled, Oriel recognized who it was—*Mrs. Nesbitt!* What was *she* doing at Bracken Hall? And at this time of day? As Oriel stared in shocked astonishment, the housekeeper pulled Suzanne back out of sight.

Fear swept through Oriel, and all her senses alerted her to her peril. The fact she was in danger moved her to action. She took a few steps backward, stumbling into a massive coatrack. Putting out her hand to steady herself, she grabbed onto the rough fabric of a garment already hanging there.

Turning her head, she saw a gray tweed cape hanging by its hood. Her hand slipped down the length of the garment. It was damp. Little beads of moisture clung to the rough, coarsely woven material. Little bits of twigs and fern were caught in the fabric. It had just been worn. Oriel stifled a gasp.

She recognized it. It was Michael's cape. She'd seen it on him many times. Suddenly she envisioned the frightening gray hooded figure she'd mistaken for some kind of apparition . . . in the fog . . . slipping through the gates of Drummond Castle. If this was *his* then . . . Fear gripped her. She sensed she was in terrible danger.

She shuddered. Her hands dropped away from the cape and she spun around. All the experiences since coming to Ireland began to fall into a pattern. It all came together—a sadistic plan to terrorize her. She knew she must get out of Bracken Hall. *Now.*

She dashed to the front door and tried to open it. Just as she reached it, she heard Mrs. Nesbitt's harsh voice calling out angrily, "Michael! Michael! She's getting away! Quick!"

Oriel's heart pounded. She twisted the door handle, desperately aware that behind her Michael had come out of the library. "What are you doing? Where are you going?" he yelled.

Oriel looked over her shoulder and saw he was standing at the library door, his face flushed, twisted. Fear gave her strength, and with one hard pull, she yanked the door open and ran out onto the porch, down the steps, and along the driveway.

She ran blindly, wildly, caring for nothing but escape. Now, she knew her pursuer, her tormentor, the one who meant her harm—and she had to get away from him.

29

Outside, the wind cut Oriel like a cold knife. The sky was now a mottled gray, with heavy clouds moving quickly across it. Not looking behind her, she started for the road then decided to take the way through the woods, the shortcut to Drummond Castle. She ran on, stumbling over twigs and stones on the woodland path. Clutching her skirt above her ankles, she kept running.

A sharp pain in her side slowed her and she staggered, brought to a stop by her agonized breathing. She leaned against a tree, gasping. Frantically, she glanced about, looking for a place she could hide. Where could she go—to Drummond Castle? She had just run away from there. Had she been wrong? Was it Michael who wanted to drive her away? But why? She had no time to dwell on reasons. She had seen the villainous look in Michael's face. She had seen hatred, something she had never expected to see in the eyes of a friend. But he was *not* her friend. Then neither was Suzanne! But Suzanne had tried to warn her. It was all so confusing.

Tears rushed into her eyes, her throat thickened, and she gasped for breath. To be betrayed by friends was hard to bear. Why had she ever thought coming to Ireland would be the solution to her problems? It had brought her not only heartache, but danger.

The fog was quite thick now, and it seemed to be encircling her. Suddenly she stiffened, alert. Did she hear footsteps on the path? They *were* footsteps—even though muffled by the heavy fog. Had Michael come after her? He was strong, athletic. He could outrun her, catch her. She had to find someplace she could hide so that he couldn't get her.

She started running again. Her foot struck a rock and she tripped, but immediately hurried on. Her heart was racing. She couldn't run much longer. The footsteps were real, and they were close behind her. She determined she wouldn't die like some cowering, terrified woodland animal. She would defend herself. She looked around her. Seeing a fallen branch, she staggered forward, picked it up, and whirled around, bracing herself to confront her pursuer.

The figure was approaching her fast. She lifted the branch with aching arms and swung it wildly with all her might. She felt the wood hit something solid. The figure ducked, but she landed another blow on the side of his head that momentarily stunned him.

She flung the stick, then whirled around. Tears streaming down her cheeks, she started to run again. But her strength was gone—it was no use. She gave a gulping sob. Staggering forward, she limped to a halt.

Suddenly, she felt a hard punch in the middle of her back, sending her pitching forward. She flung out her hands, but there was nothing to hold on to, and she fell face down onto the rough path. Someone tossed her cape over her head, then with a strong hand pressed her cheek in a grinding motion into the gritty damp sand. A gulping scream caused her to inhale a mouthful of sand. She choked.

Terrified, she tensed her body, not knowing what to expect. Then, in the distance, she heard horses' hooves and men's voices coming through the fog. Raising her head tentatively, she pulled back the cape over her head and listened. It wasn't some hopeful wish for rescue. It was real.

Through the lifting fog, she saw the two horsemen. One swung a lantern in his hand. Then she recognized the voices. One had a strong brogue—Tim, the groom! The other voice was Morgan's.

Oriel pushed herself up onto her hands and knees and struggled to her feet, her skirt and cape damp and gritty. With great effort, feeling the muscles in her throat stretch, she managed to call out, "Morgan! I'm here! Over here!"

There was a shout back. "I'm coming, Oriel!"

Standing now, she leaned weakly against a tree. Her legs were trembling, and she felt bruised and shaken from the brutal attack.

The next thing she knew, Morgan was beside her. She felt his strength as he towered over her, saying, "What is going on, Oriel? Where were you going? What happened?"

She shook her head. It was all too impossible to explain.

"Never mind, now," Morgan said soothingly. "First, we'll get you home and take care of you."

"Thank you," she whispered, and let him put his arm around her waist and lead her to his horse. It seemed strange that she had fled in fear of this man and was now depending on him—this man, who was treating her with such gentle concern.

"Hold my horse, Tim," Morgan ordered. "I'm going to lift Mrs. Drummond into my saddle, then mount. We have to get back to Drummond Castle as soon as possible. She's had a bad scare of some kind and she looks hurt."

A worried Molly met them at the door, helped Oriel out of her coat, and gently placed a warm shawl around her shoulders.

"Bring her in here, Molly." Morgan gestured toward his study, where a fire was roaring in the fireplace.

Seated in a deep wing chair, sipping on a bracing hot toddy Morgan had made, Oriel stammered out her story. She thought she might as well get the whole thing out. There was no longer any use concealing that she had eavesdropped on

215

Morgan's private conversation with Edwina just before being attacked. Now she knew there had to be some other explanation. She had to be wrong.

She drew a long breath and began. "Last night during the party, I came upstairs. As I was passing the minstrels' gallery, I overheard you and Edwina—" Embarrassed under Morgan's unmoving gaze, she paused. "I know you want to be free to marry her, and so when I—"

"I don't know what you think you heard," Morgan interrupted. "I told her it was all over between us, that I—"

"But—"

"Afterwards, I went looking for you, but you were always with someone, dancing, talking, mingling with the guests. Then, suddenly, you were gone."

"Of course I was gone!" Oriel exclaimed. "A few minutes later someone pushed me into a hidden room and I was trapped. I thought that once you realized you had a chance to get Edwina back, the two of you were trying to get rid of me!"

Morgan looked offended. "I'm humbled you think so little of me. I may be many things, but I'm not an attacker of women."

"I know that now. I'm so sorry, Morgan. But at the time—"

"How could I have seen you at the ball if you were trapped in a hidden room?"

"That's what I've just figured out, Morgan. I think the Wicklows are behind it all. I don't know why. Suzanne was in exactly the same costume as the one I copied from the portrait in the gallery here." Oriel paused, frowning. "I don't know how she knew what I was wearing, unless—" Her frown deepened. "Mrs. Nesbitt saw me making it." She stopped. "I saw Mrs. Nesbitt at Bracken Hall this morning. I don't know what she has to do with all this."

Morgan looked fierce. "I don't either. She was the first person I sent for when Molly told me about the note you'd left. However, the woman was not in her room. She had left not a trace. At least now we know where she disappeared to, though not exactly why." His mouth pressed into a grim line. "I intend to find out."

"Anyway," Oriel continued, "when you looked for me, it was Suzanne you saw. I suppose they didn't want me to be missed—at least not right away." She gave a little shudder. "Maybe I never would have been found. Maybe I would have died in there. That is, if I hadn't been able to find my way out. Thank God."

"Yes, indeed. Thank God," Morgan agreed sincerely. He looked very serious. "I didn't even know there was such a thing as a hidden room here." He shook his head. "You'll have to show me."

When she shrank back into the chair as if his suggestion appalled her, he quickly said, "When you feel better, I mean." He paused. "When I couldn't find you during the ball, I planned to talk to you afterwards, to tell you about Edwina and me. But you disappeared as soon as our last guests left and I didn't have a chance. Then, this morning, I found this on my desk." He produced an envelope. "Your note."

He handed it to her. Opening the envelope, she read, "Morgan, I'm leaving. Don't try to find me. I'll let you know through Suzanne where you can send my things. Oriel." She shook her head, handed it back. "I never wrote that. I *did* leave a note, but it was for *Molly.*"

A stricken look passed briefly over Morgan's face. "You weren't going to leave any word for me?" Then as if he had spoken too openly, he did not give her a chance to explain, but went on. "After I found this, going to the Wicklows seemed the only thing I could do. Thank goodness I did, or I'd never have found you." His eyes were troubled. "If not you, then who wrote this?" He handed the note back to her.

She examined it closely. "It's a pretty good imitation of my handwriting, but this is not it. Someone has tried to copy it, but how?" Then she remembered the missing slip from the brass bowl the night Madame Tamsin had done the handwriting analysis. "Someone must have taken the slip I wrote on for Madame Tamsin and copied it."

"No, I took that," Morgan said, looking embarrassed.

"*You?* But why?"

He reached into his vest pocket and brought out the folded slip of paper. "Listen to what it says, then maybe you'll understand. 'Never tell your love, the love that never told should be. P.S. I don't know what this is from.'" Morgan smiled. "How honest this writer is and, according to Madame Tamsin's reading of it, also sensitive, loyal, loving, and generous. It could not have been anyone else in that room that night but *you!*"

Oriel's mind was whirling with so many questions that she missed the significance of Morgan's words. She reread the note and asked, "So why did you come looking for me?"

"I couldn't let you go—not like that, not with so much misunderstanding between us. I had to explain about Edwina and me."

"Well, thank goodness you came. Hearing you and Tim coming must have scared my attacker away." Slowly, more and more of the plot against her and Morgan took shape in Oriel's mind. She thought of what she had seen and learned that morning at the Wicklows.

"Suzanne's costume was copied from Lady Lavinia Lawrence's portrait—a separate one from the one here at Drummond Castle. I saw it this morning, hanging over the fireplace in their parlor. I'd never seen it there before. Why didn't they want me to see it or know about the costume?"

Oriel paused, then said very slowly, "Morgan, what do you make of that? It was Suzanne you saw after leaving the minstrels' gallery, not me. I was already locked in the hidden room off the corridor. Someone didn't want me to be missed until it was too late. Even *you* would think I'd gone. Don't you see, it was all a plot to drive you away, to break your contract to inherit Drummond Castle?"

They were both silent a minute, then Oriel asked, "So who pushed me into the secret room? Could it be the same person who just attacked me in the woods?" Her eyes widened in realization. "The same one who sabotaged the ladder the day I was trapped down at the cove!"

She understood now. It all came together through a fog of fear and disbelief. "Michael!" Oriel gasped. She thought of the scene she had viewed from the hallway at Bracken Hall. What were the mysterious contents he had been putting in the cup he planned to give her to drink? The envelope resembled the small packets of sleeping powders Mrs. Nesbitt said she kept on hand. How was Mrs. Nesbitt involved in all this? Now convinced, Oriel nodded her head and repeated the name. "Michael. I see it all now—he was the one all along . . ."

"Michael," Morgan said furiously. "It looks like it, and he'll pay dearly for it!"

"Michael." Her lips were numb as she said his name again. "I should have seen it before. The night of the ball was supposed to be the final thing. To leave me there to die and then the note would lead you to believe I'd left."

Morgan, his fists clenched, got up and started pacing, mumbling under his breath furiously. "But how did he know? Where is that room? I've been all over this house, I never knew there was some kind of secret room."

"It might be in the book Bryan lent me. It has the original floor plans of some of the old Irish castles. It's still in my sitting room. We can check."

The books Bryan had lent Oriel were placed ready to return along with the belongings Molly had been instructed to pack. Morgan went up to Oriel's sitting room and brought the books back. Together they started looking through the one on coastal Ireland. Almost right away, they found the answer in the genealogy tables of county families. They discovered a link between the Lawrence family who had once owned Drummond Castle and the Wicklows. Michael's mother had been a Lawrence, so Lady Lavinia Lawrence was his ancestor. This explained but did not excuse his bitterness and envy toward those he considered interlopers in his heritage home.

"So you see, Morgan, Michael would do anything to drive you out. When Brendan Drummond died and the house stood empty for so long, perhaps he had hoped to buy it back. Then, when you came bringing a bride, he must have decided to resort to more drastic measures."

"He's committed unspeakable crimes—attempted murder among them. He could spend a great deal of time in jail for this."

"But we have no evidence—only my word."

Oriel told Morgan what she had learned about secret rooms being used to harbor fugitive priests. They continued to leaf through the book to see if they could find the hidden room in any of the floor plans. The Lawrence house plans showed only a long corridor running the length of the upstairs hall with rooms off of it. There was no sign of a passageway.

"Do you think you could find it and show me?" Morgan asked.

Oriel tossed aside the blanket. "Of course."

Morgan took her arm and helped her stand. Her legs still felt a little shaky, but she was eager to confirm her nightmarish ordeal.

Morgan took an oil lamp and they went upstairs. Each taking a side of the hall a few yards from the minstrels' gallery, they walked slowly along, pressing their hands up and down the wall, searching for anything out of the ordinary.

"Ah, here's something!" Morgan exclaimed. He pointed to a small button, which he then pushed. A creaking sound followed. They both watched in amazement as a partition of the wall swung back, revealing a small cubicle. Instinctively, Oriel drew back, reliving the horror of being closed up within that dark space.

"Wait until I light this." Morgan quickly struck a match and put it to the wick of a small lamp. When it flamed, he replaced the glass chimney and held out his hand to Oriel. "Are you ready? Or shall I go alone?"

"No. I'll come," she said, and stepped forward. He took hold of her wrist tightly.

With the arc of light thrown by the lamp he was holding, they stepped into what appeared to be an entry into a somewhat smaller room. This had a cot, table, and chair. Morgan slowly circled so they got a good look. "This is probably where the priest stayed until it was safe for him to leave."

"And the way he escaped was down the stairs and out through that tunnel that comes up inside the folly!" Oriel finished.

"Come, we'll go down the steps. Don't worry, I've got you," Morgan said reassuringly.

After a few steps Oriel's foot touched something hard. "Wait, Morgan, shine the light over here," she said.

What her toe had nearly crushed was the ornamental comb she had worn in her hair the night of the ball. This was the proof she needed that her terrifying experience had been real.

"Here, I'll put it in my pocket," Morgan said. "Are you all right? It's so stuffy in here. You sure you don't want to go back, wait for me?"

"No, I'm coming," Oriel said firmly.

"I must say, you've no lack of courage." Morgan's voice held admiration.

With her hand in Morgan's, the retreading of the stone steps down to the narrow passage did not seem half as terrible as when she had been alone, despairing of escape.

Within a few more minutes, they were making their way through the last part of the tunnel. When they stepped up into the interior of the folly, it was daylight, and they could see everything clearly. Morgan found a can of oil underneath the bench near the door. How often had Michael hidden in here, then donned the hooded cape to play the part of Shaleen O'Connor?

"What a devilish scheme," Morgan said between clenched teeth.

"And it almost worked." Then Oriel had another thought. "But he must have had help—someone to let him in the house, investigate, find the secret room, and devise the plan. There was plenty of time. The house was empty. Except for the servants—"

In unison they said, *"Mrs. Nesbitt."*

"Why would she want to help Michael? She worked for you." Oriel shook her head in bewilderment.

"It's a mystery, all right. But we'll solve it. And whoever's involved will pay dearly."

Oriel shivered.

At once Morgan was concerned. "You're cold. Here, put this on." He took off his jacket and put it around her shoulders. "Let's go back inside before you get chilled."

Oriel shook her head vigorously and pointed to the way they had just come. "Not back through there, please."

"Of course not," Morgan said, opening the folly door. They hurried over the soggy grass and reentered the house.

Back in his study, with Oriel again wrapped in a warm shawl, Morgan yanked the tapestry pull. When Finnegan appeared, Morgan ordered tea.

"Now we must bring this madman to justice." Morgan paced back and forth. "I will go over there and confront him—maybe take a magistrate with me—"

"I'll go with you. I have so many questions," Oriel said, "especially about Suzanne. Do you think she knew? I can't believe she would go along with such a plan. She was my friend." Oriel's voice trailed off as she remembered what she'd seen on the stairs at Bracken Hall that morning. "Morgan, I think Suzanne tried to warn me. Mrs. Nesbitt pulled her away from the balcony, and . . ."

Morgan looked at her with compassion. "Poor Oriel, you've really had a bad time here, haven't you? False friends, narrow escapes, frightening experiences. We shall try to make up for it." His gaze rested on her sympathetically.

She started to rise from the chair, but Morgan stopped her. "Not now. What you need is a good rest. You'll feel stronger tomorrow—we'll go first thing. That will be soon enough."

It wasn't. When they arrived at Bracken Hall early the next morning, they found the Wicklows gone. When Nell, looking flushed and harried, opened the door, they saw the other servants busily putting dustcloths over the furniture.

"They left early this morning, went up to Dublin." Oriel could see Nell was miffed. "From there to England, and maybe the Continent. I don't know for sure." She lifted her chin, obviously injured about something. "Mr. Wicklow wouldn't even let me accompany Miss Suzanne. Took Mrs. Nesbitt, they did."

At this information, Oriel and Morgan exchanged a baffled look.

"I'm to close the house and wait for word," Nell continued.

"When did they say they'd return?" Oriel asked.

"They didn't say. Miss Suzanne was very upset." Nell sniffed, then added somewhat grudgingly, "They did give me two weeks' wages and a reference letter." Then Nell took an envelope out of her apron pocket and held it out to Oriel. "She left this for you, Mrs. Drummond."

Oriel glanced at Morgan, then opened the letter.

My dear Oriel,

You must believe that I never meant to hurt you. Michael said it was just to scare you a little—dressing in the hooded cape to make you think it was the ghost of Shaleen O'Connor. He oiled the lock on the folly so he could wait there and watch. When the light went on in your bedroom or he saw you going out, he'd follow you. He used the shortcut through the woods known from his childhood.

To understand, you have to know the truth about us. I have another confession to make. Michael and I are brother and sister, not a married couple. He thought that was a better "front," more respectable! You see, I am totally dependent on him for everything. He is older, and our parents left him what little they had left. So no matter what, in the end I had to do what he told me.

Mrs. Nesbitt used to be our mother's maid, and when we were little, she became our nanny. She adored Michael, and filled him with stories of what it was like when Mama was a little girl and lived at Drummond Castle (it used to be called Lawrence Manor). As he grew up, Michael was obsessed with getting the castle back. He felt it was his heritage. Of course, Mrs. Nesbitt knew about the "priest's hole," so she showed it to him.

The plan was to get Morgan to leave by frightening you. They made me copy your handwriting and leave the note for Morgan. I did protest. The night of the ball, I tried to warn you. I ran across the grass to get in the folly and open the door for you, but Michael caught me and dragged me back.

You are so strong, Oriel, and have so much courage. You must think me weak and spineless to have gone along with this wicked scheme. I feel most dreadfully about lying to you. I *did* come to love and treasure you as a friend. I begged Michael not to go on with it, but he assured me all he wanted was to make you leave, and so make Morgan give up the house. Please try to forgive me.

Suzanne

Without a word, Oriel passed the letter to Morgan. When he finished reading it, she asked, "Well?"

He simply shrugged.

They drove back to Drummond Castle silently.

When they arrived, Morgan asked her, "Are you still determined to leave? I wouldn't blame you after all you've been through."

"No, Morgan, I'm not going to leave." She smiled wanly. "A contract is a contract. There's no need to leave before the year is up."

Drummond Castle

April 1896

Oriel awakened from a strange dream. She got out of bed, tossed her robe around her shoulders, and went over to open the windows. She leaned on the sill and looked out. The first pink streaks of dawn and the fragrance of flowers from the garden below gave the promise of a fine spring day.

Breathing deeply of the soft, scented air, she felt a wrenching sadness. The heaviness she had felt all week welled up painfully. Tomorrow was the last morning she would gaze out at this scene—the acres spreading out from the castle in beautiful shades of green, the narrow line of blue of the ocean beyond.

One year ago she had come to Drummond Castle. She remembered the first time she looked out these windows, the excitement she had felt as the curtain of mist parted. Ireland had promised so much. It had almost been love at first sight.

It was ironic, Oriel thought. Love had nothing to do with her coming but had everything to do with her leaving. And it was a good thing she was leaving. Another week—another day, even—and she might have betrayed herself, revealed the things she was finding it harder and harder to hide. Sighing, she closed the window and turned back into the room.

She had many things to do before she left for Dublin tomorrow. Her trunk stood open, waiting for her to pack the last of her clothing and personal belongings. She stood uncertainly in the middle of the room, not knowing where to start. When she came here, a year had seemed a long time. Now it seemed incredibly short. The last four months, especially, seemed to have flown by.

Morgan had followed up on his intention to bring Michael Wicklow to justice, but so far it had been impossible. Even though Morgan had hired a private detective, evidently Michael had parted ways with Suzanne and Mrs. Nesbitt upon reaching London. No trace of a couple or an older woman fitting the description of the Wicklows and Mrs. Nesbitt was found. As the detective reported, it would have been easy for them to change their appearance with wigs, hair color, spectacles, and other disguises. Then, if they escaped to the Continent, the trail would become even more difficult.

Bracken Hall had remained boarded up, and no one seemed to have any information as to when the Wicklows might return.

Morgan had been very disturbed that nothing could be done about Michael's vicious attempts. He told Oriel he decided to keep the detective on a retainer for a while longer. Perhaps eventually Michael would slip up and some charges could be filed.

After the Wicklows' conspiracy against them had been uncovered, Oriel and Morgan's relationship had changed subtly. No longer two people trapped in an untenable situation, they had become even closer friends. They spent many companionable times together, riding, walking, talking. Their dinner hours had become pleasurable exchanges of ideas and opinions. They had spent many quiet evenings in front of the fire, sharing excerpts from books they were each reading. Oriel had even felt the freedom to play the piano sometimes, as Morgan seemed to enjoy listening. They had discussed some of Morgan's grandfather's ideas of bringing new employment to the area—reactivating the pottery plant, encouraging cottage crafts. Oriel tried not to let herself dream that it could be anything more than a rich, interesting friendship. They could talk about almost anything—except Edwina Parker. Morgan was too much of a gentleman to say much. All he had said was that he had been blind to their incompatibility and that it was over. Oriel had to believe him.

Now it was time for her to go. She looked around. There were still decisions to be made. She had not meant to accumulate so much—clothes, books, and especially so many memories.

Stop being so sentimental, she ordered herself. *You knew this day would come.* She should be as businesslike and impersonal about ending this job as she had been taking it, signing the agreement. It was all a matter of control.

There were many good-byes to be said. She had already been to the village to bid farewell to the shopkeepers, all of whom she had made an effort to become friendly with, hoping they would lose their animosity toward Drummond Castle. She thought she had accomplished that.

For the staff here, she had small individual gifts for each of the servants, with a special one for Molly, who had been so caring and faithful. Before saying good-bye to the servants, Oriel thought she would go out to the stables and say farewell to her darling Mavourneen. How she would miss her and her daily rides.

It was a heartbreaking moment. The mare seemed to sense her sadness when Oriel rested her head against her neck and stroked her mane. Blinking back tears, Oriel gave the horse a final pat and two lumps of sugar, then left the stable. Head bowed, she started back toward the house through the garden. That was why she didn't see Morgan approaching until she was within a few feet of him.

"Morgan!" she exclaimed in surprise.

He was in riding clothes—a tweed jacket and buff breeches. "What are you doing?" he asked, his voice snapping like the slap of the riding crop he flicked against the top of his polished boots.

"Saying good-byes." She was so startled by running into him that she forgot to guard the wistfulness in her voice.

Morgan frowned. "I was just going for a ride, hoping you would come along."

Oriel was tempted. During the last several months, she and Morgan had fallen into the habit of riding together several times a week. Those had been some of the happiest days she had spent at Drummond Castle. She would cherish them. But it would be too much for her to handle today. "Sorry," she said regretfully.

She felt his presence strongly, her own keen awareness that this would be the last such day, the last chance to ride along the ocean cliffs or the rolling hillside with him. The ache of a rising lump in her throat made her anxious, so she said quickly, "Thanks, but I really can't. I have things to do that I can't put off." She moved to go past him on the path, but he caught her arm.

"Can't they wait?" he asked softly.

Not daring to look at him, she shook her head. "No. I'm afraid not."

He held her arm a second longer. "Sure?"

Their gaze met, and his eyes seemed troubled. Then he released her. "I'll see you at dinner then," he said. Making a stiff bow, he walked slowly off in the direction of the stables.

Oriel returned to the castle. She found saying good-bye to the staff very difficult. She understood the accepted code between employers and servants was strictly defined so that

228

she did not have to explain her leave-taking. No explanation was necessary—indeed, no explanation was possible.

She was touched when Mrs. Mills said, "We all shall miss you, ma'am. This year's been such a welcome change." She wiped her eyes on her flour-dusted apron, sighing. "Oh, ma'am, don't know what I'll be doin' cookin' for just t' master by himself. He don't know what he's eatin' half t' time. Takes all t' pleasure out of my work."

Molly, of course, was the most verbal of all. "I wish you'd say you was coming back, ma'am. I know a lot of bad things happened to you, but now that the Wicklows are gone . . ." She let her question hang hopefully. Oriel knew Molly wanted her to offer to take her with her as her personal maid.

Although Oriel did not know what her future held, she was sure it wouldn't include the need for a lady's maid. Knowing she couldn't fulfill that hope, she said, "Thank you, Molly. You've been wonderful." Then she gave her a small silver pin in the shape of a spray of shamrocks. Molly dissolved into tears and had to leave the room.

Later that afternoon, Oriel walked down to Bryan's cottage. He would also be leaving Ireland soon. Bryan had been as shocked and angered by Michael Wicklow's despicable scheme as she had been. He blamed himself for not picking up on what now seemed obvious.

"You were a good friend, Bryan," Oriel told him as they said good-bye. "I don't know what I would have done sometimes without your friendship." Oriel turned to go.

"Wait, Oriel, I'd like you to have something to remember me and this year in Ireland." He handed her a book of his own poetry.

"Thank you," Oriel said, knowing this year in Ireland would be impossible for her to forget.

That evening, while Oriel sat at her dressing table fixing her hair, her glance fell on the box containing the jade and pearl jewelry Morgan had bought for her. She hesitated. Should she wear them tonight for her last dinner at Drummond Castle? Or would it be too obvious a gesture? She had loved the set, more for their meaning than their value. She had lived on the memory of that happy day in Dublin. A happiness that had been as ephemeral as the Irish mist. Determinedly, Oriel closed the lid of the jewelry box. She would not wear them, not tonight, maybe not ever. She also took off her wedding ring. No point in wearing it any longer. After she left for Dublin, Morgan would contact his lawyers and make all the necessary arrangements for the legal annulment. Their bargain would be finished; their contract fulfilled. All obligations would end.

As Oriel came down the steps, she saw that the door to Morgan's study was open, a welcoming blaze in the fireplace. Morgan was standing in front of it, one arm resting on the mantel, his face thoughtful. Seeing Oriel, he smiled.

"Come in," he invited. His eyes swept over her as if searching for something. "Did you get everything done you had to do?" Without waiting for her reply, he went on. "You should have come riding with me. It was wonderful up along the cliffs today."

On the side table, she saw an ice bucket with a champagne bottle in it. Following her glance, Morgan said, "I thought since this is an anniversary of sorts, maybe we should have some champagne?"

"Yes, that would be lovely." She took the glass he handed her, and their fingers brushed briefly.

"One year." Morgan raised his glass in a toasting gesture. "But, then, maybe it has seemed longer than that to you."

Oriel could not tell if he was being sarcastic. She looked up into his dark, restless face—the smile that came and went so quickly she was never sure what was meant by it; the eyes that could be mocking or soft as music by candlelight; the mouth that could say things that hurt or soothed with their gentleness; and the charm, the maddening, Gaelic charm that had been her undoing.

Oriel looked down into the bubbles in her glass and said nothing. *After tomorrow none of it can touch me,* she thought, *not his careless words, that smile that rocks my heart, or the charm. I shall be far away, and eventually I will forget—I shall make myself forget.*

"Have you any plans?" Morgan asked. "I mean, after you leave?"

"I plan to visit Paris. After that I suppose I shall get passage back to the States," she replied evenly.

His expression was suddenly morose. She longed to ask him what *he* intended to do. Would he carry through on any of the plans they had discussed to revitalize Kilmara? Would he stay in Ireland or at least live part of the year at Drummond Castle? What before would have been natural for her to ask now seemed impossible.

The room became very quiet. A log broke, shifting in the fireplace, sending up a sudden spiral of sparks.

Oriel's heart pounded in her ears. What did she want Morgan to say? "Oriel, I love you. You're beautiful. I want you, need you." Yes, all those things and more. "I can't live without you. Stay here in Ireland and be my love." But nothing was said.

Finnegan came to the door to announce dinner, and they went in together. Mrs. Mills had outdone herself for this final dinner, cooking all Oriel's favorite foods. Oriel could only take a few bites; she wasn't able to swallow any more than that. She had to get away from Morgan. She couldn't trust herself, this last night, to keep from speaking what was in her heart.

As they left the dining room, she turned to Morgan. Her throat was so dry, it was almost impossible for her to speak. "I think I'll make it an early night, Morgan. I'm tired and I'm leaving early in the morning."

"Of course," Morgan replied stiffly.

Oriel walked to the staircase, and Morgan strode toward his study. At the bottom of the steps, Oriel's hand circled the carved post. Almost as if to herself, she remarked, "I shall hate to leave."

Morgan spun around. "What did you say?"

"Just that I shall be sorry to leave here." Oriel made a sweeping gesture with one hand. She was surprised to realize she had spoken her thoughts out loud. But it was the truth. Why pretend? "I've been happy here, happier than I've been for a very long time."

"Even after all that's happened?" Morgan asked, his voice soft.

"Yes, even after that," she said, then quickly turned and ran up the stairs.

31

London

April 1896

*O*riel had made the boat in Dublin with plenty of time. She stood at the railing and watched the coast of Ireland slip away as the steamer put to sea. This was really good-bye.

She had avoided a long farewell with Morgan earlier. She'd had Molly bring a tray of tea and toast to her room, finished her last-minute packing, then sent Molly to have the carriage brought around.

Oriel had moved in a kind of trance, not allowing herself to think or feel. When Molly came to tell her the carriage was out front, she bid the tearful maid an affectionate good-bye, then hurried downstairs. Morgan stood at the door to see her into the carriage.

"You have everything? Your ticket, your passport, enough money?" he asked.

"Yes, everything," she had said, getting into the carriage.

Morgan thrust his head in the window. "Good-bye then, and God bless."

"Good-bye," she said through tight lips.

She had stared straight ahead as the carriage started down the drive, not looking back once as it went through the gates and on the road to Dublin.

It was best that way, Oriel told herself—not to look back for a last glimpse at the castle she'd come to love, or the man she had also come to love. Both were now in her past. She had to look forward to the rest of her life, whatever that held.

Oriel had decided she would go to France. She had never been there, so there would be nothing to remind her of Morgan. In Paris, she would visit the great art galleries, the cathedrals, and all the historical places. There'd be no memories there to haunt her. Then she'd return to America.

On her arrival in London, Oriel went to the Claridge Hotel. This time, there was no question of not being able to afford it. She was a very rich woman now. However, she was not prepared for the nostalgia she felt as she entered the luxurious lobby, remembering the day of her fateful encounter with Morgan, going to tea with him in the plush dining room. She made her reservations for the boat train, then had supper brought to her room. After a good cry, she went to bed.

She spent the next two days shopping the grand London stores. She did not have to worry about price tags, but she found little she wanted to buy for herself.

She thought of going to see Nola, but there was too much to explain and her own heart was too heavy. She would not have been good company. She did, however, find a lovely porcelain tea set that she knew Nola would love. She bought it and had it wrapped to be delivered to Nola and Will's new home. With the package, she put a note: "Wishing you great happiness. You deserve it." She signed it, after a second's hesitation, with the name she had not used for a year, "Oriel Banning."

Three days later, as she stood on the platform of the railroad station waiting to board the train that would take her to the boat to France, Oriel was filled with melancholy. She had not realized how much she had changed in the past year. She had been alone for years, ever since her parents died, yet now she felt lonelier than ever before. Why? Just because one person was no longer in her life?

Then, as if in a dream, she heard her name being called. She must be imagining it. Over the noise of the busy terminal, how could she hear a voice she thought she knew?

"Oriel!" It came again, and this time there was no mistake—that *had* to be Morgan's voice.

She turned around and saw Morgan hurrying toward her, quickly covering the space with his long strides. "Oriel! Wait."

She stood there in amazement. As he reached her, she said, "I *am* waiting."

"I'm so glad. I thought I might have missed you, that I was too late—but you're here."

"Yes, Morgan, I'm here."

"Thank goodness. I was so afraid—" He halted. "Afraid I'd missed you."

"Well, you almost did. My train will be leaving any minute."

"I must talk to you. Let's go somewhere we can talk."

"I can't, Morgan, I'll miss my train."

"Miss it then. There'll be another boat train soon. Please, Oriel, it's important."

She glanced around, bewildered. She spotted the porter who was standing beside her luggage, ready to put it on the train. Morgan followed her glance, signaled the man, gave him some money, and directed him, "Keep those in a safe place until we decide which train the lady is taking."

"But, Morgan—" Oriel's protest died on her lips as the porter pocketed the money, nodded, and trundled off with her bags.

Morgan took her firmly by the arm and led her down the platform to the station tea shop. After the waitress had been given their order for two cups of tea, Morgan crossed his arms and leaned forward on the table. "Oriel, I followed you here because I couldn't bear to let you go, let you walk out of my life, without telling you."

"Telling me what, Morgan?" Oriel's heart was beating wildly.

"What you have come to mean to me." He paused. "It's hard to explain, but ever since your accident at the cove, ever since we went to Dublin, I have realized—"

The waitress came with their tea, set down the cups, and left.

Morgan picked up again where he had halted. "Realized that I cared for you. More than I knew, more than I had ever intended. I began to see in you all the qualities I'd always wanted in the woman I loved. Maybe it wasn't really until Edwina came and I saw you two together that I realized how wrong I had been about *her*." He shook his head a little. "You handled everything that weekend so well, with such grace. I was filled with admiration. I guess I knew then I loved you."

Oriel's hands felt icy. She put them around the cup of steaming tea to warm them. Through stiff lips she mumbled, "But you never let on. You never gave me the slightest reason to think—"

"I know. I thought it was the honorable thing to do. I had no idea what your feelings toward me were. I had certainly given you no reason to care for me. I was a boor most of the time. Can you forgive me for that? I was in a dilemma. I thought it would be unfair to speak to you, put pressure on you. After all, as you mentioned many times, a bargain is a bargain, a contract, a contract. Ours was a business arrangement—nothing else."

Oriel was too moved to speak.

"It wasn't until you actually were gone that I realized I'd been a fool not to let you know and beg you to stay." He reached across the table and put his hands over hers. "Is it too late, Oriel? I love you. Will you . . . would you possibly consider marrying me?"

The clatter all around them in the noisy tea shop was deafening. Oriel could scarcely believe her ears, what Morgan was asking over the banging of teacups, the shriek of train whistles, and the noise from arriving and departing travelers.

Morgan's eyes anxiously searched her face, waiting for some answer.

"*Marry* you, Morgan?" she repeated, still unbelieving.

"Yes, my darling, will you?"

Tears came and laughter too as Oriel said, "But Morgan, we *are* married."

For a second he looked blank, then threw back his head and laughed heartily. "Of course we are! I'd forgotten. Can you put up with such a man?"

Just then Oriel's porter appeared at the door of the tea shop. Spotting them, he came over to the table.

"Beg pardon, miss, the next train is about to board passengers."

Morgan looked at Oriel. "Well, what is it to be, Oriel? Shall we honeymoon in Paris, since you already have your ticket?" He paused. "But then you haven't answered my question."

"Yes, Morgan. I will." She smiled. "Stay married, that is!"

Smiling broadly, Morgan said to the porter, "Take those things on board. I'll buy my ticket on the way from the conductor."

He turned back to her. "Does that suit you, Oriel?"

"Oh, yes, Morgan. It suits me just fine."

"Come along, my dear." He got up from the table and held out his hand to her. They walked out onto the station platform together.

The next thing Oriel knew, she was caught up in his strong arms, her cheek pressed against the rough tweed of his coat. Then, very gently, he released her and framed her face in both hands so she had to look up at him.

Oblivious to the curious glances of people pushing past, the shouts of the porters, the rattle of baggage carts, and the noise and bustle all about them, Morgan kissed her. A kiss that was intense, but tender.

When it came to a slow end, Morgan said softly, "When we get to France, we'll have a real wedding—maybe in a country church in Provence. How does that sound? Romantic enough?"

Surely this was a dream come true—the words Oriel had said in the Registry Office she would repeat with her heart—fully this time, completely aware of what those vows really meant. Happily she looked up at the man she loved. "Indeed it does, Morgan."

"Splendid! Then after Paris, shall we go home to Drummond Castle?"

Oriel couldn't seem to stop smiling, "Yes! Yes, Morgan! How many American girls can go *home* to a *castle?*"

Morgan drew her close, holding her in his arms. They looked into each other's eyes, searching for something, an answer. They found what they had been looking for. They kissed again. It was not a long kiss, but one of discovery, full of sweetness and the promise of enduring love.